HOURI

D1507177

ADVANCE UNCORRECTED GALLEY

304 pp.   ISBN 13: 978-1-57962-177-3

Pub. Date: December 2009 $29

HOURI

Mehrdad Balali

THE PERMANENT PRESS
Sag Harbor, NY 11963

For information, address:
   The Permanent Press
   4170 Noyac Road
   Sag Harbor, NY 11963
   www.thepermanentpress.com

[The pious] will be in place of security (paradise) . . . among gardens and springs . . . dressed in fine silk . . . facing each other . . . we shall marry them to Hur with wide lovely eyes . . . they will call therein for every kind of fruit in peace and security . . . they will never taste death and He will save them from the torment of the blazing fire . . . as a bounty from the Lord: that will be the supreme success . . .

—THE HOLY QUR'AN

DESCENT

"No knife ever cuts its own handle," Baba used to say by way of assuring me he could never harm the son so tightly bound to him. But the knife did cut.

The plane had just crossed Turkey into Iranian airspace when there was sudden frantic activity on board.

Flight attendants hurried to remove wine and whisky from trays. Men rushed to rinse the stink of alcohol from their breath. Women donned dark *hejab*s to hide their hair and curves, scrubbed makeup from their faces. Passengers were bracing for an inquisition, or something worse. Even from thousands of feet above, and an hour before the plane landed, I caught a sense of the intolerant terrain waiting below.

I began to regret the trip. But it was too late. I was on a journey of discovery prompted by one death, and making a guilty escape set off by another. I had nothing to go back to, and no courage to face what lay ahead.

This return of the prodigal son to Iran should have happened in February 1979, when my father died in a car crash. That was only weeks before the Islamic Revolution opened its jaws on our land.

When my father died I was living in Monrovia, a sleepy town in southern California, where I was supposed to be working and studying. After a half-hearted struggle with various subjects in college, I'd totally given up and was just working dead-end jobs—gas station attendant, parking lot jockey. Now there was only my mother who needed to believe I was the industrious foreign student. No matter how much she pleaded, I refused to go back to attend Dad's funeral. I owed that man nothing, not when he was alive, and not to his decaying corpse.

I had learned of the revolution from thousands of miles away, in bits of news here and there. I'd heard about the chaos, the destruction, the orgy of killings, and the forcible campaign to veil and closet

7

women. But, strangely, my reaction to all that was a sense of relief—at the fact that my father wasn't around to witness it. The upheaval and its chaotic aftermath I saw through his eyes alone, as if this historical event found meaning in relation to one man only.

It was a timely demise for the hedonistic bastard: taking leave just when fun and joy were being clubbed to death in Iran. The trendy nightclubs my father had frequented were all raided and closed in the brutal crusade against pre-revolutionary "decadence." The stylish women he so eagerly chased found themselves bundled in dark clothes—as if their sensuous glories were something to be ashamed of. And the love songs he crooned into their ears were outlawed and pushed underground. Ironically, he met his end while driving to a rendezvous with a mistress, the last of a multitude he wooed and courted throughout his adulterous life.

As a child I had repeatedly prayed for "Baba" to die. In my mind I applauded his timing. Cruel—but that was the fittest elegy for a man whose devotion to life and sensuality touched on worship. How would he have coped with endless harassment—the daily dose of intrusion, lashing and humiliation? All he missed with his sudden departure was the long bitter hangover. He had lived life fully while it was still there. Then it was time to go.

I still hated him for his double act of betrayal, cheating me out of romance and money. First he got Houri: my childhood love, the image of the perfect woman always in my head, the earthly embodiment of fairytale Nymphs of Paradise. Then he took my money, the cache of large orange bills I had stolen from my miserly grandfather while he was immersed in prayer, the loot I had hoped to take that would let me run away with Houri. Or that's what I suspected. I vowed to find out the truth. Day after day, year after year, I spent futile hours feeding this thought, that the crippling of my life began with his betrayal. It was as though with a certain answer, I could crack the secret of his zest for life, the magic formula to a carefree existence, and somehow take it for my own.

Of course there was no inheritance to claim. That self-indulgent hustler hadn't bothered to leave anything behind, save for the corrosive question in my mind: was it really he who had robbed me of my only chance of happiness? With his premature death, he'd killed forever my hopes of learning the truth.

* * *

The airplane reduced speed and altitude, and I sat by the window watching the vast deserts pass below, broken by craggy mountains. There was a sudden thunderous turbulence and I gripped the seat handles in fear of death and uncertainty of what lay ahead. Unexpectedly I longed for Mary—my sad little girlfriend whose dying gave a decisive push to this foolish return to Iran. The thought of our forlorn relationship triggered homesickness for my pathetic life in the West. I even missed George, my asshole boss at the gas station.

"*Habibi,* you are making a big mistake," George had told me in his guttural Arab accent, when I told him I was leaving. "My friend, you want to travel, take a few days off—but don't quit! This is the fifth time you are quitting and I'm not taking you back."

"I need more than a few days."

"Remember, jobs don't come easy to Iranians these days, with the hostage crisis and everything," he said without looking at me, busy counting through a wad from the cash register and restlessly puffing at his cigarette.

The seizure of the American embassy and its personnel in Tehran in November of 1979 had created a special ethnic nightmare for Iranians living in the United States. Even after the hostages were released some fifteen months later, we encountered hostilities on a daily basis: "Piss on I-ran" bumper stickers, "Nuke Iran" graffiti splashed on restroom walls or "No dogs, No Eye-ranians" signs put up outside club and restaurants.

"I know, but still . . ."

"Still what?" he said, half listening, half counting.

"I may not even come back at all."

"Ha-ha. You mean you're going to live in that hell? *Habibi,* there's a war in your country. They'll snatch you from your house and send you off to the front to fight the Iraqis."

"I don't have a fight with anybody."

"You think you have a choice?" my boss said with a wise grin, exposing uneven teeth stained by tobacco. "I've been in situations like that. You just find yourself cutting throats for no fucking reason. After a while it becomes second nature to you."

There was no point in arguing with him. George, a Christian refugee from the Lebanese civil war, had set opinions about almost everything, delivering them with such conviction that it made you doubt your own judgment. His broken gas-station English was no barrier either, and he could talk you into anything—if his interests demanded it.

"You have a point, George, but I really have to go. I missed my father's funeral and now . . . my mother is sick." I lied to settle the argument.

"Do what you want, but I need a week's notice. I got to find someone to replace you."

I kind of expected that from him, to throw a threat my way. George was seasoned in the way of survival and considered his new home, America, as yet another battlefield. He spent his days mostly haggling with customers over trifles, or fighting off "trespassers."

"I can't wait for another week!" I said, but he was distracted again, this time by a young woman driving up in a convertible.

"Hey Shahed, check that out! You want to go for her? It may change your mind about going back," he leered.

"No, I don't think so."

"You know, man, America is a strange country. Everything costs money here except sex and matches."

"George, I have to rush to get ready. Let me have my pay."

"I'm going to have to take one week out of your check. No offense, but America is a country run by the rule of law. Without laws, these blacks and Mexicans would eat us alive."

"Take out whatever you want! Just leave enough for the plane ticket. Now goodbye. I've got to get ready to leave."

There wasn't much to pack. The content of my wardrobe was as meager as my accomplishments in my adopted land. I bundled it all into a small suitcase and went to see the elderly landlord, Mr. Johnson.

Mr. Johnson was an ailing widower living alone in an old house, just a few blocks from the gas station. My shack was in the back of the yard and there was not much to it but a small room, a toilet and a metal sink connected to a plastic hose and showerhead. But the landlord was a kind man. Although relying on a government pension, he was generous and compassionate, always accommodating my excuses for not paying the rent on time.

"You're a fine man," he'd say. "I can understand how tough life can be for a new immigrant. Just pay when you have it."

The old man had no children and his only surviving relative was an aged sister who visited him once every Christmas. Having little to do, he spent the whole day puttering outside his house, hunting for a willing ear: the mailman, garbage collectors, door-to-door salesmen—anyone who happened to stray close. Like many Americans I knew, he was upbeat, drawing excitement from little things in his humble world. But I found his company boring. He droned on from the corner of his mouth, gurgling sounds often indecipherable to me. Only once was he able to lure me into his dark living room for a tour of the bric-a-brac: boxes of old magazines, religious souvenirs hanging from walls and windows, and scraps of boards he called furniture.

"Are you sure you want to go ahead with that trip, son?" Mr. Johnson asked, as he gathered up the garden hose with slow shaking hands.

"Yes, I can't delay it anymore."

"I understand. But try and be careful—an awful lot of bad news coming out of your country these days."

"I'm sorry—I should have told you about it earlier."

"Oh, don't worry about it," he waved dismissively. "You don't have to give up your room. Keep your stuff in there and lock the door. I won't charge you rent while you're gone."

"But I don't know when I'm coming back."

"Doesn't matter, take your time, you badly need a vacation. The death of that poor girl has been really hard on you."

Next to me sat a middle-aged man with a dark bushy beard and the mark of devotion on his forehead—a black bruise caused by constant prostration. He left repeatedly for the lavatory to perform ablutions and pray in the back of the plane; when back in his seat, he pored through the pages in a thick folder. A few secretive glances told me they were filled with references to God and revolutionary clichés. The man was dressed in a dark blue suit and an open-necked white shirt, and I couldn't tell if he was Iranian or Arab, until he started talking.

"You are scared of the plane shaking?" he asked me in English accented with thick Arabic gutturals.

11

"Yes."

"Don't worry! Death comes only when Allah wishes it," he pronounced, and then looked at me inquiringly. "You are from Iran?"

I just nodded to cover for both.

"One expects fearlessness from a man coming from the land of martyrs." He smiled to temper the criticism. "So, where are you coming from now?"

"America. I've been living there for the past six years."

His face broke into a distrustful expression. "Why are you going back to Iran?"

"I don't know."

"To help the great revolution, is it not?"

I gave no answer.

"The revolution needs young men like you," the Arab urged. "*Inshallah*, it will soon spread everywhere and return the occupied Palestine to its true owners."

I looked out the window.

"What do you do in America? Do you study there?"

"On and off." I was actually doing nothing in America.

"Why on and off? Girls are a distraction?" he said with a sly giggle, risking a subject outside his moral values.

"What about you?" I didn't care but I dreaded a reprimand straight from the Qur'an. "What's taking you to Iran?"

"I am from Palestine. The great Imam Khomeini has called for a gathering to unify the struggle against Zionist occupiers. You must have heard about it."

"No, I haven't."

"Why, don't you follow the news?"

"Not much."

"But you must know about the Palestinians' historical struggle."

"I don't quite understand what the struggle is over."

His face grew hard with contempt; he took up his righteous studies again, and I turned to the window. We were circling over the sprawling capital, a grim landscape of concrete buildings shrouded in dust and smoke.

In moments I would be joining fellow Iranians in some of the darkest moments of our history. The war with Iraq was in full boil, and so was the power struggle among political factions. It was a reign of terror on the streets, with raids on homes and mass slaughters in prisons.

12

I felt sick and alone. I wanted the plane to turn around, to go back to America, where there was a place for the apathetic observer, where I had learned to be invisible.

At *Mehrabad* airport terminal, I took a long pause for adjustment, trying to get used to the grimy walls, dim ceiling lights, and the frowns of bearded guards stopping passengers at every step. There were many robed men around, in black or white turbans, all looking stern and disdainful. Before the revolution clergymen were not so visible, being confined to religious sanctuaries and forbidden from politics.

The hall leading to passport control was heavy with the stink of restrooms, but the hum of voices was soothingly familiar. After six years of American English, I realized only now how much I missed Farsi. Not just the language but the gestures and the nuances. Gazes were more meaningful, communicating subtleties, even the ferocious ones coming from callous guards. For a fleeting moment I thought I belonged. I perfectly blended in the familiar environment, drawing no hostile or curious stares. But that was too soon to tell.

In the crowded and chaotic customs station, suspicion hung in the air, an undercurrent of hostility to those arriving from western countries. There was great appetite for intrusion. While in America, I had shaved my beard hoping to look less like one of the Muslim fanatics my people were made out to be. But my clean-shaven face was now to my disadvantage, marking me as a sellout to Western fashion and values.

"Where do you come from?" growled a customs official as he groped through my battered suitcase, scattering its contents on a table.

"America."

"How long were you there? What were you doing?"

"I'm in university there . . . studying to be a doctor." A lame effort to inspire respect.

"Did you bring anything illegal with you—decadent music, nude magazines or films?"

"No, nothing like that—what you see is all I've got."

He fingered through the usual items of American personal hygiene—shampoo, toothbrush, hair gel—and picked up a box of Q-tips.

"What is this?"

"Q-tips."

"Self-indulgent objects of bourgeois luxury, huh?"

"It's just to clean my ears."

"You take such good care of your ears," he said with a disdainful grin. "Okay, go stand against the wall and wait to be called."

"How long must I wait?"

He gave no answer, just stuffed my belongings into the bag and set it on the floor beside him, before calling the next person in the long line. I stood in the same spot for almost an hour, tense and woozy. Behind a single glass door leading outside was a crush of flower-bearing well-wishers, waiting impatiently for their passengers to clear through the checkpoints. They were all in drab colors and looked tired, their faces expressing both sorrow and joy at seeing loved ones coming back. Among them I saw my mother and my brother, Arash, both jostling to make their way to the door and take a peek inside.

I remained in my place, making no effort to be seen by them, just waiting to be called. The customs official was too busy ransacking suitcases, taking no notice of me. Then I saw the Palestinian emerging, as three young clerics hurried to greet him. He had no baggage except for a carryon and the briefcase holding his fiery speeches. The mullahs waved at the guards and their guest was cleared to proceed. As they walked past, I nodded at the Arab, but he ignored me. They headed toward the exit and suddenly I followed, leaving my half-closed bag standing right by the customs official.

Mom was veiled and in mourning black—perhaps for my father, or the death anniversary of one of the saints. It was the first time I saw her in a black chador, but the dreary covering suited her. At forty, she already had the looks and air of an old woman, with a face deeply lined, a mouth missing many teeth. Her hair had turned white, judging from the few careless strands peeking from her veil.

My brother, too, looked old and worn out for a young man of twenty-two, his forehead prematurely creased and his head shaved for military service. Like most men around the terminal, he had a beard. I wondered if it was less out of piety than to hide symptoms of inner ruin. Cradled in his hand were a few stems of roses, all blackening at the edges and wilting—or so it seemed to a visitor from a colorful land.

By turns they hugged and kissed me, and I just stood there stiffly, averse to touch or sentiment. It was a relief there weren't more relatives to greet. I had strictly asked my mother to keep the date of my arrival a secret. I didn't wish to be welcomed by people who had no meaning in my life.

"I have good news for you, Shahed!" Mom said excitedly as we wedged ourselves into my brother's *Paykan*, a matchbox of a car as battered as those it transported. "You made it back just in time to attend your father's third death anniversary."

I said nothing.

"It's tomorrow! First we'll go to the cemetery and then we'll have a small service at home. Many friends and relatives will be there. You can see them all, Shahed!"

"I have no desire to go."

"It's just for a couple hours to pray for his soul." She reached from the back to take my hand reassuringly.

"I don't believe in that nonsense and I don't know how to pray."

"Bite your tongue, darling! Where did you learn to talk like that— in America?"

"I just don't want to visit a cemetery on my second day back. It's dull and meaningless to me."

"You couldn't have forgotten all about your culture in just a few years."

I said no more, not wanting to break her heart so soon after a long separation.

The next morning, my brother Arash got up early to report for his military duty in a remote province. I gave him a hug and then followed my mother to the main terminal, to take a bus to *Behesht-e-Zahra*, the main cemetery about an hour south of the capital. Roads were already crowded with buses and trailer trucks, some of them carrying coffins—of soldiers, I was sure—to the cemetery. It took us about two hours to creep along the potholed highway, blocked every mile or so by fruit peddlers and commuters begging for a ride. Mom kept talking all along the way, asking questions about my achievements in America and how much longer she had to wait before I graduated with honors. I gave few answers, mostly looking out the window in boredom. But I could not help feel sad about the changes I saw. Soot, dust and trash were everywhere and there were few green

15

patches. The big maple trees I remembered lining the roads had died or been cut down—gone, I was told, to build barricades at the warfront.

The cemetery *Behesht-e-Zahra* sprawled in the middle of the desert halfway between Tehran and Qom, a depressing religious town my father used to call a graveyard for the living. In recent years, the cemetery had grown fast to embrace thousands of "martyrs" from the revolution and the war with Iraq, as well as the unholy corpses of "traitors" weeded out.

When we arrived, there were scores of unfortunate mothers kneeling at their sons' graves, many sobbing or keening hysterically. Some ran their fingers distractedly over tombstones ruined by sand and grit, brushing dust away. Others hugged and kissed photographs of warriors still in their teens, soldier sons with the faintest trace of a mustache on their upper lips.

A bigger crowd of mourners was still arriving for fresh burials of soldiers of faith, fallen nobly in suicidal attacks against the enemy—often armed with nothing but a symbolic key to paradise hanging round their frail necks. As men lowered shrouded corpses into the graves, they shouted angry slogans—against America, against Israel, against the ruthless invader, Saddam Hussein. They wept and beat themselves, yet glamorized death and celebrated martyrdom. Defiantly, they vowed to offer up more, as many as needed until final victory.

My father's grave was in the far back, in a cursed plot called *Lanatabad*. The graveyard of the damned. Baba had not left much to erect himself a shrine. A cheap resting place in *Lanatabad* was all my mother could afford. Either way, I don't think he would have cared so much where his lifeless body was dumped.

Since Baba's burial three years earlier, the cursed plot had evolved into a dump site to dispose of political dissidents, infidels, wasted junkies and other criminals—anyone undeserving of a place in the paradise promised by the mullahs. There were no trees in this section, no lawns, no pavement and no tombstones—only a parched stretch dotted with hillocks of earth, some topped with a stick or a chunk of rock for distinction.

A dozen relatives waited at Baba's grave, and I spent an hour chatting with them, listening to endless stories praiseful of the deceased.

No one remembered him as a womanizer, a hustler, or a failure in life. They all thought of him as a good man, fun and generous, wishing his soul eternal happiness. I solemnly nodded to whatever they had to say, not contradicting a word; at the first chance, I slipped out, straight toward a nearby terminal. I had had enough.

Dozens of rattletraps serving as buses and taxis were parked sloppily in the makeshift terminal, with their drivers jostling for customers. All the way in the back of the line was a white Buick, like the one my father used to drive back in the sixties, only a bit banged up and rusty with age. I instinctively walked toward it, provoking angry honks and outbursts from other drivers first in line. Some ran in my direction, but before they could get to me, the Buick's driver swung the door open and I jumped in.

"One can't really blame them," said the young driver once we were safely away. "The economy is terrible. People don't have a pot to piss in. They are desperate for a way to make ends meet."

"I understand."

"So, where are you going?"

"No particular destination. I just want to have a look around the city. Why don't we start with Tajrish Circle?"

Tajrish, a piazza nestled in the foothills of Alborz mountain range, used to be my father's favorite evening hangout. He loved the place for its outdoor cafes, garden restaurants and breezy climate. That was actually where he was headed when he had the accident.

"Tajrish is way north, about an hour drive." He took his eyes off the road and gave me a quizzical look, as if to appraise my worth.

"Don't worry. I'll pay whatever it costs."

"You look like you just arrived from Europe or America."

"That's right—America. How could you tell?"

"From your appearance. You look . . . casually nice. People here don't dress well any more. There's no reason to, no place to go, nothing to do."

"It looks like it."

He took out a comb from his breast pocket and drew it carefully through his blow-dried cowlick, while appreciating himself into the rearview mirror. "But I try to look my best—always. I don't care who comes and who goes. One's appearance is always a good judge of his personality."

His outfit was smart but out of fashion: blue bell-bottom trousers and a black jacket tight around the waist with wide pointed lapels. His face, too, was shaved to the skin and he reeked of strong cologne.

"I don't give a damn what the mullahs preach. I live life as I like," he went on as he pulled a tape-deck from under the seat and slid it into the dash. "I won't allow them to dictate their boring theories about life and death to me. Life without fun is no life."

A pre-revolutionary song swelled in the car and the driver quickly cranked up the windows.

"You must be careful around here. You could get whipped if they catch you with these cassettes."

"That's unfortunate."

"But I can't go without music. There's nothing on the state-run radio except for dull sermons and wailing. I hardly ever turn it on." He stole a glance at me over his shoulder. "So tell me, Mr. Smart, why did you come back? Tired of the good life in America and looking for adventure?"

"Not really. I'm here to attend my father's memorial service."

"Sorry to hear that. When did he die?"

"Three years ago, but I missed his funeral."

"Now you get to attend a bigger funeral—for the whole nation."

He smiled and waited for my reaction. His cynical exaggeration was typically Iranian, a common form of speech in post-revolutionary Iran.

"Death is better than the misery we're living through these days . . . I was myself a revolutionary. But I'm over it now—disillusioned, as they say . . . anyway, let's drop the depressing talk. My name is Jahan. What's yours?"

"Shahed."

"Shahed! Witness. Interesting! So, Mr. Witness rode out the turmoil and now he's here to witness his nation's suffering?" he said with a giggle, impressed by his own wit. "I'm not a jealous guy, but I bet you're having the time of your life in America, with all the pretty blonds. Life there must be like in a cruise boat."

"It's okay, I can't complain."

"So, what made you come back? To see what has changed since you left? Do a little sociological study?"

He wanted to stretch the conversation but I wasn't in the mood and kept peering out the window to discourage more questions. He finally fell silent until we reached Hajiabad, my childhood neighborhood. Then I asked him to stop the car so I could go for a nostalgic tour.

Despite its connotation of "oasis," Hajiabad is a rundown district, traditional to the core. It was one of those neighborhoods that hadn't seen much change from the revolution because there wasn't really much to lose. Revolution meant stripping down to austerity and taking on a pious outlook, and these communities already met the standards. Even in the prime days of the Shah the neighborhood was a holdout against modernization. The only difference from the past was that some streets and alleys had been renamed after neighborhood martyrs, and Islamic activists had surfaced from underground, campaigning brazenly.

I made a quick journey round the old streets, taking in familiar sights and smells, and then I got back in the car and we headed northward, to a district fashionable in the old days. Further up, near the former American embassy, a big demonstration was underway, a daily show of defiance to the "Great Satan." Along the main route—a shaded tunnel of giant plane trees—bearded guards were present in force, all in combat fatigues and armed with Kalashnikovs. I saw them randomly stop and search cars. Jahan said they were looking for anything illegal: guns, something terrorists would use, such as radio equipment, alcohol, and even "depraved" magazines or music. At that he grabbed the tape deck and hid it under his seat again, and cranked up the radio playing mournful religious chants.

Closer to Vanak Circle, once a ritzy quarter, there was mayhem. A gang of revolutionaries whizzed by on motorcycles, screaming and throwing rocks at the windows of boutiques—the last remnants of the bourgeois decadence they were set to cleanse. The raiders were dressed in black, with checkered scarves wrapped around their necks—an emblem of the Palestinian struggle, itself a symbol of the wider conflict between Islam and the West.

"Boutique, boutique—a source of filth and corruption!" they chanted.

For its stylish assortment of trendy joints with exotic names (Chattanooga, Hot Shop, Casino Royal), Vanak was top on the crusaders' hit list. These places had sprung up during the oil bonanza in the sixties and seventies, to give a plausible look to an ostensibly modern society, a country embalmed in its superstitious religious values. They catered to the nouveau riche, a new class of professionals with modern aspirations. I was poor in those days and a stranger to the chic life, but occasionally I stole a taste of it. I used to go shopping there with the money I pinched out of my grandfather; had my fill of hamburgers, creampuffs and ice cream—everything my deprived heart desired. And they tasted so great, those imitations of American fast food and sweets—better than the originals at California mega malls.

Some of these spots I still remembered from the old days, although they looked worn out and smaller now. These treasured icons were undergoing a facelift to come out grim and humble—in keeping with the austere spirit of the revolution. The mullahs were dead set to smoke out the past, obliterate old memories. They changed street names, destroyed landmarks, all relics of former glory, as they tried to paste a pious mask on the dark ghosts they had made of our people.

"We better get out of here fast before I get one of these rocks in my window," Jahan said matter-of-factly. "I take good care of my baby . . . don't want any harm to come to it."

The tense scene was scaring me but I still wanted to hang around and watch, as if witnessing the madness would give purpose to my aimless trip back.

"Can you drive slowly so I can get a good look around?" I asked. "This place has lots of memories for me."

He came up with one of his wise remarks. "All right. I'll move like a float so you can watch the carnival. But you'll have to pay any damages to the car."

The vigilantes had arrived. They smashed their way through the main street and charged into one of the coffee shops, where they broke up young dating couples and dragged them out to the sidewalk. One of the men had a teenager by his rock-star mane, calling out for scissors or a sharp knife. Another was dragging a chubby girl on the ground by her headscarf, which was tied into a noose and slipped around the girl's neck. He was hauling her to a police van parked in front of the café.

I took a close look at the militiamen, trying to sense the logic behind their zealous actions. Most of them looked poor, members of the disinherited millions behind the revolution. And they all seemed to revel in their new status—their faith and poverty transmuted into power—and in the opportunity to bully privileged kids. They were yelling in a strange idiom, a mix of street slang and revolutionary formula, and that made them appear even more as alien invaders.

"We're all your soldiers, Khomeini, ready to follow your orders, Khomeini," they chanted with every kick or punch.

Jahan turned to me for instruction. "Can you park the car and wait for me a little? I'll pay you double."

He gave me a look as if to assess my sanity.

"Mr. Shahed, your American dollars take you a long way here . . . all right, I'll park the car, but a few blocks away."

He left and I stood watching, with a twinge of sadness. I felt powerless and frustrated, with a silly notion in my head that if my father were around, he would have stood up to these bullies. He would have ripped the veil from their hypocritical campaign and laughed out loud in their self-righteous faces. Laughed them and their phony crusade out of this land, this seat of Oriental splendor, the land of great poets, wine and lovers.

Suddenly, I began to miss him, the man I'd so intently avoided when he was alive. He was the embodiment of the old spirit and I wanted him back to take charge, steer life the way he knew best. I wanted him back to live, to celebrate life, and denounce grief and martyrdom. The past came to me in bright images and strong impressions. I felt a kinship with that place I had long lost. The childhood I was trying so hard to forget suddenly took on a retrospective sparkle in the grim shadow of the present. The past looked happy, alive and romantic, and the present had the sour taste of a hangover.

The guards packed their vans with decadent youngsters and roared off. The square settled into a gloomy silence, with only helpless whispers exchanged among the surviving ghosts.

"They are only venting their frustrations," Jahan said coolly, as if the vigilantes were just high-spirited pranksters. "If they can't have a slice of good life, they might as well ruin it for everybody."

I took it as a validation of my growing sense that my father was better off dead.

"Let's go to Tajrish now," I said.

As we passed the militia van, I caught a glimpse of the teenaged girl they had dragged away, with her sad chubby face pasted to the window. She kind of reminded me of Mary: her round figure, her

21

defiance, the brazen display of her humble good looks. The eventful day had flushed all thoughts of my late girlfriend out of my mind for the first time in many weeks. Yet now the memory of meeting her struck me forcibly. It was just after I had moved into the miserable room that Mr. Johnson rented to me.

At the far end of the old man's backyard, hidden among aged trees and overgrown weeds, was a brass bell hanging from a branch. I had spotted it when I first moved in and was always curious to know what it was for. Yet I never bothered to ask the landlord about it, lest he'd go off on a long monologue. What could that be? I thought to myself . . . a piece of junk like many others stuffing his house, a possession of no purpose or value.

Sitting bored on a bench in the yard one day, I pulled on the bell's frayed rope till it clanked loudly. After a few moments, a young girl emerged, like an apparition, from behind the fence to the neighbor's house. She was no more than sixteen, round and soft like a ripe peach, with a pleasant and smiling face. Yet her gestures were too restless, her eyes wide and agitated, as if just opened to an exciting new world. There was a gap between her front teeth and a brown spot on her left cheek, dancing up and down her animated face. She stood there examining me for a while, her squat figure framed in the wooden gate, her plump thighs and hips squeezed into tight orange shorts.

"Hi," she finally said. "Did you call me?"

"No. Why?"

"I heard the bell ring and thought—it might be Joshua," she said in a nasal and impatient tone, like many teenagers.

"Who is Joshua?"

"My ex-boyfriend! He used to live in this guesthouse with his mother. Are you the new tenant?" She didn't wait for my answer. "I'm Mary . . . what's your name?"

"Shahed."

"That's a nice name! What does it mean?"

"It's Arabic for witness," I said, surprised she hadn't asked for the spelling, as many did.

"Are you Arab?"

"No, Persian."

"Persian! How nice! I'm Assyrian." Her big blue eyes shone as if struck by a magical coincidence, as though there was a kinship between our two races.

"We're supposed to be very close, aren't we—Persians and Assyrians?" She came and sat on the bench next to me. I looked at her hesitantly. I felt no kinship with people of her race. The only Assyrian I knew was Edison, the bullyboy back home who had tormented me at school.

"I guess we are," I said, not particularly interested in the subject. I was more taken by her bouncy character, the restless birthmark on her rosy cheek. Her warm, sweet face was inviting but her round figure gave me doubts.

"Where did your Assyrian ancestors come from, Iran or Iraq?" I said, just to keep the conversation going.

"Oh, don't ask me. I don't have the slightest idea. My Baba is, or was, Assyrian, and that's all I know. I've never seen him in my life. He got my mother pregnant and disappeared."

"So you live with your mother here?"

"Oh, my mother died a long time ago."

"Sorry about that. What happened?"

"I don't wanna talk about it . . . well . . . she committed suicide," she said with the same smile. "I went to a foster home for a while and then moved in with my aunt, Laura. Now I live with her and her boyfriend, Bill. I don't like him, though."

She paused for a few seconds, playing with her nails, and then went on: "Bill is a plumber but he never works. He's such a lazy bum, and so mean. He comes home drunk every night causing trouble. But Laura still loves him, even though he cheats on her."

I could picture what kind of a character Bill was. I often ran into bullies at the gas station where I worked. They would roar up the island on gigantic motorcycles, dressed in leather and adorned with chains and tattoos. Sometimes they came for gas, but mostly to piss out pitchers of Budweiser they had guzzled. Our restrooms were for customers only, under strict orders issued by my boss. But I never had the guts to enforce these rules. "Open the fucking door!" was how these bikers made their request, leaving no doubt as to what I was supposed to do. I had no choice but to go along with their order if I didn't want to be called a fucking A-rab or goddamned Eye-ranian.

"Yeah, he's a total jerk." Mary went on. "He wants to control everyone, including me. But I'm not letting him."

"Control you how?"

"He wants to know where I go and who I see. He's such a jealous guy and I have to hide things from him. That's why Josh set up this bell, so he wouldn't have to come to the door for me."

It sounded like trouble and I half rose to leave.

"Where're you going?" she asked, looking disappointed.

"I have things to do."

"Listen, can you teach me your language—whatever it's called?"

"Why do you want to learn it?"

"I love languages. I'm gonna minor in French in college."

"What will your major be?"

"Nursing. My dream is to be a nurse. I love helping people."

"It is not a distant dream. Okay, I have to go now."

"Listen," she grabbed my arm. "Will you call me sometimes? Just pull the rope three times. I'll hear you."

Tajrish was the spot I most identified with my father. As we came to the circular intersection, I had the feeling of a man standing in the gate of a ravaged city looking onto the smoldering ruins of a glorious past. The Circle used to be a popular evening haunt, alive with color, lights and music. It was ringed with cheerful shops, restaurants, out-door shopping arcades, and always packed with sleepless revelers. On breezy summer evenings, cars lined up along a roaring canal meandering down the mountain. On its banks people ate, drank and danced the whole night. But three years on, since my father's death, the place had gone to ruins, as if their fates were somehow tied together. The channel had run dry and filled with putrid garbage. The leafy trees that lined it were diseased and soot-laden.

We parked the car and went for a stroll, with Jahan happy to play the tour guide. Nearby was one of the Shah's fallen palaces, one he occasionally used as a winter retreat. It was a sprawling mansion snaking up the hill and surrounded by high, fortress walls—though not tall enough to protect the monarch from his own people. Jahan told me a chilling account of a mob raid on the palace on the eve of the revolution, and the havoc wrought in the name of justice. The raiders left quite a litter in their wake: classic nude paintings trampled and ripped to shreds, "obscene" statues hammered to the ground, and precious antiques hauled off as booty. Signs of vandalism could be seen even on the outer wall: jagged carvings and hostile graffiti only partly effaced by dirt and soot.

We walked for some time and then headed back to the canal, just a few meters from where my father used to park his big American car and ogle young ladies in hot-pants and mini-skirts. It was the busiest spot in the roundabout, one he chose deliberately to get the most exposure. He'd leave all four doors open, and sometimes the trunk, to let the music from his Topaz gramophone spill out into the square. I could picture him standing behind a folding table heaped with hors d'oeuvres and drinks. He's joking and laughing, sharing his tales of chicanery with friends, as his eyes rove around searching for hot ladies. He is the tallest of the men, and way broader in the shoulders, dominating the stage like a prima donna. I could hear his deep announcer's voice, his booming laughter, and all the other cheerful noise that made heads turn in interested curiosity.

My eyes kept searching, looking for any sign of the cheerful past, the faintest allusion to his lively soul, and there was nothing. The stylish women he so diligently pursued had become veiled shadows flicking self-consciously along dusty pavements—all keeping their heads down not to attract attention. The curving lines of bars and sandwich shops had pulled down their shutters or were serving slaughterhouse offal, a food more agreeable to the new rough tastes.

Presently, a crane pulled up into the square and lumbering police trucks stopped to tow away parked vehicles.

"Wait here for me! I'll be right back. I have to move my car," Jahan said and quickly disappeared.

Left alone, I grew more apprehensive, becoming acutely conscious of the heightened sense of activity. Was some other drama unfolding? I wanted to ask someone, but hasty movements and frowns discouraged my questions. Everyone seemed preoccupied, not so much with purposeful activity but with worry. The smoggy air was thick with a sense of aggression.

"*Bebakhshid Khanum.* Excuse me, Madam," I said timidly to a passing shadow. But she either didn't hear or chose to ignore me.

A few minutes later, Jahan came back with news: preparations were underway for the public chastisement of a child rapist, at the very spot where he committed his crimes, in the rotting canal under a bridge.

"They usually do their hangings at dawn. The executioners must have slept over," Jahan said wryly.

By now, the crane was neatly parked in the middle of the roundabout, its long shaft shooting up in the air, with a noose hanging from the end. A small crowd was already there and more were on their way—arriving on foot, in buses, and in the back of pickup trucks. There was a general mood of nervous anticipation, as everyone waited to catch a glimpse of the convict.

We stood on the sidewalk, not too far from the infamous canal, behind a thick wall of spectators craning their heads and jostling for better position. This hanging promised relief from a mood steeped in cynicism and struggle for survival. They joked, laughed and debated with each other, but no one seemed to question the justice of the punishment about to be handed out.

In an hour the rapist finally made his appearance, mounted disgracefully on the back of a donkey—the lowest and stupidest of all creatures in our culture. He was blindfolded, wearing a gray prisoner suit, his head shaved to the skin. A cardboard hanging from his thick neck announced his crime: *The Corrupt on Earth*. A scruffy man, an old veteran of the prison establishment, was pulling the beast by a rope, parading the criminal—who faced backward, hunching over, his eyes fixed resignedly on the donkey's ass.

The old man went around displaying his freak for a while, exhibiting him at every angle—until everyone had had a good look. Then he led the donkey to the crane, where two guards came to help the rapist dismount. The man was hauled up several steps onto the gallows platform, where the hanging judge waited under the shaft, grim and pious, with a Koran in his hand.

The judge was a cleric with a domed paunch pushing out his dark gray gown, and a white turban tilted back on his bald head. He kept thumbing a string of rosary beads and stroking his white beard, trying to assume an air of reverence. A stickler for procedure, he crept through a long ritual, making sure everything was done correctly—in full accordance with divine teachings.

"In the name of God, the compassionate, the merciful," he started his sermon. "We are here today to witness the demise of a devil incarnate . . . a man who gave in to his darkest impulses . . . took innocent lives after violating their honors.

"In this very canal, under this very bridge he killed them, and in this very same place he will receive the punishment he deserves."

Here he paused to tilt his turban further back and wipe sweat from his skull with a handkerchief. Then he removed the blindfold from the convict to allow him a brief taste of light before sending him to eternal darkness. Right by the rapist the judge stood, fiddling with his appearance, as if to prepare him for the camera, give him the perfect fiendish look for maximum effect.

"Now step forward and beg forgiveness from these great people! Repent and seek salvation—although no admission of guilt will save you from your dark fate. This magnanimous nation may choose to forgive you, but the final decision rests with God.

"So we rid the world of your sinful flesh, but your soul may still have a chance. You will lose the world but may still save your afterlife. So go ahead and atone for your sins and leave the rest in the Almighty's hand . . ."

The convict made no move and remained mute, staring on impassively, showing no sign of remorse. This annoyed the mullah, and he prodded the sinner again, but he remained unrepentant. So the judge gave a signal to his men and the shaft dropped low, level with the rapist's head. The judge took the noose in his hand and slipped it around the man's neck like a wreath of flowers, as he kept intoning prayers. This must have taken longer than it should have. The crowd grew impatient and some started counting down: ten, nine, eight . . . .

The pungent smell of lamb and diesel fumes was heavy in the air and I felt dizzy and nauseous. I wanted to leave, but was transfixed with a sense of horror. Like the others around me, I wanted to see the conclusion of this black drama, the rapist's miserable end.

Finally, the execution order came and instantly the rapist rocketed up into the sky; and there he hung, swinging wide—back and forth, to and fro. A collective gasp came from the audience, followed by a climactic roar. Then everyone sang, an innocent children's song: *Tab, tab abbasi, Khoda mano nandazi.* Swing, swing high to the sky. Please God, don't make me fall.

I turned to Jahan to check his reaction. He had a grin wide with impish delight. Like the others in the square, he seemed to have become inured to such excesses—the frequent shock of raids, explosions, public lashings and hangings.

Jahan touched my shoulder. "Hey, do you get to witness shows like this in America?" he asked, still grinning. I looked around and people were starting to look at me, the only one sickened by the corpse's purple face.

"Let's go," I said.

We walked to the Buick, which was parked outside an open-air market where housewives haggled with butchers and greengrocers, unmindful of the limp shadow swinging in the sky.

"Did you have enough or you want to see more?" Jahan asked.

I ignored his question and walked weakly to the canal, where I knelt at the filthy edge and threw up.

Once in the car, my mind drifted away from the hanging and settled back to the memory of my father. I kept sniffing around the interior, for that peculiar scent in Baba's Buick—the smell of leather mixed with his cologne, sweat and tobacco.

"How long have you had this car?" I asked, wondering if it wasn't my father's car Jahan was driving.

"About a year . . . bought it from an air force pilot who fled to America . . . got it for a good price, too . . . it's in a perfect condition . . . not a dent on it."

"I love this model of Buick." I reverted to the American's easy use of love, but it comforted me.

"Look at the leather upholstery . . . not a single tear or crack . . . and check out the speakers—just like brand new, don't you think?" he cranked up the volume of the radio to prove it.

An ayatollah was on the air advocating martyrdom for Islam and the country, drawing from religious books to back up his argument:

"There is no experience sweeter than the taste of martyrdom! Martyrs don't die in vain. A palace is reserved for each of them in paradise, all made of pearl . . . each palace embracing seventy edifices of rubies . . . and in each edifice, there are seventy chambers of emerald, and in every chamber, sit seventy thrones, all covered with rugs of fine silk . . . each throne is mounted by a *Houri* sitting at a lavish spread holding seventy dishes heaped with food—carnal and spiritual nourishment . . ."

My eyes caught Jahan in the rearview mirror. The cynical leer was back on his face. He noticed I was looking.

"Sounds appetizing, doesn't it?" he said. "But I think I'm going to pass. It's too distant a promise. I'd rather go for now and ready."

The ayatollah's singsong pronouncements went on: "The Almighty bestows the martyr with superior strength. He'll savor all the heavenly dishes but has no problem of digestion . . ."

"Hell, it gives me gas just to hear about it," Jahan mocked again.

I said nothing. I was thinking about a promise of paradise that was thousands of miles away. At the cemetery that morning, surrounded by a sea of grief and black, I couldn't help remember the "Butterfly Bazaar," a colorful school parade in an idyllic seaside town called Pacific Grove. Mary was anxious to see it and I reluctantly went along, taking a drive up the California coast in her old Volkswagen. Such flashy carnivals I found rather dull and uninspiring.

True to her childlike spirit, Mary came to the parade dressed as an American Indian, in a suede outfit with beaded fringes. Her face was painted and she wore a headband bristling with bright feathers. The whole ensemble put me off, most of all the skimpy outfit exposing her fleshy legs and round shoulders. It was a struggle to hide my shame and not spoil it for her with chidings.

But when we got to the Butterfly Town, a serene environment of bright sea air and magnificent trees, I felt relaxed. There were other adults looking sillier than Mary, masquerading as fantasy creatures in colorful wings and tails; women far bigger and rounder; and frail old ladies dolled up as if for a last hot date. But no one was self-conscious or critical. They all were happy, in touch with the child within them and in perfect harmony with their peaceful surroundings. Even my cynical radar could not detect pain and suffering, or traces of grief. All were absorbed, watching their children take part with joy and pride, feeling content as parents and members of their community.

The entire scene was like those postcard images that fuelled my childhood dreams of America. But somehow those wonderful images had not seeped under my skin. With some bitterness, I wondered why the picture of a life that fired my imagination should taste so bland when I finally came to know the reality. I asked myself: what is it that keeps me from taking part whole-heartedly in these celebrations—what stops me from taking joy in simple pleasures of life? Is it the culture of shame? The twisted fascination with death and grief?

Jahan dropped me off at home and said he'd return the next day to take me for more "sightseeing." There was one more place I wanted to see: my old school. How had that one stood up to the test of the revolution?

That night I had dinner with my mother in the small flat she and my brother had moved to after Baba's death. The apartment was in a better neighborhood than our old house, but still sunless and damp. To ease the gloom, she burned a high-voltage light bulb that hung on a cord from the ceiling. There was also a kerosene heater with a long tin hood, leaking soot at the seams. On the brick shelf running along the wall sat our old transistor radio, a copy of The Holy Qur'an and a dashing portrait of my father with his roguish mustache.

Mother was full of reproach as I sat cross-legged on the red rug across from her, mechanically spooning rice and stew into my mouth. Not even the aroma of the rice and the saffron adorning it could whet my appetite, or the pickled vegetables served for relish. She herself wasn't eating and just talked—alternately exhorting me to eat and blaming me for wasting my life in America.

"You're not eating like you used to. You've lost so much weight. How can you study if you don't eat?"

"I eat when I'm hungry, Mother."

"Tell me, Shahed, what have you done in America that I can speak of with pride to my friends? What should I tell them you've been doing all these years?"

I looked away, feeling shame and irritation at once.

"So . . . you don't have anything to say?"

"There's not much to speak of, Mother."

"Then what was the point of my sacrifices, bearing the pain of separation? You know you and Arash are my only hope in this world, my only reason to go on living."

She was giving me the old guilt trip and I cringed. It was a mistake to come back, I thought. I'd come to escape the pain of Mary's death and now she's loading me with her own crap.

"I actually gave up on school. Now I'm just working."

"Doing what?"

"Different things . . . now I'm working at a gas station."

"Is that why I sent you there, to pump gas? You could have done that here!"

"You're right," I said, avoiding her eyes.

"I've had no luck with my boys. The other one couldn't finish school and now he's drafted into the army. I live every moment in dread of him being sent to the warfront."

"Why do you only blame your children?" I snapped. "What about your husband? You think you had any luck with him? I'm angry he's spared of blame."

"God bless him," she retorted." He was a good man! I wish his soul eternal peace."

It took an effort to restrain myself. Why did she have to be so naïve, paying homage to a man who had ruined her life and ours, too? What about my peace? Who's going to sing my praise? I looked at her sad eyes, her toothless mouth, the deep lines in her face, and wondered what she'd gained from a lifetime of devotion.

"All men go through a wild phase when they're young and your father was no different," she went on, her eyes filling with tears. "But he repented before dying and asked for my forgiveness."

Moron! How quickly she could forgive! A woozy apology from his deathbed and it washed away all his cheating and lies. What a lucky son of a bitch Baba is—in life and in death! My old envy of him came to seize me. I hated him for having had it so easy, gliding on the surface of life without care. Why did I have to be an heir to the fallout of his extravagant lifestyle? Why couldn't I inherit his happy-go-lucky nature?

I took a deep breath to calm down. I meant to reach for her hand, looking for a way to end our day on a note of kindness.

Instead I started on another subject. "Mother, there's something I have always wanted to ask you."

"What?" she asked distractedly.

"Do you know if it was he who stole my money, the notes I'd pinched out of Grandpa?"

"*Astaghferallah!* God forbid!" she recoiled. She struggled to her feet and started picking up the dishes.

The subject was taboo and I shouldn't have raised it. My stealing and the punishment it entailed was an unfortunate aberration not to be revisited.

"One must never speak ill of the dead! It's not fair to scandalize him as he's not around to defend himself."

"You're doing a good job of defending him."

"Why do you always blame him for everything?" She turned to me piteously, but I would give her nothing. "Shahed, he was a good man, a good father. If he punished you, it was for your own good—

31

so you would grow up to be an honest man! Besides, it wasn't your money."

"It wasn't his either—but he never had to pay for it."

My old school, once a private institute for the elite, had been confiscated and turned into a camp to indoctrinate young females, mold them into models of chastity and virtue. The school was churning out new radical ideas to overwrite the old; it was training a new generation of heroes to replace the former ones, who were now traitors.

Even the name of the school had been changed to that of a saint. Its walls were even higher to block the campus from an outside view, and give the girls a privacy they didn't want. A faded tarpaulin hung over the entrance and a fat maiden wearing a black chador sat in guard, making sure no male strayed close or peeked inside.

I stood across the street by a newspaper kiosk, unobtrusively watching the girls file obediently through the door. Hostile slogans and murals covered the outside wall, depicting the United States as the Great Satan. America, a country I once fantasized about, had turned into a monster with flaming eyes and blood-dripping claws.

It was early and students were still arriving, all swaddled in black and looking pale with no makeup. Every time the canvas curtain swept aside, I caught a glimpse of the interior where some ceremony was underway—an energetic display of hatred for America. The girls had lined up reverently before a frowning portrait of the Revolutionary Leader Ayatollah Khomeini, all veiled, their heads wreathed with red bandanas. They kept chanting slogans and punching the air with their fists. Soon their cries echoed out into the street. It was a familiar cry, in tone if not in content. It evoked a distant memory, taking me back to a patriotic ceremony in the winter of 1967.

SCHOOL

We are lined up in the freezing yard in front of a huge portrait of the Shah, the "King of the Kings," waiting for the blind principal to come and kick off the weekly ceremony—held every Saturday, the first day of the week in our Muslim calendar. It is so damn cold. My hands are frosty; my ears are red and smarting; icicles hang from my nose. Bamdad, the disciplinarian we'd rather call Bam, runs back and forth, trying to put the kids on their best behavior before his boss arrives. He makes sure no one keeps their hands in his pockets, picks their nose, or scratches their ass.

I stay in my place, as still and polite as I can be, and all too conscious of my appearance: shabby suit, sagging bag, and outsized shoes, all marking me as a hick among so many stylish boys. My schoolmates are mostly rich, snobbish sons of merchants, bureaucrats and military officers—the so-called upwardly mobile in our prospering society. They live in big villas up in the northern suburbs, come to school in private cars, driven by a chauffeur, and are often accompanied by a maid. The boys all carry a leather briefcase in one hand, cool and glossy as the one James Bond sports; in the other, a tiered lunchbox, packed with delicious lunch and dessert.

I'm one of the few in the school who comes from the poor south, a backward neighborhood of idiots, losers and religious fanatics—a community out of touch with the new exciting trends. Friendless and lonely, I spend the whole day dreaming about life up in those posh suburbs in the north, and the world beyond. I dream of being chummy with these nice-looking kids, the ones in jeans and leather jackets, looking like young American stars. My big fantasy is to visit their houses, meet their bourgeois parents and beautiful sisters, and have dinner together around a candlelit table—just like in the movies.

Our principal finally arrives, followed by his entourage. He is in a crisp gray suit, with the jacket buttoned up to his neck, and wears the usual dark glasses to protect his bad eyes. A teacher holds his arm for support, and he taps his spiked cane on the icy ground.

33

The principal is a huge man with an explosive temper, and we all fear him to death. Yet, he looks almost ludicrous, a cartoon image of a fat mogul. He is big and round in the middle, tapering on both ends.

The old man is a retired general, a "devoted soldier of the king," as he likes to be known. Some years back, in a coup people say was organized by Americans, he helped bring the Shah back to power, and the king paid him off handsomely for his service—with a fat cash bonus and a seat in parliament for his wife. He used the money to open this school and realize his dream of pioneering a modern system of education in our backward country. He wanted to train a new generation of heroes to lead the nation into a bright future—in line with His Majesty's great visions. In his relentless pursuit of this dream, the general runs the school like a military garrison, with the same discipline and rigidity, crucifying those who don't fit in and, needless to say, those who don't pay their tuition on time.

It is actually the boys who must bleed for these dreams. With the girls next door, the fat general is soft as jelly, all love and tenderness. Boys and girls are of the same institution, but the general keeps us rigidly separated to get the mullahs off his back. Our religious leaders are watching closely from surrounding mosques, waiting for any misstep to run to their pulpits and cry sin. As things stand, our society is not ready for coed education. But things may change if the "enlightened" king has his way and sweeps the nosy mullahs into their holes. Until then, the Shah and his cronies have to tread as if on eggshells, and keep a safe distance between the two sexes. Boys are never to stray into the female territory, except to enter and leave the school ground, and girls must never be left unsupervised.

But the temptation to cross the border is always there. The boys' wing of the campus is just a dump, a mere backyard to the whole establishment. There's just an old building with a jumble of sooty classrooms, and a bare courtyard for a playground. The yard, not even the size of a tennis court, is surrounded by cement walls that seem to rise flush to the sky, topped with barbed wire and shards of glass to discourage any dream of escape.

The boys have to share the main gate on the girls' side to get in and out. Every day, after the closing bell, we are held back for a half an hour or so to give the young ladies time to clear out, lest we touch and contaminate them.

34

But the boys do their best to break loose and stumble into the forbidden territory, before the angels vanish. The gate between our two quarters is a gate to heaven always mobbed by a gang of desperate kids begging entry. You can't blame us. Many of the girls next door are ripe and luscious as heavenly fruits, perhaps nothing less than the *houris* of paradise we're promised to meet in the afterlife. Even their campus is like the Garden of Eden, full of trees and rose bushes, and fragrant with the best Parisian perfumes. It is no wonder the principal has his office there, coming to our side of the school just to lead a dull ceremony and mete out punishment to bad boys.

Bam runs to greet his boss and ushers him to a faded awning over a stand in the corner of the yard, right under the king's image. It's the same picture of the monarch one sees everywhere, showing him raising a hand to a sea of black dots down below. Many teachers and office staff have already been waiting in the stand, and two janitors in blue overalls are at either side holding their brooms like rifles.

The general makes his way stiffly to the stand, his bald head cocked back pompously and his chin and stomach sticking way forward. When he takes his place, a deep silence falls before our national anthem crackles out of a loudspeaker, tied around the lone tree in the yard, and we prepare to sing in accompaniment. Bam stands in front of us like a conductor, flailing his arms and making sure we don't skip a note.

Now it's time to pray—for the health of the king and the benevolent queen. Once we've droned through that, the general lurches forward to deliver a speech, using the occasion to outline his dreams for the thousandth time and praise the hell out of his school.

"This institution is in a league with the best in Europe and America," he booms, his voice trembling with pride. "My children, you are urged to strive, sacrifice and attain. What this great nation needs are heroes to fight for our deserved place in the progressive world."

He speaks for a long time and then gives the floor to Bam to launch the dreadful part of the ceremony: the trial for the bad boys. The disciplinarian fishes out a piece of paper as crumpled as his suit, and starts reading. But the general keeps interrupting him to shout orders to the janitors, sending them to get a glass of water, his reading glasses, and finally, to everyone's horror, his notorious stick.

"Okay, don't drag it," the boss yells to Bam. "Go on! Call the names!"

"Yes sir . . . those whose names I call step forward!" Bam announces and we all stiffen.

"Edison!"

Edison is the chief brat, a stocky, barrel-chested bull given a wide berth by other kids. He is Christian Assyrian, which is why he has a foreign-sounding name. His father was so impressed with Edison, the inventor, that he named his son after him, in the hope of him turning out to be a genius too. But the bullyboy is already a big loser. He was twice recycled in the sixth grade and still gets bad grades. Edison is my biggest tormenter in school, always picking on me and trying to provoke a fight, which I go to humiliating lengths to avoid. He keeps calling me "mushroom" and "elephant ear" because of my big head and jutting ears.

Now he stands before the principal, pale as chalk and trembling like a shivering chick. I'm glad he is having a taste of his own bitter medicine.

"What did he do?" the principal asks his henchman.

"Sir, he ripped a picture of His Majesty from the wall and made a paper airplane out of it."

"How impertinent!" the general retorts, waving his stick. "It wasn't a political statement, was it?"

"No sir. He is a troublemaker, but not that kind."

"Okay, boy, hold out your hand!"

Edison twists his face in anticipation of the pain and finally extends a hesitant hand. The sightless general strikes down a couple blows, finding his target with suspicious sureness, and then dismisses him.

"Okay, who is next?"

Bam calls the next name and it happens to be mine—to everyone's shock. No one believes a wimp like me would do anything to demand punishment. I, too, think dumbly it is a mistake and stay put, until I hear my name called again, this time with a note of impatience. I nervously edge out of the line and shamble up the rows of boys, stopping dead a couple yards from the blind man. Somehow, he senses I'm not near enough and beckons me forward with a jerk of his fat finger.

"What did this one do?" the general asks.

Bam is not listening, distracted by a boy picking his nose, and he is trying to stop him with wild gestures of his hands and rolling eyes.

"Excuse me, sir?"

"I said what did he do? What's his crime?"

"Oh yes," Bam snuffles and peers at his grimy notes. " . . . this one is way too late on paying his tuition. We keep sending notices, but they ignore them. I even went to their house once, but they didn't open the door."

The boys break into a nervous titter.

"Months into the school year and you still haven't paid your fees?" the general asks.

"No sir."

"Shame on you." He dives for my ear, which he has difficulty finding at first, just clawing at my face.

"Why don't you pay your debt, stupid kid," he says, still groping and scratching. "You think this is a joke? You think I run my school on thin air?"

I have nothing to say and just hang my head in shame.

"Look at me when I talk to you!" he snarls, grabbing my chin and tilting it up.

I raise my head a notch but still keep my eyes fixed to the ground. By now he has a tight grip of my ear and is turning it back and forth like a radio knob.

"Answer me! Are you deaf and dumb?"

It's not my fault, sir. It's my father who wriggles out of his obligations. He always says he'll pay, but that day never comes. And here I am looking like a fool in front of the kids.

"You don't want to talk? Then I'll make you. Hold out your hand!"

My back breaks out in a sweat and my knees jerk. I want to defend myself but there is a lump in my throat and what feels like a clamp around my tongue.

"It's my . . . my father, sir," I finally stammer out.

"What of him?"

"He is dead, sir . . . I mean, he forgets to pay."

"He forgets . . . ha . . . then I shall do something to make him remember. Hold it out!"

I finally stick out a limp clammy hand.

"Taut! Tauter! . . . What's the matter, you haven't had anything to eat?"

The stick comes down with such a force that I fear it will slice right though my palm. But before they meet, I pull my hand away and the stick cuts through the air with a whoosh, sending the general staggering like a stalling locomotive.

The boys break into mocking cheer and that turns the old man purple with embarrassed rage.

"How dare you play games with me, stupid boy? I'll show you now! Hold it out!"

The stick flies and my hand automatically jerks away, and that sets off another chorus of whistles and catcalls. The somber ceremony is now turning into a circus, exposing the general for the fool he is. Bam scurries around frantically trying to impose order. But it is out of his control. So he leaves the boys and comes to grab my hands, holding them firmly before his blind boss like an offering tray. Blows rain down and in the frosty air, they cut like a sword. By the time he's finished my palms are in shreds and red as a beetroot.

At home, I hide my hands from mother, but of course she finds the bloody towel I try to stuff away. Her first reaction is to blame my father, as she always does.

"How can I hold it against the principal?" she says with teary eyes. "The poor, old blind man just wants his money—money he more than deserves for his hard work and creativity. People would offer their lives for the chance to send their kids to such a prestigious school. Your father doesn't understand this! You know it was a struggle for me to get you signed up there."

That was a rare win for my mother, getting me into this school, in a life of full of compromises. It took months of begging before she could squeeze a few bucks out of her husband to make the down payment for tuition. What she didn't think about was where to get the rest from or that I would be paying the price.

"I'm doing it all so you grow up to be somebody—a doctor, an engineer—anything but the bum your father has turned out to be. What a shame he doesn't appreciate it."

"Mom, maybe I'd better not go to school until we have the money to pay." I hold her hand, thinking naively that my battered palms are grounds to skip classes.

"Don't even talk about it!"

"But—"

"I don't want to hear it! All right, wait until Baba gets home and I'll have a talk with him—I mean if he deigns to show up . . . He's been out carousing all night with the money that should go to your education."

"Mom, will you make me a promise? Don't start a fight."

"Fight? What's the use? It's like talking to a stone wall. It goes into one ear and out the other."

Here she does have a point. Baba has this habit of letting things slide. It isn't just the school fees he fails to pay. Before we moved to my grandfather's house, this hellhole of a place that even rats wouldn't call home, we were always late on the rent and kept getting booted out of even the crummy places.

In fact, my father hasn't done a stroke of work in his life. For a few years he sold off the farmlands he was given by his father, piece by piece, and when he ran dry, he started borrowing right and left to feed his wasteful lifestyle. With Baba, life is either a fiesta or a hangover—and it's the latter we get to share with him. His borrowing and reckless spending is a cause of great embarrassment to Mama. He always owes a friend or relative—someone we'll have to encounter. Sometimes she is left with no choice but to take matters in her own hands, try and raise money to pay back some desperate debt. She can only do so by scrimping, which makes our already frugal meals pathetic. Or she steals from Baba. Every now and then I catch her going through his pockets, usually early in the morning when everyone is supposed to be asleep. She feels no shame at being found out. Her logic? "There is nothing wrong with salvaging a few bucks before they're wasted on whores and freeloaders."

My father is indeed a magnet for freeloaders, crooks and parasites disguised as friends. Baba loves attention and one way to get it is to spend big. His friends are more than happy to bolster his image of a generous man. Every evening, they escort him to a cabaret, eating and partying all night without having to pay a *rial* for it. Baba is always the first to reach for the bill and the others just sit back faking gratitude, doing their share by laughing faithfully at his jokes—drawn-out guffaws that make my father drunk with vanity.

Mama never stops warning her husband about these fair-weather friends:

"They're no friends—only flies around sweets!"

But it all falls on deaf ears. When there's no one to touch for cash, which is more often the case nowadays, Baba takes to selling goods from the house: rugs, appliances, kitchenware—anything the scrap dealer next door would pay for. But the one thing he'll never part with is his car: a cherished white Buick he calls the "Bride." The Bride is the most precious asset in his perpetual hunt for women, and he always keeps it shined and adorned like a carnival float. His loving treatment of the Bride is something that makes my mother very jealous, as if the car is a fierce rival.

"How come you can dig up the money to spend on the Buick but not to pay for more important things—like Shahed's school or Arash's circumcision?"

My brother is almost six and still not circumcised, as our parents keep arguing about how to get the inevitable operation done. Mama wants a professional job by a licensed physician, but Baba wouldn't hear of it.

"Why spend a fortune on such a simple thing?" he demands. "We've got the barber next door who'll do it for a pittance. His tools are sharp, and he's got more practical experience than any doctor."

This may all make my father sound like a selfish man, but he'd strongly disagree.

"I love my children and wouldn't give them up for the whole world," he says, giving my brother and me a bear-like hug and planting juicy kisses on our cheeks.

And we almost believe him.

This has been the complicated pattern of our life since I can remember: Baba indulging his eccentric habits and Mama nagging her head off. Well, she can reproach forever, until she foams at the mouth and her tongue turns black and falls off. No plea, no warning and no threat would make a dent in his resolve to live life fully, unrestrained. What's amazing is that my mother never gives up. She never stops her futile efforts to reform her husband.

My misfortune at school has now provided her with hard evidence. Here's a new chance for her to reopen her hopeless case. As soon as Baba comes home, she corners him, and grabbing my shredded hands, waves them in front of his face.

"Look! Look, Mister!" she cries with habitual panic. She won't call him by name when she's determined to shame him.

Hunched between them, I wonder why they can't just get along.

My mother is pretty, though now her face is swollen and angry. She's petite with fine light features and big brown eyes. If we had some money, lived in a rich neighborhood, I bet she would shine. She certainly has the looks, intelligence and personality, if not the educa-tion. The faux-mole sitting on her left cheek and her long curly hair gives her the look of a Hollywood actress in the 1950s, one of those quiet beauties I've seen in the old movies we watch at Aunt Fatima's house.

Baba could pass for a movie star too, maybe like a Latin lover—but he would need to have more hair. He's tall and square-shouldered, with rugged good looks, and a darker complexion than my mother. But his face is tired from debauchery, and sometimes angry.

I want to pull free and run out into the street.

Baba knows what's coming and wants to squirm out of it.

"Look at what?" he says, trying to turn away from my raw red hands.

"Don't you have eyes to see? They've punished my child for not paying the fees."

"So what if they did? He's a kid and all kids have to be punished now and then. It's part of growing up."

"What a father—really!" she says with disdain. She finally lets me go and slams a kettle of water on the ancient heater burning in our sitting room. "Just for your information, he wasn't beaten up for mis-behaving. It was because his 'caring father' dodges his responsibili-ties! It's actually you they should have punished."

"Here we go again—blaming me for everything." He's undressing, already thinking of his night out. "Is it a crime to be broke? You think I wouldn't pay if I had it?"

"You're always broke when it comes to your family. It's your Bride that's never left out. Don't you understand your children, too, need maintenance?"

"What's wrong—are you jealous of the Bride? Don't worry, I promise she will never take your place," Baba says putting on a smile, reaching to rub her shoulders.

Mama shakes off his hand and moves away.

"You always try to make a joke out of everything." The anger is gone from her voice and she even has a little smile she's trying to suppress.

"Enough of arguing now. So, what's for lunch?" He wiggles his eyebrows clownishly and rubs his hands together in anticipation of the meal.

* * *

41

The next morning, I wake up in horror, tortured by nightmares about the principal and his long stick, remembering what lies in store for me. I silently curse my mother for sending me to a school we can't afford, wishing her pain, at least a taste of the principal's stick. Mom—and no one else—is responsible for the hell I'm going through. If Baba had his way, he would have pulled me out of school immediately and let me live as I damn wish. This is not to say that he doesn't care for my future. It is just that he doesn't see very far ahead in life—for himself or his children. *Seize the moment!* is his motto. *Who knows if he'll end up dead or alive by the morrow?*

I crawl out of bed and go to the window, hoping to see a heavy snowfall, a blizzard, closing all the roads and bringing life to a stand-still. I'd pray for anything—flashfloods, earthquakes, or even volcanic eruptions—anything that might keep me out of school. Alas, there's no snow, not even a drop of rain, just a gray day with a chilling frost that burns right through to the bones. I shut the window and dawdle around, trying to think of an excuse to stay home. Then it suddenly hits me: why not feign sickness? But how? Mama is not one to fall for lame excuses. Even if I were to fall apart, she would gather up my pieces and bundle them off to school.

The Aladdin heater is still burning in the middle of the living room. I walk over and hold my head over the open top, looking straight into the wick burning with a sickly yellow flame. I freeze there until I smell hair burning and feel my skin singeing, and then rush to my mother who is spreading out a *sofreh* for breakfast, right by the samovar.

"Mom—Mom!" I say, faking alarm. "I'm running a temperature."

"That's your imagination."

"No, go ahead, feel it yourself!" I quickly grab her hand and put it on my forehead, before it turns cold. But she's not swayed.

"Have you been sitting close to the heater again? I keep telling you it's dangerous. Now go get ready or you'll be late for school."

It was my third week back in Iran, another day to decide whether to risk going out in streets ruled by fanatics, or stay home and put up with my mother's nagging. My blind retreat into a forbidding culture had already worn me out and I was thinking of leaving. With a multi-entry visa I had no problem getting back to America. What I hadn't thought of was that now I would need an exit permit to get the hell out of my homeland.

"What's your plan for today?" Mama was fidgeting nervously at the breakfast table. The small table had replaced the *sofreh*, the plastic sheet printed with flowers we used to spread on the rug and huddle around for meals. She'd kept it, using it now as a tablecloth; the floral design had gone pale and the plastic was as wrinkled as her face.

I hesitated, dreading more interrogation. "I'm . . . going to the passport office."

She poured me a glass of tea, stacked my plate with fresh bread, and then sat cross-legged on the rug, watching me eat.

"I can never get used to sitting at a table," she said. "I use it because you're here."

"You used to dream about the Western lifestyle, Mom. What happened?" I regretted the sarcasm, but she didn't hear it.

"What are you going to the passport office for?" she asked while sucking on a stale piece of bread.

"For a new passport and exit permit."

"It's not even a month since you came! You're already tired?" Her toothless mouth made a smacking sound as she gnawed the bread and I was irritated.

"Mother, why do you chew on that old piece of rubber? There's lots of fresh bread. I can't eat it all."

"Bread is bread, my son. They're all blessings from God and shouldn't go to waste. So, answer me, are you tired of being here with me?"

"Not at all, Mother. I have things to do in America," I said impatiently.

"Like what? You don't have school or a proper job. Perhaps you have a woman waiting for you?"

"Sort of."

"Who is she? What's her name?"

"Mary."

"Maria? How pretty? Is she a nice girl?" Here was something to excite her.

"What do you mean?"

"Is she the family type, one willing to live frugally and put up with hardship?"

"She definitely is." *Just like you, Mother.*

"Oh, I'm so happy. I always wanted to have a foreign bride and teach her Farsi myself. You think she would want to come and live here with us?"

"We'll see."

"Oh, Maria! I already love her, I can't wait until I see her—bring her soon, Shahed!"

The passport office was on a busy street, swarming with men and women desperate to leave the country. Those were the lucky ones. Many others on the blacklist—dissidents, entertainers and people of some wealth—would have to risk a perilous secret journey through Iraq, Turkey or Pakistan to reach the West.

There were two long queues outside the iron gate, stretching for a block on either side—one for men and one for women. It took hours to get through the stupid security stations and into the courtyard. It was also packed with a crowd waiting to get inside the vast, dilapidated warren that housed the convoluted bureaucracy.

To have an exit visa, I needed proof that I had completed military service, or a certificate to show I was studying at a university. I had neither and pinned my hope on a third option: as the oldest son in a fatherless family, I could get away without military service, supposedly to work and support my aging mother. That, however, demanded endless trips to government offices and long waits. It involved kissing many asses and taking a lot of crap from lazy and grumpy officials, if they could be found at their desks at all. I was just at the start of a surreal expedition. My purpose that day was to untangle this bureaucratic knot.

Like many other Iranian offices, the passport bureau was dominated by male workers, invariably bearded, stuffed into ill-fitting worn suits. They roamed through grimy corridors in plastic slippers, holding tattered folders, pausing frequently for long chats with their colleagues to ease the severe atmosphere.

By the time I got past the security guards and through the main building it was lunchtime. All the workers left their desks and headed downstairs, apparently to a basement kitchen. The aroma of a Persian dish had filled the narrow hallways, the only fine smell in the absence of cologne and deodorant.

I sat on a wooden bench and watched the employees climb back up the stairs, holding plates of food, and slapping along noisily in

44

slippers. They seemed excited about the humble feast, a colorful interlude in their gray day.

Once they finished eating and praying, I cautiously approached one of the public servants with my question. Without lifting his head, he pointed vaguely down a corridor.

"Can you tell me which office?" I asked.

He looked up tiredly and I recognized him at once. Edison, the bullyboy! The one who made every school day an endless hell. There were the same cold eyes, but the mischievous shine was gone. His face under a bushy black beard was no longer chubby; the fashionable devotion bruise was stamped on his creased forehead. He seemed to have met the fate Bam the disciplinarian had foreseen for a lazy clown: "You're a loser, like it or not."

A brass place on his desk identified him as "Brother Husseini." Perhaps it wasn't his desk. Maybe he had changed his name to ride out the tide of fanaticism. Without a word he buried his sad face again into stacks of memos on his desk. He didn't seem to have any idea who I was. I could have told him I was the one who had made it to the West, gloat over the luxuries and freedom I was returning to. But I felt the hollowness of such a claim; in truth, we were in the brotherhood of losers. In any event, I made no effort to refresh his memory, but turned away and headed for the next office down the corridor.

I ended up turning full circle, and after the cycle was repeated a few times, someone eventually scrawled down a note for my request to be typed.

After wandering the maze of grimy hallways, I found the typing room. The locked door had a frosted glass window. I guessed it was where the women typists and secretaries were confined. They kept as silent as they could. If they laughed, no one heard. If they talked, it came only as a whisper.

Walls along the hallways were draped with banners admonishing women to keep chaste and virtuous. *If loose dress is a sign of civilization, then animals are the most civilized of all creatures on earth!* Another dictum was more to the point: *Islamic covering (for women) is protection, not a limitation!*

Protection from whom, I thought? Us, men, predators? Are we trying to protect them from our own lust and aggression? Are we punishing women for possessing what we can't resist? Why is it they who have to pay for this utopian dream, the nightmare you pass off as a pious haven?

I knocked and the window slid open a crack, a feminine hand reached for my papers.

"Come and pick it up in fifteen minutes," said a voice muffled behind cloth.

I waited around for fifteen minutes. This time I was shown a little more, the oval of her face contoured by the black veil. As the typed page changed hands, I caught a glimpse of beauty—black eyes raised to mine, a shy smile, radiant skin. I wanted to smile too but dared not cross the boundary. Instead, I stiffened my face and dropped my eyes to appear chaste and harmless.

It was near three o'clock before I finally escaped the passport bureau, being nowhere closer to my objective. But I felt disturbed by those deep black eyes, the typist's hesitant flirtation. That subtle communication of a forbidden desire had moved my heart like no overt kiss or embrace had done in the land of sexual plenty. What was it about those eyes that haunted me so? What did they reveal that no cloak could hide?

If there's something to hide about our women, I thought, it is those eyes—not the hair, not the curves, not the smile. Or maybe that would have been in vain, too. These angels could be wrapped in layer after layer of dark quilt and they'd still radiate what they're meant to.

I took a shared taxi into the north part of Tehran, so I could walk along a broad and pleasant avenue, once called Elizabeth Boulevard, but the name had been changed to Farmer Blvd. Some of the fine boutiques still stood from the old days, and I followed a promenade running along the canal. The Persian New Year was approaching and people were out shopping, trying to revive the old spirit even for a few days. The canal, like others, had gone dry, holding more rats and frogs than water.

The cautiously jubilant mood caught me, and I found myself stepping into a boutique to buy a present for my mother. The store carried only robes and scarves for women, alternatives to the black chador, favored by more fashionable women. It hadn't been that long since the Islamic dress code had come into force, and it appeared there was still scattered resistance. A stubborn few still came out trying to look good, do a little maneuver within the mullahs' proscriptions.

I stood at the counter in the shop, looking at floral scarves, and picking a couple for my mother. I was hoping to change her morbid style, revive a semblance of her youthful past. To my left, two teenaged girls flirted with the handsome salesman. The bolder of the two had a long auburn mane flowing below her headdress, and a wavy tuft stuck out over her forehead. She was a cheerful girl, unable to keep still, talking and giggling as her friend watched in amusement.

"Is this the only color you have?" the flirt asked, holding a peach-colored robe.

"Peach looks nice on you," the man said. "It makes you look happier."

"Does it really? What makes you an expert on what women wear?"

"I have a delicate soul." He stared into her eyes, his fingers drumming on the counter.

"Oh yeah? How delicate? Give me an example."

"I collect butterflies as a hobby and design my love letters with rose petals. You want to hear more?"

"That doesn't say much," she challenged, wiggling her robed body.

"Why not try to find out for yourself? It's free to try."

He might have gone too far for the girl stiffened, and her modest friend grabbed her elbow to pull her away.

"Wait a minute. I'm not finished shopping," the cheerful girl said and turned to the salesman with the coat. "Are you sure you don't have this in blue?"

"Not in stock. But I can order it. Give me your number and I'll call you when it arrives."

"Tell me when it will come and I'll be back," she answered slyly.

I watched on for a while, lost in the gaiety of the atmosphere, and then turned to look outside. My heart sank as I saw four black figures pasted against the window, peering inside. It was the unmistakable sight of Zeinab Sisters, mannish female guards trained to crack down on nonconformist women. They were swathed in thick veils, held in place with a string around their foreheads so their hands would be free for discipline. All four were tall and one of them had the shadow of a mustache on her upper lip. Suddenly they stormed in. I didn't see exactly what happened and just heard flesh being slapped, glass breaking and panicked shrieks. I quietly slipped out, leaving behind on the counter the two scarves I had picked for my mother.

A short distance from the shop, I stopped to watch the outcome, joined by other onlookers. In moments, the girls were thrown outside and spread-eagled on the broken pavement, their faces pushed into the dust. The shy one didn't resist much, but her friend made a scene. The guards each had a foot planted on her back, and the mustachioed

Sister had the shining auburn mane rolled around her hand. In her other hand was a pair of scissors with the blades wide open. She cut through, in a jagged path, and shot the ball of hair at the sprawled figure on the ground, along with a gob of spittle. The girl strained to turn her head and directed hate-filled eyes at the guard.

"Stupid . . . scum . . . whore," she screamed, and that invited a rain of kicks.

Those watching seemed sympathetic—but they didn't dare intervene. One woman even blamed the victim in her helpless frustration.

"It serves her right," she hissed beside me. "Why can't she obey the rules? Does she think she's in Switzerland?"

At one point, two young men stepped in to help, but they froze in their tracks when a Sister pulled out her walkie-talkie for a distress call. In less than a minute two jeeps rushed to the scene with their sirens on. Male guards jumped out of the back, clutching AK-47 rifles, and I hurried away before their boots touched the ground.

Since our first meeting after Mary responded to the bell in Mr. Johnson's backyard, she was on my mind. I thought often of her sweet smile, her openness and jovial nature—everything lacking in my own personality. For weeks I made no effort to look her up, although I was curious to know her better. I wanted to know what fuelled her enthusiasm, her resolve to live and succeed despite a broken family, a cold and uncaring home, and no one to claim but an indulgent aunt and her brutish boyfriend. She was holding out well. I wanted to know the secret. Yet, I was cautious, afraid—lest I'd become embroiled. I was rather comfortable living life in the abstract and needed no distraction. A few times I walked to the bell and held its frayed rope in my hand, only to drop it and walk away.

It might have been an involuntary tug or just the wind that day that finally sounded the bell—once, twice, three times. And, sure enough, within minutes, the genie popped into view, standing at the gate with a wide grin of anticipation. She was in a tight pink flamenco dress, a wide-brimmed white hat and shoes to match. Tubes of fat circled around her waist and her lumpy tummy stuck out. Layers of powder and blush masked her pretty face. Her lips were bold red, her eyebrows thin arches, and her eyes inked in heavy lines stretching almost to her ears.

I found it an unsettling sight and just sat on the bench staring at her, feeling regret for having conjured her up. Mary's jarring ensemble stood in stark contrast to Houri—my childhood love, the phantom image of the perfect woman still in my head. I kept comparing the two, and Mary came far short—as have all the other real women I've known. Not that there were many.

"Finally!" she screamed, holding her hat in place against the draft of the wind. "What took you so long?"

"You're so . . . dressed up. Are you going somewhere?"

She didn't catch the sarcasm, or just let it pass.

"Oh, this is my favorite dress, but I don't get to wear it often—only on special occasions."

"And what's the occasion now?"

"Our date!"

She came to sit next to me and put her chubby hand on my thigh, bringing a strong scent of perfume.

"So where have you been?" she asked with a note of grievance.

"I've been busy with work—how about you?"

"Oh, everything is great, except for that little fight with Bill."

"What fight?" I was alarmed.

"Not a biggie. He keeps flirting with me when Laura isn't around, and I hate it. The other day he tried to hold me from behind and that pissed me off. He's such a jerk. I don't know why Laura puts up with that asshole."

She was whining about a man molesting her, but without any real anger. Was she really so foolishly blind to her vulnerability?

"I think you invite trouble with the way you dress and act. That worries me."

Then I felt angry for feeling concerned, giving in to this creeping sense of responsibility.

"Don't worry. I can take care of myself. It's Laura I'm worried about."

"Is he violent?"

"Oh, he's a maniac." Her accusation was so matter of fact. "He gets these fits and goes around breaking things—until Laura gives him money for drink. The other day he threw a hammer at her. It missed and hit the mirror . . . Oh, I almost forgot! Guess what? I got a job!" She bounced when she said this.

The sudden shift from complaint to euphoria made me doubt her good sense. Was it idiocy that accounted for her cheerfulness?

"You did? What kind of a job?"

"As a receptionist—at a doctor's office . . . Isn't that great? Oh, I'm so excited."

I thought she'd grow wings and become airborne soon—so I felt obliged to share in her happiness, like a responsible parent.

"Yes, it is."

It's a particularly bad day at school. Our composition teacher has called in sick and the disciplinarian comes to substitute. Bam has no teaching credentials, not even a high school diploma, but they use him to fill any gap and save money. He often shows up to change a light bulb, fix a sooty stove, or repair a leaking faucet—anything above the competence of the janitors. Once a year, on the king's birthday, for example, he even turns up as an actor, rubbing shoe polish on his face and appearing as Othello in a school play.

"Everyone on your feet," he announces on stepping into the class-room. A minute later he says: "Sit down now, with your arms crossed and observing five minutes of silence."

We do as he says, holding our breath until he gives us a rest.

"This is a new technique to control your hyperactive impulses and help you concentrate." He opens a book to give us dictation—something he usually does to fill the hour. He reads fast and mumbles and I have a hell of a time following. My hands are still sore from the beating yesterday and I can't hold the pencil in my fingers.

Bam drones on from his desk for a while and then starts walking around the classroom to check and see that everyone is writing apace, as he keeps reading aloud. There are tight rows of benches and he squeezes through them, poking his head into our notebooks. I have a double fear of being caught as a lazy student and remembered as a tuition defaulter, so every time he brushes by my desk, I bury my face into my book to remain invisible.

He inspects for ten minutes and then freezes right by my bench, his eyes fixed on my hand, which slides back and forth like the run-away cartridge of a broken typewriter. Most of what he reads I miss, but I make sure to scribble down the last word in every sentence—which is all he pays attention to. He remains glued there for some time, keeping me in a state of high anxiety, and then goes back to his desk. From the drawer he takes out a pencil and starts gouging dirt from under his fingernails with deep concentration. And we can finally rest.

With Bam so preoccupied, Edison and a few other recycled big boys in the back start teasing me. First they make fun of my looks and then begin firing spitballs at me, with my big ears as the prized target.

"Hey elephant ear, move your goddamn head," Edison says in a low hiss. "Your head is too big. I can't see the teacher dredging the sewer."

I ignore him, but he won't quit. There is something charismatic about him that I find hard to challenge—maybe his American-sounding name or his Hollywood good looks. He always dresses in designer jeans and combs back his straight brown hair like Elvis.

"I'm talking to you, mushroom head!" He pokes my back with the sharp tip of his pencil. "Are you deaf, melon head?"

I move my head sideways as far as I can and hold it there at an uncomfortable angle.

"More . . . more . . . I said more!" Edison reaches further and knocks the stationery from my desk with a rapid sweep of his hand. I turn to Bam with a despairing look, but he's too deep into his nails to notice.

"L-lay off, will you?" I stammer in a timid voice. He can't even take a mild protest and shoots up to his feet, as if insulted.

"Hey, what did you say?"

"I said . . . I said leave me alone."

"No one talks to me that way! I want to see you out in the yard, after class. Make sure you'll be there, wimp!"

Finally the bell rings for lunch break and the boys whoop out of the classroom, charging through the narrow hallway, down the stairs and into the courtyard. I'm too afraid to leave and wait until everyone is gone before tiptoeing out. I sidle along the wall like a cockroach, keeping a wary eye in case Edison springs out from a dark corner.

Out in the yard, he's trying to jump a long queue outside the cafeteria for snacks, apparently distracted from our date. That's quite a relief, and with the worry momentarily off my chest, I feel a sharp hunger. But the few *rials* I get for pocket money wouldn't take me far at our cafeteria, where almost everything is imported and frightfully expensive. So I slip into a quiet corner and watch the boys devour their fill of hamburgers, cakes and multicolor sodas in fancy bottles. Our cafeteria—it's actually just a snack shop sitting in a corner of the bare yard. But they call it that to make it sound trendy. Whatever its name, the shop is still the coolest thing we have in the whole school, and the only thing I'd miss if I ever manage to drop out of this hell. Having a shop on the school ground is actually a whole new idea in our country, a fancy addition to set our campus apart from public schools—where there's nothing to drink but tepid water from standpipes.

Our cafeteria is richly stocked with mouth-watering goodies: chocolate bars in fancy wrappings; jellybeans of a thousand colors, and different brands of chewing gums that come in exotic boxes, some with surprise gifts inside. There are also cool toys: yo-yos; puzzles; cars, trucks and airplanes running on batteries. And the variety of treasures doesn't stop there. We have such fine stationery too: designer pens, picture books with glossy pages and ribbon-bound greeting cards to mark birthdays, Mother's Day, Valentine's Day—special events I didn't even know existed before I came here.

Stuffed to their throats, the boys start messing around with the leftovers for fun, playing dodge ball with half-eaten burgers and cakes. Some shake their bottles of cola and let the fizz spray into the air, creating showers of froth and sparkles. I'm momentarily distracted from my troubles by the dazzling play of light and color. The whole scene conjures up bright images of this fantasyland they call America—a world I have come to know through films and posters.

As I go on watching, the pang of hunger grows sharper. I can wait no longer and must get something to eat. Unlike the other boys, I don't bring lunch to school—mainly because there's nothing left to bring after a meal at our home. Mama just gives me butter and jam rolled into a flat piece of bread. This is supposed to tide me over until after school; we will eat later at home when my father honors us with his presence. But her sandwiches are so tacky that I throw them to a beggar or a hungry dog before the boys can see and make fun of me.

My stomach won't stop bugging me and I keep jiggling the few coins in my pocket—the daily allowance plus the bus fare. The two combined can pay for a cake or a bubblegum, and I'm debating which one to go for. The hunger is gnawing away at my will. Lunch is a long way off . . . so, to hell with the bus! They're always dirty and packed with smelly laborers, army conscripts and perverts. It is better to travel the entire globe on foot than get on that hell ride.

Now I'm face to face with the sour-faced attendant and it's too late to back out. I slap the coins on the counter and order a cake. The second I open the cellophane wrapper, an irresistible smell hits me, sending my knees shaking. I devour the whole thing in one gulp and lick the crumbs off the cover. It's a wonderful treat but, alas, short lasting! I get a wonderful high, followed by a pang of remorse. Now I feel even hungrier and worried how I'm going to make the long trek home on an empty belly.

I struggle not to fall asleep during the math teacher's lectures. He's a tall skinny man with a thatch of white hair that makes him look like cotton candy on a stick. Every day, he comes to work in the same ragged suit, with the jacket hanging off his bony shoulders as if from a hook. His trousers hardly reach his ankles and they sag at the knees, with the seat scuffed to a shine.

I have a gnawing fear of being called to the office to answer for the late tuition. So I rehearse a few lines to hand the principal in case that happens. It's a sad story to soften his stony heart . . . like I'm an orphan, or about to become one.

Every few minutes there's a knock on the door and I jump in fright, thinking it's Bam coming to get me. But it's always the office boy delivering an emergency supply of fruits and snacks from a worried mom to her sweetheart. Once, a housemaid even showed up, dispatched hurriedly to shove food down the throat of a brat who wouldn't eat enough.

Time crawls on toward two o'clock and my hope rises of pulling through the day in one piece. I keep looking at my benchmate's watch, a stainless steel job big enough to hang from a wall. Just seconds before the closing bell, the door flies open and Bam storms in, waving my arrest warrant. He interrupts the class to bugle the reason for his mission, as if it's anyone's business, and everyone turns to look at me like I'm a repulsive criminal.

I follow him out of the classroom, heading as slowly as I can toward the office, where the Gestapo is waiting. Just before we reach the yard, the bell goes off and the boys break out as if from a madhouse, rushing to catch sight of the *houris* before they evaporate. Their march, however, comes to a halt at the gate, where a fat janitress in an Islamic headscarf stands guard. The boys have now jammed the door and are banging at the janitress with their school-bags, trying to move her out of the way. But the fat lady stands there like a boulder, pressing her hands against the doorjambs and using her big breasts as shock absorbers.

Bam is trying to weave us through the dense crowd, his hand clamped around my arm, but without any luck. The brats get nastier by the second, doing whatever it takes to break loose. When all else fails, they lock arms to form a battering ram and slam their bodies hard against the janitress in repeated thrusts. She takes the first few knocks and finally flies backward, sprawling on the ground like a turtle on its back—with the boys marching all over her like a marauding gang of ants.

The confusion allows me to break free and melt into the crowd. Under cover of rampaging boys I tiptoe toward the exit, where the principal stands seeing off the girls. This is a daily routine with the general, accompanying the young ladies to their parents' cars or the awaiting school buses.

My father has a theory on this:

"The old lecher does this to grope the girls who are in full flower," he says with a hint of longing. "He uses his blindness as a license to feel his way around."

The general is now all smiles, showing none of the severity from the patriotic ceremony yesterday. There's even a red rose pinned to his vast sloping chest to suit the tender occasion. He hugs and kisses the girls as if he's not going to see them again, his face breaking into a pained expression with every parting.

In the morning, he goes through the same routine, greeting the females as they walk into school as if taking roll.

"Is that you, honey?" he murmurs into a tender ear, cupping a pair of walnut-sized tits. "Oh, you are here. Good!" Then he moves to the next: "And you too? Wonderful!" "And you, my darling? Super!" He goes on and on—until he's relieved everyone is in attendance. Some of the girls are onto his tricks and run away with a giggle as they see him approaching. But there are always the naïve ones who walk right into the trap.

Pressed against the stone archway, I watch the old man in action, waiting for the right moment to sneak out. As I'm about to slip into a fantasy of myself in a harem with the *houris*, I see Bam still scuttling around the yard looking for me.

Finally a janitor guides the principal out onto the sidewalk to meet a fashionably dressed mother, and I see a chance to escape. I slip to the exit, throw a quick look around and duck out—keeping my eyes shut not to see the danger. I haven't taken a few steps before a huge hand closes around my arm. When I look up, there's the general towering over me.

"Who's this?"

No answer.

"I said who is it? What's your name?"

I stutter into silence.

"Stop mumbling! Tell me what you're doing here."

Frozen, I don't even have the presence of mind to lie.

"Wait here!" he says and sends a janitor for Bam.

A few teachers are in the office, drinking tea and submitting their reports. Cotton Candy is also present, doing off-duty work as the accountant. He must have been the one who first discovered my payment wasn't up to date and sounded the alarm. The men rise from their seats in respect to the general and then pull their chairs back to make room, as if I'm there to dance for them. One of the men runs to help the general settle his girth behind the desk and then walks backward to his chair like a subservient robot. The principal makes some idle chat with the teachers and then turns his full attention to me.

"Come closer!" he orders and I take a step forward.

"Come still closer."

He has me move closer and closer until I'm within striking range.

"Okay, Shahed. You have brought the tuition money?"

"No, sir," I say, looking at the floor.

"No! How rude!—to say a thing like that before these gentlemen."

Before I have a chance to speak, he claws at my ear and this time he's right on target.

"I won't allow the likes of you to hold my sacred operations up to ridicule." He begins the twisting. "Your parents want a good education for you, they ought to pay. Do you understand?"

I shake my head while squirming to ease the pain.

"So tell me when I'll get my money."

55

I want to blurt out the speech I'd prepared, but don't remember a word of it. So he gives my ear a sharp tug and I let out a shriek that sends everyone out of their chairs. First I think they're coming to save me from the monster but instead they rush to shut the door to keep the noise inside. Assured of privacy, the general lets go of my ear and gives me a hard crack across the face, so hard that it prickles every nerve in my body. Then a volley of threats and ultimatums follow: I will do this or I will do that if the money is not in my pocket by tomorrow.

"Do you hear me, stupid kid?" he shouts, his roars ringing in the room and pounding at my eardrums.

"Yes, sir," I say, feeling dizzy, shaking hard.

"I want it by tomorrow—do you understand?"

Yes, I do, old man—if that's what you want to hear. But you won't see your money—not tomorrow, not the day after, nor a week or a month from now. I won't even bother to tell my father about it. Why waste my breath?

What I don't understand is why you don't kick me out of your damn school and spare me all the trouble? Maybe by torturing me you hope to lure my father to your office—outraged and demanding explanation. Dream on, greedy old man! If Baba ever shows his hide around here, it wouldn't be to file a complaint or check on my performance—he'd come only to check out your pretty chicks, the "juicy peaches," as he calls them. Sure, I've seen the Buick pulling up outside school—its long, sleek hood sticking out and the broad tailfins blinking like a UFO. He parks it right by the entrance, opening the door and keeping one foot inside—to leave no doubt who owns this rare piece of art. There he stands for a good hour, a hand stuffed in his pocket and a lit cigarette dangling from his mouth. He surveys the girls with cool, predatory eyes, watching them march obediently into the general's loving arms. There's a flicker of jealousy in his eyes. Baba would love nothing more than to be in the blind man's place, with a "God-given" license to swim through a sea of feminine beauty. He might even be ready to offer up his eyesight, if that's what it takes to have a taste of these heavenly fruits.

NEIGHBORHOOD

I leave school with a battered ear that smarts like hell in the biting cold. My school stands on a grade, in a hilly, somewhat chic neighborhood. The sidewalks are still covered with snow from a recent fall, now turning hard and sooty. The sun is too weak to loosen the ice and snow keeps piling up, as people shovel it off their roofs and dump the mess down below. It's way past two o'clock and the streets are deserted. Shopkeepers have pulled down their gray tin shutters for the mid-day break. Only a few beggars and laborers are lounging about on the sidewalks, dozing off or drinking tea from smudged glasses.

Weak from hunger and the beating, I have no idea how to cover the three miles home on foot. I look about to see if my father is still around from one of his "peach" hunts, hoping to catch a ride from him. But he is nowhere to be seen and I set off on my own, along a shadowy and cold tunnel of trees. Boutiques, coffee shops and movie theaters line the street on both sides, interspersed with dirt lots and construction sites—where tall modern buildings are going to go up.

After a mile, My legs wobble and my knees are giving way. Hurting, exhausted, I drag myself along for a few more blocks and then turn into an alley and collapse to the ground—between a parked Chevrolet and a heap of garbage, where a few cats are feeding.

"Burger Land," an American fast food restaurant, is right around the corner, with the window of its kitchen opening onto the alley. Plumes of smoke rich with the smell of grilled meat puff out of the window fan, giving the cats the illusion of having a real feast. The beasts pause and give me a quizzical look, wondering if I'm posing any threat, and I stare back across the pile of trash. Our eyes remain locked for a few seconds and then I break into a sob, pulling my knees up to cover my teary face. I heave and sob for a long time, until there are no more tears to shed. Only a hoarse cry comes out.

Then I hear a soothing voice:

"What's the matter, little man . . . is something wrong?"

I peer up and there's a tall elegant lady leaning over me. She has no veil on, wearing instead a long white leather coat of the latest fashion. It hangs open and I see a silky dress that clings to her body and smell a delicious perfume. Her eyes are large as a fawn's, light brown under long eyelashes. Her skin glows, her long chestnut hair falls forward when she stoops to look in my face. I have never seen anyone so beautiful.

She reaches to stroke my hair but I stiffen with resistance, too proud, too ashamed to be seen sniveling with snot and dirt on my face. She tries a little more consolation, and unable to break my resistance, she walks swaying to the Chevrolet and opens the door. Casting a compassionate look in my direction, the beautiful woman gets inside and drives off, leaving me to the stink of the garbage heap.

I try to cry some more, but the interruption has broken the rhythm and I can't get it back. The outburst, however, has had its effect and I already feel better. I grab my bag, shuffle to my feet and plod along, looking forward to a delicious meal.

It would take me about an hour to get home from school, but it was like a journey to another time and space. The area around my school was not the best we had in our beautiful city, but it was still a universe apart from where I lived. Hajiabad was caught in a time warp. As one approached our street, evidence of the modern age steadily faded, coming to a sudden halt at our very doorstep. My neighborhood was a cursed landscape of broken pavements, sooty walls and stinking gutters—clogged with garbage and flowing with a pissing stream of black water.

Life in Hajiabad—it's like when there was no life. There were no cinemas; no "Burger Lands;" no fine boutiques or fancy cars; and no good-looking dames, fashionably dressed and perfumed. Our women were, like they are today, hidden under black chadors, leaving nothing but their eyes exposed, and sometimes the nose too. We got around on ramshackle buses, rickety donkey carts and tireless legs; and for restaurants, there were traditional eateries, serving greasy stews of slaughterhouse offal.

In retrospect, my neighborhood foreshadowed what was to befall this land. It presaged the gloom, the hypocrisy, the oppressiveness.

* * *

I round the corner and amble down our narrow street—past the butcher's shop, the greengrocer's, the public bathhouse, and the old mosque with its chipped dome and wobbly minaret. Then there's a row of houses with intervening shops—all decaying structures with paint flaking or gone, roofs caving in or walls giving out. Our house is right in the middle, flanked by a barbershop and a pawnshop, and overlooking a gutter lined with a stunted trees.

As I approach, there's Taj, the neighborhood idiot, standing watch against "evil." Taj is our guardian angel, so to speak, a self-proclaimed crusader against the invasion of Western culture. All day long he roams the streets praising Allah and denouncing the devil, which he finds in everything unfamiliar. At times, he gets too carried away with his campaign and attacks women showing too much hair or dogs shamelessly mating in public. That's when the police catch him and beat him senseless, as if that would deliver him of his insanity and turn him into a law-abiding citizen. But the idiot is stubborn as a bull and resilient as a cat. He always bounces back to enforce his code with even greater zeal:

"It is my calling to purge the neighborhood of sin and corruption . . . and I have no one to answer to but God Himself!"

A donkey cart is all the idiot has in this world, and he uses it to peddle rotting fruits in the summer and ancient onions and potatoes in the winter. Taj has a severe case of hernia, and his bulging testicles are the butt of everyone's jokes. With no entertainment in our community, the fool and his companion are the biggest crowd attraction—especially on Fridays and religious holidays, when there's not much to do. Of course, we have other occasional diversions, like one-man circuses and stunt shows. But the good thing about Taj is that he's always there to poke fun at and get cheered up a little when you are depressed.

Taj gets along with nobody except for my father. He likes Baba because my father treats him more decently than others do and gives him money when he has any. In return, the idiot plays the loyal stooge, offering any services his cracked brain would allow. For one thing, he doesn't harass my mother as he does other women, although Mom's *hejab* doesn't cover her enough to be acceptable by his strict standards.

On busy days, when streets are congested, Taj also doubles as a private traffic cop. As soon as the Bride wheels down the street, he jumps in the middle of the road holding up traffic—until my father eases the big boat past and parks level with the gutter running along the sidewalk.

His greatest service though comes as an informer, tipping off his master about creditors lying in wait outside our house. And this seems to be what the idiot is doing now—playing the spy again, while keeping a wary eye for obscenities. He's holding a newspaper before his face and his frayed wool hat is pulled down over his eyes—as if to keep himself in the dark as much as those he wants to trick. As soon as he notices me approaching, he cocks his head wildly, trying to warn me of a danger lurking about. My eyes follow his lead and fall on a small man standing across the street, staking out our residence. It's Khan, the notorious loan shark, and my blood runs cold. He is dressed in the usual outfit: dark suit, wide-brimmed felt hat and mismatched white canvas shoes.

Khan is the most tenacious of the bill collectors stalking my father. He's constantly on Baba's trail but never quite manages to catch up with him. My father, too, enjoys playing cat and mouse with him, getting a boyish thrill from being chased around the city by a little man. Sometimes he invites the midget to a fancy restaurant to discuss a debt, only to sneak out and leave his guest to answer for the bill. But the problem is that it is Mama and I who have to deal with the creep. When Khan can't get his hands on Baba, he keeps bugging us for news of his whereabouts.

Khan is now lurking by the coal warehouse across the street, his eyes sewn to our door. For some long seconds he surveys me, shading his eyes with one hand for better vision, and then starts walking in my direction—noisily, the rubber soles of his canvas shoes slapping hard against the asphalt. I fall into a panic and run quickly to ring the bell, but no one comes to the door—they must think it is Khan. The creep is closing in and I keep my finger pressed on the bell. But still there's no response, except for the mews of the cat we've brought to kill off the rats, breeding at a mad rate in our basement. So I start kicking and banging at the door, and the cat starts clawing. Khan is now right by my side and I feel the clamp of his hand around my arm. He slides off his hat with his free hand, exposing a thin mat of hair, oiled heavily and parted in the middle.

"I didn't mean to disturb you, young man, but there is a matter of great urgency I must bring up with you." He's almost simpering.

"What about?" I ask stupidly.

"Don't panic, my son. It is your father I want to talk about—his irresponsible behavior, his constant attempt to elude me."

"I don't know anything. Go talk to him." I'm trying to squirm out of his grip.

"My son, you are a big boy already—and intelligent, too. How old are you—twelve, thirteen, somewhere around there? You know your father better than I do . . ."

"I'm not allowed to talk to strangers!"

"There is just one thing I want to ask you: is this the way to treat a friend, to reciprocate a favor? Was it a crime to lend him money when no one else was willing to take the risk? So, why does he dodge his obligation? Why does he make sport of me? Am I his plaything or something, a ball to be bounced around?"

As he talks, he keeps closing the distance between us, until our noses are about to touch. We're almost the same height and I can smell stale tobacco on his breath, and feel jets of saliva spray into my face as he gets excited.

"Listen young man, if your father goes on deviating, there will be no other recourse but to take serious action against him . . ."

Here the door suddenly flies open and the hand of an angel yanks me inside, and before Khan can say anything, the door slams shut.

"Creep!" my mother says, dragging me through the dark, narrow corridor toward the sitting room on the left. "I don't know what he wants camping at our door all the time."

My father is also at home, as I well expected. He's in the living room, lounging against a stack of pillows and paging through a women's fashion magazine. As I stumble in, he flashes a self-satisfied smile, obviously pleased at having outfoxed his stalker.

"Come and sit by me," he says. "The talking-head gave you an earful, didn't he?"

I nod weakly and go to him. He takes me into his arm and draws me close to kiss, but I'm too angry to let him.

"So, what did Khan say to you? Tell me all about it."

"I don't know . . . wasn't really listening."

"Then let me tell you how I tricked him," he says excitedly.

"I'm listening."

He stands up to act it out, like a boy recounting an action film:

"I saw him standing there like a sentinel . . . I drove away and parked the Bride a few blocks away . . . I had the idiot lure him

61

away . . . then I slipped right in . . . Isn't that funny? . . . ha ha ha . . . But he must be wise to it now . . . that's why he's glued to our door . . ."

Then he pauses, as if struck by an important thought.

"How come you're so late, my son? What took you so long?"

"Khan was holding me up," I lie.

"Bastard! At least you had a good laugh, didn't you?"

"I guess I did."

"All right, why don't you sit and relax until lunch is ready. The meal today is taking forever, as if she's going to feed the whole Chinese army."

I sit with him and he starts teasing me to provoke a wrestling match, shoving and slapping me lightly. But I'm not playing; I'm sore and hungry and still cold.

"Oh, you're no fun! Then I'd better give you an errand."

I stiffen with alarm. Every afternoon Mama and I have to go through an elaborate ritual of preparing him for his evening out. First I have to take his clothes to the laundry and pick up the clean ones for him to wear the same night. Then I take his shoes out for a polish and after that, go to wash his car—all while he's taking a sweet afternoon nap. Once he's awake, my mother and I escort him to the blue concrete tub out in the yard and give him a thorough scrub, before he's ready to be dressed and groomed.

All this really gets on my nerves—especially when he pulls me out of a fun game to give me a chore, something he could do himself if he bothered to lift a finger. Once, when he summoned me out of a game of hopscotch to iron his shirt, I touched the hot iron to his toes. I don't know if I did it on purpose or was just in too much of a rush to get back to play. But he was furious and chased me around the yard for five minutes, hopping on one leg. Arash was too small then to understand what was going on and kept laughing. He thought Baba had come to play hopscotch with us.

I feel too weak and hungry to go out but don't have the guts to refuse his order. I go to the sink and swallow a worm of toothpaste to kill the pang of hunger, and then get his dirty clothes from the closet, bundle them under my arm and go out the door.

Outside, Khan is still nailed to his post, talking to the owner of the coal warehouse. The coalman is also a neighborhood vigilante, like Taj, but at least the idiot laughs sometimes, even when you're laughing at him. The coalman is ill-tempered as a camel, his forehead always creased in a deep frown. When business is slow, as it is all through summer, he sits outside his warehouse glowering at women who don't mind their manners or children making too much noise playing. He's a scary sight. It takes only a scowl, one twist of his sooty face and bloodshot eyes to send one running for cover. The coalman is a regular player in my nightmares, like the principal. I see him in every spooky shadow flickering on the wall when I go out at night to the outhouse toilet.

Thank god business is good this cold winter and he spends all day inside the warehouse, shoveling around bins of coal, and counting up receipts. The coalman is in a crappy line of business, as my father says, but he's rolling in money, making enough to afford two wives and house them in separate quarters. His first, a frayed, barren woman, lives right next door to us; and the younger one, fertile as a rabbit, enjoys a comfortable life in a mansion up in a more affluent area, not too far from us but populated by merchants of some wealth. The zealot himself spends most nights with the queen of his modest harem, coming to our ghetto just to hold religious services in his other house—all loud and depressing affairs that torture my father and his sense of fun.

Khan is certain that my father is at home, and as I slip out the door, he throws me a suspicious glance. I ignore it and walk on my way, looking in the other direction. Halfway down the block, I pause for a look back and see the horrible midget following me. I break into a run, bolting blindly until I skid on an icy patch and trip, sending the bundle of clothes under my arm flying around. I hear a tinkling, the unmistakable sound of coins hitting a hard surface. Quickly I search the pockets, ignoring the pain shooting up my limbs; and to my delight, there's some money—not a whole lot but enough to buy a little junk food at the local bazaar. The coins glitter in my palm with a seductive shine, and I keep staring at them, unsure whether or not to pocket them. I'm so hungry my whole body is throbbing with temptation but I'm afraid to take the risk. What if the coins are planted there to test me? What if Baba finds out the money is missing? And if he does, who is he going to suspect?

Give me a break!—is another voice I hear. *You'd be a fool not to take it.* How can this be a trap? Baba is too self-absorbed to come up with such schemes. He's too absent-minded to notice a few coins gone missing. Even if he does learn about it, I'll be ready with a culprit—the laundryman, for example, who is a notorious finder-keeper. After a few moments of painful uncertainty, the coins find their way swiftly into my pocket.

The godsend money boosts my mood and I look forward to a bender in the bazaar. I quickly return home, hang up the freshly-pressed suits in the closet and dash out of the room, before Baba can see me and give new orders. I skip down the stairs, heading straight for the kitchen to check on Mom's lengthy preparations. She says she needs a few more minutes and I go to kill the time with the cat, hoping to find it in the middle of a big fight with the rats.

THE HOUSE

Our house is a brick and concrete wreckage with two shops in the front to lease out. We've got three rooms, one opening onto the other, and each with a door so low that even the midget would have to bow to enter. The one closest to the street we use as a living room; the middle one as a dining and bedroom; and the last, which is a bit larger, to receive and sleep guests. Each chamber also has a small window, allowing a weak ray of light and a grim view of the cement wall opposite, rising flush to heaven. The wall was erected by the coalman next door to give privacy to his first wife, that severely religious soul whose face even the sun has not seen.

There's almost no furniture in this house: no chairs, no tables, no beds—only a few floor mattresses and a pair of threadbare rugs that my father has yet to get around to selling. We eat our meals on the floor and sleep on the floor—all together in the middle room. Mama always keeps the "reception hall" clean and locked, especially during the Persian New Year when it is stocked with fruits, cookies and candies. This is a cultural thing with us Persians, anxious to look prosperous even when we are not, "slapping our cheeks red to appear robust," as we say.

A narrow balcony runs outside the rooms, leading at the end to a sunken tub we use as a sink, where we wash up every morning—if the weather is not too cold and the pipes aren't frozen. A short flight of stairs leads down into the small yard where the outhouse is, and another murky flight into the basement: a damp and airless dungeon we use partly as a kitchen and the rest to store cast-off—mainly scraps of moldy bread my grandfather feeds his livestock. Every now and then, the basement turns into a temporary guesthouse for sheep or goats on their way from the farm to the slaughterhouse.

Grandpa uses rotten bread for feed because it is cheaper than hay and still keeps the milk flowing, and it also makes sure his cows don't get too spoiled. These piles of waste downstairs make a good home for rats and cockroaches, and they never stop breeding. Our poor feline does her best to slow down the reproduction rate, but there is only so much she can do—being vastly outnumbered by an enemy sometimes bigger in size. Still, she puts up a brave fight, running fierce battles that leave pools of blood all over the kitchen floor—spine-chilling scenes that disgust and horrify Mama to no end. But I find it all rather entertaining. With nothing better to do, I fritter away whole afternoons enjoying these bloodbaths and the crunch of small bones.

"We could have done a lot better if your father wasn't such a wastrel," Mama always complains. If you ask my mother, it's not really an ideal life, and certainly not one we deserve. "With the money he throws away in one night, we could have leased one of those American-style townhouses advertised on television—the ones with flowery wallpapers and tiles. We could have modern appliances."

The house belongs to Grandpa, who had it built ages ago for a place to stay when he came to the city for business—like to buy or sell a herd of livestock. The bricklayer who jumbled it together was an old man with shaky hands and no experience in home building—before that, he had only sheds and chicken coops to his credit. But his fees were small. One of the shops in front is now rented by a barber and the other by a scrap dealer—who happens to be my father's main trading partner, buying whatever household item that goes on auction. The house itself was for rent up until two years ago, when Baba hit rock bottom and we had to move in here or live on the streets.

Grandpa himself has never actually lived here. On the rare occasions he visits town, he'd rather stay with one of his six daughters—especially the eldest, Aunt Fatima, who is a good host and can really cook. Baba and Grandpa are irreconcilable as knife and cheese, fighting most of the time over money. Baba expects his father to be more generous with his money, but the old man isn't going to waste another *rial* on his "good-for-nothing" son. Grandpa has nothing but disdain for a man "whose only talent is in chasing whores."

Nor does Baba have any love to waste on "an old miser with the heart of a wolf."

"The cheap bastard even holds onto his crap for fear of getting hungry," he says of his father.

* * *

There's a lull in the fighting between the cat and the rats, as the feline becomes distracted by the wonderful smell of lamb, rice and saffron filling the basement. Mama is putting the final touches on the meal, adjusting flames in the kerosene stoves upon which rice and lamb stew are cooking in separate pots. The stoves haven't been burning too well, which is why the food is late in coming. But finally we are going to eat. The cat and I have parked our butts on the floor, impatiently waiting for the chef to start serving.

In a few minutes the floral cloth on the floor is laden with rice, stew, salad, and pickles. It is an impressive spread considering Mom's tiny budget. She really has a talent. Forced into thriftiness, she is particularly frugal with meat—which is sort of a luxury at our home. She slices the meat into tiny bits and lets the pieces swim all over the stew to ensure everyone has their fair share. But Baba always gets more than his share. He gets the lion's share, so to speak—raking the chunkier pieces to his plate, leaving the scraps for the cubs to nibble at.

He has now heaped his plate with food and is chomping away like a famine survivor, while my brother and I are waiting politely to be served. Mama ladles a spatula of rice into each of our plates and tops it with a scoop of stew, putting some pickles on the side for relish, and we hunch over, eating at a slow, measured pace. I have this habit of saving my precious meat for last to savor it longer. Baba, on the other hand, finishes all the lamb first, and if he still has any appetite, he'll hit the rice.

He's now done with his meat and I can see him darting furtive glances at my plate, waiting for the opportune moment to raid.

"Looks like you don't have appetite for meat today," he says, waving a long fork. "Which is not a bad thing—meat is not really good for you."

Knowing what's coming, I lean deeper over my plate, using my thin frame to shield it. But tiny limbs are no defense against a carnivore with a bottomless appetite and powerful muscles. Before you know it, he lunges with his fork and snatches the meat away right from under my nose.

"Ha-ha-ha!" He laughs hugely while he gobbles it up, as if it has all been a funny joke.

I pout, teetering on the verge of tears. But my father doesn't like crying children.

67

"What's the matter?" He smiles while he wipes his mouth and pats my shoulder. "Are you a kid or something, making a fuss over little things?"

"Don't forget to wash the car!" he reminds me as he makes himself comfortable for his nap.

I fetch a bucket, fill it with water and drag it out the door. The Buick is left a few blocks down the street to mislead Khan and it is such a drag to carry water so far, lapping and soaking me. I finally make it there and see the Bride parked sloppily, leaving barely enough room for other vehicles to squeeze past. It is, I notice, fitted out with a dizzying array of new accessories: bumpers, hood ornament, and a huge pair of side mirrors. The chrome tailpipe he installed just a week ago sticks out the back and fancy nickel hubcaps glitter in the late afternoon sun. The whole ensemble looks more like a spacecraft poised for takeoff or an alien machine just landed from Mars.

A gaggle of children in rags crowd around the car, marveling at the mind-boggling invention. The very sight of the Buick in our squalid neighborhood is an event in itself, something akin to a carnival or a lavish parade. When it skims down the street, my father posed majestically inside, an arm resting on the steering wheel and an elbow jutting out the window, people stand back and stare. Baba is all too aware of the appeal and tries to play it to the full—rolling past at a turtle's pace, allowing everyone a full treat.

As I open the door, the boys look at me enviously, as if the Buick is something to be proud of, as if there was more in it for me than washing it.

"Hey, mister boy!" one of the urchins calls out with mocking respect. "Would you mind if we sit in your car and play with the fancy gadgets a little?"

In your dreams, beggar boy! My father would never allow the likes of you to sit in his car or even lean against it. The nearest you may come to touching it is when he has a flat tire and needs help fixing it—and that's only the tires.

"So what do you say, mister boy?"

"No, my father would kill me if I did such a thing."

"Then up yours, sissy! And tell your Baba to stop parading his car like a trophy."

68

The boys still stand, staring and wise cracking. I don't like to be seen washing a car by the side of the road, with the legs of my pants rolled up and my bare feet slapping on the filthy wet asphalt. The worst part is when some schoolgirls walk past giggling, obviously making fun of me. Then I get so embarrassed that I want the ground to open up and swallow me whole.

Baba himself would never stoop to a lowly job like this, which is why he sends me to do it for him. He thinks because I'm a kid I don't have any pride, no reputation to worry about. Only once was Taj, the idiot, honored with the job. But he did such a lousy job that the Bride came out looking like a spotted cow. After that I inherited the privilege of a full-time job.

Another thing I really hate about cleaning the car is the leftovers I find while sweeping the inside—telltale feminine objects like an earring, a lipstick, or even a bra. Whatever they are, I quickly hide them, shove them back under the seats—before Mama could raise hell about it. The last thing I want is another fight between my parents.

By the time I get back, Baba is up from his nap, stretching his limbs and yawning pleasurably. In a few minutes, he's ready for his bath. There's no shower at home, or hot running water; for a wash, there's only the public bathhouse up the street. But it is so filthy that my father wouldn't set foot there, preferring to get his bath in the basin in the yard—even on cold winter days. Baba is very athletic and says he doesn't mind the shock of icy water—but, he tells us, it's more healthy to have some hot water. So I haul two buckets of warm water from the samovar to the yard.

Once we're done bathing him, he has to be spruced up, which is mainly my mother's job, and something she seems to enjoy. She spends an hour on him, attending to every detail, until he's finally ready to be launched for the evening. She has to see what he's wearing is a perfect match, that his jacket sits squarely on his broad shoulders and his trousers are so sharply creased as to cut through a melon. She makes sure that there's no fluff on his suit, that his Clark Gable mustache is well-trimmed and his thinning hair is combed to cover his balding pate. Mama does it all with so much care, as though she's going to be a part of the evening fun, as if she is his date. Sometimes I think it is her fault that he has turned out to be so spoiled and demanding. But, come to think of it, it is not so easy to say no to my father, a man of his magnetism and serpentine charm.

Before leaving, he gives us a generous dose of entertainment—a reward for our hard work and to sustain us through the long lonely evening. He sits on a mat at the head of the room and we kneel before him as in worship, and he reads to us from *Zan-e Rooz*, a contemporary women's magazine popular with all. He thumbs intently through the pages, looking for an episode of a melodrama or passages from the gossip or agony columns—all compelling tales of sin and betrayal: a girl losing her virginity in a flash of blind passion, a hapless pair lost in an incestuous affair, or a child led astray into a life of crime and addiction.

Baba is a master of this drama. He delivers the lines with such flair, his voice rising, falling and quivering, his eyes glistening, that it feels like we're actually living the experience. It is as if he takes our hearts in his hands and wrings them dry.

"So you're going to leave us alone again and take off for the night?" Mama asks as her husband is about to turn out the door, as if the bitter truth just dawned on her.

"Do you have to ask that every night?" he says feigning exasperation.

"We get bored sitting here with nothing to do. You could at least take us with you."

"You think our tails are tied together? Give me some room to breathe!"

She stands in the door, eying him with uncertainty. "At least leave some money so I can take them out—to the movies or something."

"Are you crazy, with all the wolves prowling around the town? I wouldn't feel safe about sending my young, beautiful wife alone out in the streets."

"Then you come with us. You wouldn't die spending a night with your family."

"Not tonight. I'm seeing some important people."

"Who are these 'important' people you always hide from me? Bring them here so we can meet them."

"They're not the sort one would trust with his family."

"Why? Are they whores or pimps?" I wish Mama would stop. She will only make it worse.

He doesn't answer and steps out, leaving a cloud of cologne and a pile of aching hearts.

For a few minutes I sit there remembering the lost souls in the melodrama, trying to be glad someone suffers more than me. Then I grab my jacket and duck out the door, heading straight for the bazaar to spend the godsend money.

In our little bazaar, I wander about for a while taking in the all-too-familiar scenes. It's a maze of dark twisting alleys with dim evening light coming through a ceiling of latticed skylights. I push my way through mobs of shoppers who browse and bargain with scruffy merchants in crowded cubicles. The strong smells of oriental spices, rosewater and cheap perfumes are mixed with the stench of the ever-present gutter. Haulers with enormous loads weave and jostle through the dense crowd, rushing to reach their destination and dump more cheap junk in the stalls. The shabby neighborhood bazaar is as far as I can go with my few coins.

I pass rolls of cheap fabric stacked up to the ceiling, bushels of legumes and spices displayed outside stalls, and plastic or metal household wares hanging from hooks. Then I stop off at a vendor selling pin-up posters of movie stars and famous athletes. Among them is a dashing portrait of James Bond flashing a pistol, flanked by two pretty blonds. I always wanted that picture and almost buy it. But a few yards away is something more enticing: a mound of syrupy sweets sitting in a large tray. The peddler himself looks awful with his gnarled brown limbs baked by the sun. His face is full of scabs from wounds not healing too well and his nose is running from either a flu or drug addiction. Even on a chilly winter day, a swarm of flies shuttle back and forth between the pus on his face and the sweets in the tray, as if not sure which would make a better treat.

I can't decide between the poster and the sweets, but eventually go for the sweets. I hand the peddler my coins and he drops them in a tin pot at his side. Then he puts a sticky pretzel in a cone of newspaper and sends me on my way. I can't take it home because my mother will kill me, so I nibble at it walking along, totally lost in its deliciousness. It tastes so great that I'm already plotting a heist to finance another trip to the bazaar.

When I walk back down our street, I see Usta, the barber and circumciser, sitting outside his shop. He's undressing women with his unchaste eyes, something he always does when business is slow. The barber seems to have lasers for eyes, able to penetrate the thickest veils, even in the shadows of twilight. As soon as a feminine shape looms out in the distance, he locks his radar on her and won't let go until she passes down the street and fades into a dot. Usta is married, but his wife is too skinny to satisfy him in bed—that, I guess, gives him the right to lust after other women, especially the white plump ones. This I know because he tells me everything about his private life.

"My wife is just a skeleton . . . she must lie in the bottom of a grave, not in my bed . . . with all those bones she'd make a great meal for a dog." His complaint is familiar by now: "You know what, I get more turned on touching my own ass than hers . . . she's like stale bread. Listen, Shahed, I'll give you a word of advice: try to marry late and even then, someone with a quilt of meat around her bones."

Usta is not my idea of great company but I'm drawn in by his talk of sex. He has an answer to all my questions, offering them with such juicy details that blow me away. He's actually the one who first told me how babies are made. Such facts I could never get out of Mom, no matter how much I squeeze her. She just goes on insisting that my brother and I came through a slit opened in her belly, and she even has a scar to prove it.

But the barber has a nasty side, too, which usually comes out when he's sore at something, like when my grandfather raises his rent. Then he takes it out on my brother and me when we go there for a haircut. First, he brandishes an array of sharp tools he uses in his trade, and cracks his razor strop next to our ears with a loud snap. He gnashes his rotten teeth and smacks his tongue, as if in anticipation of some great fun. He plays at this for a long while and once we're scared and subdued as lambs, he takes out his clippers and sheers us like sheep.

The worst part is when he shaves the back of our necks with the rusty razor he also uses to circumcise babies. He works at a leisurely pace, scratching his way around, and then rubs in a green musk that burns like acid. Through it all, we're expected to sit up ramrod straight, without so much as wincing or blinking. If we slump under, he'll give us a whack right where it hurts the most: on the back of our raw necks. It's a full session of torture, and we always come out badly scarred and with teary eyes.

My brother is terrified of Usta because he knows he'll one day pass under his razor. But I don't have as much to fear, since I've already been circumcised. Still, you never know where you stand with the sadist, and it is always better not to get on his wrong side.

The barber is now perched on his stool resting a foot on his knee and twirling a string of prayer beads around his index finger while whistling. As he turns to check out a veiled figure, I slip past and head to the door. But his eyes catch me and I hear my named called.

"Hey, Shahed, come here. I want to show you something."

"What?"

"Look at that whore! Look at what she's wearing under that chador."

I peer at the woman—probably just a housewife passing down the street—but she's covered from head to foot.

"See, I'm trying to warn you not to fall for the wrong woman or you'll get stuck with a whore all your life. Why carry a weight around your neck forever when there are so many of them begging for it?"

But women absolutely hate Usta and change their routes once they see him staring, even if that means extra blocks to walk. His only chance is with street women he sometimes sneaks into his shop, usually on quiet afternoons when folks retire for their midday break. I sometimes hear noises coming through the hatchway set in the common wall of our houses. The hatchway is there for escape in emergencies, but we use it more to eavesdrop on each other.

I clawed myself out of a ditch only to fall into a well goes a Persian expression. That well describes my hasty return to Iran in the winter of 1982. What was intended to be a bout of convalescence in my homeland I spent mostly trying to find a way out. At dawn every morning, I went to the military recruitment bureau with my mother, waiting in long lines and crying for attention from rude public servants. Still I was not getting any closer to my goal: a military discharge to pave the way for an exit visa. On the Iranian weekend—which consists of only one day, Friday—I roamed about the streets, losing myself in the buzz and hum of the city, with no purpose but to be free of my mother's suffocating care.

* * *

One Thursday evening, I was frittering time away outside Play Town, an amusement park once called Luna Park. It was one of the few recreation centers that had somehow survived chaos, violence or neglect.

The brick wall hemming the park bore paling images of Disney characters, along with the scars of bullets and tiresome political slogans. Inside was a primitive rollercoaster still creaking along, giving the grateful children of this land a modest thrill. There was also a rusty Ferris wheel and a few merry-go-rounds, all stuffed beyond their capacities with revelers.

I was sitting on a bench watching children file through the entrance with their parents. There were separate lines for men and women, as in most public places, with their separate male or female guards ripping tickets and searching visitors. People seemed impatient and frustrated, but largely subdued. It was in whispers that they complained of growing repression, rising prices and declining living standards.

"They've made life hell for everyone," muttered a woman accompanying her adolescent daughter to the park. "I really feel sorry for these kids being deprived of a happy childhood."

Moments later, a bus stopped to let off schoolgirls headed for the park. The girls were clapping, laughing and cautiously teasing passing boys—the whole scene a welcome break from the persistent gloom. Then I heard a commotion at the front of the queue. I stepped closer and saw the guards throwing out a flower-boy who had tried to sneak in.

"I'm not here for a ride! I just want to sell flowers!"

"Get lost! You can't fool us. Everyone knows you," one of the guards barked and pushed the boy, sending him crashing onto the pavement. He got up, shook himself and stood aside, still holding his few stems of roses.

I sat on a bench and started writing my impressions in a notebook, an occasional hobby when the mood prompts me. Then I heard a voice.

"Hello, mister. Would you like to buy a flower? This is the last one left."

I looked up. The flowerboy stood in front of me holding a rose. His pants were still dusty and his white shirt grimy. He was about ten, dark and bony with big striking eyes, shining with hope and intelligence.

"Please, Engineer. Buy this for your wife?" Engineer was a catch-all respectful title addressed to educated-looking men.

"I don't have a wife."

"Then your fiancée?"

"She's not here," I said brusquely and resumed writing.

"What're you writing, Engineer?"

"A letter."

"You have a nice pen. Where did you buy it from?"

"I don't remember."

"It must be American. Only Americans make such cool stuff."

"That's right."

"Are you writing to your fiancée?" he said and sat next to me.

"Why do you ask all these questions?" I leaned away, bothered by the smell.

He plucked the wilting petals from the rose in his hand and handed them to me. "Here, stick them in the folds. It makes your letter smell good."

"That's a good idea. Okay, I'll pay for the flower."

"Is she in America? I bet she is. That's where everyone wants to go. I'd like to go there myself . . . to become a jet pilot and come back with lots of presents for my mother."

"Where's your mother now?" I asked, impressed about his sense of devotion.

"She's at work now . . . cleans houses." He reached for the note-book in my hand and kept rubbing it. "This is American, too?"

"Yes. What about your father?"

"He's a junkie, too lazy to get a job. That's why I have to come here to sell flowers."

"What do you do with your money?"

"Save it. I want to go to America one day."

"Doesn't your father take it away from you?"

"No way. Keep it all in my piggy bank. Don't even spend it in a park. Whenever I can, I sneak onto one of the rides—but haven't made it on the rollercoaster so far."

"Do you want to ride it now?"

"Of course, but I don't have enough money with me."

"I'll pay for it."

He stared at me with uncertainty, some disbelief, and maybe a little distrust.

"But even with a ticket they won't let me. I have a bad reputation here. They think I'm a cheater, looking for a free ride."

"I'll walk you in. Tell me your name, in case they ask about our relationship."

A wide smile swept across his face and his eyes shone brighter. He rose to shake my hand like an adult. "My name is Ahmad. And you are Engineer."

We waited in the queue, which moved slowly, but still faster than the women's line. The female guards, *Zainab* Sisters, found fault with everything: traces of makeup, strands of hair sticking out of scarves or a line of flesh visible around the ankle.

In a bare cement room by the entrance, we were frisked and then allowed into the park. There was no great amusement. Everywhere you turned, murals of the revolutionary leader and martyrs of the war assailed your eyes. The garden, dusty and neglected, was still there, but there was no festive music, just religious hymns and occasional announcements reminding revelers to watch their behavior. Moral cops were out in force to make sure everyone conformed. Many rides were broken, rusty and still in the late afternoon heat. Modern coffee shops had been closed, replaced by makeshift counters serving tea from industrial-size samovars.

Even so, Ahmad was very excited to be there, and that was enough for me. He had me by the hand, pulling me around to show off interesting features of the park. I was a bit self-conscious about the uninhibited display of male affection, still conditioned by norms in America. A few times I shook off his hand, but he reached to grab it once again unconsciously.

Eventually I relaxed and began to enjoy the promenade. Smells of corn cooking on spits and spicy soup in cauldrons filled the garden, mixed with the scent of flowers sold by so many jobless young men. We bought two cobs of corn to nibble while walking, and then headed for the rollercoaster. There was a long line and I withdrew in discomfort.

"Go stand in the line and I'll wait for you here."

"You're not coming with me?" He sounded disappointed.

"I'm scared of roller coasters. You go ahead."

"It wouldn't be fun going alone. Then let's go for another ride. How about the bumper cars? We both can fit in one."

I couldn't let him down again, so I went along.

"I love fast cars," he laughed, as he kept turning the wheel in excitement. "One day I'll buy one of these, the real ones of course."

"I'm sure you will. What else do you want to ride after this?"

"The Ferris wheel."

When we soared to the sky on the Ferris wheel, his eyes glazed over with a dreamy expression.

"You know, Engineer, I feel so happy here so high in the sky. I wish this car would get stuck and never go down."

"So do I."

"*Mashallah* (Praise Upon Allah)—it feels like an airplane ride. One day I'll be in an airplane off to America . . . you know, mister, they say America is like paradise."

"Why, have you seen the paradise?"

"Mullahs talk about it all the time. They say you must be a martyr to go there. But in America, you only need a visa and some dough."

The sound of evening *azan* suddenly boomed through loud-speakers, followed by a call to prayer. Rides creaked to a halt and merrymakers were ordered to get off. The faithful rushed for ablution at a row of faucets by the public toilet.

"Spit on this luck!" Ahmad snapped in frustration as he and I stepped off the Ferris wheel. "Here goes an hour of my time down the drain. You see, Engineer, what we have to put up with?"

"Don't worry. We'll find something to keep busy. Let's go for a sandwich."

His face bloomed at the mention of a sandwich: "But, mister, I don't want you to spend all your money. I sold a few flowers today." He drew his skinny body up with pride. "Let me pay for the sandwich at least."

"No, Ahmad. Save your money . . . for the trip to America."

My father hasn't come home. As soon as I wake up I see his bed is undisturbed, and there's no one singing. That means that after his swaggering exit, he was out chasing skirts all night. Mama doesn't care how late her husband comes home, as long as he is there in bed beside her when she opens her eyes in the morning. This is another of her bizarre logics I don't understand. I'm now very afraid. We're certainly in for a big fight. I close my eyes and huddle under the blanket.

She's sitting in her bed moping and bemoaning her fate, and I know she's waiting for me to get up so she can give me an earful. Reluctant to give away family secrets, Mama uses me as a confidante, a companion in misery, stuffing me with all kinds of crap I don't care to know about.

I go on pretending to be asleep and she's getting impatient. She frets a little and then goes to light the samovar for the morning *chai,* and comes back a few minutes later to roust me out of bed.

"Hurry, hurry. You'll be late for school."

I crawl out of bed, my back hurting from the lumpy mattress, and lumber up groaningly to the sink, with my eyes still closed. I splash a few handfuls of icy water on my face to wake up, and it stings more than the principal's slaps. With a dirty towel hanging by the basin, I dry my face and return to the room, where Mom's sitting cross-legged on the floor at a flimsy spread of breakfast: stale bread, a lump of feta cheese and tumblers of sweet tea. I sit across from her and after a few minutes of tense silence, she finally lets it all out. There's a long list of complaints against Baba, the usual litany of grievances, well-documented and preserved. Some are old, some new—but to me they all sound like the same depressing tales. What's bothering her these days is "this new whore" clinging to her husband and sucking him dry. She knows of her through Reza, my trouble-making cousin and her reliable spy.

"Reza has been shadowing your father every night and gathering information," she says while cleaning up, carrying the tumblers down to the little pool in the yard to wash. "I know exactly where he hangs out, who he sees and how much money he throws away every night—on gifts and lavish tables. This whore has a good grip on him."

She rambles on: she's done everything to break the hold but nothing seems to work. She's seen a mystic, the best in town, and even taken up praying again—but God, too, is deaf to her pleas. To dry up the financing for Baba's evening parties, she's even increased pre-dawn raids on his pockets. Still the money is coming in from somewhere.

"I tell you, this bitch is a tough nut to crack, impossible to dislodge."

She laments on and on and there's nothing I can say to make her feel better. I hate to say it, but I don't even feel sorry for her any more as she kind of asks for it. I hate to be so harsh on her, but I've heard all of this so much, she sounds foolish to me. Where did she think her husband was off to last night when she was grooming him to such perfection?

I have my own worries. This rotten tuition has become the curse of my life. I can't have a moment of peace. A heart-to-heart talk with Mama may help, and I cautiously approach her to give it a try. She's now back sitting by the samovar, making a sandwich for me. I slip down by her side, wracking my brain for an opening, but her face is so grim that I have second thoughts. She smears a thin layer of butter over a flat piece of bread and tops it with jam, working absentmindedly with resolve.

I finally start with a rambling introduction, talking in circles, not making sense even to myself. Anyway, she's not listening. It might have been the cat meowing for all the difference it made to her. She lets me babble on for a few moments and then stuffs the sandwich in my bag and packs me off.

When I come to think of it, Mama is not to blame at all. She doesn't have her own life and lives entirely for her children. She was hardly fourteen when she was married off—too naïve at that age to stand up for herself. In those days, my father was wilder than he is now. She had to play to his every whim to keep her marriage intact and spare herself the shame of divorce. When it comes to her own rights, Mama is willing to surrender, as is expected of a good wife in our culture. But for her children, she fights in whatever crafty ways she can: waging useless battles that actually make our lives harder.

As I'm about to step out, she opens her purse and hands me a few coins—the usual chicken-shit for daily allowance and bus fare. The two *rials* look even more ridiculous after the ten *rials* I clipped out of Baba, and I'm thinking to give it away to one of the street beggars along with the sandwich. The taste of yesterday's treat is still fresh in my mouth and I can't wait for another visit to the pus-faced peddler. I wait around hoping she'll leave the room so I can give Baba's pockets a search.

She finally heads down for the basement and I quickly run to the closet and turn Baba's pockets inside out, but she must have gotten there first and made a clean sweep. As I'm about to call off the search, my father shows up with a mean hangover. He looks frayed and disoriented. His handsome face is broken into deep lines. His eyes are drooping, his hands shaking; he's already in need of a shave. The suit that so perfectly fit him the night before is now hanging like a rag. He doesn't seem to see Mama or me. As he walks past along the balcony, I smell alcohol on him, mixed with perfume—that spells trouble. I decide to stick around just in case, too worried about leaving the two of them alone together—as if I can be any deterrence!

Baba changes into his pajamas and comes back to the living room, where he sits chain smoking, sunk in deep despondent thought. Mama leaves, probably off to give his pockets a fresh search to see how much he has pissed out in one night. She tries to keep close tabs on his spending by demanding a full accounting every morning—but gets a "go to hell" wave of the hand for answer.

I stand inside with my back to the door, waiting nervously for the inevitable. After a few minutes, Mama comes up from the basement, her face flushed with self-righteous anger, about to explode. I try to think of something to say, but all I can do is be a helpless observer to their fight, another bout in their never-ending war. Still, that beats going to school and facing my own doom. Luckily, Mama is too blind with rage to notice that I'm still around. She just stands in the doorway staring at him in wordless outrage. There are a few seconds of tense silence and then she lets off:

"Shame on you—all the shame and curses of the world for lavishing on strangers what you deny your own family! You take the bread out of your children's mouths and shove it down the throat of whores and scroungers."

"Don't go starting that again!"

Mama runs outside to fetch one of my busted shoes to use as hard evidence.

"Look! Look!" she says holding out the dusty shoe. "He doesn't even have decent shoes to wear to school and you shovel money out like dirt . . . ."

He's leaning back against the cushions, staring at the ceiling. "Let me be, will you?"

"The other one," she goes on, speaking of my brother who's away at my aunt's house, "will soon reach puberty and is still not circumcised . . . the skin around his penis is growing as thick as the bark of a tree . . . soon it'll take a saw to cut it off!"

Baba sits upright for a better offensive position, and she's still standing, holding the shoe like a gun.

"Who's to blame for that?" he asks plaintively. "I could take care of it in the wink of an eye if you dropped this unreasonable demand of hiring a nuclear scientist do the job."

"Yes, but then I'll have to watch my baby bleed to death."

He rolls his eyes in fake exasperation. "Here you go exaggerating as always. Usta is more skilled at it than any doctor I know. He can peel it off like banana skin."

"Look who's exaggerating now."

"You know what, I don't even understand why you want to cut him up. I'd give anything to have that extra inch back." This one is meant as a joke to defuse the row. Humor is his best weapon to calm down his wife and still have his way.

"That's all you think about—your size. You know, there are more important things expected of a man."

"Like what, washing dishes?"

"What about trying to be a good husband and father?"

His hand waves dismissively. "Anyway, Usta is all we can afford. You know I'm flat broke. Lice are rolling dice at the bottom of my pockets," he says, using one of his self-coined sayings to make a point.

"You wouldn't be broke if you deigned to spend time with your family more often."

I can see his patience wearing thin.

"You think I wouldn't pay for my son if I had money?"

"But you have it to buy expensive gifts for your mistresses."

"What mistress? You're hallucinating."

"Don't deny. I know everything," she says, assuming a knowing air.

"Who is she then?"

"How do I know? One of those tarts you dig out of trash dumps. The streets are crawling with them."

"Watch your language in front of the kid." He jerks his head toward me. I've been hunched by the door all this time.

She leans back a little, startled. "Shahed, go to school!"

Quietly, I back out the door onto the balcony, leaving the door slightly ajar to keep watch. I'm terrified, shaking all inside, unable to breathe well in the hostile air. The cat is crouched at my feet, staring inside in disbelief. A few yards away, the hatchway is flung open, with the barber's head sticking out. I ignore them both, just praying quietly for Mama to come to her senses and see the pointlessness of her struggle.

Mom's voice goes up. "I don't need to watch my language! He learns it all from the barber—the all-knowing expert you have so much faith in."

"Enough of your arguing! Don't you see I'm in a bad mood?"

"You're always in a bad mood around your family. You save your good humor for strangers."

He shoots to an upright sitting position again, a warning in his eyes. "Cut it out I said!"

She's scared but still defiant, her eyes filling with tears. "You think you owe it to everyone except your wife and children."

"Shut your mouth or—" he springs to his feet, raising a finger.

The battle grows louder, and I open the door a crack more, hoping to find my mother still in one piece. They're still at it, the air charged to the point of explosion. She seems determined to fight to the end, bracing for a do-or-die finale with her pig-headed husband. He, too, is standing his ground as always, dead set to have the last word in a crucial battle.

"Please drop it!" I say in a timid whisper.

He ignores me and charges toward her. She shrieks—a pathetic sound too painful for me, but no doubt melodious to the barber. I see the trapdoor opening wider with Usta sniffing out for blood. I ease the door shut and wait outside, trembling and chewing my nails. Her screams wither to a sob, then to a whimper, and I finally work up the courage to peek inside. She's curled up in the corner, all but vanquished, reduced to an unresisting bundle. Baba towers over the wreck like a triumphant boxer, peering down with a sneer. She finally struggles to her feet and out of the room. Without turning to look at me, she walks past and heads down the stairs into the basement, where she can quietly grieve her dark fate.

* * *

Is this the moment that gave birth to the gnawing fear in my soul, a formidable impulse underlying all other senses? Did this horrible feeling of powerlessness come from the failure to stand up and defend my mother? From that moment, I think, something began to steadily eat away at my soul, eventually leaving nothing but a hollow shell.

Never after this crushing moment was I able to rise up for myself—or anyone else for that matter—urgently as the situation may have called for intervention and justice. Never again would I love or trust anyone, intense though my need was for friendship and love. Running became my first response, the main drive that took over my life. My dread of responsibility and involvement became so strong that I chose not to live at all.

On January 16, 1979, Mr. Johnson woke me in the early morning with two pieces of news: first, the Shah of Iran had fled the country. Second, there was a telephone call for me from Iran.

I lumbered out of bed and followed him to the house. His black and white television was on, broadcasting live from Egypt, where the Shah and his wife had just landed to take refuge. The announcer intoned that revolution was now certain, rolling down like a deadly avalanche. I passed by indifferently and picked up the receiver. A shaky voice crackled into my ear. It was my mother sobbing, unable to speak.

"Your father died . . . in a car accident . . . in the hospital . . . a week later."

I waited for something to hit me. Something like grief. Some tears. Some sadness. But it all sounded to me like secondhand news, triggering no shock, no alarm. It was as though I had expected the outcome, just like the news of the Shah's escape.

My father's presence had been on my mind like a constantly rolling movie, with him ruling the poor streets of our neighborhood like a petty brazen shah. I never had contact with him after I left Iran, but always saw the familiar scenes: the gaudy Bride would be cruising in search of ripe peaches, Baba would be conning someone to pay for his next extravagance, and only my mother would be bathing and pampering him before the night's revelry.

Suddenly grief did hit me, but it took a bizarre form: I missed him. I cried. I writhed in pain. Yet I was relieved. It was as if I had been delivered of a huge burden, an obstacle preventing me from living a natural life. Yet the world felt empty without him. He was a controversial presence, unnerving and exhilarating at once.

So what now? What does it all mean? Am I finally free? Can I go living life the way he did, the life I've been dreaming about? I doubt it. But at least his shadow is removed and I feel lighter. I can chart my own course in life. But where will I begin? Which direction will I head? And what about that nagging question in my mind?

A couple weeks after that, Mary came to see me one evening. She still didn't know about my father's death, as I hadn't told her—partly due to laziness, but mostly to spare myself a predictable expression of condolence.

She appeared distraught, and in the dim light of my shack I at first missed the bruise on her face and the scratches on her arms. She ambled over and snuggled by my side on the couch-bed. Then I noticed.

"What happened?"

"Bill and I had a fight. He called you a 'fucking Arab' and I had to defend you."

"You shouldn't have. I don't care what he says about me."

"I know, but I care. I'm not gonna let him disrespect you."

My relationship with Mary was out in the open by then and Bill was upset. He kept pushing her to leave me, trying absurdly to play the role of a protective father. But she wouldn't hear of it.

"But he's dangerous. He could have hurt you worse than this."

"I know how to take care of myself. You should've seen the shit I gave him."

"That's not good, either. You should have called the police."

"I was going to but Laura talked me out of it. She thinks he'll eventually accept you."

"Accept me as what?" I said, alarmed.

She reached to caress me with a loving smile. "My future husband."

"We're not planning to get married," I said, holding back.

"Don't get defensive . . . you're such a drag sometimes, Shahed . . . well, never mind . . . listen, guess what? I got a car . . . an orange VW—my favorite color!" Her voice rose to a shriek and she squirmed against me. "Oh, I'm so excited . . . you know, it's yours, too. You can drive it whenever you want."

84

"Thanks, but I don't need a car. I have nowhere to go."

"Sure you do. We can go to lots of places: movies, Disneyland, Magic Mountain. We can even drive up the coast . . . there's a real pretty town called Pacific Grove where they have butterflies and great carnivals." She turned to me and finally spoke softly. "Listen, you mind if I stay here tonight? I don't want to be in the same house with Bill. I can't stand the jerk."

"Well . . . yes . . . of course."

"Are you sure?"

"I don't know. I've never shared my bed with anyone for a whole night. It makes me kind of nervous." I didn't want her to get in the habit of sleeping at my place every night.

"Don't worry, I won't rape you . . . I'll wake up early tomorrow morning and make us breakfast—how about that?"

As we lounged on my sagging bed, jammed up against piles of scraps, Mary slipped into a dreamy mood, pouring out her big plans for the future.

"I think I'm ready to move out and rent my own place."

"How can you afford it?"

"I got money saved up—enough to pay for a month's rent and the deposit."

She rolled over and straddled me, staring lovingly into my eyes. "Listen, you think you might wanna move in with me?"

I said nothing and the expression of love turned to uncertainty, her eyes begging for a "yes." "Hah? Hah?"

I stared at her blankly for a few seconds and then my eyes drifted away. They traveled over the grimy walls and stopped dead on a cobweb hanging from a corner of the ceiling. For a moment I gazed at the tightly-spun web and then shook my head.

"No, I don't think so. That's not a good idea."

"Why not, what's keeping you in this dump? We can start a new life together. You'll quit the gas station and find a better job."

"I don't know how to do anything else. I'm not the one to make you happy."

She locked eyes with me again, searching for an answer she already knew was not there. It was a painful gaze piercing through my very heart. I couldn't think of anything to say and our conversation waned along with her spirit. I switched off the light and we slipped under the cold blanket.

In the dark privacy of my room, the comfort of her soft embrace, my fears abated and I came in touch with my senses. I felt content, perhaps even blessed, to have the company of Mary, as if she was the only gift the world had to offer. It was easier to let my guard down in this dim cave, hidden from the prying eyes of the public, enjoying a respite from my own ruthless self-examination.

"I love the way you touch me," she said. "I wish you'd do it more often, though—not just when we're in bed."

Uh huh! Here it comes again, that needling demand, another push in the steady campaign to pin me down. Why doesn't she keep quiet? Can't she see the pointlessness of it, trying to squeeze juice out of a hollow shell?

I tensed up and went limp—inside and outside.

"In private, you're more intimate. But when people are around, you don't show your emotions. You're just a totally different man."

I kept that same silence that neither satisfied nor discouraged her. She turned on an elbow and ran her hand over my bare, bony chest.

"Don't you have anything to say?"

"I get rather self-conscious around people."

"I don't understand—what's so embarrassing about showing your feelings? It's the most natural thing."

Was she leading me into a trap? My mind retreated from her, even as our bodies were entangled. I couldn't think of an answer that would both justify my coldness and spare her feelings. Instead, I tried one more time to figure out why I was trying to make a go of it with her.

"My father died," I said suddenly, just to save the conversation.

She jumped up and stared at me in disbelief. "You can't be serious! When did it happen?"

"Two weeks ago, in a car accident."

"And you're telling me now?"

"I . . . didn't have the chance before."

"I can't believe how coldhearted you can be sometimes. I thought you're only like that with me . . . anyway, are you okay? It must be awful to lose a father, especially so young."

"It is, in a way."

"Do you miss him?"

"Yes, now that he's dead."

"What's that supposed to mean?"

"Our relationship wasn't so good. We were more like rivals."

"Rivals in what?"

"In everything: romance, money, life in general."

It was the first time I confided my secrets to anyone, but I wouldn't give too much detail. I said nothing about his lies, his deception, his acts of betrayal.

"Are you at all like your father?"

"In what way?"

"I mean, was he also afraid of commitment, of intimacy?"

Yes, the bastard was fully committed to his own fun. He was ready to move a mountain for his dick, but not raise a finger for his son . . . but how could I convey all that to Mary? "He . . . he was . . ." Trying to push down the feeling choked my voice.

"Did he have a dull attitude toward life, too? Was he cold to women like you are?"

"Not at all. He squeezed the last drop of juice out of all of them."

"Why are you dawdling out there on the balcony?" Baba shouts to me after the fight with my mother. "Come here and keep me company."

He's obviously sorry for what he did to his wife and needs someone to help ease the spasm of guilt. I reluctantly go in and sit stiffly by his side, wondering what he expects me to say to make him feel better.

"How're you doing, my son? I'd like to do something for you. You fancy going out to lunch?"

It's strange but after a fight with Mama or his father, Baba becomes affectionate toward his children, doing things he normally doesn't do. Last time he gave me a cash reward, as if I'd cheered him on during the bout, and now he wants to take me out to lunch. His offer is tempting but I don't feel so right about partying when Mama is in the kitchen crying her heart out. Well, that's tough. One has to be heartless now and then, especially when there's a good reason like skipping school. I definitely need a break from my troubles, even if it's for one day. As my father wisely puts it: *Seize the moment! Who knows if you'll end up dead or alive by the morrow?*

"But I have school," I say hesitantly.

"Forget school. The sky won't crash down to earth if you miss a day."

"Mama wouldn't like it."

"Don't worry. I used to cut classes almost every day and nothing happened. I bribed the schoolmaster with chickens and turkeys I stole from our farm, and that shut him up. Let's go now. You'll be okay."

We hop in the Buick and hit the road. It's too early for lunch, so we drive uptown, to the wealthy commercial district, checking out fancy auto parts and then visit Baba's tailor to order a new suit for him. He is still feeling down from the fight, silent and moody. From the glove compartment, he pulls out a record and sticks it into the Topaz player, cranking up the volume to the max. A sentimental Iranian song spills out and he plunges into melancholy. His head sways from side to side and his eyes well up with tears, as he holds up a finger to enforce a hush. He plays the song over and over, still guarding his ecstasy with the finger, savoring every pulse and word in the lyrics: *My heart has gone mad again with love . . . hopelessly lost in a lonely alley . . . knocking desperately on every door . . .*

The blue mood hangs on until we get to the fashionable district and streets take on a brighter look. Women, too, seem to undergo a metamorphosis: first wearing fewer thick black veils, and then sporting colorful scarves. By the time we reach the main drag, sidewalks are crowded with coquettish mannequins in miniskirts and hot pants. He drives slowly, his head revolving, picking up every feminine pulse around. Every time a "juicy peach" steps into view, he slams on the brake and shouts a compliment, nearly causing an accident. Some ladies don't like it and give us dirty looks, but that only stimulates his instinct to chase. I'm embarrassed and wish he'd quit it, worried that one of these women would call the cops on us. What I don't understand is why he has to go after these strange women when Mama is so young, smart and pretty.

For lunch we go to the main bazaar, my favorite place in the whole world to dine. Eateries in the bazaar are modest but the quality of rice and kabob is superb. We enter the medieval brick archway and walk along twisting passages, brightly lit by lamps and the gleam of gold from a double row of jewelry shops. The restaurant we pick is almost hidden from view, tucked deep at the end of an alley with no signs.

The place is packed with customers and there's a long wait. But since it seems that my father is a regular there, and probably a generous tipper, the headwaiter runs to clear a table for us, hustling out a party not quite done eating. Many people there seem to know Baba, and as we walk down the aisle, they rise to show respect and invite us to join them. It's just a courtesy, but Baba feels proud all the same for being well known.

We take our seats and watch the headwaiter at his antics. He is a comical old man in a greasy smock, walking around with a tray of sizzling kebobs, throwing slabs of meat onto plates—whether they have been ordered or not.

"Shut up and eat!" he snaps out good-humoredly to protesting customers,. "I make the decisions here."

Baba, amused by the scene, leads the waiter on in his mischief, until he notices one of his friends, the Colonel, standing by the door waiting for a table. The Colonel is one of those freeloaders Mama always warns her husband about. The man never carries money, yet usually goes home with a stuffed belly. Many people fall for his impressive uniform and glittering medals and race to please him. The officer, too, acts as if everyone owes him, just because he's in the army, as though he's single-handedly saved our country from a barbarian invasion. He shows up everywhere in uniform, even in the public bathhouse, where he gets a thorough scrub and rubdown free of charge. No one knows him by name—everyone calls him by his military title, as if he has no personality outside his uniform.

The Colonel remains nailed in place, waiting for a party to crash. He's not having much luck this time. People either don't notice or flat out ignore him. But the officer is not one to give up so easily; he'll stand there forever if that's what it takes for a free meal.

He stands there nervously shifting on his feet and scratching his skull, and Baba cracks jokes about his stinginess:

"He's such a tightwad . . . never puts his hand in his pocket except when it's cold . . . the slacker orders pocketless suits so he has an excuse not to carry money . . . give the bastard free rope and he'll hang himself."

"So, Baba, why do you hang around with him if he's such a sponger?"

"He's a good friend to have around. His pull may come in handy one day."

My father lets the tightwad suffer a little more and then gives him a shout.

"Hey, national hero, come here."

The Colonel runs like a kid coming for a candy, falling over himself. At the table he stands a few seconds beaming his camel grin and tousling my hair in false affection.

"Hi prince, how are you, prince?"

He calls me prince to make my father feel like a king and be more forthcoming with his royal gifts.

"Aren't you going to shake hands, prince?" he continues, his huge teeth protruding beyond his thick lips.

I hold out a hand and he feigns shock at seeing my sore palm.

"Oh my god, what happened?"

Baba starts to explain but his friend's eyes follow the waiter passing by with trays of kabob.

"Eh—don't worry, it's nothing. It builds character . . . makes you tough as a soldier." He lets out a braying laugh that turns heads.

"Have you ordered lunch yet?" he asks. "Hey waiter, we're hungry!"

We order a lot of food and the Colonel works through it hurriedly, rooting among slabs of meat like an overexcited dog. When we're done eating and it's time to pay, he finds an excuse to disappear as usual.

"Hey, my stomach feels strange. I think it's the food here," he says and rushes to the restroom. He remains invisible until the bill is settled and then comes back hitching up his pants.

"Kabob here is terrible. We've got to find another place next time."

Back at home, Baba looks for a way to make peace with his wife without diminishing his pride. He tells a few jokes to melt the frigid atmosphere, but Mama turns a cold shoulder. She obviously doesn't want to settle for anything short of a heartfelt apology, and that's something she'll never get from her husband. Baba would die first before begging forgiveness from a woman.

Then Mama gradually goes soft, knowing all too well she can't play hard-to-get forever.

"If you see me smiling, it is because of the children," she says in a lame effort to save face. "You're finished for me. I'm just here for the sake of the children. I've always made sacrifices for them—I won't stop now."

"Oh, you deserve a prize for that!" he mocks. "I'll stay home tonight to spend time with the family."

"That's probably because you don't have any money to go out."

"Why do you always have to be so cynical?" He laughs and rubs her back cautiously.

"That's the truth. You know it well . . ."

He starts on another tack to deflect her:

"I have a full bag of stories to keep you all entertained for the night. Shahed, go get the magazine!"

Baba reads more of the sad, mushy stories and then, for comic relief, makes fun of Khan and the Colonel—both objects of his mischief. In an hour a jolly mood fills the house and we're all laughing hard, even my mother. He wrestles with my brother and me and then gives Arash a long ride on his back, pretending to be a horse. He also tells outlandish stories of his childhood, and then of his brave fights with wolves out in the wilderness. One tale that really blows me away is a boyhood punishment he received from his father: the feudal lord strapped the boy to his horse's belly and launched the beast into a gallop.

"You think I'm a bad father?" Baba says every time after telling the story. "You should have had that monster for a father."

The highlight of the evening is the popular quiz show on the radio. We huddle around the transistor box listening to tricky questions asked by the presenter. Mama has the answer to most of them, and if we had a telephone to call it in, we could have won a toaster or a rice-cooker, one of those imported appliances they give away as prizes. Baba, too, has a crack at it but he can't make even one right guess.

"These are silly questions they ask," he says, obviously embarrassed. "Your mom may have the answers but that doesn't make her any smarter."

"Then what does?" she shoots defensively. "If they're just silly quizzes, why can't you answer even one?"

"That's because I got more important things on my mind."

"I wonder what they are—maybe which skirt to chase tomorrow night?"

After a light dinner of cheese, bread and cucumber, we switch off the lights and pile in bed—all in a row and next to one another. I pull the quilt up over my eyes, and feeling exhausted, fall asleep immediately—even before my head touches the pillow. As usual, I wake up in the middle of the night to pee. Tonight there's whispering coming from the other end of the room, where my parents are huddled together. I prick up my ears but can't hear well, just getting a drift of their conversation. It is Baba mostly talking, in an excited trembling voice, a tone I'm not used to hearing. The two seem to be up to something weird, but I can't be sure what exactly. I just have this awkward sensation. I hear Mama speaking briefly, maybe starting up her old complaints, only in a hushed pleading tone. Maybe she naively thinks she has a willing ear in this rare, tender moment.

I pull the quilt over my face, but sleep doesn't come to my eyes. The noise grows, the noise of life packed into his soul, and she's dead silent. I'm both disgusted and curious. My fingers nervously clutch the edge of the quilt, slipping it over and under my eyes, back and forth. Peak-a- boo!—as if I say to the baby in the making.

The kerosene lantern sitting by the door gives off a lazy glimmer, enough to highlight silhouettes. My twitchy eyes chase the shadows. One is full and restless, the other flat and still. The first mounts the latter and bobs up and down like a boat riding over waves. This is as far as I see and his groans are all I hear. She's is dead still, drowned in her worries. The groans last for a few minutes and then end with a gasp. The shadow rolls over and lies still and in a minute snores come to fill the room.

BLOOD FEUD

I can't wait for the dinner tomorrow at Aunt Fatima's. Her elaborate feasts are a welcome relief from the meager meals at our home, and there's always a colorful cast of characters to meet: mostly Uncle E's opium-mates. I look forward to taking a stroll in their big garden. They grow so many kinds of trees, bearing fruits of all seasons, all ripe and edible but with no one to pick them.

Today, we have a drama of a different sort. The coalman, our next-door neighbor, is commemorating the *Ashura*, the death anniversary of Imam Hussein, the third and probably the most important of the twelve Shiite saints dating back to the seventh century. Everyone, even every child, knows Imam Hussein and his seventy-one disciples died in a lonely battle against a vast Sunni army. We know that Sunnis were the enemy, because Iranians are mainly Shiites. Hussein's martyrdom is supposed to inspire our people's thirst for justice and integrity.

Anyway, the coalman's service is very noisy, as it is being broadcast to the whole neighborhood through scratchy loudspeakers. The preacher invited to bless the event with his voice doesn't actually need speakers; they are built into his lungs. His hoarse, mournful chanting is going on and on, irritating the hell out of my father.

"He yells as if they're driving a nail up his ass," Baba says, exasperated. He scrambles for a way to shut him up, or to cut the noise somehow. But there's no way he can persuade our neighbor to turn down the volume. The man lives for such days, when he can show off to the whole world what a pious and charitable soul he is.

So Baba is at the end of his rope.

"Some Arab died fourteen hundred years ago and I have to pay for it. Is that fair?" He goes on grumbling and shaking his head.

"What a life this man lives! What a waist of life!" Now he's speaking of the coalman. "He's a walking cemetery! He carries death around with him everywhere. He should have been born as a tombstone."

He complains for a while and then starts clapping his hands together and singing at the top of his voice, hoping to disrupt the service. But all the noise he makes has no chance of penetrating the thick wall between us and the coalman, and it bounces back at us like a squash ball.

"Okay, I know what to do." Baba says and runs to grab the ladder. "Shahed, you go get a big pan and a couple of sticks. I'll wait for you up on the roof."

I know what he's up to and am embarrassed, even a little horrified at the thought of the blasphemous act. Yet I have no choice but to comply. I go up to the roof and find him sitting along the edge looking over the coalman's yard, which is draped in black and packed with men. They're all beating their heads and crying hysterically.

Baba takes the big pan Mama cooks rice in and settles down to drumming with an African beat, making all kinds of weird sounds. I lean away embarrassed, trying to distance myself from the circus.

"Why are you just watching? Do something."

"Do what?"

"Sing! You have a good voice."

"I don't know how to sing." I try to stay back so I won't be seen.

"Okay! Just make a noise! Here, do it like this." He starts howling and tapping his mouth in rhythm like an Apache Indian, until I finally join the band. We bang and scream away as loud as we can, until our breaths fail. But all our shrieks and drumbeats have no chance of subduing the sound of faith booming out of the loudspeakers.

Aunt Fatima's function is in honor of my uncle, Baba's younger brother who's going off to Europe to pursue a higher education. All but giving up on his firstborn son, Grandpa has pinned all his hope on the second, whom he lovingly calls "the light of my eyes." The old man's big dream is for my uncle to be somebody—a doctor, to be sure—to wash away the shame that Baba gives him. He already calls his sweetheart a doctor and swells with pride every time his name is mentioned. This is something that makes my father fume with jealousy alienates him further from his old man.

To make sure her husband would attend the farewell party, Mama had informed Baba about it a week before. But now he says he has other plans and can't make it. Baba and his father are on the warpath again and he wants to punish Grandpa by boycotting an event so dear to him. So the minute Mama brings it up, he sails into a tirade against the old man, digging up age-old grudges to make a strong case.

"There's no way I'm coming," he says while we give him a bath in the blue tub in the back yard. "I won't go anywhere that old miser goes—not even to the moon."

"You're not going for your father. It's for your brother," Mama says rubbing his wide back with a coarse cloth.

"It doesn't matter. They're all in this together; they feed from the same trough. I'm the black sheep of the family, treated always like an orphan."

"Come off it. It's only for one night. Just show up and leave."

"Not even for one minute! I don't want to have anything else to do with this family. I'm ready to sever all ties." He towels himself dry and shakes deodorant powder over his hairy chest and under his armpits. Mama keeps talking while him dress, trying to calm him down, but he flares anew every time Grandpa's name is mentioned.

"He's not a fair father . . . never stops playing favorites," he grumbles while pulling on a white linen shirt and looking into the mirror, obviously enjoying the contrast with his tan skin. "His darling son has everything going for him and now he is trotting the globe. What do I get . . . nothing . . . always the shitty end of the stick."

He keeps it up for a while, taken by his own sad tale; his eyes fill with self-righteous tears. Mama and I begin to feel sorry for him and that encourages him to juice it up even more.

"I never get the respect I deserve—or the money. The tightwad keeps count of every *rial*, begrudging me even a cup of tea. I could drop dead before him and he'd march all over my corpse. Do you call that a father? . . . No, there's no way I'm going to the party. If I were you, I wouldn't go either."

Mama and I look at each other in alarm, worried he may expect us to boycott the event in solidarity with him. He often does this, using my brother and me as a bargaining tool to blackmail his father. The tactic doesn't always work though, as Grandpa finds it easier to part with his grandchildren than his money.

"I love the boys . . . miss them a lot when I don't see them for a while . . . but I won't cave in to blackmail," the old man says, flashing his calloused hands for all to see. "I haven't worked my fingers to the bone to give my money to a loser to piss away."

* * *

I don't like to take sides in the family feud, but Grandpa has a point. The feudal lord has already given his son many acres of good land, a would-be inheritance as a head start in life. But instead of working the fields, Baba has been selling them piece by piece until he's left with just a worthless tract that nobody wants to buy. Now he's become too lazy to get a job and relies on his wits and dregs of credit to survive.

But my father would never own up to his mistakes. "It's all your fault," he told Grandpa the last time they fought. "You loved and spoiled me when I was a cute little boy and now you've washed your hands of me, leaving me high and dry. You're actually reaping the fruit of your own rotten seeds."

"Bullshit!" the patriarch shot back. "No one can fault me with the way I raised my children. It's your own evil streak. You've always been like this."

"Look who's talking—a man who has screwed the whole world over for his selfish aims!"

"No one had a moment of peace with you," Grandpa went on, ignoring the accusation. "Remember—you used to sneak into the village mosque and hammer nails heads up into the imam's pulpit? The poor mullah! His ass was like a strainer from all the holes punched in it."

"That was to put more fire in his sermons," Baba said with a mischievous wink at the audience.

"Even my chickens and turkeys you didn't spare," the old man said, not getting the joke. You stole them and gave them away as bribes to your teacher so you could pass.

"But," Grandpa was quick to add, "You were so dumb that even bribing couldn't take you beyond third grade."

"Okay, it's my turn now," Baba swiftly counterattacked. "Remember how corrupt you were working as a young cop, committing every sin for a fast buck?"

"I was an honest policeman! No one can question my integrity."

"That's right. You blackmailed whores, shook down shopkeepers and asked for a cut in illegal deals in alcohol and gambling. Everyone knows this even if they don't say it to your face."

Grandpa shook his head as if listening to a lunatic. But everyone knows he made his fortune during World War II, when our country came under British and Russian occupation and our people lived through unimaginable hardship. There were few jobs to go around and little to eat, all the food went to the Allies advancing on the Nazis through our land. The chaotic situation created a golden opportunity for Grandpa. He hoarded scarce food and commodities and sold them later on the black market at inflated prices. It didn't take long before he amassed enough wealth to buy hundreds of acres of land and get into farming, which was his passion.

Along the road to success, he sometimes had to be ruthless. The one who paid most was his wife. Many a night the tyrant came home drunk with one or more prostitutes in his arms. He made out with them in the same room where Grandma slept with her children. The room was their entire living quarters in a house shared by other tenants, and poor Grandma had nowhere to go with her children. All she could do was fall like a blanket over the little girls to spare them the obscene sight, and chant prayers aloud to muffle the drunken noise.

All this happened at a particularly low point in Grandpa's life, when he was bitter over fathering three girls but no son to bless him in old age.

"I want a son to carry my coffin on his shoulder when I die," he bargained with God.

After Baba's birth, he made a pilgrimage to Mecca to thank the Lord and atone for his sins. He became a *Hajji*, an honorable title in Islam for those rich enough to make the coveted pilgrimage. Consequently, he built a wholly new personality around that holy experience. He stopped drinking and promised to abstain from worldly pleasures—like boozing and whoring.

But maybe Hajji didn't repent with a pure enough heart, because after Baba's birth, he was cursed with another trio of daughters. The poor man had to go through many more sleepless nights and tearful prayers to stop the flood of bad luck and win another baby boy.

While cutting his sons plenty of slack, Grandpa was brutally strict with his daughters. He molded them into dutiful housemaids and then rushed them into mismatched and loveless marriages, even before they began menstruating. He just gave the nod to any bum who happened to knock on his door with a proposal.

Five of my aunts are timid and dull characters. But the eldest, Aunt Fatima, is of a different order. She's pure, loving and helpful—always there to help people in times of hardship. She's also fearless,

97

never cringing when handling things others find disgusting, such as helping deliver babies or in circumcisions and burials. I've seen her wash corpses, clean up after invalids and even help restrain a lunatic—doing it all with care and patience.

Despite her good natured qualities, Aunt Fatima was the last in the pack of girls to go to the "House of Fortune." Grandpa did all he could to get rid of her, but no one came for her hand—even after the old man waved *mehrieh*, the customary bride price meant to tie the groom to the marriage. This was because my aunt is not exactly a beautiful woman, on the outside anyway. Her legs are fat, and hairy if she doesn't shave them, and her face is scarred with pimples popped over the years as she pondered her black fate as an old maid.

It wasn't until she was thirty, the age her sisters became grand-mothers, that an opium addict with a monster of a son came with a proposal. But he was such a lousy candidate that even Grandpa had doubts about giving him the last daughter. He was mainly worried the addict would be sexually impotent, like many opium and heroin users, and not be able to deliver a grandson. My aunt though decided to go ahead with the marriage, and raise the *enfant terrible* as her own.

GRAND ILLUSION

Aunt Fatima's husband, Uncle E, is an odd man with a prickly soul, as if made of porcupine spikes. On the outside, he is short and round, with full rosy cheeks. My dad likes to say that his brother-in-law is flushed with pig hormones.

In his delusions of grandeur, fed by his drug habit, Uncle E puts himself on the higher planes of kings and queens, snubbing us family members as too common. In his pipe dreams, he hobnobs only with the crowned heads, above all Queen Elizabeth of England. In one flight of fancy, he had dinner with the Queen. She was so taken by his charm that she offered to divorce her husband and marry Uncle E. My uncle refused of course, being too wary of *Englisiha*—the English—and their endless evil schemes.

That's what is weird about Uncle E. When he is deep in his stoned world he talks tenderly with Queen Elizabeth. But other times he rants against the Brits. This hatred goes back to Britain's having colonies in this part of the world. Uncle E, like many people in their middle age, believes in conspiracies, and blames *Englisiha* for everything from revolutions to the high price of dates to earthquakes and typhoons.

But when I listen to him I get angry too. I've heard him talk about what the English did to our people in their greed to dominate the world. They looted our oil for half a century. Then, just fourteen years ago, they made sure our good Prime Minister Mohammad Mossadegh, who wanted to keep our oil for us, was defeated—they tricked America into toppling him. America, which is in my opinion the best country in the world, didn't want to do it at first, but the Brits knew how to persuade them. Anyway, Mossadegh was gone and the Shah, a traitor who had chickened out of the country, was brought back. Uncle E said he was installed as a puppet.

After that Uncle E lost his faith in *Englisiha*. But the funny thing is that while endlessly cursing Great Britain, he dresses and acts like an old-style English gentleman, sporting a fedora and an ivory-handled cane. And while impeccably suave with his imaginary friends, the so-called courtiers, he is disgustingly crass around his family. He picks his nose and breaks wind all the time, and might have even taken a crap in front of us had his bowels not been paralyzed by opium sedation. Thank goodness he is always solidly constipated, getting the urge to evacuate only once in a blue moon. This, too, he blames on *Englisiha*:

"They are the ones who brought opium to this land from China. They wanted to lull our nation into a stupor so they could squander our riches. I curse them every time I struggle to evacuate a drop in the bathroom."

Every now and then my uncle suddenly vanishes, supposedly off on a long vacation with the Queen. He keeps his adventures a top secret, sharing details with no one, not even his wife. If someone asks about them, he flashes a mysterious grin, as if his exploits are beyond ordinary minds to grasp. Uncle E keeps all his secrets and refinement for the royalty; with us commoners, he only has his farts and boogers to share.

My father hates his brother-in-law so much that he'd probably look the other way if he saw him drowning in a river. This is partly due to jealousy. Uncle E is loaded with money and has a lot of free time on his hands. He's never worked and the family carpet business his brothers run turns a good profit, of which he gets a share. All day, the bum does nothing but smoke opium in the sunny parlor of his big house and pop candies to counter the bitter taste of opium. If not that, he's making unreasonable demands on his wife. My poor aunt has to wait on him like a slave and put up with his every complaint: why the rice is overcooked, why the kabob is underdone, why the persimmons are too ripe.

Uncle E has a scheduled habit at each hour of the day, a gentle stream of activities that don't upset his delicate constitution. Once he wakes up in the morning, usually at ten or eleven, he orders a bowl of soaked peaches to loosen his bowels. Seeing that it is all in vain, he leaves it and goes to take a few puffs from his *vafoor,* a china opium pipe he treasures more than his life. That helps lift his mood and whet his appetite for a meal. So my aunt turns up with a tray of juicy kabob and grilled liver, a nutritious treat to boost his health and flush more blood into his plump rosy cheeks. After that he takes a light stroll through his garden, picking savory fruits and flowers to design the elaborate spread that complements each bout of smoking. Then it is time for lunch, tea and a long, sweet siesta.

The main séance of opium smoking gets underway around six in the evening, as soon as he emerges from his nap. He lounges with a few friends in the parlor or out in the shaded veranda, if the weather is not too cold. For hours they lean on their elbows, drinking tea, puffing away and playing backgammon, while following the world news on BBC or Voice of America. Uncle E absorbs every bit of news and analysis, but he doesn't believe a word. He tries instead to read between the lines, catch the ploys of English colonialists and American imperialists.

"I can see through them like crystal," he says with an elfish smile on his pink face. "If our king had any sense, he'd come to me for advice. I could show him how to foil foreign plots."

"The bum is so full of himself!" my father says of his brother-in-law and I can't agree more. Uncle E talks as if he has all the answers to life, projecting this image of himself as a superman, one who can steer life according to his whims. He always compliments himself—about his wit, his wisdom and his sexual triumphs. Even his addiction he touts as an achievement, something everyone should try to emulate. He tries particularly hard to get my father hooked.

"You see, opium isn't a narcotic," Uncle E started with his familiar lecture the last time we were at his house, beaming at Baba with his pink face. "It's a tonic, a panacea for all ailments."

He takes a pleasurable puff from the china opium pipe. "What they say about opium causing sexual impotence is just a myth. On the contrary, it delays ejaculation and drives women crazy. That's why they can't leave me alone."

While talking about his imaginary conquests, he puckers his mouth and raises a fully ripe red persimmon to his lips, trying to create a sensual image.

"Umm . . . that's how I like them—plump and luscious, with a silky feel."

My father just stares at him, as if to pop the airbag with his intense gaze. The men constantly fight with each other, a battle of wits, each trying to make the other look ridiculous, especially in front of women.

"The King of Farts," Baba often calls his brother-in-law. Uncle E, too, is a sly one and often comes back to score a surprising point. He makes fun of Baba's receding hair, his beer paunch, and the bags of skin under his eyes, knowing how sensitive he is about his looks.

"Look at you! You're not even forty and your hair is thin as that last pair of rugs in your house," Uncle E says, trying to stir up the competition in his rival. "I'm fifty-five and still have so much hair, enough to carpet a palace."

"An old fox doesn't look his age either," Baba fires back. "Besides, what's so good about having so much hair if it looks like a ball of cotton?"

"It's not just my hair. I'm in such perfect health, too. I eat like a cow and my stomach never complains. You can't even drink a glass of water without taking a pill to digest it."

As the old fox goes on boasting, he slowly sucks on a hard sugar candy, as if to show how sweet life is for him.

"You want to know the secret of my full hair, baldy? Opium. That's what you need if you want to grow back your hair. You don't have to smoke it all the time—just a social puff now and then. You want a hit now?"

I can see Baba gradually rising to the bait. He's so desperate to have hair that he'd try anything. Fortunately, before it is too late, Mama jumps in to save her husband:

"What's the use of having a lot of hair but no drive for sex?"

The bad blood between the two men goes back to the night of Uncle E's wedding to my aunt. I was only a little kid then, but the story has been told so many times that it feels as though I was there in the bedroom with the couple.

Feeling a bit nervous, the groom has smoked too much opium, more than his usual dose, and that makes it hard for him to consummate the marriage. He feels so numb, in fact, that he can't even raise a finger, let alone that lazy organ of his. So he's taking too long with it and the guests being present as witnesses are growing impatient. In the traditional Muslim culture, they have to be on hand to confirm that the bride is a virgin.

Everyone is waiting for him to get it over with and march out of the bedroom in triumph, waving a bloodstained handkerchief. The whole scene is full of suspense for the climactic moment. A group of musicians is on hand to break into the celebratory anthem. Children have their palms filled with lucky coins and sugar balls to throw at the newlyweds. And young ladies are itching to erupt into a wild, euphoric dance.

Time grinds on and there's still no sign of the groom and the bloody handkerchief. Anxiety sets in, gossip begins to fly. Aunt Fatima is a rather old bride and many among the guests wonder if she's not the source of problem, whether she's actually the virgin her father claimed her to be. Grandpa in particular is very antsy, eager to prove to the world that he hasn't tried to palm off a defective merchandise onto the groom's family.

Grandpa decides to take matters into his own hands. He commandeers an old spinster to collect the evidence, and plants her outside the wedding chamber to rush the newlyweds on. A tactless boor, the spinster keeps kicking and banging on the door, as if to recover a long-overdue debt. The groom storms out of the room in his long shorts.

"Will you please stop this stupid ritual?" he pleads, distraught and dripping with sweat. "Leave us alone or at least have more patience!"

Always the prankster, Baba tries to make a joke with this.

"What's the matter superman, you have trouble finding the hole?" he shouts. "Grope around a little, or leave the lights on . . . one more thing, try not to rush into it . . . take the persimmons one at a time."

The eunuch slips back into the room to give it another try. By now he's all but ready to throw the fight. Like a defeated soldier, he walks out of the bedroom, his head hanging in shame. It is here that my father dives under his crotch, hoists him on his shoulder and runs out to the pool.

"Please don't! It's icy cold. I'll have a heart attack," the groom keeps yelling.

"It'll shake you out of your stupor. Then you can perform like a man," Baba says and throws him in.

Uncle E came out of this therapy no more of a man, but with a stinger as sharp as a wasp's.

I would come to know what Uncle E went through that night. I would endure bitter failures with women, if I could even bring myself to approach them. It was the sense of degradation that rooted itself in my being the night I witnessed my mother lying like a corpse under my father's grunting thrusts. At that age my knowledge of sex was confined to dirty images pounded into my head by Usta, the pervert next door. With contempt and leers, Usta had pointed out the women who sold their bodies, the prostitutes he sneaked into his shop on quiet afternoons.

"What a lousy lay, the fucking whore!" he spat out later. "She just lay there like a corpse."

In my youthful confusion a terrible idea took hold of me: Mom's reluctant submission, offering her body in return for meager domestic concessions, made her like a prostitute. After that night, her sacred aura evaporated and suddenly she was just a woman with a soiled body, her once pure soul defiled. The deep disgust I felt then stayed with me forever. It was a stigma I would find impossible to shake off. My pursuit of love, especially in my years in America, became tainted by that recurring bitter nausea.

Aimlessly driving Mary's VW one day, I saw a woman hitchhiking outside my college campus, not too far from Monrovia. She was tall and attractive and I slammed on the brake, as my father used to do when he saw a foxy lady.

"Thanks for stopping," she said quickly and jumped in. "I parked my car somewhere around here but can't find it now. I've gotta get home before my kids come back from school."

"Where do you live?"

"Up in Arcadia—not that far. Take the 210 West . . . I'm Suzette by the way. What's your name?"

"Shahed."

She was a slim brunette lady, with long brown hair puffed up in the emerging style of the 1980s. Her face was long and bony with a few lines around her full mouth. Her big brown eyes were dreamy and a bit weary.

"That sounds weird . . . how do you pronounce it? . . . oh, never mind. You go to college here?"

"On and off."

"I'm taking Italian here . . . my boyfriend, Marcello, is Italian . . . met him last summer during a tour of Europe. He doesn't speak English which is why I'm learning Italian . . . would be nice to be able to communicate. With Italians you don't really need a language. They're so spontaneous. Am I talking too much?"

"It's okay."

"Where are you from?" she asked, her head turning restlessly.

"Iran."

"Oh, Persians aren't like Italians. You folks revel in pain and sorrow too much . . . you patented tragedy, like the Greeks . . . I always see you crying and beating yourselves on television."

"That's more for the camera."

"Oh, I miss Italy so much. Can't wait to fly back there." She talked fast and her bony fingers jiggled nervously on her knees.

We finally reached her house, in an upper-middle-class suburb, at the curved end of a quiet street.

"Thanks for the ride. Here, take my number and call me sometimes," she said as she rushed out of the car. "You'll call me, won't you?"

"Yes. I—think so."

"Don't call after six, though. My husband is at home."

"Are you married?" The question was less out of principle than to make sure of her intentions before I wasted my time.

"Yes—technically. We're not happy, though . . . are together just for the kids . . . his choice."

"What about your boyfriend, Marcello?"

"He's too far away. I think Mediterranean men are sexy." She flashed a mischievous wink, exposing her straight but cigarette-stained teeth, and quickly shut the door. I still had my beard then, but that didn't make me Mediterranean. I let it pass.

I thought about it for a few days and finally decided to give her a ring. I needed to date other women to keep alive my search for the perfect woman: someone who even remotely resembled that earthly image of the Nymph of Paradise. With more candidates, I figured I had a better chance of success, of figuring out the jigsaw puzzle of my love life. Each piece, I thought, could offer something new, a trait lacking in the previous piece: long legs to make up for Mary's stumps, curved-in waist to offset another's bulges, convex butt to fill the flatness of the one before.

I would call Suzette because I thought her to be trouble-free: a middle-aged woman out solely for sexual gratification. But as I fantasized about this, I sensed the adventure was already doomed. I didn't feel so guilty about wooing a married woman, but haunted, for at the edge of my fantasy lurked the memory of my mother and her taintedness. It had cast its pall before.

One morning, I drove to Suzette's house in Mary's car. It was the safest time of the day. My girlfriend was at work and Suzette's husband and children were away, too. I rang the bell and had to wait a few minutes before a distant voice called: "I'll be there in a sec."

She finally came to open the door, dressed in a pink robe with curlers covering half of her scalp. The hair of the other half gleamed an unlikely black from fresh dye. Her living room was equally untidy, littered with paint brushes and canvases, unwashed glasses and full ashtrays.

"Please excuse the mess . . . It's been a crazy day . . . lost one of my contact lenses." She dropped to her knees to search for it.

"Let me know if your eyes accidentally fall on it."

I looked around the room, not for the lens but for clues to her neurotic personality. The walls were covered with garish oil paintings of John Travolta in disco dancing poses, and some loud abstracts. There were also family pictures amidst exotic souvenirs and antiques that spoke of foreign travel.

"Why don't you sit down? I have to finish my hair. It won't take long."

Along the way she paused, looked around distractedly and then turned sharply toward a chest of drawers to grab a stack of photos.

"Here are some pictures. Get started with them and I'll get the drinks. What would you like?" She didn't seem to remember my name, but didn't bother to ask. Through the entire rendezvous, she didn't call me by name. I must have been just a generic male with the sexy bearded Mediterranean look.

"You like apricot schnapps?"

"I don't want alcohol—just a soft drink."

"That's right. You're a Muslim. I forgot."

"Has nothing to do with that. I just don't drink in the morning."

She disappeared into the kitchen and came back with a Coke and a tall cocktail, and then her eyes fell on the picture in my hand.

"That's Joel, my Jewish friend . . . I've no idea why I always end up with Jews. You're not Jewish, are you?" She blushed. "Oh forget it. You already said you're Muslim . . . you want a tour of the house?"

106

"Of course."

I got up and followed her, but she couldn't decide what to start with. Finally she walked to the paintings, some of which featured Travolta in a pitch-black beard, heightening the green of his big eyes and red of his full lips.

"These are all my work. You know John, don't you?"

"Who doesn't?"

"He's sexy, isn't he? John is my dream man, especially with the beard."

On the buffet was a picture of a chubby man with a bushy blond beard embracing three blond children.

"Is that your husband?"

"That's Steve, my husband. He's an engineer . . . more preoccupied with the bridges he designs that his marriage . . . he looks like a wimp next to John, doesn't he?"

"He seems like a nice man."

"Nice he definitely is . . . well-informed, too, in his field. But has no idea how to establish a love-relationship with a woman. He approaches love as though it's another field in science."

"So that makes it okay to cheat?" Instantly I regretted my comment.

She turned away and shook her head, then looked at me with narrowed eyes. "Look, it's not cheating—all right? The heat went out of our marriage long ago. We're only roommates now . . . let's sit down. I want to show you Marcello's picture . . . oh I miss him so . . ."

"Don't you want to finish your hair?"

"Can do it later. Why, don't you like me this way?"

"It's okay," I said and plopped down on the couch, already thinking of leaving. But I felt I had to take this date to its pre-ordained conclusion, whatever it was. To me, it was more important not to disappoint her than follow my own desires, which were as dull and unfocused as always.

She went to the bathroom and I sat there looking at the pictures again. When she came back, she looked beautiful and desirable again. She had a photo that she handed to me.

"I wonder how I seem to men.

"Attractive."

"All men say that: attractive and smart. What made you stop for me?"

"Need, I guess."

"Tell me, what kind of woman did you think I was?"

"I haven't made up my mind yet."

"You're hard to get through."

Her eyes searched me. She looked innocent and cute, and I reached to kiss her. But she hung back: "Uh uh. No, I can't let you do it."

"Why not?"

"I don't know . . . I mean you're an attractive man, but it takes a lot more to knock me off my feet. You understand that, don't you?"

"Yes."

The rejection had sharpened my lust and awakened a rare spirit to fight for a woman. She gave me a long uncertain look and then edged closer. But I waited for her to make the next move.

"You go to church?" she asked.

"No."

"I may start going. I feel like I'm morally declining."

I didn't know what to say and suppressed a yawn. She crept closer and put a hand on my thigh: "Listen, if I let you kiss me, you won't get violent?"

"Why violent?"

"It's funny."

"What's funny?" I couldn't follow her.

"Did you give it the slightest thought we'd end up cuddling?"

"Well . . ." I got tense. Before going to her house I imagined that something would happen between us and I kind of looked forward to it. But now I was nervous, even frightened. What brought the sudden death of passion, I wondered. Was it the faint lines around her mouth and under her eyes, her forward teeth, the slight swell of her belly— supposed imperfections I must have missed at the first glance?

She took my stiff hand in hers and stared into my eyes.

"Why are you so uptight?"

"Am I? I don't know why."

"What's the matter, don't you like me?" she persisted. She buried her face in my chest, her nervous fingers running through my hair and under my shirt. I cringed, hanging my head down, either from shame or to keep from seeing the flaws under her brittle beauty. But her fire raged as I kept thwarting her advances. She ignored my resistance and wanted to rush it along, perhaps thinking that with perseverance she could rekindle extinguished passion. She maintained the thrust and I kept retreating in torment, until my back was against the armrest and I was trapped. Panic seized me and I struggled to drag a breath. I tore away from her, ran to the door and burst out onto the street and fell into Mary's car.

Baba sticks to his vow and refuses to come to my uncle's farewell party. So the rest of us take a taxi to Aunt Fatima's house. She lives not too far away, in a more affluent area of the neighborhood, an area populated by merchants of some wealth but still religious and traditional. It is a community obsessed with the afterlife but still keeps a practiced grip on the material world. Most of these folks live in big houses with impressive brick facades, fronted with lush gardens of rose bushes, persimmon and pomegranate trees, with tendrils of ivy trailing the walls.

The coalman also has a mansion there, living with the queen of his modest harem and their many children. And that's where he hosts the happy functions of his life: weddings, birth celebrations and circumcision rituals—although they're not as frequent as the sad events held at his other house. In any case, wedding or funeral, it is always the same somber gathering segregated by sex. There's just more food, more flowers and more morose faces.

We arrive a little early to find there's a vicious fight underway between Uncle E and his monster son, Reza. Reza is going through adolescence and has become even more impossible. The boy is hardly fifteen, with some fuzz on his chin for a beard, but he drinks vodka from the bottle and smokes like a wet log in a chimney. He also chases much older women, taking his dates to fancy restaurants to look important. To support his expensive habits, Reza resorts to blackmail, shaking down anyone he can. Reza rarely shows up at school, and when he does, it is only to gouge a passing grade from a teacher at knifepoint. He also has no shame about breaking long-held taboos. Just last week, he set fire to a curtain hanging for privacy outside a ladies bathhouse, sending naked bathers out onto the street clutching to their clothes. Today, the boy is angry because his father refuses to send him to America to pursue his education. He's heard his uncle is going to Europe and that has given him the itch to travel too.

"Europe is too small for me. I'd rather go to America to study. It's big and there's more action."

His father meets this remark with a derisive chuckle, as he prepares his china opium pipe for a fix. "Hah—go to America to pursue a higher education! What education—to learn to become a full-blown gangster?"

Reza turns to his mother plaintively: "Did you hear that, Mom? He wants to make fun of everything. If I turn out to be a failure you know who to blame."

"Why don't you listen to him just once?" my aunt pleads with her husband. "You ought to have a little faith in your son."

"Don't be a fool, woman. I have as much faith in him as in a wolf."

"Watch your mouth, nasty old man!" Reza shouts back.

"You're a born loser. You can't even count to twenty without using your fingers and toes . . . ha-ha-ha . . . You've never passed a course without holding the teacher at knifepoint."

This throws my cousin into a fit of rage and he starts breaking china dishes stacked up on the table.

"Please don't provoke him," my aunt begs. "I need the plates to serve dinner. Why don't you argue it out later after the guests leave?"

"The little rascal can't even go through the elementary school and now he wants to become a rocket scientist," Uncle E says with a shriek of laughter. "You know it reminds me of that old maxim: this fool wasn't even welcome to the village and he was already counting on a treat at the chieftain's mansion."

This settles it for Reza. He makes a mad dash for the opium pipe and snatches it from his father, and runs with it to the window.

"Hey, what do you think you're doing?" Uncle E yells in panic.

"This is your life in my hand! I'll smash it to smithereens if you don't pay me," the boy shouts, holding the antique out of the window, a few yards from the brick pavement below. "You do what I say or this will sail off to heaven to your imaginary lovers."

"This isn't a joke! Put it down immediately!" the father says and bounds to his feet like an acrobat.

"Will you cough up or not?" Reza is now pinching the pipe by the end and dangling it like a pendulum.

"All right . . . all right . . . will you calm down, please?" Uncle E pleads, holding both hands up and circling around his son, as if to tame a wild tiger. "Can we sit down and resolve it amicably like two civilized people?"

Reza becomes bolder and starts throwing up the china and catching it in mid-air. The fate of Uncle E's lifeline now hangs by a hair-breath. Utterly desperate, he turns to my mother for help.

"Will you please stop him?" he says, his fat cheeks flushed red from exertion.

Mama finally steps in and averts a catastrophe, but not before Uncle E pays a hefty ransom.

My parents are the only people in the world that Reza would listen to, otherwise he's totally unmanageable. Sometimes, when he gets too wild, my aunt comes to her brother for help in restraining him. Baba appears to promise help, but he does his best to stoke the fire and put more venom in the brat. This he accomplishes by playing the loving uncle, showing sympathy for his nephew for all the hell he has to go through in the hands of a "vicious" father. He fills him up with rage and conflict and then lets him loose on his old man like a bloodhound.

"Why do you put up with all that shit? Don't let yourself in for such abuses," Baba says in an avuncular voice, during an intimate moment with his nephew over a bottle of vodka. "Stand up for your rights. Go claim what's yours. I'm with you in it right to the end."

"Oh Uncle, what would I do without you?" says Reza, dropping to his knees, his eyes filled with tears of gratitude. "You're the only one I have in this lonely world. Please let me kiss your hand."

"No need for that. What do you think an uncle is for?"

"Oh dear Uncle . . . "

Reza utterly worships my father and tries to imitate him in every way—his swagger, his sartorial splendor, his extravagant habits. Every night he trails him like a stray dog to trendy night-clubs, places he's too young to be admitted; and there he waits by the door, dreamily watching my father hobnob with his big shots and glamorous ladies. Poor Reza tries so hard to be taken into the circle, allowed a piece of the action, but my father has only one use for him: as a lethal weapon to train on his brother-in-law. Sometimes my dim cousin suspects he's being taken for a sucker. Furious then, he comes around to take revenge by tattling to my mother, telling her things about her husband she shouldn't know.

With the money he gouged out of his father, Reza wants to show off, so he urges me to go out to the movies. I get permission from my mother and we run to catch an early screening of a James Bond film. Iranians like to eat dinner late, so we can get back by nine and still enjoy the feast.

James Bond films are my favorite. I find the lead actor extremely handsome and hope to grow up to look like him. I especially admire his smooth way with women and the fact that he doesn't take shit from anybody, handling crowds of thugs all at the same time. I wish I could kick ass like he does and teach the bullies at school a good lesson.

We buy our tickets and wait outside the theater checking out stylish ladies. Both of us have a twelfth-grade textbook under our arms to make us appear older and to impress women. Two good-looking girls stand a few yards away and we barely take our eyes off them—but they're a bit stuck-up and look away every time our eyes meet. We keep staring at them for a while, until the girls become uneasy and start giving us dirty looks. I immediately stop looking but Reza won't quit; he even makes some provocative remarks that make the girls very angry. Suddenly, one of them shoots over and slaps my cousin hard across the face and then starts making a scene and calling for help. A big crowd forms and two young policemen turn up to investigate.

One of the cops has my cousin by the collar, slapping him to impress the girls, and the other one seizes my arm in a crushing grip. Reza isn't afraid of them and keeps calling them "pigs" and "pussy-lickers." Furious, the policemen kick him to the ground and put hand-cuffs on his wrists. Luckily an old fellow intervenes and pleads for our freedom. The cops finally let go but make us return our tickets and never show our faces there. I'm really upset about missing the film and make a vow to never again follow my rowdy cousin to the cinema.

HOURI

When we get back, the party—or the funeral, rather—is in full swing.
The guest room is crowded with family members. Grandpa sits on a
thick mat at the head of the room, grieving over the imminent separation from his darling son. He looks miserable, as if coping with a
depthless tragedy. His thick fingers are pinching his leathery forehead
and his sun-baked skull sways mournfully. With a big handkerchief
wadded in his hand he dabs his wet eyes and cheeks. It is an old yellowish piece of rag and I wonder if it is not the same one Uncle E failed
to grace with my aunt's nuptial blood. As my uncle goes to pack his
suitcase, Grandpa breaks into an uncontrollable sob, shaking so hard
that some of his potential heirs run to get paper so he can write a will.

Out in the parlor, Uncle E and his fellow addicts are sitting
around a grill of blazing charcoals, puffing away and discussing politics. All the hot topics are on the table: the Cold War, the threat of
a nuclear holocaust, the decline of the British Empire and America's
rise as a superpower. Uncle E, dressed impeccably like Churchill, is
painting a macabre picture of the future, spine-chilling scenes that
make our hair stand on end:

"An atomic war will spell the end of life as we know it today. It will
usher in a gray landscape of ashes and charred bones.

"This may well be the outcome wily *Englisiha* are after. They're
hell-bent to regain global hegemony and will stop at nothing. Such
masters are the Brits in the art of deception, so cunning that even a
crafty intriguer such as myself can't fathom them.

"*Englisiha*, I've no doubt, are behind every conflict, every mal-
aise. No good has ever come from them to anyone, except maybe to
bring opium to Iran from China."

He punctuates each grim prophecy with a deep puff from the
vafoor, the same my mother miraculously saved today. He exhales a
plume of smoke, and feeling content, he comes back with an eloquent
pearl of wisdom: "So, my dear friends, what's the use of it all? One
might as well go on and enjoy life while it lasts."

* * *

The wives are in another room chattering, all veiled and jingling with gold shining from their necks, their wrists, and their fingers. Some are rubbing my grandmother's shoulders in comfort. The old woman is in even worse shape than her husband, fearing that she may not live long enough to see her son again.

My grandmother is a stooped figure with a puckered face and hanging breasts, a pair of milk reservoirs withered to creased bags. Like my mother, she is a worrier, suffering mostly from the irreconcilable conflict between her husband and her older son. To maintain a bridge, she often comes to visit us and stays for long stints. But she's quiet as a sea breeze, a shadow treading around the house. More often than not she's in a deep trance, fingering worry beads and mumbling prayers that only God would understand. If she makes it out of her trances, she's always patching something, usually articles of clothing beyond repair.

It is finally time to eat and guests gather in the big hall around the *sofreh*, the fine brocade cloth on the floor, surrounded by cushions, where a colorful spread of food awaits us. We're all hunched over eating intently when the door suddenly bursts open and Taj, the neighborhood idiot, storms in. He stands by the door, pulls off his filthy hat, paws at the shags of white hair flowing down the sides of his head, and fiddles with the tufts shooting out of his ears. He stands there for a while staring at people, as if through a mist, and then lets loose:

"I'm here to lodge a formal protest on behalf of my master, declare why he had to boycott this event," he utters like a mad guru in a booming voice, and everyone knows he's talking about my father.

"His Highness chose to decline the invitation . . . because this gathering has no legitimacy . . . due to its prejudicial nature . . . it is downright unjust and immoral to favor one son over another. God created all men equal . . . He won't stand for such a breach of justice.

"And shame on you, Hajji!" he rages on, pointing an aggrieved finger at my grandfather. "Shame on you for violating the divine order . . . the natural rule of succession . . . bypassing a deserving son and bestowing all your wealth and favor onto his younger brother."

Grandpa gazes at him intently for a few seconds, his face reddening, his eyes flaming, and then bolts to his feet and charges.

"You son of a dog, what's it to you how I treat my sons," he thunders, grabbing the fool by the collar and smacking him back and forth with his big peasant hand.

Taj is unrepentant. He raises his arms, clumsily pushing back. "It has everything to do with me, tyrant! I'm the champion of the poor, the guardian of the oppressed," he shouts defiantly. "It's my calling to fight injustice and bring decency back to earth.

"Go ahead, tyrant! Go on and beat me! But I'll resist injustice until the last drop of my blood. I'll hold a sit-in here until His Highness' legitimate rights are fully restored to him. I will incinerate myself right in this house if my demands are not met . . . ."

Before he can finish, Hajji gives him a square kick in the butt and the idiot goes wobbling onto the street like a loose tire.

A few minutes later, to everyone's surprise, my father shows up, as if to reap the benefits of the idiot's dramatic intervention. Or perhaps he has a hunch about what will be waiting for him at his sister's house.

He walks in the room with a grim face, not looking at anyone, as if we're all traitors. He takes a seat and leans back, acting bored, trying to show he's done everyone a favor—and himself a big disservice—by attending this wretched gathering.

Just as the effects of Baba's carefully timed entrance are wearing off, the door swings open. Only a few of us turn to see who's arrived, and it's the shocked look on our faces that stops the chewing and chattering.

Who is this incredible lady! I think as the mesmerizing beauty walks in with her husband. Where did she come from—out of which land? Certainly not this neighborhood or anywhere near. She must be from a different realm, the realm of dreams, made of a different soil, the dust of precious gems!

Then it suddenly strikes me! She's the gorgeous lady in the leather coat and a poodle in her arms, the angel who descended from heaven to succor me at that lonely moment in the alley. What is she doing here? Did her Chevrolet break down and they're here to seek help? But no! She's my aunt's new neighbor. I'd heard of this foxy lady moving into our neighborhood and was dying to meet her. But I had no idea it was this glamorous and ravishing woman.

115

Her name is Houri, the Persian word that means the "Nymph of Paradise." What a perfect name for this heavenly creature! So fitting, like everything else about her. She's in a sleeveless dress of the latest fashion—a sheath in geometric patterns that shows the curves of her body. Her eyes are shining even brighter this time and her silky hair is done up in a beehive.

The poodle is not with her. It wouldn't be welcome in our orthodox neighborhood, where dogs are considered impure. But Houri's allure itself is likely to ruffle feathers and rattle nerves, upset the dull harmony that has pacified us for ages. The way she dresses, the way she carries herself, will no doubt be an eyesore to the zealots in this community. Look at how Grandpa is looking at her, giving her a glowering appraisal! It's the force of her animal vitality, her luxuriant self-confidence that offends a world where women are cocooned in black.

I still remember my religious teacher at school raving about *Houris,* those lovely creatures and their luscious habitat, so often mentioned in the Qur'an. They are promised as the ultimate reward to the pious, those with the strength of character to resist earthly temptations, defy the lure of lawless passion.

The holy book gives vivid images of the "Garden of Delight," where fair-skinned *houris* with big lovely eyes breeze amongst the faithful, anxious to serve. Where the book falls short, Muslim leaders and scholars are quick to draw from their imaginations.

I remember how Edison and other class clowns yawned and joked around as the young mullah read from the book, promising salvation in return for good behavior:

There in Paradise, atop thrones of gold and precious stones, perfected souls are placed gloriously, all dressed in fine silk, reclining in serenity by streams of fresh water under the cool shade of banana trees. Forever these men are freed of worry and the torments of Hell. Fruits are in abundance where they roam, the bounty of all seasons and tastes, one sitting atop another, rising high beyond reach. There is fine cuisine, too, the flesh of any fowl one's heart may desire, food as nourishing to the soul as to the body.

This is just a glimpse of the Promised Land, the book reminded us, as the "matter of the *houri* is not but as a twinkling of the eye."

Fifteen years on, having searched in vain for that obscure object of desire, I now wonder if by some divine favoritism, as a bounty from the Lord, I came to get a hint of this land of plenty: "lovely maidens of special creation . . . made of a more precious soil."

Could it be that for a split second the sky moved asunder and one of these amazing nymphs burst forth like a thunderbolt, showing me a flash of heavenly might and resources? Was this aberration in divine order meant to convince an infidel like me of the truth of the Lord's promises? Was it intended as an irrefutable touch of evidence for those who need to see things plainly before they believe, those who need to be lured down the path of truth?

I must confess this brief glimpse of heavenly offerings raised my expectations to levels unachievable in this world. Never again did I encounter a woman who came remotely close to that image of *hur,* that blinding flash of charm that struck me with ecstasy. Never again could I love or desire an earthly being, perfect as they came by worldly standards.

My father is hit even harder by the sight of Houri. He stands back in trembling rapture. His jaw is hanging loose, his eyes popping out, and his Adam's apple is bouncing up and down like a Cossack dancer. As Houri walks over to shake hands with him, he blushes like a shy girl meeting her first suitor and has to grope around to find his own hand.

It takes some time before he shakes off the spell. Then he starts to hone his skills and oil his tongue, a tongue that can lure a snake out of its hole. It is the usual routine: firing flattering one-liners that make his intention clear but still leave some room to back out if necessary. At first he has difficulty catching her full notice, as she's busy with introductions, dividing her attention equally among everyone. But it's just a matter of time before she yields to his charm, slipping quietly down in his snare.

Baba decides to brighten up the whole party, something he's an expert in if there's someone he wants to impress. With Houri around, he's bursting with bounce and mischief. He leaps, bounds, whoops, doing anything to make an impression. Soon everyone forgets about my uncle and joins the theater. The nymph, too, has an easy laugh, and that encourages my father to try harder at being the irresistible entertainer.

While he's busy performing, Uncle E steps in to order tea for his guests, and Baba turns the point of his jokes on him.

"Where did you get that hat, Your Majesty?" he says. "It looks great on you . . . must be a new gift from the Queen."

"Don't strain your brain. You can never understand," Uncle E hits back.

"Of course—it takes a hallucinated mind to make sense of fantastic tales."

"What's the matter? You found a pretty cheerleader and are taking off like a rocket again?"

Baba didn't expect the swift counterattack and his face falls for a moment. He recovers, takes on an aloof silence until his brother-in-law waddles out of the room, and then resumes the flirtation. Houri's husband is sitting right by her side, staring at my father like a zombie. But Baba must be taking him for a cuckold or a fool, ignoring him. Nor does the zombie show jealousy or anger—he's more like a bodyguard, sitting back stoned-faced and waiting for the lady to finish her visit so he can escort her home. Houri is as oblivious to him as to a piece of furniture. They look so mismatched and have brought no children. He is squat, bald and hairy as a gorilla—not the type of man I want to look like when I grow up.

Well, he can be cool as a cucumber, but I certainly do feel jealous to see my father flirting with Houri so brazenly. I try a few times to grab her attention away, telling jokes I've heard at school, but they have no chance of getting through with the noise Baba is making. He's taking it rather too far, making a fool of us all—especially my mother. Yet Mom, too, unsuspecting as ever, laughs at his jokes and cheers him on like a loyal fan. She's always slow getting these things, coming to realize her mistakes when it's too late. I feel so disgusted with it all and walk out of the room in futile protest.

Out in the parlor, the men are still puffing away and trying to solve the problems of the world. The room is now filled with smoke, looking more like a scene from the apocalypse Uncle E has predicted. Grandpa has also joined the talks, seeking outraged refuge from Houri, this embodiment of Satan he finds himself in the same house with.

When I get there, the old man is in the middle of a harangue, cursing the king who is trying to make our country modern. Grandpa views the Shah as a weakling, an unworthy successor to his powerful father, Reza Khan.

"Reza Khan was a man," he says passionately. "He had balls. I mean balls—not testicles. Testicles anyone can have, any cock chasing hens—like that gigolo in the other room I'm ashamed of calling my son.

"The one thing I disliked about Reza Khan was his campaign to let women go naked. But that, too, was imposed on him by godless America."

As a policeman, Grandpa took active part in the campaign to force women to remove their chadors—Reza Shah had prohibited veils as part of his plan to make Iran a modern country. In his haste to illuminate women quickly, Hajji sometimes went too far, ripping off undergarments along with the chador. You know, Grandpa, as Baba says, was a decadent young man, but at old age he turned pious, like many hypocritical Muslims.

"The present king doesn't have the balls to stand up to the superpower," the old man goes on. "Under his rule, our country has turned into a big whorehouse."

What eats Grandpa is this new law to take lands from feudal lords and distribute them among poor farmers, something that has cost the old man acres of fertile plots. He says the Shah is doing it on orders from his American masters and in order to stay in power.

"This is outrageous, unjust and anti-Islamic—taking my hard-earned lands and giving them to good-for-nothing bums," he thunders, his face glowing red as the pile of charcoals in front of him. "What they're doing is punishing hard work and rewarding laziness.

Hajji is also mad as hell over this "women's right shit," which the queen has started.

"This, too, is ordered by infidel America. May God unleash all the furies of hell on President Lyndon Johnson! What do they want to make of our women—turn them all into whores—like that giggling bubblehead in the other room? What's her name, Houri? What a name to give herself, the tart. I would rather go to Hell if they have *hours* like her in paradise."

After midnight we all go to the airport, meeting another batch of well-wishers from the village. They've brought sacks of rice, live roosters and turkeys for my uncle to take with him to Europe—in case there's nothing to eat in the godless land. Uncle E has come with an embroidered silk bag containing bird seeds. "This is a present for Queen Elizabeth," he tells my aunt with a wistful smile. "Throw them to Her Majesty's swans for me, will you?"

My uncle stuffs the bag in his coat and goes to wait by the gate, and the whole clan follows. As the departure time draws near, Grandpa's grief and anxiety overflow. He keeps consulting his fob-watch, tied to his loose trousers with a length of rope, and when the passengers are called to board the plane, he bursts into another disconsolate sob—grieving as if sending a loved one to die at the front. At one point he's so carried away that he orders his peasants to invade the tarmac and stop the plane from taking off. But his long-time dream of having a doctor-son gets the better of him and he finally lets go.

Back from the airport, Hajji is in a cranky mood, snapping at everyone for no reason. Soon, he has a good reason to be angry, when he realizes his watch fob is missing.

"It was securely tied to my pants! It couldn't have fallen. Someone stole it!"

He points the finger of blame at Reza, my disreputable cousin. Poor Reza is a natural suspect in any wrongdoing. His mere presence on the scene of a crime is plain proof of his guilt. Grandpa, still spoiling for a fight after the dustup with the idiot, grabs Reza by the collar and slaps him back and forth, trying to force a confession out of him. The boy finally manages to pull free, but before running out of the house, he breaks whatever china he had spared during his earlier fit.

When I was off to the *godless land* six years ago, I received no ceremonial farewell like my spoiled uncle did. There were no rivers of tears shed, no proud moments, no roosters or sacks of rice donated. Mama just slipped me a couple hundred dollars she had scraped from the bottom of her husband's pockets and sent me off with her tearful blessings. The rest of my venture she left to my own nonexistent ambitions, trusting filial devotion to a mother who'd given all for her children.

My mother thought the separation, painful as it was for her, would be good for me. It would open my eyes to a new world and keep me out of trouble: the drugs, the subversive political activities that were in vogue in the twilight years of the Shah. Even more important was to keep me apart from my father; my resentment toward him burned more and more with every passing year. She had a keen sense of my hostility and didn't want that blown up into another father-son vendetta in the family.

And it may all have been a wise move. It's hard to imagine how things would have turned out had I not left for America, what path I'd have taken to vent my bottled-up frustrations. Maybe I would have jumped on the revolution bandwagon and burned everything I found in my path—like those disgruntled youth with a mania for devastation. Perhaps I would have marched to the warfront and died a martyr. Or even worse, scaled the wall of the U.S. embassy and taken American spies, cooks or janitors hostage . . . and then, day in and day out, led the masses in confused, aimless demonstrations against the *Great Satan.*

LIFE IS CINEMA

My father has been out on another of his nocturnal binges and he's yet to come home. Reza, my rowdy cousin, dropped in this morning to give Mama a blow-by-blow account of the information he collected on his uncle the night before. And she's in panic again—not so much over her husband's unfaithfulness, but because she needs money to prepare dinner for our guests tonight. My brother is finally going to have the circumcision, and a dozen kinfolks are coming over to witness the momentous event.

It was my aunt, the usual savior, who finally stepped in to break the deadlock. She called on the barber to come and remove the foreskin before it grows too thick for even a saw to cut through. Mama is still reluctant to put her son in Usta's hands, but she had to submit as usual.

Just before seven in the morning, Baba finally shows up, once again broke and with jangled nerves. He drinks some tea to steady himself and then changes to leave the house again. Mama says nothing about Reza and his revelations, but she keeps needling her husband about the money for meat and groceries.

"Get off my back. I've got no money."

"What should I feed our guests then?"

"How do I know? It wasn't me who invited them."

"You don't expect me to watch my son bleeding all alone? I need people around for comfort."

"Why do you always have to make things difficult for me? As if I don't have enough responsibilities as it is."

He takes a few deep puffs from his cigarette and has a second thought. "All right, let me see what I can do. I have to borrow it from someone."

"From who?" She's alarmed, worried he might again ask a relative for a loan.

"I don't know . . . whoever's available."

"I hope not someone we have to see everyday."

"Now, don't split hairs."

"Just be quick about it. Guests will soon start arriving. And make sure you're here for the ceremony."

"What do you need me for? I'm not the one being circumcised."

"The boy is terrified . . . needs his father around to give him courage."

"We'll see," he says distractedly, gazing past her at the door.

I know he won't be there. Baba dreads the sight of blood, and he can't stand a child screaming his head off—even if it is his own boy.

He hurries out the door as if he has someplace important to go, then I hear him shout to me. "Do you want a ride to school?"

I jump at it and we hop into the Buick.

"Hey listen," he says as the car takes off. "You want to forget about school and go see a friend of mine?"

I don't know where he's taking me, but anywhere is better than school. We drive for half an hour and then stop at a service garage outside the city limit.

"I'm going to see a mechanic friend of mine, maybe get that money your mother is nagging me for. You stay here."

It turns out to be a long wait and when he returns, he doesn't look so happy.

"No luck here. Let's go somewhere else." He turns the ignition and steers the glittering Bride toward the main bazaar, where merchants issue high-interest loans. There, he goes from shop to shop, talking to gold traders, rug merchants and all the other wheelers and dealers raking in money. But they all turn him down because of his bad credit. He gets in the Buick again, and grips the steering wheel, staring ahead.

"God damn it! What a shitty deal I've been handed in life."

I'm sad to see him in despair and begin to understand what my mother means when she says all his friends are *flies around sweets*. He sits hunched behind the wheel, smoking and sunk in thought. A lottery peddler sidles up to the window and that cheers him a little. He spends everything in his pocket to buy a set of tickets and the shine returns to his eyes for a few seconds, before he's distracted again by something else.

He steps out of the car and walks toward a kiosk around the corner to buy a newspaper. Back in the car, he opens the paper to the ad section, looking for a buyer so he can sell his last tract of land. There seem to be no such advertisements, but his eyes fall on a

123

government announcement offering low-interest loans to farmers to cultivate their barren lands. He whoops out, "That's great!" His jaw stiffening with resolve, he cranks up the engine and off we roar to a state bank he's done business with before. On the way, he's full of hope and keeps talking about his grand plans.

"I'll get the loan, farm the land and then sell it at a good price. A fantastic idea, isn't it?"

I shake my head.

"I could pay off all my debts and even take care of your school fees," he adds, patting my shoulder, trying to press his optimism onto me.

At the bank, Baba goes boldly to see the manager: a little man with a hollow face and outsize glasses. He sits behind a gray metal desk as cold as the expression on his face, scanning documents and adding his signature. Baba slaps the application on his desk and waits for an answer, confident it will be positive.

The banker lets the form sit there for a while and then gives it a superficial glance, before pushing it aside.

"So?" my father asks as he rests both palms on the desk and towers over the official.

"What do you expect to hear?"

"When should I come to pick up the loan?"

"What loan?"

"You know what I'm talking about. The farm loan."

The small man gives him an icy stare through thick glasses, but no answer.

"Are you finally going to deign an answer, Your Excellency?"

"You don't qualify for a loan. You're not a reliable customer."

"Who are you to say that? The government is offering me a loan. Here, look at it!" He holds the page tautly in front of his eyes.

The banker gives an exasperated sigh and shakes his head.

"What's that supposed to mean?"

"You're not getting any more money until you settle the outstanding debts."

"Listen," my father says, trying a different track. "I've been down on my luck. But things are looking up now. In fact, a nice piece of fortune is coming my way. I'll soon be able to pay back all my debts."

"So let's wait until then." The banker resumes his work to end the conversation.

"Hey, why don't you look at me when I talk to you?"

The manager lifts his face a notch and gives my father a tired look.

"All right, I'm looking at you now. Are you satisfied? Now, let me go back to my work."

"Listen, man! It's been a bad day for me and I can't take another letdown. All my hopes are pinned on this loan. So, see if you can bend the rules a little . . ."

"I said no! Be off now!"

My father jerks and his face is getting red. I half expect him to knock the wind out of the banker right there. *Doesn't the nerd know better than to shoot off his mouth like that? Doesn't he know Baba has steel in his hands, and it takes only one blow to bring him to his last gasp?*

"What's that attitude you're giving me?" he says in a cool voice. "This is no way to speak to a customer."

"I speak as I like—don't you give me lessons in manners. Now, beat it! I'm busy."

Baba's square jaw sets hard as a rock and a ferocious blaze comes to his eyes; I can see his grip tightening around the roll of newspaper in his hand. There's a tense pause and then his arm swings out and smashes hard across the banker's face, sending him spinning like a top and his glasses flying off. Baba's taking off his coat to free his punching arm, but the banker takes to his heels, screaming for help. Baba goes after him, corners him in the courtyard behind a big tree. Trapped, the little man claws up the tree and settles in a fork like a monkey. All the bank employees rush out of the building, as if to escape a fire, but no one does anything to help. They're either too afraid of my father or just happy to see their mean boss get his ass kicked.

"You think you're safe there, wimp?" Baba yells up to him. "So stay there until your ass freezes. Just make sure you've got enough leaves to feed on."

We wait by the tree for an hour or so until two cops come and take us away. My father must not have seen this one coming. At the police station, they hassle Baba through a rude interrogation, calling him names and making threats. If not for the Colonel's intervention, they might even have kept us overnight. But Baba calls his friend and he comes to bail us out. All the Colonel has to do is flash his badge and our status suddenly changes from prisoners to guests. The magistrate orders tea for the adults and ice cream for me, and then he gets down to explaining why he has to be mean sometimes just to please his bosses. Then, still pouring forth his apologies, the magistrate and his deputies escort us to the door, and his driver takes us back to the Bride, still parked outside the bank.

"Thank you, Colonel," my father says to his friend after the ordeal. "I'm so glad that all the lunch treats have finally paid off."

Baba notices the Colonel staring at him blankly, and smiles to bring it off as a joke. "Hey, let's go celebrate our freedom! How about lunch . . . and then we can go to the movies," he adds.

That's rather surprising because my father has never liked movies. "Why would anyone want to sit in a dark room and stare at a blank wall for two hours?"—is his logic.

He must have noticed my mouth hanging open. "I usually don't care for movies, but this one is different. Everyone's talking about it. Let's go catch a matinee show when the theater is less crowded."

"But it's no fun to go to the cinema in the afternoon," the Colonel objects.

I lean over the front seat. "He wants to waste time until they're done circumcising my brother." It slips out of my mouth.

"Who asked for your opinion?" Baba snaps with a frown. But I can't help grinning because we are going to eat, and go to a movie, while those other idiots are in school listening to the math teacher.

On the way to the restaurant, we stop at Aunt Fatima's house to borrow a few notes for the escapade. My aunt is one of the few people in the world who would still lend money to my father, although she has to keep it a secret from her husband.

At the restaurant, there's nothing unusual except that the Colonel doesn't run to hide this time when the bill comes.

"I more than deserve the treat for saving your butts," he says half-jokingly.

So complacent he is, indeed, that he orders double the usual portion, skipping the rice and bread to save his appetite for meat. There's a large plate of juicy lamb in front of him, and the glutton works through it like a hyena, sinking his fangs and ripping the meat from the bones. By the time he's finished, his uniform is spattered with red juice, as if he has just come back from a commando raid.

The cinema part is the most fun, except for the beginning of the show when the audience has to rise and salute the image of the king on the screen, with our national anthem playing loud. It's the same image of the monarch posted on every public square, showing him extending a taut Hitler arm, with his arrogant nose sticking out.

At first, I'm a little too lazy to get up and salute, feeling stuffed and sleepy. But the Colonel is so gung-ho about it that I feel awkward on my seat. He keeps clicking his heels, doing right-face, left-face and about-face, as if he's marching on a training field.

The commercials and sneak previews are even more entertaining than the main feature. They show stylish suburban homes, in cheerful bright colors, occupied by beautiful blond families. All of the houses have spacious kitchens, squeaky-clean bathrooms and dazzling modern appliances: television sets, stoves, refrigerators—everything my mother dreams about but will never get.

The movie itself is a local melodrama, like the Indian musical films—a combination of songs, dance, action, and of course tears and laughter. It is the story of this wealthy old miser who keeps hoarding, but has no idea how to enjoy life. So selfish and greedy is he that his friends leave him one by one. So every night he sits alone at a long dinner table, with no company to stimulate his appetite.

His life becomes empty and unbearable; one day, during a lonely stroll along a bridge, he jumps into the river to end it all. But before it's too late, fate intervenes and a Samaritan who happens to be around jumps after him, saving him body and soul. Although a simple mechanic and penniless, the savior is a happy-go-lucky fellow, with nothing to do in life but sing, dance, and beat the shit out of bad guys.

The men become close friends, and the mechanic rolls up his sleeves and tutors the depressed old man in the art of living. He teaches him how to spend, and how to enjoy life. The miser, too, turns out to be a good student and it doesn't take long before he's shed his fears of sharing his riches with others—above all, his down-and-out savior. So indebted the old man feels, in fact, that he offers his daughter, the sole heir to his vast fortune, to the mechanic. After that, life is hunky-dory and there is nothing to do but sing, dance and party.

My father is absolutely spellbound by the story and the amazing parallels with his own life. He leaves the theater in a daze and with moist eyes, as if walking out of a fairytale.

"The miser reminds me so much of my father and the Samaritan of myself," he tells me, after we drop off the Colonel and sail the Buick home. "The movie well describes my philosophy of life—that money is for spending not hoarding. All these years I've been trying to pound that into your grandfather's head, to no avail."

I know what he's getting at and keep quiet. It's another one of his schemes.

"The old man must absolutely see this movie," he announces, "and realize this is no life he's living. It's the life of a dog."

"You know," he goes on, as if bombarded by sudden new discoveries. "Life is really cinema. This film can be an eye-opener. It will stir his dead soul . . . God willing, it will loosen the strings of his pocket."

If life is cinema, as my father said, then I was watching an epic film of ludicrous proportions and absurd characters in post-revolutionary Iran. Running into one of these daily demonstrations against the *Great Satan* was almost inevitable, hard as I tried to shun them. Just days after I arrived, it was the third anniversary of the seizure of the U.S. embassy, right outside the fallen compound renamed the *Den of Espionage*. A huge demonstration was announced to send another sobering message to America, land another blow on the crooked mouth of President Ronald Reagan. The cowboy-president had been tilting toward Iraq in the war and his secret services were supplying Saddam with intelligence and sophisticated weapons. His purpose was to do away with the "barbarians" once and for all. But these barbarians were undaunted, ready to take on the whole world if needed—they had plenty of cheap blood at their disposal.

Streets around the former embassy were closed off to traffic, allowing only pedestrians and buses to dump loyal protesters picked up at city corners like day laborers. I happened to get caught in the drift, melting into the roaring tide of anti-Americanism. Many in the crowd carried placards scrawled with tired slogans, and U.S. and

Israeli flags to be burned. There were people from all walks of life: schoolchildren out on a field trip, military conscripts glad for a day off from degrading service and workers organized by Islamic unions, and, of course, those who truly believe in the cause. All voiced hatred of America, but it didn't take too close a look to see that their slogans sounded as hollow as the promise of glory bestowed on them.

Senior clerics arrived to bless the event with their spiritual weight, along with their foreign guests: dignitaries from the Middle East and Africa aspiring to our revolution, the same cast of characters I saw on the plane when returning to my country. In fact the Palestinian was among them, the bearded devout who sat beside me.

The dignitaries took off their shoes and sandals, aligned them, and stepped onto a carpeted arena fenced off from the foot-soldiers of the revolution. There, they knelt down on the floor in a humble gesture, watching obligingly a trite parade they'd witnessed too many times, but one deemed essential for their political survival. Among the celebrities were war-disabled—young men with a leg blown off, or grim faces disfigured in chemical attacks. There were also Siamese twins, a pair of sisters welded together at the head. For some obscure reason, they'd been invited to endorse the sacred cause with their anomalous physique, perhaps to add their bizarre touch to a grotesque show.

A veteran sloganeer respected for his booming voice climbed up the podium and read an uncompromising resolution against "arrogant powers," vowing endless struggle for a dull dream. Then came a speech in Arabic by the Palestinian, the guest of honor from a brotherly nation. The speeches were capped with a scathing oration by a grand ayatollah, a long sermon of political parlance and outlandish metaphor.

"America, even if all your ancestors emerge from Hell and line up before us, we will stand on our sacred principles and fight on until eternity," the turbaned ayatollah roared.

Among the audience were scattered a claque of professional rabble-rousers, goading the crowd to respond with passion: "Death to America!" . . . "Death to Israel!" . . . "Death to Saddam!"

Toward the climax of the event, flags were rolled out on the street and people were urged to soil them with the dirt on the soles of their shoes. Then pickup trucks arrived, all mounted with loudspeakers blaring revolutionary songs. They weaved their way through the mob trying to whip up enthusiasm, and then came to a halt outside the embassy compound. Men in black jumped off the trucks to set the stage, unroll more flags and douse them with kerosene.

Finally, the time came to set the flags alight and a few diehards bravely attacked them with their torches. Flames shot up into the sky, mirroring the blaze of hatred in their souls, with the forced roars of the crowd and martial music in the background. Once the flames subsided a little, several men jumped around stamping their boots on the charred remains, displaying a dramatic rage, as if crushing the very mouth of the U.S. President.

One of the men I recognized from a long time before. He was the younger son of the coalman, my boyhood neighbor. He looked a lot like his father, minus the layer of soot on his face. I had an urge to walk over and greet him, but rebuked myself for a dangerous nostalgia that would make me vulnerable. I didn't want him to remember me as the son of a man who mocked their religious services with his pagan music. My thoughts went to my father again. What a timely death! He would have been hanged in these days as an infidel. Even if not, he would have been forced to live life in a hole, hiding his pleasure to spare himself the lash of the whip.

When Baba brings me home from our day of recreation, my little brother is lying naked on a cot, his *dool* shriveled to a peanut, waiting in terror for the barber to come and take him through the bloodthirsty rite of passage. A team of opinionated old ladies is clustered around him, exchanging crock-pot ideas on the situation. All they actually do is talk; Aunt Fatima is the only one being helpful. Out in the yard is a sacrificial lamb donated by my grandfather, tethered to the pipe by the little pool, enjoying its last drinks.

Seeing that the operation is still on hold, my father makes his excuses and leaves again. I go to sit by Arash to comfort him, but the women get on my nerves with their scratchy voices.

Khaleh, Grandma's nosy sister, is the one talking the most; she wants to show how indispensable her presence is so we'll keep her longer as a guest. Khaleh doesn't have her own place and is bounced around by her daughters-in-law like a football. Her tongue is as stinging as a cactus, and if she stays in one place for too long she may incite a family feud. When there's no one else to take her, she comes to stay at our house, often for such long periods that she becomes a part of the gloomy landscape—among the rats and the cockroaches. Her company is really annoying to me, as she sleeps and prays in the guest room, the same room my father hangs his clothes—and that makes it hard for me to go through his pockets.

The barber sticks his head through the trapdoor to announce his imminent arrival, and the women rush to don their chadors. A minute later, Usta walks in holding his surgery kit: slabs of rough plywood nailed together into a box. He kneels on the floor by my brother's bed, rummaging through the clutter in the box, looking for his notorious razor. As he unfolds the rusty blade, Arash lets out an earsplitting yell and makes a run for the door. But before he gets too far, my aunt scoops him up and pins him to the cot again.

"I don't want it short. I want it long," he pleads through screams, as he struggles to free himself.

"Don't worry, I won't cut too much—only a tiny bit," Usta responds with a leer, showing a narrow space between the sooty tips of his thumb and forefinger.

He tests the blade on his thumb for sharpness. Unsatisfied, he grabs a shard of china from his bag and runs the blade against it back and forth. He hones for a good five minutes before he's ready to cut. By now Arash is trembling in my aunt's arms, his face wet with silent tears. Usta takes off his glasses and drops his head for better vision, so low that it almost touches my brother's pee-pee. Then he takes the foreskin between his fingers and starts rubbing at a leisurely pace, as if to test a fabric before buying. And suddenly, without warning, he takes the blade to the skin and slices off a good chunk and throws the piece into a tray beside him. Blood spurts and spatters his face. Mama shrieks. And Aunt Fatima rushes to cover my brother's eyes to spare him the horror.

Usta fetches a strip of cloth and wipes blood from his face, and then uses the same cloth to bandage the wound. While he's busy wrapping, Grandma, ever superstitious, swipes the amputated foreskin from the tray and runs with it outside, as if to defuse a nuclear bomb. I follow her and see she's giving it a thorough wash at the sink, before coming back to run a thread through it with a needle from her sewing kit.

"What are you doing, Grandma?" I ask.

"You'll see later."

"Why are you doing this?"

"Just wait and see."

Once done with the sewing, she takes the skin and hangs it from a nail sticking out of the doorsill.

"What's that for?" I ask again.

"To let it dry out in the sun."

Not until later am I told the wisdom behind the ritual. That shred of skin, aired and sunned properly, may work miracles, if swallowed with a full glass of water. It could cure incurable diseases, heal the deepest wounds, mend trodden spirits—spirits as shattered as her own. Who knows? Maybe my stooping grandma will get to walk straight again one day, erect and proud as her egomaniacal husband. Maybe the very fact that she's still alive and moving after all the abuse is due to the enduring effect of my own foreskin still in her system.

Done with my brother, the barber rushes to take care of the sheep, which turns out to be even less cooperative, fighting till the last breath. But Usta finally overcomes it and spills out its guts, slicing some meat separately to make kabob. My mother is busy making a fire in the yard for kabob when Baba finally shows up.

"Smells good!" he says.

"Where the hell have you been?" She's hissing so the guests won't hear.

"I got snagged."

Fortunately, before Mama can start a fight, my grandfather walks in through the front door, with a proud grin on his face.

"Congratulations! Congratulations! Let's celebrate. Where is my grandson, the circumcise-boy?"

"He's in the bedroom, dancing," his son answers sarcastically.

The patriarch runs upstairs, where my brother's wrapped in blood-stained linen, writhing in pain. Grandpa holds the boy in his arms, showing unreserved affection, as if the amputated foreskin has removed an unholy barrier between them.

"My great son, now you're a good Muslim—with that damn thing taken off."

Arash just cries, and to cheer him up, the old man makes funny faces and slides his dentures in and out. In spite of how he treats Baba, Grandpa is immensely patient with children and he has many tricks up his sleeve to entertain Arash and me. He doesn't even mind it when my brother mounts him like a rocking horse, while the old man is kneeling in prayer and touching his forehead to the ground.

In a break with habit, though, Grandpa digs deep into his pocket and gives the circumcised boy a large banknote. He has foot-long pockets, so deep that he has to stoop to touch the bottom—the pockets are sewn that way so he won't lose his money.

I hover near, hoping to get a present too. But no chance. One has to have his dick cut off before he sees anything out of the miser.

The thieving thoughts come back and I start thinking maybe I should help myself to the wad. That little dabble in crime has put a restless bug in my head and *my hand is going astray,* as the Persian saying goes. So I wait impatiently until he takes off his trousers and hangs them from the coatrack in the guestroom, and changes into pajamas. Grandpa feels more comfortable now as we sit and eat on the floor.

With Grandpa around, Baba decides to raise the issue of the house, once more. The house, the dump we live in, is a delicate matter that has brought the titans to the brink of open war several times in the past. Baba wants the property to be transferred to his name so he can sell it or take a loan out. But the old man is too wise to fall for it. Still, the issue crops up every now and then, with my father giving it a fresh, futile thrust.

Knowing it will be tough bargaining, Baba doesn't dive straight in. He steers around the subject a little until he comes to talking about this "wonderful movie" he's just seen, the happy-go-lucky musical he hopes will open the miser's eyes to the meaning of life.

"I know you don't like movies, Hajji, but you ought to see this one." He calls his father by his venerable religious title, which is more impersonal. "There's a late show tonight and I'd be happy to take you there. I'd see it a thousand times myself."

Grandpa still misses his younger son stuck in the godless land hundreds of miles away and is no mood for a joke. He rejects the offer with a mean snigger, but Baba keeps trying to wear down his resistance.

"I know you're feeling depressed, Hajji, but this film will cheer you up. It's light entertainment that makes one forget his problems," he says with childish excitement. "Trust me just once! Let me show you the door to a wonderful experience."

I already know how Hajji is going to react, and cringe at it.

"Do you know what you're talking about?" Hajji thunders. "I took a vow of abstinence from all worldly pleasures after pilgrimage. You think a devout Muslim would stoop to a vulgar practice?

"Listen, Hajji. You don't understand . . ."

"No way. It's immoral to see a movie, especially a musical."

Baba looks with a hint of mockery in his eyes, obviously trying to suppress a chuckle. He has his work cut out for him, but I can tell he likes the challenge.

"I understand, Hajji, but this isn't a show with corrupting influence. It's educational, illuminating."

Grandpa considers it a bit and shakes his head again.

"No, I cannot. It's bad for one who should set an example. What would people say if they saw me queuing outside a movie theater?"

"Don't be stubborn, Hajji! This is the chance of a lifetime. I swear! Let's rush and catch the film before they take it off the screen."

Baba charges ahead until finally, to my surprise, the old bear goes a little soft and agrees to see the film—on one condition: "There must be no nudity."

"Hajji, I'll give you a manly promise on that—a little flirting, yes, but no one takes off their clothes.

"Anyway," he goes on with a furtive wink meant for the audience, "A man of your spiritual standing is immune to temptations."

"Okay, let's go," Grandpa says. "but I must consult my prayer book for divine guidance."

He picks up the book from the mantle and patiently flips through it. It turns out there are no objections and he is finally ready to take the leap. Before heading out, my father takes him to the sink to tidy him up and make him more presentable. He puts on him one of his own floral shirts and a bright tie that make the cattle raiser look ridiculous. He wants to shave his beard too, but the old man puts up fierce resistance.

"What's the matter, Hajji? You act like I'm aiming at your balls. It's only your beard I'm trying to cut."

"Why don't you tag along to make his company bearable?" Baba whispers to me as we follow Grandpa to the door. I jump at it. The men sit in the front of the Buick and I scramble in the back. We get to the theater a little early and a traffic of trendy young couples is milling outside. We take our turns in the ticket line and Hajji is quite ill at ease among so many "lost souls" in the showy lights. The old man is sweating and seems to be painfully conscious of his ridiculous appearance, the clashing ensemble of jazzy clothes and farmer's rags, his shoes thickly caked with mud.

"Look at him!" Baba murmurs. "It's as though he just plowed a field of cow dung . . . it would take two cows to lick all the dirt off his face."

We buy our tickets and wait beneath the marquee, next to a poster of a belly dancer propped on an easel. She's a curvy woman with full crimson lips and huge black eyes outlined in kohl. Her arms are spread, ready to embrace, with one fleshy leg thrust out. Her big bust is spilling out of a red bra.

Grandpa stiffens with apprehension, displaying the look of someone who finds out too late he's been duped. His eyes dart back and forth uncertainly between the vivid image and his mischievous son.

"What's this?" He's pointing at the poster but not looking at it. "She's not going to be in the show, is she?"

"Oh no. This is just to attract customers."

Hajji examines him in confusion and keeps wiping sweat from his forehead with a wadded rag. His eyes begin searching for a way out, but his son is holding him in place with a hand clamped around his arm.

"Yes, I was saying, Hajji . . .the miser becomes so desperate that he tries to kill himself . . . it's why . . . no one likes him because he's so cheap . . ."

"Eh—don't give the whole plot away! I'm going to see the movie myself, am I not?" Hajji snarls. "And let go of my arm! I am not blind."

Baba knows when to keep quiet. Then we go inside to buy popcorn and Pepsi Cola, which Hajji refuses to eat. Instead, we get him a bag of sunflower seeds to keep his dentures busy.

For the first few minutes inside the auditorium, Grandpa is stiff as a rod, as if sitting on a bed of nails. But once the lights fade, he loosens up and a satisfied smile breaks across his face—especially during a trailer when the belly dancer advertised outside puts on a sultry performance. That old farmer watches it all with bedazzled eyes, and when the movie starts, he looks enchanted by the music and color. By halfway into the movie, he's tapping his dung-caked shoes on the floor, keeping time with the music. Towards the climax, he's so involved that we have to keep him from running into the screen to join the antics of the happy-go-lucky cast. My father has him under surveillance the whole time, and seeing that his experiment is working, he flashes me triumphant winks.

After the movie, we crowd up the aisle full of chattering people, still aglow from the happy ending. Baba's waiting impatiently for a response, something to show a deep change has taken place in Grandpa. But Hajji is sulky and silent, marching a few steps ahead as if we may contaminate him with some disease.

"So what do you think?" Baba hurries to catch up.

"Leave me alone."

"It was a rare experience, wasn't it?"

"What experience?"

Baba has to lay it out for him. "Did you finally see the light?"

"What light?"

Disappointed, my father turns to me for explanation, but I'm equally surprised.

"Maybe he's still under the spell of the movie," he whispers, "still digesting the deep meaning."

Outside, Grandpa pauses for another look at the poster of the belly dancer. A look of horror flashes across his face, as if facing the devil himself disguised under the mask of a seductress. He nervously fingers his prayer beads and mouths prayers to ward off evil.

"What's the matter, Hajji? You look as though your ship just sank."

"Take me straight to the bus terminal! I want to go back to the village," Grandpa growls, and starts walking again.

"Why are you acting so strange?" Baba asks, running after him.

"You forced me to watch a stupid show with a bunch of clowns in it!"

"Calm down, Hajji."

"And that whore, too. Her eyes are cesspools of sins . . . oh Lord, why did I trust my mind and judgment with this rogue? Why did I allow him to trick me into sin?"

136

"Wait a minute, Hajji! Hold your horses and let's ride together . . . I exposed you to a whole new experience and is this what I get for thanks?"

"What did you expect, a trophy? Are you happy to see a life of worship and devotion threatened by this filth?"

Baba keeps pushing and begging his father until the old man finally cools down and agrees to stay the night at our house.

It was this same cinema that I revisited with my brother Arash when he was on a brief leave from the warfront. Arash came in his military outfit, his head shaved to the skin, his beard a blue-black stubble. He looked healthier than the day I arrived, or maybe I was getting used to gaunt grim faces. My brother was taller than me, about six feet, but his back was stooped, and we looked the same age.

We went to a matinee show of a war movie. There wasn't much else on the screen in post-revolutionary Iran, save for religious and Third World propaganda. A scruffy man in a wheelchair sold tickets from the small bare kiosk: a disabled veteran of war rewarded for his sacrifices with a job. The lobby was gray, cold and stripped of colorful posters. Walls were covered with grime, chandeliers dark, and romantic music had fallen silent, replaced by the forlorn sound of the Qur'an.

The snack bar at the end of the hall looked more like a junk dealer's stall. No corn was popping, no fancy logos of American drinks flashed through the refrigerator against the wall, which was unplugged, its shelves stocked only with plastic pitchers of lemonade and tap water.

Arash picked up two sandwiches from a pile on the counter, boiled eggs rolled in flat bread, and we stood in a corner eating. In the lobby only a dozen young men milled about, and a few others huddled in privacy with their veiled wives and children.

Inside the auditorium we sat on folding wooden chairs with the other stags, at a safe distance from the family section. Instinctively, I expected to hear the old national anthem and see the boastful image of the deposed king on the screen. Instead there was a grainy picture of the revolutionary leader Ayatollah Khomeini, eyes downcast and frowning as always, with martial music enhancing the effect.

After the movie, we went to a sandwich shop at a busy square, another spot replete with memories. The Armenian owner was still there, but his food tasted bland. "Religious Minority" announced a big sign hanging from his window.

"What's that sign?" I asked Arash.

"It's to warn pious Muslims of the impure food served here," he said with an apologetic smile. "All religious minorities have to put it outside their shops, if they're selling food."

We sat in a private corner and my brother told me about the horrors he saw in the war with Iraq: the long frontier littered with mines and human limbs, the killing marshes floating with swollen corpses. His nights out in the desert were lonely, filled with threats of ambush and screams of shell-shocked soldiers. His accounts were too painful and I tried to steer him to the distant past.

"Remember, Arash, how Baba used to spar with Uncle E?" I said and his eyes turned to mine with some hope.

"Yes, kind of," he said, straining his mind.

"I rather miss the fox. Is he still around?"

"Oh yes. He wouldn't kick the bucket so easily. He's come down with Alzheimer's, though . . . is now bedridden, unconscious."

"Tell me about Baba," I said. "Did you two ever get along?"

"Oh yes. We never had any problem. He lived his life, I lived mine. But you did have a problem with him, and I never understood why."

"It's . . . my biggest regret."

I went on digging into the past, with the sense of nostalgia whetted by a rare union with my brother. He didn't seem to remember much from the old days. His life had been too harsh to allow for nostalgic thoughts. My attention hovered elsewhere for some moments, falling on the next table, where a woman sat with her son and daughter. They seemed to be back from school shopping, their table scattered with stationery items. A pair of new schoolbags and bagfuls of binders and folders sat on the floor by their chairs.

The boy, perhaps twelve, had spread out his purchases in front of him, joyfully sorting through them. He kept smelling at a pink and blue eraser and gently biting into it. The girl, a year younger, was busy with her own treasures, trying colored pencils individually on a white napkin.

I watched them for a few whimsical minutes, taking a journey back to my own childhood. I smelled that peculiar smell of the two-toned eraser and tasted its dry taste. What immense joys those back-to-school sprees gave me, the long walks relieved by anxious visits to restaurants or confectionaries. I remembered the day Edison, the bullyboy, knocked my pencil and sharpener off the desk, and crumpled the new stationery I so cherished.

"What are you looking at?" Arash asked.

"At those people."

"She's a mother . . . Shahed, don't let your eyes stray like that . . . this isn't America."

"You're right." I turned back to him. "I wanted to ask you something, Arash."

"You're in a talking mood today."

"What were Baba's . . . final years like? Did he change at all?"

"Well, yeah, you could say that. He chased women even more. Teenage girls even came to visit him in the hospital, all that time while he was dying slowly. But sometimes he was in a confessional mood. He'd pour out his sins and beg forgiveness." Arash shook his head and stared out the window with a faint smile.

I drew a breath to force out the question that threatened to choke me. "Did he mention me—the money he stole from me?"

"What money?" Arash looked puzzled.

"Never mind."

"Shahed, what—"

"It's okay, Arash. Let's go." I was almost relieved that I didn't have to dredge up what had steamed in my guts for so many years.

We stepped out of the shop and saw, just across the square, a gathering of high school kids, all dressed in olive green Mao-style outfits and holding hands in a chain.

"Bread, Housing, Freedom," they chanted.

"They're Maoist youth activists," Arash said. "They're looking for trouble."

"What's the demonstration for?"

"They want to take the country from the mullahs and make it into a communist country. They're dreaming."

A thin crowd of bystanders stood around, cheering or staring in curiosity. A minute later, the woman and her children also stepped out, clutching their bags. The kids were still sipping from their cola bottles, and looked scared by the sight of the rally.

"Let's get out of here, Mom," the girl pleaded.

"Don't worry, darling. These protests are common. Nothing will happen."

She hadn't finished her sentence before four military trucks lumbered into the street and ground to a halt outside the shop. Guards jumped out waving long clubs. Some also pulled out knives, blades flipped out of the handle and gleamed in the late afternoon sun.

"Now!" their leader shouted and the platoon charged at the protesters. Angry roars, painful cries, the crunch of bones . . . puddles of blood. People dashed for their parked cars, before they were smashed, and sped away. Shop owners rushed out to pull down their shutters and pedestrians scurried about like frightened cockroaches. In their madness and confusion, the guards kept hitting at anything: live bodies, immovable objects, shadows. Every blow was followed by a blind stab of the knife; every stab, by a manic shriek; every shriek, by painful groans.

The little girl was right next to me, stooping over and cupping her knees, screaming. The boy trembled and dropped his cola.

"Please, Mom, let's get out of here," the girl begged.

"I think we ought to leave, too," my brother said to me.

"Where to? There are roadblocks everywhere. Those guards are beating everyone."

For some strange reason, I wasn't perturbed—rather odd for a man who's done nothing in his life but escape. It wasn't braveness or coolness. I'd been shaken enough, maybe too much—to the point of numbness. Presently, the children's mother turned to slip into the sandwich shop for cover, but the Armenian blocked her way.

"Please, madam, don't make trouble for me," he said, while dragging down the shutter.

The shutter was half-closed and the woman tried to squeeze through, dragging the bags and her children along.

"Please, madam! They might think I'm harboring communists."

"Move out of my face, you coward. We're your customers. We just had a meal here."

"You're welcome anytime, but now I have to protect myself. I'm Christian. I don't want any trouble!"

140

"You're human, aren't you? Open the door or I'll make a bigger trouble for you."

She pushed herself in, dragging the children along.

"Let's slip in, too," Arash said and shoved through.

Once we were all inside, the owner locked the door and stood there behind the window holding up his hands in surrender.

"I don't want my windows broken. We're a minority in this country . . . don't take sides . . . just want to live in peace."

Through the window we watched the battle shifting to the other side of the square, where some of the dissidents still standing were waving their bloody shirts and shouting anti-government slogans. The lull on our side gave a chance for people to jump into their cars and flee. An old Chevrolet was parked right outside the restaurant, and a middle-aged man with a shock of white hair ran toward it. As soon as he opened its door, the mother stormed out of the shop with her children in tow. She jerked open the back door and pushed in the kids and her bags.

"What are you doing? This is not a taxi," protested the driver, still standing on the street, holding his door open.

"I'll pay you. Don't worry." She closed the back door and herself jumped in the front seat.

"I said this is not a taxi. Get out! Quick, before the guards come back."

"Then you better get in quickly and drive away."

He jumped in and tried to push her out of the car. "Get out, whore!"

"Shut up and start the car."

"I'll call the police."

"Hah, the police in this wild jungle?"

"Then I'll beat your ass myself if you don't leave."

As he raised his hand, the woman pounced on him and grabbed his hair.

"You get us out of here or I'll kill you. Your cheap blood will be wasted in the sea of blood in this square."

The man threw a hateful look at her. Then he shook his head, started the "taxi" with a roar and took off.

"What a woman!" Arash said admiringly. He chuckled. "You think they can bring souls like her to their knees?"

141

"Not if there are enough of them."

Back at home, Baba settles to discuss the movie again, before its magic evaporates. He wakes up his wife and his mother to sit and listen, as if he needs witnesses and an audience for his lecture. Mama makes tea, tries in vain to shoo me into bed, and then we all sit expectantly.

Baba starts, circling in on his main theme.

"That miser learned a good lesson, didn't he?" he says, throwing a side glance at Hajji to catch his reaction.

Grandpa keeps a morose silence, his sunburned forehead deeply wrinkled, his bushy eyebrows knit together in an angry frown.

"It's amazing how a movie can change one's life, more than a lifetime of worship," my father goes on.

Hajji doesn't even lift his head to look at him. His eyes are fixed on the fading patterns of our rug. From a silver holder, he removes a cigarette and lights it with a match, putting the charred stump frugally back in the matchbox. He takes a few puffs and then puts a big lump of sugar in his mouth before taking a sip of his tea.

"Some people hoard and hoard, thinking that's all life is about," Baba starts again. "They only realize their mistake when it's too late. This is exactly what the movie wants to say: that money is for spending, not . . ."

This last is so lame that Grandpa chokes on the ball of sugar in his mouth. His mouth sets in a disgusted smirk and his denture almost slips out of his mouth, but it all seems lost on my father.

"Anyway, it's never too late to turn your life around and make something good out of it—something that will bring you rewards on the Day of Judgment."

The scornful expression on Hajji's face shifts into outrage and he bolts upright.

"Cut the bullshit and come to the point!" he barks out. "What are you trying to get at with these childish insinuations?"

"I beg your pardon?"

"I said get right to the point! Reveal your satanic intentions!"

"What's the matter with you?" Baba pauses in his routine.

"Do you want me to learn from that stupid clown and give my hard-earned money to you to shit all over? Wake up! These things happen only in movies, in fairy tales. Why can't you grow up?"

142

Baba might as well have been lashed across the face. His jaw drops a few inches and all blood leaves his face. He wants to fire back, but he is tongue-tied.

"What . . .what's that attitude?" he finally says. "I . . . I'm just saying generosity is virtuosity . . ."

"Don't hand me that crap about the virtues of generosity. You want something from me, be honest."

"You know what I want. I want the house. I'm not asking for the moon, am I?"

Hajji jolts as if hearing a sacrilegious remark. "What! I'd as soon turn this house to cinders."

"Okay, keep it, then. Just let me put it on the market for you."

"You want to make my grandchildren homeless? This house is all they have left. You would have carted off every brick in it if I hadn't fortified them with mortar."

This is the last straw and Baba goes off his head.

"I can't believe it! You've got one foot in the grave and still guard your money like you have a thousand years to live. What're you keeping it all for—a vacation in Hell? If you can't enjoy it, there are others who can."

"Ha—only in your dreams," Hajji chuckles. "I'd as soon throw it to the goats to feed on or give it to charity, even pagan charity— anyone but you."

"Then keep it. Take it to the grave with you. You've always wanted a son to carry your coffin on his shoulder and I can't wait for the honor."

"I wouldn't even trust you with my corpse. Let me tell you loud and clear: you won't see another *rial* from me. So tighten your ass and get a job!"

Grandpa grabs his hat and shoots to his feet.

"I slave my whole life away and look what I get for a son: a pure loser. You're forty and what have you got to show for it save that hulk of a car?" he says and stomps out of the house, leaving Grandma behind.

Baba stares at the door in shock, as if knocked over the head with an iron bar, and then explodes.

"The bastard will come to regret this. He'll pay for it with his cheap blood . . . he'll soon crawl back begging for mercy . . ."

As he yells, window panes rattle and we're all worried he might do something foolish in a flash of rage—like take his hunting rifle and blow the "miserable life" out of his old man. To appease him, Grandma reaches under her shawl and digs a knotted kerchief from under her big breasts. She opens the cloth and gives all the money in it to her son. That takes the edge off his anger, but he still goes on to blacklist his father from family visits.

My father's plight may have seemed pathetic, but that indignant fury, born of his own self-pity, gave him a destructive strength in his relationship with me. There was a ferocious intensity about him that nipped the bud of manhood in his firstborn son, stunting his growth as a confident and assertive person.

One night, Mary invited me to her house for dinner. She'd long been insisting that I should meet her family, if you could call it that, and try to get close to her aunt and her boyfriend Bill. I'd done my best to wriggle out of the obligation. First, I didn't want to create an impression in her mind that our relationship was going anywhere. Second, I didn't have the guts to face Bill—what I knew of him from Mary—his prejudices and his weird dislike of me as a rival.

Eventually, I caved in. The pain of disappointing Mary was more unbearable than submitting to her annoying demands.

"Laura is making your favorite Persian dish. I spent the whole week teaching her how to cook it," she said by way of tempting me. "I wouldn't worry about Bill, either. He's really not so awful when he's not drinking. Laura and I made him promise not to touch alcohol tonight."

It was about six o'clock when I rang the bell. Bill's pickup truck was parked outside, identifiable by its sensational bumper stickers: Plumbers have bigger tools and dig deeper, I'm ripe—Eat me. The last came with the picture of a banana peeled off and penetrating a rouged mouth.

Mary and Laura came to the door and I entered apprehensively. Inside the hallway by the door, I paused with a dizzy sensation in my head, feeling like a shy little boy entering an unfamiliar territory, hiding behind Mary and half turning back to the door. A present was in my hand for Laura, and I wished I could drop it like a delivered pizza and take off. It was a box of Persian candies I'd brought from Iran but never bothered to open.

The house was typically working-class, not unlike Mr. Johnson's: poorly-lit and crammed with knick-knacks from yard sales. Bowls of cookies and candies sat on tables and the kitchen counter—probably treats piling up from previous Halloweens.

Laura herself was a big woman with platinum-blond hair, wearing a turquoise blue blouse and peach-color pants. Her frothy bright appearance and cheerfulness invoked the image of a wedding cake, and I wondered about the bruise under her eyes spoiling the picture. Like Mary, she was bubbly and talkative, with every word trailed by a flurry of giggles. She could be a future version of her niece and that rather scared me, sharpening my doubts about the relationship I felt trapped in.

I presented her gift and she was as happy as a child to receive it, gasping and screaming at the top of her voice, as if no one had ever shown her such kindness. She put the gift on a table and opened it with relish, spending a lot of time studying the gilded wrapping, the gaudy ribbon and the Farsi inscriptions on the box. With every discovery, she let out a gasp, followed by a shriek, marveling at the exoticness as she placed the candies in a cut glass dish. In my head, I praised her quintessential American spirit, her lack of inhibition in expressing her excitement. It was a marvel to me that a battered woman could take joy from such a simple thing. I would have tried to look unimpressed even if presented the whole world—so deep is my fear of showing emotion . . . my needs, privations.

Bill was lounging against a beanbag chair, sipping from a bottle of Michelob and watching television.

"Hon, why don't you come and say hello to our guest," Laura said to him.

He got up lazily and took a few staggering steps, stopping dead a few feet from me. He was wary, as if facing a wild animal outside its cage. Contrary to my expectations, Bill was a small man with a shrunken face and prominent cheekbones. His intense blue eyes, set deep in his reddish face, exuded weariness, a lingering hangover. His jaws were tight, closing together in a taut crack of the mouth. The clothes he wore conformed more to the picture I had in my mind: boots, Levis, T-shirt and a red baseball cap.

145

"Umm . . . yummy . . . what's it made of?" Laura asked, biting into one of the white chewy candies.

"I have no idea."

"I'm really not supposed to be eating this, but as you see I love sweets . . . Bill, you wanna try some of this?"

"Uh uh . . . not for me," he answered with distaste, as if she were holding a bedpan before him—the candies were either too weird or too sweet for his alcoholic taste.

"What's wrong with you, Bill? Aren't you going to shake hands with Shahed?" Mary asked.

He took another reluctant step and extended a limp hand.

"I'm Bill." His voice was low and smoke-hoarsened.

"Nice to meet you."

"Yeah."

Laura ushered us to a huge brown couch; Mary plunked down next to me. Bill went straight back to his beanbag to watch baseball and Laura to the kitchen. Across from the sofa was a buffet cabinet with a shattered window.

"Bill threw a hammer at her. It missed and hit the glass," Mary informed me quietly.

"Why did he do that?"

"She caught him making out with a bar lady in the pickup. They had a fight and he hit her."

Laura's attempt at Persian cuisine was not so great, but my culinary judgment may have been colored by my anxiety. The women were the only ones eating the gluey rice and the undercooked lamb spiced with Mexican herbs. Bill and I just sat morosely picking at our plates. Mary tried to stimulate conversation, talking nervously about food, weather, etc., but it all failed. My eyes avoided the cowboy and fixed on the bluish skin under Laura's eye, wondering what she'd done to deserve it. She was so kind and loving, the only source of warmth in a cold house, the only reason I didn't rush back out the door. The air inside was unbearable. I couldn't stand Bill's stifling presence, his hostile gaze, his mean spirit, the smoke he puffed out. A few times I caught his eyes and they bored through me, a hollow stare hard to read. Was it hatred, obtuseness, offensive curiosity, or what?

"So, what's your opinion about the mad dogs running your country?" he finally said.

"Mad dogs?" I feigned ignorance.

"The rag-heads, the barbarians taking our folks prisoners," he said in hard-jawed defiance, his thin lips closing tighter.

I slowly moved my gaze from his eyes down to the tattoos on his slender arm, fading and blending into thick blue veins.

"I don't have an opinion. I'm not into politics." I became stiffer, but my legs jiggled under the table, my sweaty hands held together between shaking knees.

"Bill, come on now." Mary rushed to help me, but he ignored her.

"What do you mean you haven't got an opinion? You're alive, aren't you?" he said while striking a match to a Camel. "You think America is out to be bullied?"

"Of course not."

"Then why do you treat our folks like shit?"

"It wasn't me who took them. And they've been freed now anyway."

"That's because our president scared the shit out of you guys. We would have nuked the crap out of you if you hadn't freed our folks."

"It's fortunate that it was averted."

"Not quite. The towelheads will eventually pay for it. And you'd better go back and help them. You got no business staying here." He flicked ash onto the dinner plate.

"Bill, you'd better stop drinking that beer," my girlfriend tried again. "You promised, remember?"

"I didn't make no goddamn promise," he snapped back. "I'll stop drinking when I fucking feel like it."

Mary looked at her aunt for help, but Laura looked like she was worrying about the Persian food.

"Come to the kitchen. I want to talk to you," my girlfriend told Bill, and he hauled himself up and followed grudgingly. At the table, an awkward silence hung between Laura and me, as we heard the two arguing it out.

"Don't be so mean, Bill."

"I don't like this guy. I want to put my fucking fist in his face."

"Please—we just wanted a nice dinner."

"I trust no goddamn A-rabs."

"I told you a hundred times he's not Arab. He's Persian."

147

"Same fucking shit. It's just another name for barbarians. I want him outta your life and outta this fucking country."

The day after the fight between Baba and Grandpa is Friday and there's no school. As usual after a fight, Baba is affectionate and stays home to spend time with us. He seems to appreciate us all of a sudden, as if we were all he had left in the world. We have a raucous day with a lot of joy and laughter, lots of games, wrestling and "horse riding," and drop into bed very late.

I hate getting up this morning to go to school. It's Saturday again and we're supposed to have a stupid ceremony, and another trial for "bad boys." Nothing has changed since the last ordeal and I'm certainly in for another round of beatings. Damn it! There's no end to this nightmare. I wish I could stay at home like my brother. I wouldn't mind having another circumcision if that would keep me out of school.

As I'm about to leave, Baba slips me a few coins to spend as I like, a fruit of his lingering tenderness—but that doesn't help ease my anxiety.

I step out of the room, passing under my brother's scorched foreskin swinging like a chime in the winter breeze. The skin is now dry as ash, but Grandma still won't take it off the doorsill. This one doesn't seem to be for swallowing. She wants just to let it hang there to ward off harm. I pass under the lucky charm back and forth, hoping its miraculous powers will save me.

Walking to the bus stop, my feet feel heavy, as if there's lead in my shoes. It's a cloudy day with a chill. Above flat rooftops, the sky is a gray sheet for as far as I can see. The air is choked with dust and smoke, rolling into a giant ball, blotting our view of the mountain and the upper-class world spread out over the foothills.

I plod along and pass by the mosque. Its wobbly minaret has tilted further, ready to fall at a touch. By the crumbling steps leading up to the entrance, a beggar is camped out, just a dark bundle of cloth wrapped in a frayed chador. She reaches a grimy hand to me, moaning and praying to soften my heart, and I take the sandwich out of my bag to hand her. She throws a dirty look and waves it off, directing her palm and eternal blessings to someone else.

Further up Seyed, the grumpy greengrocer, is arranging his display of persimmons and pomegranates, and all the other delicious winter fruits. From a hook sticking out of the wall hangs a tantalizing, fat bunch of bananas. Bananas are an exotic fruit in our neighborhood and outrageously expensive, and Seyed is the only one here to sell them. There's always a bunch of hungry children crowding outside the shop and staring, as if the fruit has just descended from heaven. But Seyed won't tolerate window shopping, and he's especially rude to children. If you can't pay, the mean bastard barks and waves you on your way.

Mercifully, the ceremony is called off because the principal is sick with the flu and has to remain in bed for several days. That's one hell of a relief and I go to celebrate the news at the school cafeteria, with the money Baba gave me. The old lecher can wither and die for all I care. Who's going to miss him, except for the *houri*s next door fond of his magic touch?

I order a hamburger and a soda, and a bar of chocolate-coated ice cream for desert. It's quite a party but again too short. The problem with these occasional treats is that they sharpen your appetite for more mouth-watering treats and you want to repeat them. So here I'm once again looking for lost coins everywhere—in closets, under the rugs and even out in the gutter. In the streets, I roam about like a bum, with my eyes sweeping the ground for any metallic glint. Occasionally, I hit upon a few rusty coins; but that's rather rare in our neighborhood, where there are more people scavenging for coins than losing them.

I wonder why I didn't get this idea of stealing before. It's becoming second nature to me. What I need to do is hone my skills and expand my field of operation, open new frontiers. I haven't had much luck getting anything off of my father lately. Mama is always sure to get there before I open my eyes in the morning. So I've all but given up on my father and am looking for juicier prey. This of course is a little risky, but the payoff is great too. So I start with Grandma, the ambassador of good will, who is on a long visit to our house again, trying to maintain that rickety bridge between Baba and Grandpa. Grandma is a soft target, too naïve and spaced out to notice someone is groping her boobs searching for her piggybank. Her eyes are always fixed on a length of thread she's trying to run through the eye of a needle. But that's an impossible task with her vision getting dimmer and dimmer. Nowadays she needs my help to mend a sock or something, and that lets me snuggle by her side. But I'm learning something from her, too. Actually I'm getting quite good at sewing, even thinking maybe I should become a tailor when I grow up, in case I don't make it as a doctor.

The last time I opened her bank, the crumpled handkerchief, there was nothing in it but the ashes of my brother's foreskin. The poor woman is growing too attached to the fetish and I have no idea when she's finally going to throw it to the winds. Anyway, that was the last time I stole from her, or any other woman. Men make better game. They carry more cash and are less likely to notice if a few coins go missing. Every time an uncle visits, a husband of one of my six aunts, I give his pockets a quick search while he's taking a nap or stands to pray. Unfortunately, they're mostly broke dudes and there's not much to be found. I'm waiting for the lucky catch, one to keep me afloat for life and even finance my trip to America with Houri. But that has to wait until Uncle E visits, or even better, Grandpa. That however is unlikely, given their relationships with my father.

One thing that ties my hands is the endless presence of great aunt Khaleh, Grandma's homeless sister. She's still here with us since my brother's circumcision and I don't know what she's waiting for before she takes leave—maybe for the little boy to grow back his weenie. Anyway, she must feel welcome at our house. My parents are both generous people, but Mama has to make up for the shortage of food at the *sofreh* with plenty of filling bread to eat with rice and stew.

The witch is running deep roots here, scratching her mark all over the place and prying into everyone's business. Our every movement is under Khaleh's eye. She inspects every hole and crack in the house, opens and closes doors like the caretaker of a bank. She has eagle eyes, too, and extra-sensory ears—all of which make it impossible to trick her radar. So I've put it all on hold until she leaves, if that would just happen in my lifetime.

Finally one day, I have a piece of luck and Uncle E comes for lunch. His coat pockets are filled with coins and candies, and he keeps jingling them to show off. Once he takes off his jacket, I notice a fat roll of cash bulging out from the pocket of his shirt. Bingo! This is the big break I was waiting for!

I roll up my sleeves and brace for action, if I can only find a way to distract the nosy aunt. It turns out to be a stressful day. My poor little brother has developed complications in his *dool* and can't make pee-pee. He's in pain and bawling his head off, and there's nothing anyone can do to help. Mama just stands there wringing her hands and mouthing prayers, and Khaleh spews rubbish ideas that find no ears. It's Aunt Fatima again who has come to the rescue, with her steely nerves and timeless patience. As she removes the bandage for a look, we're all horrified to find what used to be his weenie. The appendage has swelled into a grotesque mass of blood and pus, with twisted bubbles breaking out all over the surface. Mama buries her face in her hands and runs out wailing.

My aunt fetches a washtub, fills it with warm water and permanganate and has my brother sit in it, until his penis is thoroughly soaked and clots melt away. With a scissor, she painstakingly picks off every shred of bandage melted into the skin. It's a devil of a job to clean up all the mess, but the boy can eventually piss again.

While following the ordeal, I keep an eye out for Uncle E and the wad of bills lodged next to his chest. I have his every move under watch, just waiting for him to change into pajamas, which I'm sure he will so as not to wrinkle his trousers while sitting on the floor.

He finally takes off the trousers but, to my chagrin, leaves his shirt on, with the orange notes winking at me through the white polyester. I estimate there are at least five thousand *rial*s, enough for me to put my feet up for the rest of my life. I can pay off our debts to the principal and still have some left to splurge around the school and buy friends. Most of all, I have been dreaming of a way to run off with Houri, and now I can ask her to go with me—I can tempt her with every luxury. I work myself up to such wild fantasies that I almost jump and snatch the wad away from our guest.

At lunch, my father and I sit across from Uncle E, staring at his bulge, which sticks out like a single breast. He's stoned once again, traveling through space in search of his mythical love, but alert enough to slyly notice our interest in his wad. To torture us more, he casually slides up a big orange bill, letting us catch a glimpse of the corner, as a seductive woman lets her skirt ride up a silky leg.

Uncle E slurps a big bowl of soup, thick with noodles and chickpeas, and feeling heavy, announces it is time for a siesta. Before retiring, he gives my brother and me each a hard candy to suck on while he's resting, and holds out the promise of more bribes if we keep the noise down. I pop mine and stand by the door to the guest room where he's bedding, waiting for his snores to rise before jumping into action.

As is my bad luck, Baba is in a playful mood again, looking for a trick to play on his brother-in-law. Unable to find one, he starts stomping around the rooms and slamming doors shut to jolt him out of sleep.

"Candy, candy, I want a candy too," he yells over and over in a childish tone. "How come they all get candies and I don't? Come on, give me a candy or I won't let you sleep."

I have to wait until he has his fun before returning to my surveillance post. In a few minutes, Uncle E's snores fill the house and it's finally time to act. I tiptoe into the room and kneel by his bed. My fingers crawl into his pocket like a spider. But as I lock my thumb and forefinger around the outer orange bill, the door flies open and Khaleh barges in holding her prayer mat.

At George's gas station, on the graveyard shift, I used to come across all kinds of weirdos and outcasts: thieves robbing brazenly, perverts masturbating in full view, and hermaphrodites appearing nude and looking for a bedmate—all turning up like vampires after midnight, when weariness and slumber gives way to lawlessness.

One lonely Halloween night, I snapped out of a doze in the office and found several giants towering over me. All wore stocking masks—and one of them held a rifle. At first, I thought they were Halloween revelers coming for "trick or treat," and wasn't so alarmed. But then, suddenly, like manic racehorses, they vaulted over the counter and pushed me to the ground, with the gun pointed to my head.

"Where's the safe, mother fucker?" one of them yelled. "Come on, where's the fucking safe?"

I unlocked the cash box and they made away with the pathetic contents. A minute later, while I was still lying on the floor, shivering with belated fear, one of the hold-up men slipped back in through the door and stood there eying me through slits in the nylon stocking. I could see his eyes, and froze in fear he'd come back to shoot me. But after a moment I realized he was just staring at me as if pleading for understanding. Then he pulled off the mask and muttered something indecipherable. He was a child actually, a tall black boy with cold red eyes speaking of suffering. He looked innocent and menacing at once, and my impulse was to embrace him in forgiveness, tell him how much I understood—so he wouldn't leave with a bad conscience. But as always, my fear got in the way and I lay there shaking like a coward.

"Please . . . leave," I said with a trembling voice. "Customers aren't–aren't allowed inside the office after midnight."

He threw another confused, almost remorseful look at me and turned out the door.

The next morning, I had to justify my cowardice to my boss and explain why I hadn't the guts to stand up to the raiders.

"They looked vicious and determined."

"Don't give me that shit!" George shot down my excuse. "These lowlifes are like dogs. They smell your fear. You show them weakness, they're all over you."

"You're probably right," I said shamefully.

"The gun, too, must have been fake—a toy."

"Maybe, but it looked real to me."

"Everything looks real here, *habibi*. This is the land of fantasy, Hollywood,—don't forget!"

"I don't know what you mean."

"You have this romantic picture of America that isn't true. I found it out right after I got here. But you go on dreaming."

"What else is there?"

"Let me tell you something. When I first came here, I didn't lock my car door—hell, they don't do it in movies. But in a few weeks, my car was stolen and I learned a lesson."

"So . . . I have to learn a few lessons too."

"Do you remember what they looked like—the thieves? Were they black?"

"No." I lied because I didn't want to reinforce his prejudices against blacks, or against thieves.

"Why, didn't you take a good look at them?"

"They all had masks on. I didn't see their faces."

"They must have been black. It is their style. You mean you didn't even see their hands?"

"No, I was too nervous."

THE BUTCHER

Losing all hopes on getting the house from Grandpa, my father puts every effort into getting rid of the last strip of land he owns. He's moving heaven and earth to find a buyer, but no one comes to even look at it. The lot has stony soil where even weeds don't have a chance to grow; for now, villagers have turned it into a dump-site. Baba's utterly frustrated and never stops cursing his father for "palming off a piece of shit" onto him.

Back from school one day, I see a truck parked outside our house, unloading a flock of sheep. The door stands wide open, the animals squeez their butts through, heading down to the basement to join the rats and the cockroaches—they bleat happily and swing their shit-smeared tails as if going to a swell party.

I walk in and see my brother greeting the animals with excited laughter. He wants to hug them all but they keep knocking him to the floor. He gets up, makes another attempt but falls backward again. I grab his hand, lift him up and give an older-brother warning to behave, and then go to the basement to check things out.

In the basement kitchen, Mom's sitting by the kerosene stove, frying shovel-loads of onions to store away for winter. She looks stressed out, her bony fingers are shaking, her eyes red and tearful from the fumes and onions. With the beasts invading her territory, she's rushing to cover the frying pans from dust. Then she bursts into a sob, pleading with Allah to deliver her from a crazy husband.

I feel sorry for her but isn't she overacting? It must have something to do with her bulging belly. Another baby is on the way and she's not so excited about it.

I overheard her talking to my aunt the other day. "I already have my hands full taking care of these two. Anyway, it's God's will and I have to go along with it."

I don't think it has anything to do with God though. It must be from that night when I heard her hissing to my father. You see, I'm an old boy now. I understand everything. The barber is teaching me everything I need to know about sex.

I try to comfort her, throwing my arms around her shoulders.

"Mom, this isn't the first time we have livestock as guests. Please don't make so much fuss."

She cries a little and then goes upstairs to interrogate her husband, who's standing outside the door paying off the truck driver.

"Why are these sheep here?" she asks as soon as he comes inside.

He gives a triumphant grin then sighs with relief: "I finally found a fool to buy the land. He's a cattle raiser and wants to turn it into a livestock farm."

"What are these sheep here?"

"Oh . . . the sheep. The guy had no ready cash so he paid me in sheep."

"And you accepted that?" Mama raises her hand as if to beat on his head.

"Yes, I decided to take the offer. Sheep you can at least eat. What're you going to do with a piece of shit?"

Rats and cockroaches are horrible pests, but they at least keep their traps shut. Sheep bleat constantly, taking sleep away from us for weeks, until my father finally finds a butcher to buy them, at a ridiculously low price and in installments. The deal itself isn't much to speak of, but it sets off a bizarre relationship between my father and the buyer.

The butcher looks like all the men of his trade. He's a big fellow with an overhanging belly and a big curved mustache. His nose is broken and skewed, his eyes bulge; and his ears, like a wrestler's, are pounded into lumps of scrambled eggs. In action, he's even more colorful: loud, phony and vain beyond imagination. He's also got a mean streak.

Like the idiot and the coalman, the butcher is a guardian angel, but a vigilante of a different kind. He's not exactly a fanatic, maybe not even religious, but he has this code of honor that everyone in the neighborhood must respect—everyone but himself. He sets himself as a model of chivalry to be emulated, if one wants to be a "a real man."

A "real man," is a humble guy, a man who walks with his head down. While humble, he must also have "big balls," big enough to impress my grandfather. He can booze and whore around all he wants, but he must never lust after neighborhood women, threaten the honor of their husbands or fathers.

When the butcher is in a bad mood, he charges down the street like a drunken bandit, roaring like a lion. He has his sidekicks in tow—at a respectful distance—all waving daggers and cleavers. The big thug himself appears in a tight shirt of crimson red, symbolic of the bloodbath he's about to start.

"Is there anyone with the balls to rise to my challenge?" he screams. "Come on, I want to see a real man."

Of course, no one is so foolish as to stand in his way. All give him a wide berth and even the police don't interfere. The butcher has money to bribe his way around and good contacts to bail him out of trouble. Grandpa says he and his gang of thugs helped bring the Shah to power through the CIA-British coup in 1953. They fanned out through the streets and clubbed and stabbed everyone who bad-mouthed the king.

But there's something I like about the butcher that comes out when he's hard at work in his shop. I love to go there and watch him cut fine slices of meat from sheep carcasses hanging from ceiling hooks. I admire his speed and skill when he breaks a bone, slicing clean through it without sending chips flying around.

Another thing that both fascinates and horrifies me are the religious frescos painted all over his walls. They're bloody scenes of ancient battles between saints and infidels. One awful picture shows an apostate chopping through the wrist of a holy man with a cleaver, and the next sequence shows the severed hand flying and dripping with blood. The theme of blood runs through the whole painting and blends gruesomely with the stained surroundings. I always wonder why he displays scenes like that in his shop. Maybe he finds them appetizing.

My return to Tehran furnished me with too many bloody scenes on the streets. I witnessed them enacted against our own people, men and women whose innocent or hopeful lapses in conforming to austerity earned swift and cruel censure. People no longer dared to celebrate with noise and music and color.

Even the commemoration of *Ashura*, the death anniversary of Imam Hussein, a saint who inspired our national pride and historical grief, had taken on an official air. The ceremony had become regulated, stripped of its spontaneity, reshaped to serve the political interest of the new rulers. The happier musical instruments were banned, a repressive code of dress and behavior was instituted—and of course young men were kept apart from young women.

Watching the gutted travesty of Ashura made me long for those dazzling visuals I lapped up as a child. Those pictures lingered so preciously in my mind because they were mournful events ironically taking on a festive fervor. They were dramatic affairs with the air of a carnival—an occasion to lament the death of a precious leader, but more, to celebrate his indomitable spirit.

In those days, colorful processions started from various quarters in the city and converged at a main thoroughfare, creating a spectacle of epic scale. For our humble neighborhood, the butcher was the master of ceremony, throwing his money and manpower into the cause, mobilizing his whole gang for an ostentatious show. At times, there was rivalry between him and the coalman, with each trying to outshine the other.

There was a Hercules for every street—men with barrel torsos, tattoos and handlebar mustaches—who carried the *Alam* in front of each parade: a giant cross hanging with cumbersome symbols in bright colors, and topped with peacock feathers. It was a coveted job, an honor with the burden, an act of penance that could wash away sins—and also show off muscles and endurance.

Children and veiled women would pack the sidewalks, watching in captivation the exhibitions of joy and grief float by, intoxicated by the magnificent air, the martial music and the bursts of color. Marching bands played drums, cymbals and accordions, as men in black beat themselves to the rhythm: some struck their chests, and others their shoulders with lengths of chain, and always a few zealots slashed at their own skulls with long swords.

Taj the idiot was always present in the bloodiest displays, his sword cutting a little deeper than the rest, his face and shroud dripping with blood. He drew more laughter than praise, his antics adding to the fun and exuberance. Scores of sheep were slaughtered along the way—a carcass every hundred yards; the meat was quickly whisked away to be cooked in huge cauldrons for charity meals.

158

In the afternoon, the event reached its zenith. Different bands came together in a big square. The Hercules leading each procession took the stage and began to turn around, floundering under the colossal weight, as he tried to outspin others. Mourners rushed to throw money at his feet and behead cows and sheep. Drums of iced water lined the edge of the streets, a welcome relief in hot summer days. Above every barrel stood a painting of the battle of *Karbala*, in a parched desert in present-day Iraq, between Imam Hussein and his Sunni enemies. Hussein's forces were vastly outnumbered by infidels led by Caliph Yazid Ibn Muawiyah, the corrupt ruler of BaghBaba, but they fought heroically until martyrdom.

The stages of the "passion plays" were as humble as Hussein's spirit. They were performed in dirt lots, all the rubble and trash swept away for the occasion. Props didn't exceed a few swords and daggers, and pairs of cymbals, drums and bugles. Someone would paint a large image on a wall, showing Caliph Yazid propped on his undeserved throne, holding a dagger and the severed head of a saint.

The play went on for three days in a row, enacting different episodes of the tragic conflict. On the first day, the coalman himself played the role of a chief disciple to Hussein, and his sons two orphan boys. They put on the white gowns and headdress of Bedouin Arabs, their chests emblazoned with Arabic symbols. A mustachioed monster in a shiny red outfit and a helmet topped with feathers whipped the boys, trying to make them betray their father, the most loyal follower of the Imam.

The two other days, the coalman appeared as Hussein himself, in a gown and green headdress, his face covered in respect for Imam's holiness. He would hold a doll swaddled in cloth and painted red, its throat stabbed with a spike. The baby was laid to rest in a tub and white pigeons landed on the corpse to mourn, and to promise. Melodies surged in the air and the beats of drums and cymbals whipped up frenzy and drew cathartic tears.

The event lasted well into the night and then mourners went for dinner to the coalman's mansion and makeshift structures outside, draped in black and lit up with candles.

All these touching details were absent in the winter of 1982. Islamic radicals tried to disrupt the innocent procession and direct it toward their political end. They chanted trite slogans and voiced hatred. The cry for justice had given way to a cry for death and destruction. Martyrdom, a symbol of noble aspirations, had been given a literal expression and become a convenient tool to further selfish causes.

Every time my father hits the jackpot, he quickly runs to get himself new clothes and more frippery for his car. The Bride is now slung way low under loads of glittery ornaments, looking like an invention by a mad scientist. The jackpot this time is the money from the sheep sale which still flows in installments.

He also goes out partying every night, celebrating the loot with his good time friends, shoveling money around like sand. All those who turned their backs on him in his hardship are back once again renewing allegiance and picking him clean.

The Colonel, too, is around for the party, and so is Khan, the persistent bounty hunter. Khan smells Baba's change of fortune and has been hot on his trail. One day, as we're off to collect another payment from the butcher, the midget finally catches up. He's been waiting in ambush in a dark corner and we walk right into his trap.

"Greetings, reverend sir!" he starts with his usual exaggerated tone. "I apologize for engrossing so much of your time, but I thought it is best to catch you in these prosperous moments and recover this long-overdue debt of gratitude."

Baba tries to hatch up an excuse and break loose, but the creep is hanging tight, holding his arm and planting a big foot in front of him.

"Hey, Khan, which hole did you crawl out of?" Baba dispenses with any courtesy.

"Sir, please try to use appropriate speech. Have you the money ready?"

"Just give me a few days—I'll settle it all. Right now I gotta run, Khan."

"I know you're in a hurry, my good friend," Khan says with a wise grin. "You're off to see the butcher about money. That's why I'm here, to collect my share before you go spending it all."

"So clever of you, but let me at least see how much he'll give me."

"Ha-ha. My good man, you have such an oily tongue, slicker than fish. You could actually dress up a wolf and sell it as sheep. But I won't fall for your tricks any more."

"I'm not trying to trick you, Khan. Just give me . . ." Baba is getting impatient and keeps looking around, as if for a route of escape.

"No, sir. You've reached the end of your wits. My partners are losing patience with you, and, God forbid, I don't want anything to happen to you on the eve of the New Year."

"All right, give me a couple days and you've got your money."

"No, my dear man, not even an hour. We have to take care of it right now. This is your last chance—don't blow it."

Baba moves restlessly like a tiger in a cage, but all the doors are closed. "All right, why don't we meet later for lunch to take care of it?"

"Ah-ah . . . no more lunch dates with you. I don't want to end up paying for your meal again. Actually it may not be a bad idea if I join you for lunch with the butcher."

"No, Khan, That's a terrible idea."

"Don't worry, I won't make you buy me a meal. I'll just take my money and leave," the midget says and tags along like a bell strapped around our ankles.

We don't go straight to the restaurant. Baba stops outside the neighborhood *Zoor-Kahneh*—the House of Champions, a traditional gymnasium. It is a mysterious place I've always wanted to see but never dared to approach, with all the giants going in and out of it. I have heard much about *Zoor-Kahnehs* and their role in the CIA coup. From these same places the butcher and his like recruited muscle-men to rally in support of the Shah and beat up his opponents. The rumor is that they were hired to do their dirty work by the Americans.

The green wooden door is open and a rag curtains the entrance. The door is intentionally low to oblige the *pahlevans* (champions) to bow in humility before stepping in.

"What are you doing?" Khan asks.

"The butcher is down here working out. Let's go watch him a little," Baba answers. He sweeps the curtain aside and stoops through, and I obligingly follow, with Khan reluctantly last. After edging down a dark narrow staircase, we come to an octagonal dungeon with no windows. Dim sunlight shines through a hole cut into the arched ceiling, casting eerie light on the outlandish scene inside. Muscular men wearing only tight breeches of brocade are busy displaying their arts. Their massive arms and chests are covered with tattoos: pictures

161

of mythical Persian warriors battling lions and dragons with swords and spears. More of these lurid pictures are painted on the walls, festooned with tiger and leopard skins and resplendent feathers. A large portrait of the Shah and his wife also hangs, showing the Empress kneeling before her king during their recent coronation ceremony.

The air is filled with the stink of sweat, and grunts from the giants straining every muscle to show their phenomenal strength.

In the middle of the dungeon is a pit, about two feet deep and ten yards across, where hulks of bodies are entangled in wrestling. Other spots feature tumblers displaying acrobatic feats: some spinning and some juggling *meels*, huge wooden weights in the shape of bowling pins.

On a carpeted platform facing the entrance sits the Ravi, the Narrator, dressed in a flowery robe and a conical red cap, the exotic costume of ancient Persia, reading from Ferdosi's *The Book of King*, our epic saga of mythical warriors. A drum is tucked under his arm and he beats and sings martial music to uplift spirits. The giants keep tumbling and spinning and my fear soon gives way to fascination.

Baba peers through the crowd looking for the butcher. Obviously nothing is on his mind but the money he is owed. Finally we spy him lying on his back, lifting two huge slabs of dense wood in tandem, surrounded by awed admirers. After a dozen strokes, he rolls over, kisses the floor in respect and gets up. An old man runs to him with a towel, with others chanting in singsong an Arabic verse from the holy book: *Peace be upon Mohammad and his family . . . peace upon Ali, the lion of God.*

Baba keeps waving, but the butcher is too engaged in receiving his tribute. Khan, looking nervous and out of place amidst giants, is getting frenetic. "By heaven, why are we here? Let's go and wait for him in the restaurant."

Baba hisses, "I didn't invite you, did I?"

The butcher finally notices my father and calls him over. Baba takes off his shoes and sets foot on the sacred ground, and Khan sidles up to me.

"May God add to his life, but your father is a naughty soul. I can never figure him out."

I pay no attention, just watch the sweaty action, and wait for Baba to return. In a few minutes he's back, smirking.

"Let's go. The butcher will join us soon."

162

"My good man, let me beg leave to state . . ."

"Are you coming or not?" Baba says and winds up the eerie steps.

We go to the same restaurant in the bazaar and, sure enough, the Colonel is waiting by the door, hungry as a goat, his eyes begging for an invitation. As we walk in, his big face lights up and he rushes to hug my father.

"I'm so glad you are here. Where the devil have you been?"

"Are you waiting for a table to parachute on again?" my father answers.

"I heard the good news," the Colonel says, ignoring the gibe. "You finally got rid of that piece of land."

"Yes, the money is flying out too," Baba says.

"So what? Money is for spending, isn't it? Now, should we go ahead and order?"

"No, let's wait for the butcher."

"Oh, he's never on time . . . always makes a point of arriving late to seem important."

"Why, do you know him?" my father asks.

"Who doesn't? He's the most notorious thug in town. Wait! Here he is. Let's order now. Where's the menu? Waiter!"

The butcher swaggers toward us, his arms half spread out to look tough. He's in a glossy black velvet suit, with the jacket draped over his shoulders in the cool style of street goons. The black felt hat, sitting on his head in an angle, has the same sheen as the suit and his white shirt is open to the navel, exposing a gold disk hanging from a thick chain.

Baba pulls a chair and the butcher sits on the edge of it, as if his butt is too precious to commit fully.

"This is Khan, the world's most persistent creditor," my father says mockingly by way of introduction. "He's hanging off me like an umbilical cord."

The thug gives the midget a cursory look, obviously contemptuous of his size.

"And this is the Colonel, the big spender."

"Yes, everyone knows the Colonel. He's a public liability."

The butcher turns his back on us at the table and speaks directly to my father about his exploits.

"Every one knows I worked my way up from nobody. I had to be a man everyone fears and respects at the same time," he says in a street drawl. "It wasn't easy. There were too many bums to move out of the way. But, thank god, it's all behind me.

"But let me tell you something: I never forget my roots—who I am and where I came from. I've touched too many lives. I've taken lots of orphans and widows under my wings."

He goes on complementing himself and the Colonel is growing more restless. His eyes beg my father to order lunch. But Baba seems impressed by his friend's feats and listens intently like a curious student of life.

"Hey, shall we order now?" the Colonel interrupts, rubbing his belly and yawning.

"Hush. Adults are talking," my father answers.

"Stop torturing this great soldier!" Khan intervenes. "You'll give him an ulcer."

"Okay, what do you all want?" Baba says.

"I'm not eating," Khan says.

"Don't worry, it's on me this time," Baba says.

Khan throws a disbelieving look at him and then orders a big dish of rice and a double skewer of kabob: both steak and ground lamb. He's a hearty eater, too, for his size, putting away everything in front of him and scrubbing the plates clean with bread. The Colonel, likewise, polishes off dish after dish of appetizers and then opens his belt a few notches to make room for the main course. The only one not eating is the butcher. He just sits there twiddling his mustache and thumbing prayer beads as big as his eyeballs. The only attention he gives me is to open my bottle of cola with his teeth, which impresses me more than all his other feats.

By the time we're done with the meal, the Colonel is so stuffed that he can't even make the effort to run away from the bill. He's tucked his chin under and keeps puffing up his cheeks to suppress burps. Presently, the waiter comes with the tab, and the butcher reaches to grab it. But my father intercepts and sets the tab on the table, without making an effort to pay. Khan and the Colonel keep exchanging uncertain glances, worried they might have to pay their shares after all. The Colonel finally gets a hold of himself and lumbers away; Khan remains in his seat nervously fidgeting. He's obviously waiting for the butcher to pay my father so he can grab his share.

164

At the table, there's some idle conversation and then the butcher takes out a roll of cash, hands it to my father, and splits. Baba puts the money in his pocket, but still doesn't pay the bill. He just sits coolly, hands in his pockets, with a sly look on his face, ignoring Khan's expectant glances.

On the other side, from behind the bathroom wall, I see the Colonel craning his head, waiting for the all-clear signal before emerging. My father watches Khan suffer for a few minutes and then takes the wad out to count, and the midget jerks like a Doberman on leash.

"Hey, what're you doing?" Baba objects, leaning away.

"Let me see, how much did he pay you?" Khan asks excitedly.

"Wait until I finish counting," my father says, guarding the wad between his legs. He flips through the roll and then stops—his face freezes in a surprised grimace.

"No way!" he shouts. "This is way short of what he was supposed to give me! You guys wait here!"

He dashes for the door and Khan runs after him. Baba pauses to stop the midget.

"Where are you going?"

"Wherever you are."

"No, you wait here. I must catch up with him quickly. I'll be right back."

"I don't trust you."

"Listen, Khan, you think I'd leave my son with strangers and take off? Be reasonable. You know I'm a responsible father."

"And a responsible debtor, too," Khan says sarcastically and follows.

"No, you stay here. I need you to watch over my kid."

Khan gives him a hesitant look and slowly backs up to his chair. The Colonel, too, finally emerges to find out what's happening. So the three of us sit at the table staring at the tab and waiting for my father to come back. Hours pass; all the customers leave, but there's still no sign of him. The head waiter comes repeatedly to inquire and we plead for patience. Finally, it is time to close for afternoon break and we have to leave. So the men split the bill angrily and we go out. Outside, they call a taxi, pay the driver and shove me into it—not too gently. When I get home, Baba's nowhere to be seen.

* * *

165

After the row with Bill over his rudeness to me, Mary moved out of her aunt's house. She rented a studio apartment near her work, pouring all her heart and talent into designing it, turning the Spartan flat into a cozy model of her future dream home. I took to spending almost every night at her place, enjoying the warmth and the comfort, but careful not to make it seem like a permanent move. Stubbornly, I refused to play the role of a reliable lover. To ease my guilt, however, I tried to lighten my burden on her. I fed from her refrigerator and drove her VW now and then—and that's as far as it went.

Mary was totally available to me, attuned to my every mood, willing to love and provide for as far as I allowed her. Money was no problem for me. I would have given her all if I had it. The problem was that I had no job. I was going through one of the periodic quarrels with George, prompted by our conflicting characters. Once again, I'd angered him by allowing "trashy losers" to use his restrooms. But I could not have done otherwise. How could I tell a pregnant woman and her little children to go piss in their car? Even worse, how could I risk a fight with a redneck over such a silly thing?

One night, Mary was in an anxious mood. She kept raising her usual demands and I tried to wriggle out.

"Did you give it more thought?" she asked while we were having spaghetti for dinner at her little table.

"What about?" I laid down my fork.

"Moving in together—permanently."

"I don't think it's a good idea."

"Why? You're practically living here. All you need to do is bring your suitcase."

"My life is scattered all over. It doesn't fit in a suitcase."

"You don't give all of yourself to this relationship . . . don't do things for me . . . I like to go to the movies sometimes . . . out dancing . . . get tender little gifts now and then . . ."

"I told you I'm not the right person . . . you deserve better . . . really mean it."

"That's not what I was trying to say." She threw her head down, rolling and unrolling a long noodle around her fork.

I held her free hand. "But it's true."

"You think you're wasting your time with me?"

"No. I think just the opposite."

"But you don't look happy."

"This is as happy as I get," I pleaded.

GREAT FEASTS

Before my father squanders the sheep money, Mama squeezes out just enough to pay for my school, and throw a religious feast. The sum won't cover the whole tuition, but it's enough to get the principal off my back for a while. A huge burden rolls off my shoulders and I can concentrate on my thieving. I'm making good progress, too, learning new tactics. For example, I no longer limit my prey to close relatives, and my field of operations to our own house. When we go to a party, I sit politely in the beginning, going through routine formalities, and then get into action.

One Ramadan evening, after my father goes out to party, Aunt Fatima comes to take us to an *iftar* dinner at the coalman's mansion. My angelic aunt is always concerned about us feeling bored in that ghastly house and takes us out with her whenever she can. *Iftar* is the supper that breaks the dawn-to-dusk fast during the holy month of Ramadan, and rich folks offer big treats on this occasion.

The coalman's house is just the opposite of his scruffy appearance. It's a dome-shaped structure with ceiling mirrors and ornate medallions. Full-length mirrors are everywhere, set in marble walls and framed by golden iron. The furniture, too, is glittery, with snaky arms and legs painted in gold, and marble pedestals stand at every corner of the reception hall.

There aren't too many people except for some veiled women and children. My brother and I sit in two fancy chairs and stare at mounds of candies and pastry in crystal bowls and trays, right by big dishes of winter fruits. But nobody is eating yet except for the kids. Adults are still fasting, waiting for the evening *azan* to be broadcast on the radio before they start. My agnostic mother is not fasting but pretends she is, and she wants me not to eat either, for a different reason.

"Make sure you don't eat too much because the host may think you don't get enough at home," she keeps whispering to me.

As soon as Mama turns away to talk to a guest, I slide up to the table and fill my pockets with candies and cram cookies down my throat. My little brother tries to copy me, but I make him sit down and behave. Eventually I have to bribe him with a few candies to keep his mouth shut and make sure he doesn't tell on me to mother.

The *iftar* time approaches and we all go to sit around the elaborate *sofreh*. Everyone is waiting for the sound of *azan* to die before they raid. I no longer have any appetite and sit there politely with my arms crossed to impress Mom. But she's too engaged in faking devotion to pay attention. Like the other women, she's mouthing prayer and raising her hands to heaven. Arash is sitting next to her, doing as he damn wishes, rubbing food on his face and stuffing his pockets with a chicken leg and a wing as I did with the candies.

Once the *azan* ends, all hell breaks loose. Guests attack bowls of soup, dishes of saffron rice, and plates of saucy stew arriving in riots of smells and colors. With all the noise and frantic activities, it is time for me to sneak out and scour closets. In a chamber with mirrored walls, there's a safe. But there isn't much I can do except stare at it and run my hand over the cold steel surface. My reflections are everywhere and I wonder if the soot-laden owner ever bothers to look at himself in these mirrors.

Above the safe there's a curved marble mantle, where a few coins sit on the glossy surface. I sweep them into my pocket and run back. The house is so big that I get lost in the maze of hallways and foyers, and it takes a while before I find my way back to the dining hall.

With coalman's money I go to visit the sweets peddler the next day and then the liver-man down the street, treating myself to lamb liver and kidney cooking on skewers over the open fire. Something that melts my heart, but I can't afford, are the bananas hanging in splendor outside the greengrocer's shop. I love bananas. I love their taste, their look, and the fact they're so easy to peel. But I've yet to have my fill of them.

Mama wants to hold her feast at Aunt Fatima's house, because ours is too small for so many guests and our furniture too shabby to reveal to strangers. *Sofrehs*, religious feasts, are common in our culture, like any party in Europe or America. But unlike parties, our feasts are off limits to men, even to boys who have reached puberty.

Women use every chance to throw a *Sofreh*, which is to thank God for a wish of theirs that has come true: a sudden fortune; miraculous healing of a patient; or reformation of a wayward husband, brother or son. I have no idea why Mama is holding one. What has she in the world to thank God for? There's no sudden fortune coming our way, no turn of luck, and no sign Baba's ever reforming. So why go for such an expensive treat when the money could be spent better?

Maybe she wants to bribe God so He doesn't forget her and eventually gets around to answering her prayers. Perhaps the Almighty's blessings will soon begin to shower, once my mother has proved her good faith and best of intentions.

Either way, I'm glad we're having the party and looking forward to the orgy of food and all the fun—though not necessarily the hysterical sobbing and self-beatings. It's a delight to be around so many perfumed and bejeweled ladies, even though they're covered up. One problem is that these women, presumably devout Muslims, lock men and even boys my age out of the house. But this never stops my cousin and me from sneaking in and catching some of them in comfortable positions. Ensured of their privacy, they drop their veils to relax, and sometimes lounge in seductive positions.

What turns me off about these feasts is that they become a venue for affluent women to show off: their big houses, gaudy furniture and jewelry. Guests come wrapped in black chadors, but underneath they're dolled up—in tinsel dresses, heavy makeup and jingling with tons of gold. The only person who lives up to the spirit of the event is Aunt Fatima. She, too, is religious and a regular host of *Sofrehs*, but that's because she truly believes in them. My aunt keeps religion in her heart and doesn't wear it on her forehead. One could commit the worst sins before her and she wouldn't so much as frown. The only thing she does is look away, as her mother did with Grandpa.

Mama finally holds the shindig and the usual crowd of plump bejeweled women turns up, all tinkling like a caravan of groomed camels. My cousin Reza and I are just standing by the door appraising them, adding up in our minds the gold they carry.

"Can you imagine how much gold you could get away with if you held them up all at once?" Reza asks me while playing with a slingshot.

"What do you mean held them up?"

"I mean rob them at knifepoint or even with this slingshot."

"Come on. Don't say these things." I look away from him, my attention with a woman entering the house.

"No, seriously—can you come up with an estimate?"

"I don't know and I don't care. All I want to know is how to infiltrate their tight cell and catch them with their guard down."

"For that, you have to wait until the caterer comes to deliver food. Then we can slip in right after him."

"Not a bad idea!"

We wait by the door for an hour until the last of the guests arrive and they close the door. Then we stroll down the street looking for something to do. A few blocks away, the idiot is sprawled on the sidewalk dozing off, his head lolling on his chest and both hands cupping his swelling testicles. The jackass is parked off to the side, unhitched from the cart and tethered to a tree. The beast happens to have a ferocious erection and Reza takes out his slingshot and aims. He takes a few shots from different angles. The target is too wide to miss. The ass takes the first few pebbles bravely, just flicking an ear, but then lets out an agonizing bray that jolts the idiot out of his snooze. Taj rubs his eyes with his fists, throws a bleary look around and then grabs his donkey spur and jumps to his feet.

"You sons of whores, leave the tongue-tied beast alone." He roars and lunges with his spur, punching the air with the weapon like a Samurai warrior.

Reza raises his arms, feigning surrender.

"Why blame us? It's your donkey who doesn't behave. We're just teaching him a lesson. Didn't you say one must fight obscenities?"

"This is no obscenity, moron. It's just an innocent beastly hard-on."

"Come on, Taj. You know that's not true. You know what's your problem? Your double standards and hypocrisy—no wonder people don't take you and your mission seriously."

As they go on arguing, I see a gorgeous figure walking gracefully toward our house. She's unrobed, dressed provocatively, in skin-tight black pants and a pistachio-green blouse that shows one of her shoulders. Her high heels clack noisily on the uneven sidewalk, as if to call attention to her dramatic appearance. Houri! It's the first time we meet since my uncle's going-away party. What a breeze of fresh air after the sight of those steamrollers in morbid black! I'd almost forgotten she existed, but seeing her again rekindles my passion.

As she draws closer, some street loafers let out whistles and cat-calls, and that attracts the idiot's attention. He puts down the lance and runs to his wooden cart to grab a handful of rotten tomatoes to throw at the nymph. But, before it blows into all-out war, Reza and I rush to provide cover and safely escort the lady into the house.

In a little while, my cousin gets bored and takes off. But with Houri in the house, I'm dead set to sneak in. When the caterer arrives, I slip right after him, running to hide in a cold-room in a corner of the garden, where my aunt stores persimmons and pome-granates during fall and winter. Minutes later, they close all the doors and seal the boundaries of their privacy, and I crawl out of my hole, sneaking up to a window to the reception hall to take a peek inside. The window is curtained, but there's a seam—I can get just a blurry view of the uninhibited scene inside.

Some of the women have taken off their robes and head cov-erings, revealing tight spangled dresses, exposing their hair and patches of pale skin. I treat my eyes to a good look. It's a precious view wholly my own, unshared by any other males; that fills me with vague lust, a sense of triumph. It is as if I have all these women to myself, possessing them in a way their husbands don't.

While waiting for the mullah to come and officiate the ceremony, Mama goes around serving tea and introducing her new friend, with a proud look on her face. Everyone seems impressed by Houri, looking at her with avid curiosity.

Agha the cleric finally arrives and the women rush to fling on their veils. The relaxed air gives way to glum piety and faces set in grief. The preacher walks in with a self-important air, groaning and coughing to remind the women of his presence. He climbs the high chair and settles there like a sovereign, scouring the room from his vantage point. He is the only man in the room and wants to make the most of it. His eyes search around, feasting on any neglected lock of hair or spot of flesh, and finally settle on Houri. She has slipped under a gauze black chador just to keep a pious appearance, but she is sexy all the same. The mullah seems to be dissecting her with his eyes and I almost let out a yell. But the women don't seem to mind the lecher. Maybe they think his spiritualism outweighs any human weaknesses.

* * *

Anyway, the lecher wraps and unwraps his robe around him with rapid sweeps, as if to enchant the audience, and then breaks into a sermon.

"Guard your chastity like a treasure. Your utmost duty is to fulfill your obligations toward your husbands—in the kitchen and in the bedroom."

"If your husbands and your children are happy, the doors of paradise will be open to you . . . ."

He talks like a celestial insider, one in the know of divine secrets, painting vivid images of heaven and hell, as if he has been to both. Mom, wearing a chador, runs back and forth serving tea, to make sure Agha doesn't lose his voice in the middle of a divine revelation. The mullah graces each glass with a sip and leaves the rest for believers to finish and benefit from its holiness.

Done with the sermon, he clears his throat and breaks into an elegy that stirs all like a heavenly ballad. As he belts it out, women sob, shriek and claw at their hair, and a few even pass out. This is the scene I'd hoped to skip: this disgusting display of grief. But the mullah likes it and keeps it going for too long, until everyone is reduced to a coma and his own voice to a screech. Finally satisfied, he steps down, receives his money in an envelope from my mother and strides off.

Once he's out the door, the mood shifts from mourning to celebration. Here's the scene I've been waiting for. A lady bursts into a happy song and others clap their hands and click their fingers in rhythm; some even dance. There's such a racket that it can be heard blocks away. I cock my ears and glue my eyes to the window, capturing every bit of this forbidden sight and sound. It's all so sinfully delicious!

GIFT FROM HEAVEN

The butcher has finally paid up the money for the sheep, and Baba has pissed it all away—his pockets are cleaner than a cat's ass. But this time, he at least has a friend to rely on. He and the butcher have become close pals, inseparable as finger and nail, spending almost every night out together. The butcher loves to show off his generosity and takes insult when my father puts his hand in his pockets, even in pretense. Baba has no problem with that and, to make his friend feel better, he even borrows money every time the opportunity arises. All he has to do is keep massaging the butcher's ego and that keeps the funds flowing.

It would have been an ideal situation if the thug didn't expect my father to take part in his drunken brawls and gang wars. Baba doesn't mind kicking a butt here and there to have things go his way, but he generally doesn't have a taste for violence. Still he sometimes has to take part in these obligatory fights just to prove his loyalty to his friend. Fortunately, he manages to emerge from them with just a few cuts or bruises.

Of course the butcher is disappointed that his bosom pal is not giving his whole heart to his cause, but still he likes to have him around. He loves my father's sense of humor; if there's a joke he really likes, he makes him repeat it over and over, until everyone has heard it. No matter how many times the joke has been told, the thug roars with laughter and slaps himself or anyone sitting dangerously close. The butcher himself is so humorless that he can't even make a baby smile.

My mother is worried that her husband is hanging out with a goon. She thinks the butcher is a bad influence on my father and a worse friend to have than the Colonel.

"The Colonel is generally a harmless guy except for his bad habit of not paying for his meals," she says.

There are in fact good reasons to be worried. Baba has taken on a wholly new persona. Of late, he dresses like the butcher—in jazzy clothes, with a gold disk shining from his hairy chest. Sometimes when the two are off together to a nightclub, they look like a pair of magicians performing in a cabaret.

With Baba busy escorting the butcher around the clock, Mama has found her own steady company—Houri. The women have been seeing a lot of each other since the feast and become as close as sisters. Houri's husband, an engineer with the state oil company, is often away on business assignments, and she spends most of her time at our house. This is like a godsend and I wonder what I've done to deserve it. Maybe it is the magic *Sofreh* Mama threw recently, the feast that made God indebted to us and unleashed His eternal favors.

Perhaps she's one of those *houri*s who descended from paradise, and I don't even have to do good things to qualify. My religious education teacher says if we don't lie and don't steal we go to heaven, where we're fed and lulled into sleep by these fabulous creatures. I had all but given up on this promise with my 'crooked hand' going astray all the time. But it looks like God is far too compassionate and merciful. He doesn't disappoint even imperfect subjects of His.

Whatever it is, Houri's company has filled my life and I no longer need to go to the basement for entertainment. She gives me all the attention I need, endlessly complimenting me on my good looks, intelligence and manners. Never before has anyone told me these things, and they've gone to my head. I spend hours in front of the mirror appreciating myself, putting on various expressions and comparing them, trying to find one that suits me the best. There's one that I particularly like, when I arch an eyebrow and freeze it right up there. Then I look so like James Bond that I wonder if I'm not really him. I would paste it on permanently, if not for fear of being laughed at in school.

The bell rings and I rush to the door, knowing it is Houri. She looks ravishing as usual in a red pleated miniskirt, a tight black blouse, and sheer nylon stockings—a sexy ensemble that has drawn fierce stares from the barber next door.

"Where's your Mom?" She sounds upset.

I point at the sitting room, and she flashes past cursing and groaning.

"Jerk!" I heard her voice coming from the room. "The man is a horror! He rips you apart with his eyes."

174

I know what she's been through, but in that outfit she asks for it, as the barber puts it. She ought to be more careful with the way she dresses. What if Taj the idiot had seen her? He'd have again pelted her with rotten tomatoes; or even worse, let his jackass on her with that "innocent hard-on."

Houri grumbles for a few minutes and then goes to the guest room to lie down, complaining of a headache. After resting a little, she walks with her usual sway back to the sitting room, giving Mama and me belated hugs and kisses; then walks to the mantle to turn on the radio, tuning it to a foreign music station.

"How're you doing my sweet little boy?" she says, holding me tightly in her arms.

"Do you want to feel my biceps?" I ask, emboldened by the attention.

"Sure. Show me what you've got." She pats my head, giggling.

I grab her hand and drag her back into the guest room where we have a tall mirror. I stand before it, flex my arm and grab her hand.

"Okay, feel it now!"

"Oh, you're so strong! Do you lift weights or is it all natural like your Baba's?"

The mention of my father and his manliness is like a bucket of ice on my fire. The muscles I've been trying to flaunt go limp, like the donkey's prick under the rain of pebbles. I turn away and leave the room, as she follows unaware of my feeling.

"I'm invited to a wedding this weekend," she tells Mom. "Would you pluck the hair from my legs?"

"Sure. Wait here—I'll go get thread. Shahed, why don't you leave the room to give us privacy?"

"Oh, let him stay. He's like my son."

Mama accepts reluctantly. The nymph rolls down her stockings, seductively, and then lies flat on her belly flipping through a magazine. In a minute, my mother comes back with a length of thread; she loops it across her palms and settles to mow away.

Houri pulls up her miniskirt until I can see her underwear, giving my fantasies a free play. As Mama plucks away, I run my hand smoothly over Houri's silky skin to make sure no hair are left, and if I hit one, I immediately alert my mother. With every brush of my hand, pleasure surges though my body and it is all I can do not to pinch her. At times I may be letting my hand stray too far, for Mama turns to

175

stop me with a steely glance. But the nymph giggles and follows with a kiss on my cheek for reassurance. Once she even sits up to peck me on the lips, and that almost melts my heart.

"Don't go spoiling him too much!" my mother protests mildly. She apparently senses the revolution taking place inside me. "He's just a kid and may get the wrong ideas."

We're about to wrap up when Baba walks in, and his eyes pop out when they find Houri in that sexy position. He pulls in his belly a couple of inches and puffs up his chest like a turkey, getting ready to greet his guest.

"Welcome Lady Flower! So humble of you to strain your feet and step to my door," he says, using a Persian pleasantry reserved for special guests. "My eyes have come alight with the sight of you! I thought it was the moon shining too early."

"Thank you," she giggles and sits up, covering her legs. "I'd have come more often if not for that weird neighbor of yours."

"Who, the barber?"

"Yes. He eats me up with his stares."

"Who can blame him? You'd make a corpse rise from the grave and stare."

"And the idiot, too—he always taunts me."

"Never mind him," Baba says, as if talking to a little girl. "How can you make a rabid dog shut its mouth?"

"Oh, you have such a flare for metaphors."

"They all come from the heart. Stay here. I'll be back."

Baba goes out to the sink to spruce up, freshen his breath and comb a tuft of hair from the side of his head over the balding patch. Then he comes back and tries to pick up where he left off. "You look lovelier with your husband away. Why is it always the jackal that gets the best grapes?" That's another of his proverbs.

"Doesn't she look gorgeous today?" Mama asks her husband, as if he might have a problem seeing that.

"Please you all, stop flattering me." By now Houri is totally unaware of the "sweet little boy" she was doting on a little while before.

"She's looked better before," I say, rabidly jealous.

"Who asked for your opinion?" Baba says, half-joking. "You're just a kid. The smell of baby milk is still on your breath."

I blush and curse him silently for barging in on my date. He thinks he stands a chance with Houri, but she's sending him up. He should have seen how far I got with her before he stuck his head in, when I was running my hands freely up those legs. Even in his wildest fantasies, he could never reach that far. For now, he has to be content with her teasing stares and phony giggles. I'm so angry!

Mary has put her foot down to get married. With the quilt of meat around her bones, she perfectly meets standards set by my boyhood mentor, the barber. But I can't imagine myself in the role of a groom, crammed into a black wedding suit and walking down the aisle with a phony smile on my face. She raises the issue every now and then, and I know our relationship is heading toward a resolution—one way or the other. I either cave in to her demand or she'll walk away, looking for a more reliable partner.

It's Bill and Laura who're pushing Mary to be assertive. Bill knows a "nice guy" for her to meet, someone in the Navy with a bright future ahead of him. But she says she's not ready for another commitment, perhaps hoping that there's still a chance with me. I'm not quite sure if this "nice guy" actually exists or is just an invention to goad me into action. Either way, I can't make myself respond. I go on waiting for that dream woman.

It was a hot smoggy Sunday, and Monrovia was a ghost town, like Fridays in Hajiabad, my childhood neighborhood—only a sanitized version of it. George had taken the day off to spend with his family and I had to work a double-shift, from seven in the morning to twelve at night.

I spent the whole day sitting lazily on the front stoop of the office, wiping sweat from my forehead and staring ahead at the void. The red and yellow sign of the rival gas station across the street dimmed through the haze and its Mexican attendant dozed off on his own stoop. To my left, on each side of the crossroad, were two sales lots full of cars with red dollar signs splashed across windshields.

Now and then, a hulk of a car pulled up to the pumps for a dollar or two of gas or free air: the familiar cast of scruffy white guys with red eyes, aggravated single mothers with lots of children, young black studs with much older white girlfriends.

It was around three that a teenaged girl wandered in, walking barefoot toward me, popping chewing gum. She was in skimpy tight shorts, revealing the lower half of her round buttocks, and just a bra for an upper garment—her full legs and slim shoulders glowed with a sexy hint of sunburn.

"You wanna suck on my tits?" she said abruptly, through the inflated bubblegum in her mouth.

"What!?"

"For twenty dollars, I'll let you suck on my tits."

"How old are you?"

"Are you interested?" She shifted on her feet, waiting impatiently for a response.

"Tell me how old you are first."

"Twenty." The bubble burst and the gum became pasted on her small nose.

"That's not true. You're barely sixteen, maybe even younger," I said. But she was in full bloom and seductive for her age. Still, I wasn't interested in her offer, tempting though it was. Suddenly, a weird fantasy gripped me: maybe I should adopt this sexy doll as a lover, give her the home and education she hasn't had, and a good lesson in middle-class morality—everything she needs in order to be converted into a perfect lady. She looks promising in a strange way. There's something about her that sets her apart from many other women I've known: a catching fire in her hazel eyes, a raw sexuality aiming at your very guts—a magnetism beyond class, culture, and upbringing.

I saw a likeness with Houri, but also glaring differences. She had all the allure but none of Houri's bold assurance, that command of her seductive powers. Still, I was smitten enough to idly consider breaking up with Mary for an affair with the young prostitute.

"What do you want the money for?"

"I owe it."

"To whom?"

"Some guy who sold me weed. He says he'll kill me if I don't pay him back."

A banged-up Cadillac was waiting for her outside, and a black man was standing by the car looking in our direction. He was in a brown leather jacket, tight beige pants, and thick-soled shoes of brown and beige. His hair was oiled and styled in large curls, and a golden medal sat on his bare chest.

"Why do you use stuff like that?" I looked apprehensively toward the black man, still staring at us. He had the easy confidence of a practiced pimp-hustler.

"Hey, you wanna do it or not?"

"No, not that way."

"Can you at least give me a dollar to get a Coke?"

"Here, take this twenty dollars, but promise to stay away from bad people. You ought to be in school . . ." I counseled her lamely.

"All right . . . promise . . . bye now."

She ran happily toward the car and the two took off.

No sooner does Houri leave, than the barber gives me a shout through the trapdoor.

"Hey Shahed, business is slow. Why don't you come for a chat?"

I go out and he's perched on his stool, flicking his head around like an owl.

"I saw the whore leave. Come on, tell me what happened."

"I touched her legs and she kissed me on the lips."

His eyes flash and he seems out of breath.

"See! See! What did I tell you? She's crying for it. Go for it! What're you waiting for? Strike the iron while it is still hot. If you don't move, your father will get her."

The next morning, my father is up bright and early, drunk with victory, chipper as a *bulbul*. He's feeling great about Houri and wants everyone to be up to share it with him. So he goes around kicking up a big racket, making it difficult for everyone to sleep. First, there's the rustle of a newspaper he's pretending to read; then he starts crooning fragments from a syrupy love song, clicking his fingers in accompaniment.

It is love's doing . . . don't blame me . . . it's the heart's doing . . . don't scold me!

Hey, lady flower . . . it's becoming so hard for me to bear . . .

He's lost in the song for a little while and then comes back to roust us from bed. When we still cling to our pillows, he starts shaking our shoulders playfully and kicking butts—next he might run up to the roof and shout his joy to the neighborhood, like an early call to prayer.

There's a brief lull, as he's distracted by something, and I fall back into a sleep. A few minutes later I wake up to the boom of a poem, by the Persian poet Omar Khayyam. He loves Khayyam for the message of life and pleasure in his poetry.

How Sweet is Mortal Sovereignty! – Think some
Others: How Blest the Paradise to Come!
Ah, Take the Cash in Hand and Waive the Rest
Oh, the Brave Music of a Distant Drum!

I certainly don't share his joy and want to go back to sleep. But kicks keep coming from the other side, and one of them knocks me out of a catnap, right in the middle of a wet dream about Houri.

"Up! Up! Get ready to go for a hike."

"Leave me alone. I hate going for a walk so early." I hug my pillow.

"Don't be lazy. We must keep in shape. I've been eating too much lately."

"Then go alone. I don't need to watch my weight."

"What's a son for, if I'm supposed to go alone?"

I crawl in the Buick and Baba drives us to this exclusive neighborhood up on the hills, with modern villas, five-star hotels and lush green parks. It is the swankiest part of our city and the side we show off to foreigners in tourism posters.

Baba parks the Bride, glittering with adornments, outside a huge compound and we walk toward the gate, guarded by two men in blue uniforms and chauffeur hats. He talks to one of the guards and oils our way in. Once inside, I feel as though I'm in a different world. Everything shines with newness, the brilliance of wealth— dimensions are staggering: perfect white mansions fronted with lush lawns and bordered with dense hedges, set off majestically against the turquoise blue sky.

We stroll up a winding path, taking in the glare of luxury and fresh mountain breezes, filled with the sweet smell of roses and jasmine. Some foreigners and rich locals in their tennis whites are jogging, a few with dogs in tow. I have an uncomfortable sense of displacement, feeling as though I have invaded their privacy. But Baba seems proud to have crossed the social divide and to be getting a taste of opulence, even for one brief hour. Every few seconds, he pauses to make an appreciative comment and pinpoint a marvel I may have missed: a fancy car, a sprawling manor, or a gorgeous lady.

"Imagine if Grandpa had the sense to buy land here instead of that godforsaken village," he says. "Then we could have been millionaires."

"Maybe."

"Can you imagine how much a square meter of land is worth here?

"Have no idea," I mutter, but he keeps nudging me for an answer.

"Just guess. Ha?"

"I really don't know, Baba."

"Then what do they teach you at school? You can't even make a simple mathematical calculation. Why are we wasting all that money on tuition?"

I ignore him, sinking deeper into my thoughts, wondering what's going on in those luxury suites, on king-size beds. We walk in silence for a few minutes and he seems irritated that I'm not playing along with his fantasies.

"What's this sour face you're giving me?" he finally says.

"What sour face?"

"Why are you sulking? What's eating you, son?"

"I'm not sulking."

"Yes, you are. Wipe it off your face! You asked to come along— now be a good sport!"

It's amazing how selfish this guy can be, always expecting people to synch their moods to his. He can go to hell this time. I'm not playing by his whims. If he keeps bothering me, I may even run away, go somewhere with Houri. All I need to do is dig up the money from someone's pocket, someone as rich as Grandpa.

Whenever it became too much for me to bear, I went straight from school to Aunt Fatima's house, where I could take temporary solace from my sorrows. There, I enjoyed absolute freedom and could say and eat what I wanted. Like a barren angel brimming with unspent love, she fed and nursed me, as if to make up for her brother's failures as a father.

181

On the silk rug in her sun-lit parlor, she spread a *sofreh*, placing before me whatever edible she could find in the house. She sat by my side, encouraging me to eat, asking questions about my school, my health and life in general.

"You're so skinny, my dear Shahed! Your clothes are falling off of you. Don't you get anything to eat?"

I do, aunty, but not enough, not as much as my heart desires.

"Eat, my darling. Eat as much as you want. *Nooshejan Azizam.* Food to your soul. God willing, they'll turn into meat around your bones."

Sometimes, I stayed long enough until her husband woke up from his siesta. Then I had the pleasure of watching him at his main séance of opium smoking, and the elaborate preparation that preceded it. Uncle E would dress and perfume himself and then go to decorate his opium spread—with flowers, persimmons, pastry and candies. Then he sent his wife out to the yard to light the charcoals, the messy part of the ritual he preferred to skip.

While waiting for the hot coals, he'd turn on the radio and tune it to his favorite American station, playing romantic songs by Nat King Cole, Frank Sinatra and other crooners. From a walnut chest in a corner of his study, he'd retrieve the *vafoor,* sheathed like a treasured sword in a fragrant leather jacket. He peeled off the cover and gave the instrument a long appreciative look, fondling the bulbous china head where the drug would stick.

As he'd go on rubbing and removing imaginary dust, he'd talk whimsically about the history behind the antique, for the thousandth time, to anyone who happened to be around. The *vafoor* once belonged to an English lord, a colonial master, to be sure—an explorer who scoured the world collecting rare pieces. The lord himself used the instrument while he was still alive, taking an occasional "social puff" from it. Then, on his deathbed, he bequeathed it to Uncle E, his closest friend and the man he most trusted.

In a china tray sitting by his side, also rich with love and history, sat a dozen rolls of opium in different hues, like crayons. He'd pick one, break off a small piece and press it against the hot porcelain bulb, next to a tiny hole. The pipe was finally ready to be lifted in splendor and laid like a magic flute between his lips. With silver tongs, he'd grab a glowing charcoal and hold it over the opium piece, until it melted and smoke flowed down into his lungs, through the wooden handle.

In a minute, the room would fill with the fragrant scent of the narcotic, along with the smell of charcoal and the aroma of vintage tea. It was such a stupefying ambiance, heightened by Nat King Cole's soothing romance, that I would be lulled into a trance—as if I too had had a taste of that tonic, that "panacea for all ailments."

Those random interludes in the house of plenty, with an idyllic view of snow-laden trees, became the most delicious memories of my life, from which I could still wring a taste of beauty when the rest of my life was an unforgiving landscape mirroring defeat.

The next time I see Houri it is at my aunt's house, where we're all invited to dinner. She looks as smashing as ever in her pink Jacqueline Kennedy-style dress; her hair is in an elegant coiffure, and her lips and neck are delicately rouged and perfumed.

Uncle E tries to engage the adults in a poetry game, in which one recites a line of poem and another responds with a verse beginning with the last letter of the previous line. Uncle E has an amazing memory and he knows thousands of classical verses by heart. This is an art he has mastered in games of *moshaereh* with his opium buddies out in his veranda on moonlit summer nights.

No one except maybe for my mother is a match for the host. Houri and my dad are not into literature and Houri's husband, the potato, is too dull to be poetic. Baba quickly gets bored and he starts trying to get Houri's attention. He even wants to go a little further, trying to lure the seductress into the garden for a private moment. But the nymph is kicking like a filly, playing untamable. "No, I prefer to stay and chat with Uncle E," she tells him with glowing eyes.

Baba hates rejection. His eyes glow with jealous rage. He starts poking fun at his brother-in-law to make him look ridiculous in front of Houri, teasing him about his addiction, chronic constipation and sexual impotence. To further embarrass him, he even recalls his dismal performance on his wedding night.

"Everything this man says about his conquests are pipe dreams," Baba says. "He's just a drum, all noise and empty inside."

Uncle E just listens impassively, showing no sign of irritation or shame—he must be too numb to feel the sting of the assaults.

"This guy has smoked himself way past sexual desire. He needs a crane to lift it up," my father goes on. "You should have seen how pathetic he looked on his night of *zafaf*—it was as if he'd been called upon to split the moon."

He keeps looking at Houri to see if she's appreciating his wit, but her face is set in an unreadable indifference. Baba ignores this lack of appreciation and charges ahead, while Uncle E maintains his cool silence. The fox just picks his nose and stares at the pile of coals in front of him burning with a red hot glow. One can tell he is in deep concentration and it is just a matter of seconds before he strikes back.

Slowly, Uncle E reaches for the *vafoor* and places it in his mouth, savoring the taste of the walnut wood before inhaling. He takes a few pleasurable hits, props the instrument against a metal holder, finally ready to plunge the dagger.

"Your hair looks so full tonight, fuller than the moon," he jests from the corner of his mouth. "What have you done, composted the follicles?"

My father suddenly tenses up, sensing a threat.

"I wonder if the new treatment with sheep droppings is working." The host goes on, exhaling a big ball of smoke.

This time Baba blushes to his ears, wondering how in the world the fox learned about his secret experiment with sheep droppings.

"Did you know, Houri, he fertilizes his bald pate with dung? It's the barber next door who prescribed the medicine . . . ha-ha-ha."

Houri bursts into laughter that hurts my father more than the joke itself.

"You know something?" Uncle E goes on. "I think you and Usta should market your secret formula and make a lot of money . . . ha-ha-ha,"

My father looks if he's sitting on the heap of hot charcoals in front of him. A few times, he tries to turn the table, but all his jokes fall flat, with no one laughing. So he frowns and falls into a glum silence.

"And you should see his car, the Bride. It is smothered under loads of junk, looking more like a groomed camel. Next, he'll put red lipstick on the front bumper and fake eyelashes on the headlights . . . ha-ha-ha."

Houri lets loose with another shriek, a malicious laugh that draws her husband in too. Even the cold potato is now chuckling and that makes my father sure there is some conspiracy against him. He looks at Houri with such hatred that I half expect him to pick up a blazing coal and throw it at her.

"You're all ganging up against me. What have I done to you?"

Mama and I feel so bad, but all we can do is try and not laugh at Uncle E's jokes.

"So what're you going to do with your rejuvenated hair, grow it long like the Beatles?" Uncle E says, maintaining the offensive.

"That's it! I'm out of here," Baba says, bolts to his feet, and turns to us. "Come on, let's get out of here! I'll wait for you in the car."

He storms out and my aunt hurries after him, explaining and pleading—all in vain.

"Can we go out to Disco tonight?" Mary asked.

"Why Disco? This is our last night together."

"I like to end it on a happy note. I'm happiest when I'm dancing."

"You know I hate dancing."

"It won't kill you—one night."

"You're right—just one night."

She ran to get ready and came back a while later in a pink flamenco dress, her festive attire. This one I hadn't seen coming and cringed.

"Do you like it?" she asked, lifting up the puckered skirt.

"Yes, if it makes you happy to wear it. Are you ready?"

"Let's wait for the limo."

"Limo?"

"Yes, I called for a limousine. I want everything to be perfect."

"You want to put me to shame?"

"No, I want to spare myself the shame. This place is too high class for our beat-up VW."

The limousine pulled up outside Chez Moi, a fancy nightclub in Beverly Hills frequented by wealthy Middle Eastern men and good-looking women drawn by the exotic opulence. A crowd of men in designer suits and tall women in revealing gowns were standing by the door, eying new arrivals with interest.

Our chauffeur jumped out to open the door and I was too uneasy to step out, with so many gazes fixed upon me. I felt the pretense of wealth was more of a reason to be ashamed than my poverty.

"Please move along quickly. A line of limos is waiting behind you," the nightclub doorman urged, and Mary pushed me out.

The club was packed, full of smoke, and the crowd blinked like trout under the strobe lighting. A band played a mix of Western and Mediterranean music, and a foreign singer crooned romantic songs in various languages.

Mary ordered glasses of cognac and soon was half drunk. She kept looking into my eyes and flirting.

"Don't be a bore. Say something," she said loudly, her tongue heavy.

"It's too noisy here. My voice can't reach you."

"Let's dance then."

"I don't want to dance." I looked away at the table to our right, where two foreign women sat wiggling their shoulders to the music. One of them I guessed to be Iranian; our eyes met a few times and she quickly looked away. Mary must have caught that. She grabbed my hand and put it around her soft fleshy waist.

"Come on, let's go dance." she said and pulled me toward the floor. I followed grudgingly, trying to overcome my inhibitions, as if the dance was a worthy price to pay for my imminent liberation.

I'd seen it coming and had taken a few drinks to limber up—but alcohol couldn't ease my anxiety either. My limbs were unyielding; my head was in turmoil. Mary writhed in exaggerated Salsa motions, theatrical movements that I was sure drew the amused contempt of anyone watching. She spun, arched her body and threw up her squat legs, using my stiff hand as a peg.

"Why don't you move your body?" she urged me breathlessly.

"I told you I can't dance."

"Don't be silly. Anybody can dance—just try. Just let go."

I don't know what it is about dancing that makes me so uneasy, what about jubilation that gives me shame. I could already taste the bitterness of a hangover in my mouth for the next day, when I'd wake up brooding over the idiocies of the night before.

"I can't. It is not in my blood."

"So what is in you blood?" Sweat shone on her round happy face.

"I don't know. Pain . . . grief."

"Don't be a bore. Just shake it off."

We stayed there until two in the morning when the place closed. Limousines and other fancy cars pulled up at the entrance, but many lingered, as drunk patrons tried to make the good time last. Several stags dawdled around hunting for any untaken girls. Some jumped in their sport cars and revved the engine to show off their power, and a few stood by the door inviting company.

Mary, too, wanted to stay and survey the fancy surroundings, the glamorous people she didn't get to meet often. Then I saw the Iranian woman walking out with her friend, and the young stags pricked up with interest. She threw a glance at me and I responded with a doubtful shrug.

"Can you wait here? I'm going to use the little girl's room," Mary said. The Iranian kept looking and I kept hesitating. Then one of the young men approached. She turned to him with a smile and was gone quickly.

My father licks his wounds for weeks and plots madly, trying to find a way to get even with his brother-in-law. There's also this grudge to work off against Houri, the traitor, but that one can wait.

The opportunity eventually arises one day when my aunt comes crying for help to save her husband from addiction.

"He's sinking deeper and deeper into opium," she tells her brother in desperation. "His dose has rapidly increased. Lately he eats it instead of smoking—in fistfuls, enough to poison a horse."

"I see . . . go on," my father says, his eyes calculating.

"He pops it in like candy and gets so sedated that he can't even make the effort to pick his nose. His constipation, too, is getting worse. He eats like a cow, but doesn't evacuate as much as a sheep dropping."

"Then he needs a plumber."

"This is no time for jokes, brother. We ought to do something before it's too late."

"Don't worry, nothing can kill a weed. He's more toxic than any drug he can take. You want my opinion, don't waste any grief over him."

"Please don't say that. I'm going mad with worry."

"Like it or not, death is coming to him and I wish it well."

"Please . . . please. Let's do something before he goes to waste."

"He can't be any more wasted. Anyway, it's too late now. He's headed or his miserable end and nothing can stop it."

"How can you be so cruel? He's my husband, your brother-in-law. You owe it to him."

"I certainly owe him a lot . . . well, you tell me what to do and I'll do it just for you. I myself don't give a damn whether he lives or dies."

"I don't know. Just do something," she says, wringing her hands helplessly.

"Do you want me to call the police?"

"No, I'd rather keep it in the family. It's too embarrassing to expose to strangers."

"Mm . . . let me think . . . okay, I'll get back to you about it."

Days go by and there's no word from my father on the subject. Aunt Fatima comes to query every day but he's mysteriously quiet. The devil is obviously up to some trick, but he won't let it out.

He just reassures her vaguely. "Don't worry. It's in the works. I'm trying to find a lasting solution so he won't slip back into addiction."

He finally comes up with a brilliant idea that he presents to my long-suffering aunt.

"I told you I was on the case. When I take a job, I see it through to the end."

"What? Tell me quickly!"

"I talked to my colonel friend. He doesn't mind doing some side work for extra pay."

"How much does he want?"

"Not a whole lot—about a thousand or so."

"A thousand!"

"He doesn't actually get the money. It goes to set up a task force, a crack unit, so to speak."

"Why a crack unit?"

"To pull off a fast clean job. You said you didn't want a lot of noise about it, right?"

"Right. But that's too much."

"It is money well spent, a small price to pay to save a husband, even a good-for-nothing husband."

"But I don't have that kind of cash on me. You know he doesn't trust me with his money."

"Then you have to steal it from him, Fatima. It's for his own good, anyway."

"I can't steal. It's a sin."

"Give me a break. All wives steal from their husbands."

"No, I won't do it."

"Then I can't help you. Let the bastard overdose and rot with all the shit inside him."

"No . . . okay, let me see if I can raise the money."

The money eventually comes and my father quickly settles to work, as planned. But there's no crack unit, no sting operation, no commando raids—just Baba, his colonel friend and Taj, the idiot, recruited as a hired gun.

"I set a honey trap for him at that empty garage in the next block," Baba later told us. "I sent out word there's a revel in this den of vice where men do nothing but smoke opium and play backgammon, and women serve wine and do belly dancing. And the bum fell for it like a mouse for feta cheese."

It turned out that he, the colonel and Taj sat in ambush behind a wall and as Uncle E approached, they seized the bloated addict, and stuffed him into the garage. Then they pulled the shutter and locked it.

Uncle E, according to my father, was roaring like a wounded lion, but no one was there to help.

"I'd already informed the neighbors," he said. "I told them the junkie was in a drug program and he was best left alone. But I left enough food and water to last him a week—by which time he was to make full recovery and check out of the program."

A week after that my father and I go to check up on his patient. As he opens the shutter a crack, a terrible stink hits our nostrils, as if opening a mass grave. Baba opens it a little more, and there is Uncle E lying motionless on the ground, in a pool of his own urine and loose excrement. Going without opium for a week had triggered a violent diarrhea attack and the crap wouldn't stop coming.

"These are tons of grilled lamb and liver the bum gobbled up over ages," Baba says to me. "No plumber could open him up better than I did."

"Is he alive, Baba?"

"You think he'd let go so easily?"

In a minute, the patient stirs a little and then sits up, rubbing his eyes. With some effort, he struggles to his feet and lurches toward us, flashing his shit-smeared claws and long nails.

189

"He looks like a monster emerging from a swamp," Baba says.

"What's he going to do to us, Baba?" I ask, terrified.

The monster looks so angry and I fear he'll leap at my father and tear him apart. But instead he reaches out to hug him.

"Thank you, my friend. I owe you my life. I feel reborn," he says. "At the very least, I can move my bowels again."

I wish my father had also given me a dose of his therapy to help me shed my inhibitions like Uncle E shed his crap. I wish he'd settled scores with me as he did with his brother-in-law—with an eye toward my well-being. Instead of beating the piss out of me over the stolen money, he should have kicked off the bottom of this barrel of compacted angst I carry inside—fear accumulated over ages and not evacuating as much as a sheep dropping. I wish Baba had walked me through the ABCs of life, as the Samaritan did with the miser in that feel-good movie he forced Grandpa to see, teaching me everything I need to know about the tricky art of living.

After the incident at the garage, Baba and his brother-in-law became friends, using endless pleasantries to address each other. Uncle E is still more generous with words than his money—but that, too, my father hopes will change with time. In fact, there's so much at stake in this new alliance that Baba decides to dump his beloved protégé Reza, and invest in the precious friendship with the boy's father.

A few weeks after Uncle E's miraculous drug rehabilitation, Reza has a vicious fight with his father over money, and as usual, he comes to see Baba to complain.

"You know, Uncle," my cousin cries. "The fox is no longer the soft touch he used to be, now he's off opium. Before, at least I had the *vafoor* to scare him with, but now there's nothing. He stands his ground no matter how much I twist his arm.

"So I'm absolutely desperate . . . have no idea how to get some dough. Swear to God, Uncle, I even gave up Winstons, got the cheap smokes . . . and no more Smirnoff—you know, industrial alcohol works for a buzz . . . But even those cost money."

"I know, boy. I know." Baba takes a harder look at Reza. "What do you want me to do about it?"

190

"I don't know. Let's find a way to shake him down together. We can ambush him on the street, wearing masks. You know—mug him."

"Are you crazy? He's your father, my brother-in-law. We've just begun talking to each other and you want to ruin it?"

"Friendship with a wolf, Uncle? Are you out of your mind?"

"What I want to say is . . . look, I can't coach you like I used to."

"Uncle, I'm beginning to lose faith in you." Reza is a wreck. His face is puffy and his eyes are bleary and wet. Baba relents a bit, takes out his cigarettes and offers one to Reza. The boy takes it with a shaking hand.

"Let me see what I can do, Reza. I'll see him tonight and have a word with him about you. You know I've always put my reputation on the line for you."

When we get to my aunt's house, Baba sends Reza out to the garden to wait while he talks to his father. He starts off pleading for his nephew, with apparent good intentions.

"You know, dear E, the boy is going through adolescent rage, and it's all normal . . . well, it's a bad age . . ." He keeps pausing for effect, using lines from the advice columns in pop magazines he reads to us. "Reza does get a little irrational now and then . . . but it's all understandable."

Baba pauses again and lets out a few dramatic sighs. "He is a tormented boy, tends to be cocky at times. But deep inside, he's a good kid . . . needs help to make it through this difficult phase."

Here he waits for a response, but Uncle E's eyes are amused and cynical, as if to say: "He can fool you, but not me."

"I feel deeply sorry for the boy. He feels unloved, misunderstood," Baba resumes, sounding increasingly like a guru. "He needs an outlet to release his anger, a channel to direct his energy toward a positive goal."

"All right, let's change the subject," our host says impatiently. "You're not here to talk about that loser . . . So how're things with you?"

"Ah . . . life is unkind as usual. I'm in debt up to my neck again and there's nothing in the horizon."

"Really? That's too bad," Uncle E responds, finally showing a spark of interest.

"Yes . . . nothing in my pockets but spider webs," my father moans.

"Why didn't you say that sooner? You know you can always count on me." Uncle E fishes out a roll of cash and holds it out to his brother-in-law. "Take this. It should help you out of your financial straits."

Baba is thrilled, but a little guarded, obviously fearful Uncle E is playing an old trick.

"Why do you keep staring at me? Take the money."

"You're not putting me on, are you?"

"Of course not!"

My father's face blooms like a sunflower and he falls into a stutter.

"I . . . I don't . . . know how to thank you, my friend . . . don't know what to say . . . how to phrase it . . ."

"Don't mention it at all. This is just a token of my deep gratitude for what you did for me, saving me from the evil claws of addiction."

Aunt Fatima and my mother come out of the kitchen and their eyes are wet, apparently touched by the amicable atmosphere.

"But—it was your own strong will power. I really did nothing . . ." Baba shoves the roll back meekly. "I hope you realize I didn't do it for money. My sister and I were so damn worried about you."

"I know, I know, and I thank you for it all. But you must take this. It's yours. I insist!"

Baba fakes a little more resistance and finally pockets the money. Then he rushes to hug the generous lender and plant juicy kisses on his plump rosy cheeks. The two are locked in a loving embrace when Reza drags in from the garden and pauses at the door. He freezes in shock as he hears his "loving uncle" offering his parents tips on child rearing.

"You know, this is not the way to raise a kid . . . to pamper and spoil him all the time. Try not to encourage him in his bad habits." Baba is too into his role as expert counselor to see Reza behind him.

My father turns to his sister: "And you, stop nursing him along, spoon-feeding him all the time. Let him stand on his own two feet and see that life is not all play. Sister, you're all heart and no brain."

Reza goes on watching in disbelief, biting his nails. His dilated eyes dart around the room to read our reactions, to see if everyone is hearing the same thing. Then he bursts out:

"Uncle, is that really you talking? Do you understand what you're saying?"

Baba turns around sharply to look at him, but tries not to lose face.

"Hey, Reza, you shouldn't butt in when adults are speaking. Go back in the yard and wait until we finish."

"But, Uncle, you promised . . ."

"What promise?"

"I thought you were on my side."

"I said get out! We have business to finish up."

"But, Uncle, . . . don't you understand? This is a trick. The bastard is trying to drive a wedge between us. Before long he'll sink in his teeth and spit poison."

"Shut your trap! This is no way to speak of your father. Your old man deserves some respect. Now, get lost!"

Reza bursts into a sob and storms out of the room, kicking at everything in his path. He stays out all evening and doesn't come back till after dinner.

When we're about to leave, my father calls his sulking nephew aside to counsel him, make sure there are no hard feelings. He's hoping to have it both ways. "Listen, boy, don't get all riled up about it. You know I came here to help you."

He takes out Uncle's E's wad and peels off a few small notes to give the boy.

"Here, this is for you. I don't want you to think I forgot you. Now go get yourself a drink."

My cousin throws a hateful look at his uncle and spits on the ground.

"I don't want your goddamn money. Keep it! You're a traitor . . . cringing to a wolf for a bloody roll of cash . . ."

"Hey, don't push your luck. This attitude will get you nowhere."

"Go to hell! I don't need your advice."

"Hey, Listen to me! I'm trying to help."

"I said I don't need your fucking help. Get out of my face!"

Reza snatches and rips the bills, and throws them down.

"You've sold out your best pal for a lousy wad of cash." He spits on the shreds of notes on the ground.

"Watch your mouth, boy! No one can talk to me like that."

"I said go to hell. I'm not taking any more orders from you. You're finished," Reza shouts, and storms out the door with a wail, a little boy betrayed.

That's how far my father would go to put himself first, how easy it was for him to betray a "pal." Yet, as much an indication of his deceit and manipulation, this episode reveals his lusty drive to live, unhampered by scruples and fears of being judged. These two are at the root of my ambivalence toward him. How should I really judge my father . . . based on which trait: his dishonesty or his obstinate zest for life? Should I curse him forever for pulling a fast one on me, or worship him as an earthy prophet?

Sometimes, I'm silly enough to think that he was among the few with the gift to live. He savored life in a way one hears in songs, poems and tales of fantasy. He was among the handful in the human race who lived to the hilt, making the Lord Almighty proud of His chief creation. Baba was no whiz kid at his Qur'anic school, but he was brilliant in the school of life. He succeeded where his father, the coalman and all the other "tombstones" were utter failures. He may have been slow in catching those holy verses, but he made life electric in ways that his low-wattage son can only dream about.

NEW YEAR

Our New Year is fast approaching and the country is full of bustle and good cheer. Persian New Year falls on the first day of spring, the exact time of equinox. With the sweet promise of spring comes joy, optimism, and dreams of a better life—hollow as they may feel to many people. In the spirit of the new season, people are to look their best, their house and furniture their shiniest, and their souls their purest—cleansed of hatred and malice. Everyone is expected to participate in the jubilation. If, in reality, there's no reason to, they should at least make a pretense of it. The whole country must take on a look of festivity.

Even the sick trees lining our street germinate new leaves, despite the scum they draw for nourishment, and our sidewalks sprout shoots of grass through cracked pavement. The coalman scrubs the yearlong soot from his face; our clumsy math teacher the stubborn spittle off his mouth, and even the idiot feels obliged to get a shave and haircut and go for his annual bath.

My mother, too, gives the house a thorough cleaning, inside out, from top to bottom. She scrubs the walls, dusts off the little furniture we have, and beats the moth-eaten rugs, sweeping rats and cockroaches away—for a while at least. Quilts and blankets get their yearly laundering and the cotton beater comes to fluff up the lumpy cotton in our pillows and mattresses, so we enjoy a little sleep before they go hard again.

In the guestroom, Mama sets a *haftseen,* the spread of seven traditional items starting with the letter S in Farsi, each symbolizing an essential element of life: beauty, love, joy, rebirth. Among these are painted eggs, small beds of wheat shoots, stems of hyacinth and red fish swimming in a glass bowl. A mirror stands to reflect and enhance the effect of life, tall candles on each side shed light and give warmth. The spread is meant to survive intact during the two-week festive period, but ours is already patchy before it even starts—as I nibble at whatever is edible in it, even the shoots of grass.

For weeks leading to the New Year, we go shopping, with Mama leading the way and my brother and I shuffling obligingly along. We're hunting for an identical pair of suits Arash and I can wear year-round like uniforms—something that is both affordable and sturdy enough to last the whole year. We're also looking for shirts that don't wrinkle, and shoes one or two sizes too big to make sure we don't outgrow them too fast. From shop to shop Mama drags us, searching frantically, haggling her head off, until we walk our legs off and almost drop dead. With her measly budget and unrealistic demands, it isn't so easy to find what she wants. It happens quite often that we're bawled or laughed out of a store.

Back from shopping one evening, staggering under loads of bags, we come across a *Hajji Firooz,* one of the street entertainers who fan out through the streets with the first breeze of spring, bringing the promise of a new dawn. They wear baggy outfits of shining red, blacken their faces with soot, and put on a shimmering hat—singing and dancing joyfully.

This fellow is a small man, with a drum tucked under his arm, beating and singing away:

It's a time of joy, my master, why aren't you dancing?
It's a time of joy, my master, why aren't you laughing?

A crowd of children and some adults have circled him, watching the show in delight. Arash and I also force my mother to pause so we can have a look. *Hajji* entertains a little and then starts walking toward us, drumming and singing as he closes in:

I'm Hajji Firooz . . . incarnation of the jovial spirit . . . I'm never around but once a year. . . .

Once he's within a foot of us he stops and removes his hat. It is unmistakably Khan, the loan shark who constantly stalks my father. His stringy, matted hair is freshly dyed and looks greasier; it stinks of sweat and cheap pomade.

"Is that you, Mr. Khan?" my mother exclaims in surprise.

"That's right, madam. It's your very devoted humble servant," he says with a wise grin and an exaggerated bow, holding his glossy hat by his side. "I hope you don't mind my ridiculous outfit . . . but sometimes one needs to appear in disguise to beat people at their own games."

He's obviously referring to my father. Mama anticipates a long dreary monologue and tries to escape it. "It's late, Mr. Khan, and we have to run."

196

"I know, my sister. I have no intention of being an imposition . . . just wanted to take the opportunity to extend my best New Year wishes . . . ."

"Thank you. Now let us go. We had a long day shopping and we're tired."

"Please let me finish, madam. I wish you and your family a good prosperous year. May God never withdraw His blessed shadow from over your heads . . . ."

"Khan, I appreciate that, but it's getting late . . . ."

"No need to remind me of that, sister," he reaches to stop her as he does with my father, but freezes. Touching an unrelated woman would bring serious trouble. "Let me just present my case and you are free to leave."

"I know what you're going to say, but there's nothing I can do to help." Mama says and walks away, dragging us with her. This is what we have to put up with, thanks to Baba's need to party all the time.

"Wait madam! I must warn you, this is very important," he talks in an urgent low voice as he follows. "My partners are considering tough action against your spouse, and I'm most unhappy about it. God forbid, I don't want any harm to befall him in this blessed time."

Mama is alarmed: "What do you mean by that? What are your friends going to do to him?"

"If that happens," he goes on, ignoring the question. "I would be most ashamed. The last thing I wish for an honorable family is to be deprived of its breadwinner on the New Year eve."

Mama is in a panic and starts begging for mercy, but that further emboldens the creep.

"Listen, my sister, my partners are not just ordinary creditors to be given the run around. If they're not dealt with in good faith, they have other means at their disposal. So my advice to your husband is to settle this debt quickly."

He puts on his ridiculous hat, gives a long threatening glare and ambles off, singing and dancing.

On the last Tuesday of the outgoing year, hours before observing the Festival of Fire, Mama tells me to take my brother to the public bathhouse, as he hasn't had a good bath since circumcision. This is something I hate to no end. The bathhouse looks awful and smells terrible, from tons of human filth extracted and deposited there over

197

the ages. Its marble walls are cracked and stained yellow, and its floor is covered with a thick layer of fungus and depilatory substances. It's so slippery that one has to walk on tiptoes to keep from slipping. Even worse, bathhouses are a magnet for perverts, always on the lookout for young smooth flesh to diddle.

Going for a bath was fun up until I was six, when they still allowed me in ladies' bathhouses. It was a long, amusing affair, with bathers holding a picnic with lots of fruit, snacks and gossip. They were also a perfect place for women to hunt for a bride for their brothers or sons, where they could thoroughly appraise candidates and run a background check on them with nosy *dallaks*, professional cleaners: Is the potential bride chaste? Does she have bad breath or too many moles on her body? The inquiries go on and on and I greatly enjoyed the gossip, also the opportunity to roam freely among so many hairless bodies. There were ugly sights too here and there, old ladies with puckered breasts and folds of loose skin hanging off their stomachs, but they were sure outnumbered by young fresh bodies.

Anyway, I cherished those moments, until some stupid prudes began to complain that I was too old and curious about sex to be among naked women and Mama stopped taking me along. The job was then left to my father, who chickened out as usual. He said he'd go to a public bathhouse only if they had female *dallaks,* like in Japan. After that, I was on my own with my brother to take responsibility for, too.

When we get there, the bathhouse is jammed with New Year bathers, all rushing to get cleaned before the calendar turns. A grotesque cast of cripples, hunchbacks and men with one eye or a pockmarked face are on their haunches scrubbing away. They're the professional cleaners, wearing a red cloth around their waists, some rolled up into a loincloth. But the loin is just the spot least covered. As they wrestle with mounds of hairy flesh, heaving and twisting massive limbs, their big knobs swing like the pendulum of a clock tower.

For hours my brother and I sit waiting on a grimy platform, also with the red *lowng* wrapped round our waists, watching row after row of hulks undergo a thorough scrub and rubdown. Some of them look like elephants emerging from a mud bath and it takes an hour before they shed all the grime. The *dallaks* rub away with patience, extracting every flake of dirt and rolling them into thick ropes. The more dirt they dredge up, the fatter their New Year tips will get.

I keep waiting for our turn, but influential merchants and good tippers have to go first, no matter when they arrive. I make one meek objection but the hunchback *dallak* gives me such a dirty look that I shrink.

Our turn finally comes and I hold Arash's hand, take him to the hunchback, and stand close to see him through a safe wash. The *dallak* rubs the abrasive cloth too hard on his body and the little boy pouts and looks at me plaintively. That sharpens my sense of responsibility and I order the washer in a firm voice to take it easy.

"Why do you worry so much?" he shoots back, with a wink. "No wonder you're so skinny."

I ignore that and go to sit down on the floor for my own bath. He reaches to open the knot of my *lowng* tied around me, so he can scrub my legs. That's the routine, but I hold the knot firmly and he's getting pissed off.

"You want to be scrubbed or not?"

"Just a soap wash would do."

"You legs are caked with filth! They won't come off with soap alone.

"Yes, they will."

"As you say—I just don't want your mother to come here and complain."

"Okay, go ahead and scrub, but don't rub too hard."

"Children of this generation are such sissies," he huffs.

But it is all worth it because the Festival of Fire we celebrate that same night is awesome. It is as extravagant an affair as we can afford, held in our humble little backyard, with the family participating. Grandma is there, but her husband has to stay out because he still is on Baba's blacklist.

The Festival of Fire is an old tradition, going back to our Zoroastrian heritage. Zoroastrians, as we learned in school, worshipped fire, which they believed could purify you. Now, thousands of years later, families still gather dry bushes on this day, line them in small bundles at intervals and set them afire. Flames rage. Men, women, and children hop over them like horses over obstacles, hoping to shed their illnesses and bad luck. *Take my (sickly) yellow hue and give me your (healthy) crimson red*: is the verse they repeat over and over as they jump.

Children like to take it a little further. They burst firecrackers and launch crude toys rockets and torpedoes. I've spent much of my stolen money on noisy explosives this year. No one seems to notice there are more than we ever had before. That's something I have to look out for, but sometimes it's hard to keep my mouth shut when I know I'm providing more than Baba ever did.

Mama cooks a sweet dish of rice and dates for the occasion and prepares a bowl of nuts and raisins for us to munch on all evening. Baba too skips the party with his friends and stays home with us, helping to make fire and adding fun to the celebration. The big surprise is that Grandma is finally ready to part with her treasured talisman. After we all throw our bad luck into the flames, she opens her cloth-bank and spills the ashen foreskin of my brother's weenie on the ground, running a trail of ash from the entrance to the far end of the house.

"This immunizes the house against any bad luck," she promises.

My trip back to my country didn't take more than five months, but it was long enough for me to witness an observance of the New Year in post-revolutionary Iran. Instead of *Hajji Firooz* in red garb and soot-blackened faces, there were ghosts in black veils and pallid looks. Instead of invigorating flames and firecrackers, there were the horrifying sounds of gunfire as guards burst rebels out of their hideouts, and the swish of whips chastening youngsters. The cheer, the bustle, the spirit of expectancy in outdoor markets had all given way to long lines of aggravated citizens fighting amongst themselves for rationed essentials.

The ruling powers frowned upon pagan celebrations, and there was a reason: the blood of hundreds of thousands of martyrs had not been shed for others to seek selfish joy. Instead of special New Year programming, government-run radio and television broadcast religious chants, long sermons, war movies, and hostile slogans. Moreover, there was this constant fear of Iraqi missile attacks, which Saddam Hussein repeatedly warned of.

One day, during one of my aimless strolls, out in a park, a *Hajji Firooz* suddenly popped up singing and dancing—quite a rare sight in those days! He was typically dressed in shining red, clutching onto a tambourine, banging and twisting away.

What a frightening sight!—the gaudy image of a street entertainer filling the grim air with his music. People stepped back in horror, trying to distance themselves from this act of rebellion—*Hajji*'s cheer had either faded from memory or no one saw a reason for it any more, with all the gloom.

The musician closed in and the crowd retreated, further and further, fading back like ghosts. Some nervously looked about to make sure no guards were around and a few even eyed the clown with hostility. But *Hajji* was undaunted and obstinately pressed on, as if on a mission from the devil to undermine this spiritual land. He wiggled and swirled and leaped through the crowd of zombies, trying to put smiles on their weary faces and urge them to participate.

It's a time of joy, my master, why aren't you dancing?
It's a time of joy, my master, why aren't you laughing?

As he sang, he reached over and grabbed a young man by the arm, thrusting him forward. The man blushed; his eyes nervously darted around. Finally, after some enticement by *Hajji*, he threw up a shoulder in rhythm with the tambourine. Next came a timid movement of the other shoulder, and then a twist of the hands and sensuous tilt of the hip—all in tandem. The beat picked up and the amateur dancer hopped in abandon, as others looked on in guarded satisfaction. In a few minutes, masked faces softened into smiles, stiff limbs stirred and hands rose in the air, as everyone dared to clap and sway. All seemed momentarily distracted from their conditions, and the fear that engulfed them. It was as if there was a lapse in history, a brief journey back through a time portal.

The first three days after the holiday we receive a lot of visitors—aunts, uncles, cousins, all coming to pass on New Year's wishes to my grandmother, who's staying at our house. We return some of the visits, but my father sits them all out, preferring to spend time with his friends. My brother and I however are having great fun with the orgy of food and all the cash gifts we get. We've banked enough to each buy a toy or something. It's a pity though we're barred from visiting Grandpa. The old man is tight with his money, but he likes to give big New Year presents just to show off.

On the fourth day my grandmother comes to my father with a bold demand:

"My good son, why don't you put your resentment aside and make peace with your father in the happy spirit of the new season?"

"You must be kidding, Mother. No way." He's striding back and forth along the sitting room to digest his food. He feels too lazy to go out for a walk.

"Please. He's still your father. It's your duty to visit him on the New Year."

"I don't have a father."

"Please do it for my sake," she throws herself at his feet, pleading. "I don't have much time ahead of me. I want to die with peace of mind . . . finally see you two in harmony . . ."

"Rest assured you'll survive him," he says, rubbing his paunch and trying to hold back burps. "I'll soon finish him off so you can leave the world with peace of mind."

"Then do it for the children. They miss their grandfather . . . let them get their New Year presents."

Baba softens at the mention of presents and his eyes flash, but he still acts angry.

"Presents from that cheap bastard? He recycles and eats his crap to save money."

"Enough of such talk! Please, my son—put on your clothes and let's go to the farm."

"All right, I'll take you there, but I'm not going to talk to him."

Arash and I rush to put on our most festive clothes. Mom, too, is very happy, almost jumping to kiss her husband, but she's reserved in front of others.

We all pile into the Bride, shining with new gear, and drive out to the farmhouse, where the patriarch is holding court, receiving well-wishing peasants. He sits on a thick mat at the head of a long hall, leaning against a mountain of cushions. By the door stand a row of farmers, all in new clothes and keeping their hands to their chests in respect.

When we first arrive, the mood is tense. Grandpa remains seated, waiting for his son to come and kiss his hand, but Baba stands by the door, facing away. Mama and Grandma grab Baba's arms, trying to drag him to the patriarch, but that's like moving a boulder.

But in time the ice melts a little and the adversaries force out a few words, though still not looking each other in the eyes. In any case, we're all glad to have Grandpa back into the family fold, and I'm even happier because now I won't miss out on my New Year present.

"How are you, my darlings," Grandpa says, holding both Arash and me in his arms, eyes brimming with tears of joy. "Come here, I've got something for you."

He digs in a pocket and draws out two large notes, both new and glossy, and hands them to us. Baba stands back, trying not to look interested, but I'm pretty sure he's estimating the value of the bills in his mind. He's been keeping a close tab on our intakes so far and been waiting for it to reach a sizable amount before making a claim for it.

"This is your money. Don't let your father take it from you!" Grandpa whispers in our ears as he presses the bills into our palms.

I stand aside and play with my note, savoring its crisp feel and fresh smell, and then I carefully slide it into my breast pocket so it doesn't bend. While the adults are talking, I walk outside for a stroll through the farm. Off to my right is a barn, and I watch the cows feed on moldy bread and crystal blocks of salt. Outside it a flock of chickens peck and flap under berry trees. A rooster with a fat red crown and resplendent feathers charges through the hens, puffing its chest, fluffing its feathers, and cock-a-doodle-dooing boastfully. His cocky air reminds me of my father. As I approach its females, the bird braces for attack; his proud neck cranes; his wings lift and spread out. I steer clear and walk through the orchard of blossoming cherry and apricot trees. It is a balmy afternoon, the air filled with scents of flowers and freshly-turned soil. From the north blows a soothing spring breeze which opens up my heart after months of being cooped up in a dingy house.

When I return to the house Baba is standing by the door; just like that rooster, he is in a hurry to go back to the city and into action. Mama is not quite ready to call it a day, still trading pleasantries with Grandpa, but she soon follows. The Bride's white fenders are now all muddy, but Baba opens the doors with a flourish. We all pile in with plenty of room, even for Grandma, who comes back with us to return a few New Year visits.

Back in the city and our dingy house, Baba scurries to get ready for his evening out, and I go to wash the car, which is caked in mud from the drive through the countryside. After the car wash, Mama and I parade him through the ritual of the bath and anointing him with cologne. Just before he leaves, he asks for our piggy banks.

Mama protests. "Hands off! It's their money."

"It still is theirs. They're giving it to me for safekeeping," he says and hurries us along.

"Who're you trying to fool? You do that every New Year . . . chip away at their savings with a pickaxe."

"What do they need money for? They've got everything they need."

"What do you think they are, your tax collectors? As soon as their savings come to something you take it away."

"I don't have time to argue . . . Shahed, get it quickly!"

Arash and I hide behind our mother, as if she can shield us from the raid.

"Come on . . . fast!"

I fetch the earthen pots choking with coins, with a few notes sticking through the top slit, and hand them over like presents to a conqueror. I wanted to buy a bicycle or a mechanical toy with the money, but my hopes turn to ash. What I pilfer now and then doesn't amount to much and I quickly spend on goodies.

Baba walks with the banks out onto the balcony and smashes them against the hard plaster. A mass of rusty coins spills out, scattering all over the cement floor in a shrill jangle. He drops to his knees and sorts through them like a frantic gold digger, pocketing the notes and larger coins, leaving the cheap coppery ones for the vanquished.

To make the loss more bearable for us, he entertains with a story, this time the sad tale of a delinquent boy taking a tailspin into misery.

"It all started with a crooked hand that went astray," he says by way of commentary. "Then it led to more serious crimes."

It gives me a chill to follow the boy's story. It starts with petty thefts. Then he starts smoking cigarettes and drinking beer. Next is hashish, then opium, and finally heroin. The boy goes in and out of prison and his parents kick him out of the house. He has to spend the nights under a bridge with other junkies, sharing scavenged food and needles with them. Baba pauses now and then to throw an ambiguous glance at me, and I wonder if he suspects something. He also stops to insert a comment, add his insight to the sad tale.

"Can anyone guess the moral of the story?" he asks but doesn't wait for answer. "It says that parents shouldn't trust their children with a lot of money."

It is a self-serving conclusion, I know, but still convincing. I'm actually glad he plundered my savings before it's too late.

"Some parents don't have a clue how to raise a kid," he sums up. "If I had a son like that I'd kill him to spare the family the shame."

It wasn't a bluff. Mary finally left me, and I already feel the pinch—both emotionally and financially. After that tense night at the discothèque, we ended up staying together several more uneasy weeks. But one night she called, breathless and excited, stuttering and mixing up her words, to tell me she had found someone else, a real man much better than me. Then she said we were through and told me not to call her ever again. The sense of relief I'd anticipated never came, or was eclipsed by a drop into emptiness, unbearable pangs of depression. I felt jealous of the "nice" Navy guy she started dating, the man who perfectly met her needs for order and stability. It was the first time I felt envious toward anybody in many years . . . maybe not since I'd lost Houri to my father.

As opposed to the loser Shahed, Mary's new beau had a promising career ahead of him and a sense of direction as accurate as the missiles he fired. If I could believe Mary, the couple had already planned their wedding and the big family they could not wait to start. Resentment stirred a weak flame of ambition in my soul, a confused desire to outperform the soldier. I even began to consider offers of partnership made by my boss, a gesture I had earlier spurned with a sneer.

"Shahed, I like you," George told me just a few days ago. "You're a nice guy and trustworthy. The problem with you is that you don't have enough aggression in you . . . your feet aren't planted solid on the ground."

"You're right, George. I don't always know what I want."

"You do know what you want. You just don't have the guts it takes to go after it. Tell me, who in this world wouldn't like to live in a nice beach house, drive a red sports car, and date lots of sexy women?"

I didn't tell him that's what he wanted, that I stopped myself from wanting it because I knew I'd never get anything like that. But losing

Mary had really shaken me . . . there might be something in what he was offering to fill up my life.

"George, you deserve some credit here. You really know me better than I do."

"Hey, I may not read a lot of books, but I know a man with balls when I see one . . . anyway, there's a gas station for sale. The owner is a junkie and not up to running a business. I can take it off of his hands for nothing. You think you can manage it for me?"

"Sure."

"But I want a long-term commitment. Yeah yeah yeah . . . I don't know why I should have any faith in you. Anyway, let's go take a look at it next week."

"Next week" was when Mary was getting married, but I wasn't welcome to attend. She had actually invited me, if only to see the look of remorse on my face, but Laura and her boyfriend were fiercely against it. Bill had threatened to shoot me if I showed my "fucking eye-ranian face."

THE BIG COUP

As protocol dictates, Grandpa must return our New Year visit, some time before the end of the holidays. One lucky day, he finally makes it. His visit comes a few days after Baba's raid on my piggy bank, which I'm still mourning.

While in town, Grandpa takes the opportunity to sell a herd of sheep. He comes to our house straight from the deal, and like a laboratory rat I jump to greet him with expectation of a reward. One of his pockets is loaded with cash and sagging with the weight of it. Reza is also there when he arrives, but my cousin can't stand the sight of the old man and takes off immediately. Since that incident over the missing watch fob, the two haven't been getting along.

Mama hurriedly dons her *roosari* headdress to greet Hajji. She usually only does it when a religious man comes to our house, to show respect. Grandpa likes his daughter-in-law and feels sympathy for her over all her problems with my father, although the old man has done even worse things to his own wife. He still doesn't openly acknowledge Grandma, although it is obvious he loves her. For some strange reason men in our family are ashamed of showing their feelings toward their wives or even their sisters.

With Reza gone, Grandpa feels more relaxed, takes off his hat and hangs it from a hook in the sitting room, where he hunkers down. His bald head is extremely pale next to his sun-beaten face and neck. Even at seventy, Hajji is fit and strong, with such a strong grip that can open a Coca Cola bottle.

Mama brings tea and then goes back to the kitchen. Grandma is sitting in a corner, patching something, oblivious to all, and my little brother is by her side playing with his own toes. Grandpa has a sip of his tea and then takes the wad out of his pocket to count, right before my hungry eyes. It is such a fat appetizing roll that I blush, as if I've caught a glimpse of forbidden female flesh. I turn to leave in respect for Grandpa's privacy.

"You don't have to go anywhere, my son. I fully trust you," Hajji says. "Reza and your Baba are a different story. When they're around, I even sleep with one eye open."

Hajji fumbles through the fat roll and it gives me a thrill just to watch him count and recount. His old eyes peer closely at the notes and he keeps licking his crooked brown fingers to peel each one back. It is even more tempting than the one Uncle E was waving before my eyes the other day. A ruthless assault is all but imminent. Luckily, my nosy great aunt is not around this time and I have more room to maneuver.

Grandpa finally finishes counting, puts the money back in his pocket and changes into pajamas. He takes his pants to the guest-room, and hangs them from a coat rack. Then he comes back to the sitting room to knock back several tumblers of tea while waiting for lunch. He is in a hurry to get back to the village with his money intact, knowing his son will be coming home soon. But he's in a bind because it is rude for him to leave without eating.

We spend some idle minutes until Baba shows up. He's unusually warm to his father. I'll bet he knows Hajji just came from a lucrative deal.

"Hajji, I heard you're here to sell some sheep."

"No!" Grandpa responds quickly. "The deal didn't go through."

"You probably asked for a fortune and scared them off."

"What did you expect? Give them away for free, as you do?"

Before it boils into another conflict my mother rushes to distract them.

"Lunch is ready! Let's go to the guest room."

We follow her back to the guestroom and sit to lunch. Grandpa is tensely cautious, with Baba in close proximity to his trousers hanging from the hook. He keeps throwing sideway glances to make sure he doesn't stray too close. He's so edgy in fact that he doesn't even go to take a leak or a nap after lunch. That's unfortunate because I'd hoped to hit his pocket while he's asleep.

But I have a plan B: jump into action while he stands to pray, the long mid-day prayer which is supposed to take at least fifteen min-utes. That is something he can't skip, come hell or high water.

Mama hauls away the lunch *sofreh* and goes down by the pool to wash the dishes, and everyone else but Grandpa returns to the sitting room. The old man stomps out to the sink to perform ablutions and I quickly run to spread his prayer mat in the same room where we had lunch. Being alone there with Grandpa's trousers, I'm tempted to carry out the job there and then. But before I can act, my brother wanders in looking for Grandpa. He wants to jump on his back and enjoy a ride while the old man is praying, especially when he kneels to touch his forehead to the ground. I snatch his ear and drag him out of the room, ignoring his screams, and then go back.

I'm all wound up when I hear Hajji's plastic slippers slapping hard on the landing. His shirt sleeves are rolled up to his armpits, his arms dripping wet.

"Praise upon you, my dutiful son," he says, happy that the stage is set for his devotion. "*Inshallah*, you will see the rewards of your good deeds—both in this world and in the other."

"Grandpa, can I stay here and learn from you how to pray?" I ask, confident that he won't turn me down.

Hajji's big dream has always been for his grandsons to grow up to be pious like him, especially since both his sons are nonbelievers.

"Of course, my darling." He dries off his arms with a handkerchief. "Just stand behind me and go through the motions, until I have time to teach you the verses."

Grandpa faces reverently towards Mecca, palms held up, eyes shooting heavenward. Then he starts a loud monotonous chant. I stand right behind him, mimicking like a monkey: bending with my hands cupping my knees, kneeling on the floor and touching my forehead to the ground. For a touch of reality, I drone nonsense for verses that I have yet to learn. The gestures actually seem to have a soothing effect and for a few seconds I forget what I'm there for.

After more bobbing around, Hajji slips into a trance, kneeling down and staring into his palms, and here I see my chance. I turn around, tiptoe over to the hanging trousers and dig my hand up to the elbow into the deep pocket, my heart racing and my knees trembling. I fish out the wad, hurriedly peel off a few outer bills, the large orange ones, and put the rest back. The loot has to be hidden quickly and I run to find a safe place. Everyone is still in the sitting room and I go to the middle one, looking frantically for a recess. Unable to find any, I open the closet door and stuff the bills into a dirty sock, and then go back to finish my prayer.

Grandpa is still at it, totally lost in meditation. The money's still there in his coat pocket. My heart is still pounding, but I like this feeling. Why not take more? When will I ever get this chance again? So I take one more dip into his pocket, remembering this time to take a few smaller notes—they'll be easier to pass off. I turn to take a quick look at Hajji and he looks so stiff, as if his soul has taken off leaving just the corpse behind. Before his spirit finds its way back to earth, I keep shuttling back and forth between his trousers and my dirty sock, until the wad sheds half its weight and even more of its value.

By a rough count, I must have made away with ten thousand *rial*s or so, an enormous haul by any standard. More than what a doctor makes in a month! With that money, I can buy the whole school cafeteria, or a lifetime ticket to all the James Bond movies. I can finally take that dream trip with Houri. There are just so many exciting possibilities before me that they wash through my head like a river—I don't know which one to pick.

Hajji finally finishes his prayer, drinks some revivifying tea and takes leave. Then I go to find a more secure place for the stolen money, a hideaway not even a whiz kid can figure out. I stuff the smaller notes in my pocket for current expenses, then shove the rest in a dirty sock—they fill it up like a fat sausage—and hide it deep inside a mattress, one of the futons my mother plumped up for the New Year. The mattresses are staked up in a corner of the middle room, and the one I've marked is right in the middle.

Grandpa doesn't make the discovery until the day after, and then what a stink he makes about it! He comes roaring back to our house looking for the culprit. Everyone is at home—Mom, Grandma, Arash, even Baba, who's going through his favorite women's magazine. Hajji yells so loud that my brother bursts into tears and jumps into his father's lap.

"It must be Reza, the usual suspect!" the old man growls.

"Please, Hajji Agha," my mother pleads. "Sit down and relax a little. Don't worry. Your money will be found."

"I won't sit down until I find the thief. I know it's that little scoundrel."

"But Reza wasn't even there," Grandma says like a public defender. "He left right after you arrived."

"You take the side of all losers like a public defender." Grandpa and Grandma don't address each other by name for reasons I don't understand. "Then it was your brother!"

"Her brother died recently—did you forget? He has a rock-solid alibi," Baba jokes and leaves the room. He can't bear his father's screaming his head off.

210

"If it's not Reza then I know who it is!" Hajji hisses to his wife, trying to lower his voice. Arash and I are squeezed on cushions in the corner. I strain to hear every word.

"Who?"

"It's definitely your gigolo son."

"Don't go accusing my poor son," Grandma objects. "He didn't even see your money. You had him under watch the whole time."

"My eyes must have slipped. He's like a wizard . . . can rob blind-folded . . . with his hands tied behind his back."

"Maybe it didn't happen in this house. Maybe someone picked your pocket in the bazaar."

"Are you crazy, woman? I counted the wad right before this kid. Didn't I, Shahed?"

I stiffen with terror, and probably blush, too.

"Y . . . y . . . yes."

"See!" Grandpa says to his wife.

"Then why not accuse Shahed, too? You're just lashing out at everyone."

I'm about to have a heart attack even before spending a *rial* of the stolen money. The money is in a safe place, but what about the smaller notes? I run to transfer them from my pocket to the secret folds of my schoolbag. Mama has a bad habit of turning my pockets upside down before laundering my clothes.

"Shahed? Never!" Grandpa objects. "This saintly boy would never do a thing like that. He has taken the path of prayer . . . asked me to teach him the verses. No, it's most likely your impostor son."

Days go by. Hajji's suspicion flares into strong conviction that his son is the culprit. He says that when Baba is not around, and when he is, the old man drops sarcastic hints, hoping to bluff his son into confessing.

"This can't be the work of a novice. It takes a hardened crook to pull off a job like that," he says. "But have no doubts about it. I will find the coward and bring him to justice. I'll take my pickaxe and dig through every hole for him."

Baba is either too slow to catch the hints or feigns ignorance, but he's dying to know who was behind the job just for the heck of it.

"I really want to know who this clever guy is who took the lead from me in screwing Hajji," he says when his father is not around. "He's done such a great job of covering his tracks."

But when Grandpa is there, Baba talks differently:

"I'm so embarrassed by this taking place in the sanctuary of my house. It has ripped my reputation . . . raised questions about my integrity. If I find the thief I know what to do with him."

The house is abuzz with rumor. Everyone is anxious to get to the bottom of the mystery, but no one is coming anywhere close. Was Hajji's pocket picked? Did he lose his bankroll on the bus home to his farm? I ignore it all and go on to enjoy the fruit of my masterstroke. Everyday after school, I sail through the bazaar spending the loot, having my fill of lamb liver, pretzels, and even bananas. Bananas I order in bunches and shove down my throat whether I have any appetite or not.

"You throw around a lot of rials these days," Seyed the greengrocer says pointedly. "Where do you get them?"

"It's my monthly allowance . . . just—in a lump sum," I answer.

He takes it for the nonsense it is and keeps his mouth shut, as his greed dictates. In any case, the rude bastard has taken on a wholly new attitude. Every time I pass by his shop, he rises from his chair, tips his hat and bows in respect.

These binges, needless to say, kill my appetite for meals at home. During lunch, I sit back contentedly, allowing my father to make away with the meat in my plate, or whatever else it is he has designs on. *Nooshejan.* Food to your soul, Baba, I laugh inside. You more than deserve it for taking the fall for me in the scandal.

Mama though is worried over my loss of appetite.

"Look at you! All color is draining from your face! You should eat more . . . need some flesh around your bones . . . a little juice under your skin."

Poor woman always has to be worried about one thing or another. I certainly owe her a lot for all her sacrifices. I'd have bought her a present, something she really needs, if not afraid of being asked how I could afford it.

For a couple weeks, I shop in the local bazaar and then get tired of it. Then I'm ready to dabble in the domain of wealth and fashion, where all the fancy boutiques, toyshops and American fast food restaurants are. This, though, is a bit difficult, as fashionable districts are far from where we live, and I have only so much time to spare. But there's a solution to that, too: taxis. Then I take cabs right and left—to go to school, shopping, or wherever else I need to go. Like an idle millionaire, I lounge in the backseat and we go straight to *Vanak Circle,* where glitzy malls are sprouting like mushrooms. There, I give my fancy a free run, splurging money on anything my heart desires: food, toys, designer pens, you name it. There's a lot to do and I'm in a hurry. Unfortunately, these toys I can't bring home, as they arouse suspicion. So I keep them in a drawer under my desk at school, and when I go back the next day, they're usually gone. But who cares? I have lots of money and can replace them.

My new riches have also brought me fame and respect at school. All those who teased and bullied me are now competing to be my friends.

"Shahed, you've got very nice toys. Can I play with them?" asks Edison. The nasty bully's suddenly full of brotherly love.

"Of course, go stand at the back of the line."

The search for the heist-man is in full swing. Grandpa has left his work at the farm to take the bus to the city and hassle us almost every day. He says he's closing in on the suspect, but doesn't still give a name, keeping us in miserable suspense.

"I know exactly who he is, but I'd rather not reveal his name yet. But you won't wait long. Soon, I'll haul him into the basement and hang him from the ceiling."

One unforgettable night he finally comes pointing a brown gnarled finger at my father, in front of the usual crowd in our house.

"Thief! Thief! I found the thief," he screams, eyes ablaze and his voice quivering with anger. "Here he is, sitting right before your eyes!"

My father goes still and all blood leaves his face.

"What did you say?"

"Don't play ignorant . . . you have no route of escape . . . better own up to it."

Baba bolts to his feet to defend himself, but he's tongue-tied.

"You—you don't mean—to insinuate—"

"I'm not insinuating. I'm accusing you with all the proof I need. You didn't think you could get away with it, did you?"

"What a nerve you have to call me a thief! I won't take that from anybody."

"Stop this game and give back the money. Hurry up! Hand it over! Give it back or I'll go to the police."

Baba stares in disbelief, tense and about to burst into flames. Ropes of veins stand out on his thick neck, throbbing. His eyes keep searching around the room, as if for something to throw at his father. Smelling catastrophe, Mama runs to hide her husband's hunting rifle, and all sharp objects sitting around. The men keep shouting insults at each other and we watch helplessly, wondering where it will all lead. The shaky peace we worked so hard to bring about is blowing up in our faces and we're sliding fast back to square one. I feel so bad that I almost break down in tears and make a full confession, just to get my father off the hook. But if I do, all this rage will be turned on me. I just keep my scared mouth shut and pass the point of no return.

"You're a disgrace to the family and to the whole human race," Grandpa shouts, ignoring his son's cries of innocence. "I'll disown you . . . remove this stain of shame forever."

"Hajji, I swear on my father's grave I had nothing to do with it. God strike me dead if I'm lying."

"Cut the blasphemy! I've yet to buy my grave and you're already swearing on it."

"If that doesn't do it for you, I'm ready to swear on the holy book."

"You might as well swear on a dead pig for all the difference it makes. You don't have a whiff of faith . . . never pray except maybe for my death."

"Okay, enough of insults! Get out of my house right now—you dirty old miser!"

"*Your house*? You only wish it was yours."

"Okay then, I'll move out," Baba jumps to his feet and turns to his wife. "Pack our stuff! We're leaving here right now."

"Please cool down," Grandma pleads.

"He can keep this rat hole for himself. I'd rather camp out in the streets than live a wretched life here."

Grandma freaks out, knowing her grandchildren have nowhere to go and are facing a miserable life as gypsies. Mama is even more worried, but there's nothing she can do.

"Please get off your high horses, if only for the sake of the children.," the old woman begs again. "God, what did I do to deserve this fate, suffering until my last days?"

But neither man is willing to climb down.

"I'll do whatever it takes to restore my honor," Baba vows. "I'll stand firm even if all the stars crash down to earth."

Grandpa raises the stake a notch higher: "I'll do anything to recover my money . . . hold my own even if the whole universe goes up in flames."

"Hajji, please stop him," Grandma cries. "They have nowhere to go."

"He wants to leave, let him leave. I'm not going to beg him to stay in my house for free. The ingrate had never appreciated it anyway."

"Hurry up, go pack!" Baba orders Mom. "Why do you stand there looking at me?"

My mother leaves to pack and Grandma pleads some more with her son, until she scores a small victory: Baba agrees to let us stay the night and move out the first thing in the morning.

It's like a funeral at our house that night. We sit among bundles of shabby luggage, with the women weeping nonstop. No one gets a wink of sleep, except for the adversaries who are snoring away in separate rooms, feeling light after spending their rage.

The day after the storm, Grandpa wakes up early to pray and then leaves for the village. Baba stays in bed until his stomach grumbles too loud to ignore. He gets up and orders a big breakfast of omelet and lamb steak, which Mama goes to prepare in a miserable state. While he's eating, Grandma makes one last plea, but nothing can sway him.

"A man is as good as his word," he says. "I'd rather live like a bum than under his debt."

As George had promised, we went to check out the bargain gas station in Oceanside, a quiet town north of the Mexican border. The town hosts the United States' biggest Marine Base and at that time was a transit route for drugs smuggled across the border.

It was a brisk spring day, the sky cloudless and the town serene. A mild breeze blew from the ocean, and I had the sense of being on

215

vacation after years of isolation in dull Monrovia. Through the two-hour drive, George babbled his opinionated theories and I kept looking out the window.

Max, the owner of the gas station, was a skinny blond man in his midthirties and bound to a wheelchair. He was a Vietnam War veteran with disheveled looks and a cynical attitude, but friendly and talkative, once he made our acquaintance. The problem was that he rambled too much, jumped erratically from one subject to another. As soon as we arrived, he rolled a joint and took out a tiny bottle of white powder, which I later found out was meth.

"Go ahead, have some," he said in an intoxicated voice, his eyes red and weary.

"I don't do stuff like that. I get high on money and pussy," George said with a satisfied grin.

"I do, too," the veteran responded with his own leer. "But drugs just . . . enhance it, you know, man?"

George was edgy and impatient, hardly concealing his disdain. "Let's go get something to eat and discuss business."

"There's a Jack in the Box around the corner," Max said while snorting a line from a piece of mirror.

"Forget Jack in the Box. Let's go to a fancy place in La Jolla. I'll pay."

La Jolla is a seaside resort in San Diego and on a beautiful clear day, the spacious landscape and vivid colors conjure up the image of Paradise. Visitors were out with bright smiles and colors, invoking another postcard image in my mind. Maybe I could fit in that picture one day, when I can afford the nice beach house and the red sports car George had promised.

We moved along the path running near the beach, enjoying the cool breeze and the saffron hues of the ocean sunset, and then went to a seafood restaurant for dinner. The place was packed with senior citizens, probably attracted by the discount price lobster. Next to our table sat two young women, engaged in a heated conversation, and George kept ogling them.

"Let's invite them to join us," he proposed but Max dismissed it.

"Nah . . . They seem too stuck up. I know a couple of easy ladies if you're horny."

"I thought we were here to discuss business."

"We can do both," the soldier giggled.

"Where are the whores? Call them." George said.

"They don't have a phone. We'll go see this lesbian couple. They go there for drugs."

The lesbian pair lived in a dilapidated house by a row of trailer homes. An eight-year-old mulatto boy played on the mangy front lawn with a pair of Dobermans. One of the women was thickset, and very white, with an attitude both friendly and blustering. The other, the kid's mother, was skinny and brittle and had bad front teeth.

We went inside and sat on a sagging brown couch in the living room. The skinny woman didn't pay us any attention. She took her son to the kitchen and then they disappeared. With the boy gone, the dogs wandered in and for some reason climbed all over me. I sat stiffly in a corner of the couch but didn't protest, not wanting to offend Janet, the rough-cut host.

Janet made some idle conversation and then disappeared into the garage. A few minutes later she came back with a bag of a yellowish white powder and set it on the table.

"That's all I got for you," she said gruffly and went on to make a row of lines. "Help yourself."

"We don't do drugs," George said defensively. I watched him getting more uptight: he didn't like drugs and he sure didn't like homosexuals.

"You're smart," she answered tersely and snorted a couple lines herself. "Where you guys from?"

"They're from the Middle East," Max said. Invoking those words unleashed a political commentary he seemed to have practiced. He covered hot topics of the day, including Iran. He was more critical of the U.S. government than the enemies in Tehran.

"I don't blame the Iranians for taking hostages. They got some legitimate demands that we should have listened to. We have no right to stick our nose into everyone's business."

He had a surprising knowledge of America's past intervention in Iran, the CIA's role in toppling a democratic regime in Tehran in 1953 and restoring the Shah to power. He was critical of the U.S. backing for the deposed dictator and its current support for Iraq in the war with Iran. I recognized Max as one of those well-read underachievers.

His macro views and obsession with politics seemed to prevent him from seeing minor details, and that may have been why he was losing the gas station he had inherited from an uncle. At that moment, too, his interest was focused on my background, not my struggle with the drooling dogs.

"So, what do you think Shahed?" he asked, his kind blue eyes dulled by the drug.

"I'm not really interested in politics, Max," I said, pushing dripping jowls away from my face. "I don't like to be identified with my government."

George liked this and smiled. He was bored and fidgeting.

"Stop raving, Max. What happened to the girls you promised?"

"Oh yeah." The soldier didn't seem insulted, perhaps used to interruptions. "They live in a motel right near here. Let's go get 'em."

George pulled into the motel's parking lot and got out to take a leak behind a wall. I helped Max get out of the van and he wheeled down to one of the rooms on the first floor. Ten minutes later he came back:

"She's with a guy but it's okay to go in."

The door was open and the three of us crowded inside. It was a small flat with a large dirty bed filling most of the space. Besides the bed, there was just a chair for furniture. A skinny woman sat on the edge of the bed, while a young man in jeans and long blond hair was sitting in the chair rolling joints.

"Have a seat," the woman said in a sedated voice. She had rough skin and a big bony nose, looking like a man made up as a woman. Her teeth protruded way too far and were stained yellow. She seemed totally spaced out, her tongue spinning in her mouth like a wheel in mud.

"Where you guys come from?"

"L.A." George said quickly before Max could go off on another political diatribe.

"Sweet. I go there a lot with my boyfriend." she asked me and uttered a few French-sounding words.

"Let's open some wine, Steve," she told the long-haired guy and pulled out a corkscrew from a canvas bag. "Do you know why I carry this? To scare off rapists. I'd just plunge it into their bellies."

"Where's Tracy, Debbie?" Max asked.

"How the hell do I know? Probably fucking some guy . . . ."

Before she finished, the door opened and a girl entered with a young black man holding a briefcase. I immediately recognized her. She was the child prostitute I'd met at the gas station, the one I converted into a lady in my mind. This time she didn't look so fresh and voluptuous, and was garishly dressed in a pink spangled outfit. She had on too much makeup and looked as if she had aged years in just several weeks.

The black man opened his case and spread out its contents: bags of marijuana and speed. He was not the same pimp I had seen her with at the gas station. Everyone had a few lines of speed, except for George and me, and then the men started negotiating a deal. It was my first contact with this underworld and I felt depressed around all these wretched lives.

"Come sit here, honey," the big-nosed woman said to the young prostitute. "Guys, this is Tracy, my roommate."

"Not bad at all," George said to Max. "Where should we take her?"

"Right in this motel," Max answered.

George looked at me questioningly, trying, in the midst of this squalor, to be discreet and generous in a Middle Eastern tradition: "You want to go first?"

"No, you go ahead." I said despite my inner dismay. I hoped naively she would turn George down.

He walked over, took Tracy's hand, and they left the room. I stayed behind with the pimps and the junkies, pretending to share their conversation and enjoy their company.

It wasn't even fifteen minutes before George came back.

"Go ahead. She's waiting. I got her hot for you."

I hesitated for a moment, then stepped out and opened the door to the next room. She was lying naked in bed, her curves looking enticing, now that they were exposed and stripped of the gaudy pink outfit. I eased myself on the edge of the bed and looked at her shyly, as she appraised me with restless eyes. I wondered if she remembered me at all and the promise she'd made not to use drugs.

She was impatient. I ran my hand over a smooth thigh and up over her breast. There were needle marks on her arms, but I still felt a tingling sensation. It wasn't lust, though. Something deeper . . . concern, pity.

"What the hell are you waiting for?" she snapped.

I don't know If she was bored or scared, but I had a need to prove I was different, not just after her body. "I don't want to sleep with you," I said. She looked back blankly. "Do you go to school?"

"No. Quit a long time ago," she answered uninterestedly. "What's the problem? You don't got money on you? Tell me, if you aren't serious?"

"I'm too serious." I still didn't make any move and she got up to get dressed. Her scuffed purse was lying on a table and she went through the contents to fish out a piece of bubblegum. Her meager belongings said she was a child in a rush to grow up. There was a Barbie doll in pink amid the clutter of nail polish, lipstick, and mascara.

A knock came on the door.

"Shahed, are you still there?" George shouted. "What are you doing in there, man? You surprise me with your strong back."

"I'll be out shortly."

"Hurry up. We'll have to get back. My wife will kill me."

Tracy looked at me as she refreshed her lipstick in front of a spotty mirror on the wall.

"Which way you guys headed?"

"Los Angeles."

"You mind dropping me off in Long Beach? I have to see a friend of mine."

Tracy and I huddled together in the back seat of the van as George drove through the night. She was quiet and thoughtful, resting her hand on my knee. I held her hand and closed my eyes, savoring the touch, drained of my tension and confusion. Soon she laid her head in my lap, curled her legs up on the seat. I put my hand over her thin shoulder as she fell asleep.

A few times George flicked on the dome light and peeked at me in the rearview mirror, grinning. I looked away every time and he finally gave up, fixing his eyes on the lonely road to the north. Maybe he was making up a lie to hand his wife; maybe he was thinking of the new gas station he had bought for a pittance. My mind was blank, but my senses were sharp. It was a self-contained moment. The forty-minute ride felt like a glide through a moral vacuum—a world devoid of judgment, fear and hang-ups.

PLEASURE LAND

One man we can always count on for temporary shelter is a great uncle of my father. He and his wife live in a big house on the fringe of Pleasure Land, our city's red light district. The house has eight rooms, or nine, if you count the shit house in the corner of the yard. One of the rooms the ancient landlord and his wife occupy, and the others are rented out to a troupe of lowlifes and lonely hearts that populate such neighborhoods. Since these are mostly transient souls, there's always a vacancy.

We're actually lucky to get two adjoining rooms, one of which Mama converts into a kitchen. She's at first a little uptight about living among a bunch of riff-raff, but soon she gets too wrapped up in domestic cares to notice. Slowly we fall into routine and there's also the mandatory company of the elderly couple—whether or not we like it.

The old couple have no children and all day they do nothing but fight. The husband is particularly cranky, constantly chiding his wife over petty things: why she leaves on the lights, why she skins the eggplants too thick, why she makes too many trips to the toilet.

"You must not be following the diet I gave you," he barks, his hands shaking like a vibrator. "or your bowels would work like a Swiss watch."

"Leave me alone," the wife shrieks back. "I go to the toilet to hide from you, have a moment of peace."

"I'm the one who doesn't have a moment of peace. My only quiet time is when I go to visit my mother at her grave on Thursday evenings."

"Then stay there with your mommy! Why do you come back to torture me?"

The old man has imposed strict rules to keep down water and electricity bills, including a power blackout after nine at night, and he makes random checks to make sure no one cheats. Such antics make perfect subjects for my father to make jokes about, and he never stops playing pranks on his stingy uncle. He's rigged up a high-voltage light bulb inside a chest and left it burning around-the-clock. The old miser runs in panic from room to room, trying to find the source of the leak.

Baba also makes fun of his uncle's invention, the spool he's jammed up the spout of the watering can used for a wash in the toilet.

"The spout allows only a tiny stream of water that freezes in the air before it reaches my ass," my father says humorously.

Baba has an interesting theory about his eccentric uncle: "He's so cheap because he came down with syphilis as a young man . . . whorehouses were so near and he couldn't resist the temptation.

"But the stud eventually paid for his unruly dick, when his oven suddenly went cold," he goes on, using his term for infertility. "After that he could only shoot blanks like an antique gun."

The neighborhood around our new house is really a wormhole of filth and decadence. Streets are narrow, dirty and packed with scruffy-looking men: beggars, junkies, laborers and military conscripts on an outing—all heading toward the compound of brothels deep into the quarter. The main strip is lined with stores selling used clothing and a string of shady cabarets, theaters and playhouses. Not a single mosque or school can be seen for miles around. The first we don't have any use for as my parents never set foot in a mosque, except to attend a funeral. But school is a problem. Mama insists that I stay in my old school, which is even farther away now. That's her condition for staying in the seedy house, in the company of all those losers.

Despite the sleaziness surrounding us, the neighborhood has its allure after dark. Every night I watch from the roof the main street glowing like a smoldering bonfire. It's a mesmerizing sight, full of secret promises, and I'm dying to have a closer look, a taste of the nightlife—its glitter and its shadows, its glamour and its vices.

But Mama has me under strict orders not to wander off into the forbidden territory.

"It's dangerous and full of diseases," she warns again and again. "Learn from the fate of your great uncle. Syphilis ruined his life. You keep your distance, Shahed!"

For a few weeks I listen, but then go to check it out myself. It is a thrilling discovery! To me, the place is a true land of pleasure, so it is rightly named. It is so alive, so full of color and dazzle—a wonderland of restaurants, theaters and nightclubs.

At first I'm cautious, standing at a distance to take it all in, with gaping eyes and a swirling head. There are so many billboards with belly dancers in bright silk, posters huge as theater marquees, showing actresses with plump legs, fiery eyes and red hungry mouths. Playhouses stage burlesque adaptations of classic dramas, with sooty-faced actors playing Othello and flashy white women Desdemona. By the entrance to each theater stands a dwarf, holding a bullhorn to his mouth, announcing the latest arrival, revealing just enough tantalizing details to lure customers.

Whenever possible, I sneak out to catch a double or triple-feature show at one of the movie theaters, offered at the price of one. The one I go to is a rundown place, an old pavilion gone to seed. Its red carpet is patchy and stained with dirt and the lobby reeks of dampness, tobacco and piss. The auditorium itself is a gutter bed, paved with nut shells, fruit skins and cigarette butts, smeared with snot, phlegm and sperm. The hall is packed with bums, heroin addicts and pedophiles, and there are never enough seats for everyone. Late arrivals have to bring their own seats, usually a bundle of cloth or a tin box. I use my schoolbag all the time, whether or not there are chairs available. The good thing about a portable seat is that you can move it around if there's a pervert sitting next to you and harassing you.

The movies they show are all several years old. I try to catch all the spy movies, including the James Bond film "Gold Finger," which I've seen over and over again. What appeals to me about spy movies are the good looking actors, red sports cars, and the sleek gadgets. It is a picture so at odds with the look of life here and it keeps my dream burning.

Money of course is no problem. I still have some of the smaller bills I stole from my grandfather, and haven't had the need to rip into the magic mattress, where the cache of the big orange notes is hidden. The futon is safe in a closet in our new house. It was moved here along with the rest of our flimsy furniture.

I've seen all the razzle-dazzle but have yet to catch a glimpse of the brothels in the heart of Pleasure Land, and the nymphs that live in them. I can't wait to see them in flesh and action, everything Usta has been telling me in juicy details. But I don't have the guts to get too close, with all the scary things my mother has been saying. A few times, I will myself to take the jump, but each time I find an excuse to chicken out. The whores' compound is a bit far and inaccessible. You'd have to take a narrow winding route and it is a fifteen minute walk, if you don't have to dodge too many beggars and perverts along the way.

Finally, one afternoon I throw caution to the winds and drift in with the tide, my stomach sick from fear. I walk for a few blocks and then stop for a peepshow, touted as "Magic Spectacle." It's just a metal box with a hole punched into one side, through which you can see images of naked women. I give the vendor a coin and he allows me a brief peek. But there's nothing magical about his show. The pictures are blurry and some of the women without a head, presumably to cover their identities.

I walk deeper and deeper into the strange land, and the deeper I get, the scarier it becomes. For one thing, I have this fear of running into my father, or worse, one of my teachers. But it's a baseless worry. There's no one there I know; no one I actually care to know. All are creeps, looking sick and dirty, or junkies huddled over a heroin fix.

At the entrance to a narrow alley, there's an ambulance parked, with its attendants collecting the stiff corpse of a man who probably overdosed. I pass quickly but then pandemonium breaks out. A scruffy young man is running madly, as he clutches a briefcase, with several others in hot pursuit.

"Catch the dirty thief! Catch him!" the pursuers shout as they run, kicking a cloud of dust. I run along only to watch. More people join in the chase, galloping like a herd of buffaloes. The thief zigzags through a maze of alleys, bumping against people and vaulting over stooping junkies, until he hits the end of a cul-de-sac. Trapped, the young man backs up against the crumbling brick wall and slips to the ground, as the vigilantes close in with furious eyes. Kicks and punches rain down and switchblade knives flash in the sun. A bigger crowd gathers to watch, but no one interferes. The beating lasts for too long, until the wolves are too tired to pummel any more, the quarry too lifeless to be any fun. I stand there aghast, watching with a confusion of emotions, glad to see the thief pay for his crime but questioning the justice of it.

I hurry away and reach the *Garden of Pleasure*, but I'm hardly prepared for what I'm about to witness. There's no sign, and no warning. The secret world of my dreams opens up in the most casual way: short narrow cul-de-sacs leading at the end to wooden doors. Outside each door is a tattered old man, once a glorious pimp ruined by addiction. He sits on a tin can, selling tokens and directing customers to different rooms. One of the doors stand ajar. I pass by slowly, seeing a small courtyard inside, planted with a few trees and holding a small pool and a fountain at the center. Wooden beds are arranged under the frugal shade of trees—all covered with a red rug and laden with hookahs, samovars, and opium grills. Husky mustachioed men sit there smoking, drinking and talking to painted dolls. Some of them look like the butcher, sporting the same shiny velvet suit, the same felt hat and the same gold medallion.

I want to get closer for a better look, see if those dolls are for real, discover the secret of their hold on my imagination, but fear and confusion held me back. I slip past several alleys, realizing that the quality of whorehouses degrade steadily, as does the lure of their tenants. The very last brothel is in the *Pissers' Alley*, a cursed patch of land reduced to a public lavatory. A dozen shabby clients have lined up outside, poor men with rich lust. They're in a hurry, elbowing their way through the door, trying to get to the whores before others.

Beyond that last alley is a dirt lot, where sickly boys with shrunken faces and sooty hands play strange games. Some roll sheep knucklebones on the dirt ground and another group piss over a wall, betting money on who produces the longest arc.

Then I see three frazzled women emerging from the Pissers' Alley, heading toward a grocery stall across the street. They all have sad faces and thick figures and are dressed in loud colors, tottering on broken heels. They look like they just woke up: their faces are puffed up, their hair is bedraggled and their eyes are red. None of them resemble the belly dancers featured on the main strip, or the vision of seductresses the barber implanted in my mind.

"Hey, whores, will you hold our dicks for us while we piss?" one of the boys shouts, and the others laugh.

"Let your mother hold it for you, son of a dog!" one of the prostitutes yells back and takes off a shoe to throw.

"You put that down, bitch, or I'll smash your face," the same boy says, picking up a rock.

"Faggots! Sons of whores! Pimps!" the woman screams and charges, with her friends trying to hold her back.

Her anger is so intense and terrifying that I turn to run away. Now I understand why Mama has been trying to keep me out of this place. What if it's too late now and I won't be able to make it back in one piece? What if I end up like the thief who was pummeled to a pulp? Or the incorrigible boy whose sad tale Baba was reading to me the other day? My mind races with horrible thoughts, my legs tremble hard, as I break into a trot, running blindly toward home, dodging through the human clutter littering the streets.

In the midst of my endless futile visits to government offices in pursuit of an exit permit, I made my way to Pleasure Land one day to observe its fate. The red light district had been sitting squarely on the moral fault line—I knew it would be the most vulnerable should divine wrath fall on this nation one day. And I was right. The messengers of faith were dead-set to root out that infested armpit of our city, the ultimate expression of pre-revolutionary decadence. They wanted to level that cursed patch of territory and rebuild it from the ground up, turn it into a park or a fitting institution for the spiritual haven in the making.

I happened to arrive the day its denizens were being taken away. Armed guards were posted throughout the district, taking positions at the head of each cul-de-sac and turning back horny clients. Along the main strip, all the theaters and cabarets were closed, their facades draped with black cloths. The whorehouses themselves had been raided and their occupants herded into police cars to be taken away for public chastisement. I passed by the vans and caught a glimpse of the prostitutes. They were all swaddled in black chadors and stripped of makeup, already looking like the chaste maidens they would become—after rehabilitation.

Hanging at the entrance to each bordello were banners declaring the end of Pleasure Land and exhorting men to behave.

"Rein in your sinful impulses and seek happiness in faith," said one.

Others were even more to the point, appealing directly to the male sense of honor:

"How would you like someone doing it to your mother, sister or daughter?"

To some clients, this came as a flash of insight and they left with their heads hanging in shame. But most stuck around, hoping to outlast the invaders, thinking naively the siege was temporary, a random kick in the ongoing convulsions of the Revolution. But the guards were there to stay. They drove around in jeeps, bellowing ultimatums through bullhorns. But threats fell on deaf ears, and crowds still massed before the alleys leading to whorehouses. Then the militants charged with their boots and the butts of their rifles. There was resistance from the indignant horny, but eventually all the stallions retreated and dispersed.

Stripped of its whores and stallions, Pleasure Land was reduced to a junk heap of beggars, derelicts and junkies. It looked sad and desolate, like a citadel fallen to a savage raid. I stood there mourning silently, as if for the loss of something very dear to me. For some strange reason, I felt a kinship with that place and its displaced whores. I wanted to champion their cause, their right to remain and work their cunts off.

One of the militants, a young man with a downy beard, walked past smiling to me. He looked harmless enough for me to risk a mild criticism.

"Why are you folks doing these things?" I whispered.

"What?" he turned to look at me, his eyes intoxicated with blind faith.

I tried to rephrase my question: "With all due respect, sir . . . ."

He'd already heard me. "You asked me why? Let me tell you why: it is our national and religious duty to wipe corruption from the face of earth . . . ."

He paused as if to invite another challenge, and I felt obliged to carry on with the debate.

"But do you think this is the way to do it?"

"What better way can you suggest, brother?" he flashed a confident grin. "Go on, tell me. I'm ready to listen."

He seemed genuinely interested in a philosophical exchange. My impression of him as a mule-headed fanatic was beginning to soften a little.

"I don't know. I haven't given it a thought."

"Well, we have and we have found the answer . . . the promise of a lasting glory and eternal blessing . . . ."

"I beg your pardon, but what lasting glory? To me it is just a construct of lies to create a hollow myth."

"Don't say that, brother," he said, staring down and playing with his rifle. "The truth of what we promise is measured by faith, not reason. This world is just a mirage. Man's true destiny awaits him in the afterlife."

"It doesn't make sense to me," I said, looking at the gun. "So what's man's role in this life?"

"Fight to martyrdom in order to pave the way for that ideal world."

"It still doesn't make sen—" I spoke unwittingly and the last word faltered. He was fidgeting with the gun and looking around to assess the situation.

"It will make sense to you once you start to believe," he smiled wisely. "One can't bring justice to earth with flowers."

"Your thirst for justice is abstract," I said with renewed courage. "You don't want to change the world. You want to destroy it . . . destroy it because you can't enjoy it. Look at what you're doing here!"

He shook his head at my stupidity, then gazed at me. He was tall and wore the ill-fitting uniform and carried the Kalashnikov with confidence, though he was no more than eighteen. His eyes were full of purpose, hardly seeing me through the mist of his distant dream, and I began to doubt my own position. I thought maybe there was a noble cause to his campaign, a vision beyond my understanding.

"What if you were on the receiving end of this misery, if your sister was the object of inhumane lust?"

"I don't have a sister."

"It doesn't matter! All women are your sisters. You ought to have a sense of duty to all children of God."

"A sense of living is all I've longed for."

"These two go together, brother! One must believe first before he can live."

PEDERAST

The problem with our new home is that it's too far from my school and I have to take a bus. It's a horrible trip, since the buses are all old and always stuffed with perverts hunting for a pretty face—male or female. To beat the rush hour, I leave home early, but there's never any slack in the traffic of sex-starved men shuttling back and forth to Pleasure Land.

Buses arrive packed to over-flowing, with passengers hanging onto outer rails and ledges. Drivers often don't bother to stop, and if they do, it is just to disgorge a few passengers. If I do make it on board by some miracle, the chance of finding a seat is almost zero; if there is a seat, one is better off leaving it alone than bear the reproachful stares of the elderly, the disabled and pregnant women— who think they deserve it more.

On one of these rides one day, I feel a hand groping me from behind. I turn to have a look, but it is too dark inside and I only see the vague outline of a giant, and a pair of glowing eyes. His hand keeps working over my back and I'm terrified. I wiggle to free myself, but my body is wedged tightly into a corner, facing the wall. I cock a shoulder to force him back, but the giant is immovable. His massive paw closes over my hand on the rail and I'm nailed to the spot. My head turns to give him an imploring look, but that only encourages a leer, exposing a row of jagged teeth. I think of screaming for help, but that would only call attention. People might think I'm a faggot.

Presently the bus stops to let off some passengers and somehow I squirm free from the creep's grip and squeeze through the dense crowd toward the door. I jump off, dodging across the street through lashing rain and heavy traffic.

I run for a few blocks and then pause for a look back. The giant is following, in long determined strides. My heart goes into a freefall and I quicken my steps, running madly with no clear direction. My legs are tired and my knees are giving way. I look back again, and every time he is closer. I give one last thrust, run on blindly, and then *BANG*. The world goes dark.

I come to finding myself lying by the side of a road, soaked in rain water, with a crowd of people circling me. I throw a quick look around to see if the giant is there. He's not and I feel relieved, but become aware of a pain shooting up my right arm.

"You crashed into a crate being loaded onto a truck," one of the witnesses says.

"Let's call an ambulance," says a man and I panic. I bolt to my feet and run away.

"Oh my God, what happened?" Mama asks in horror, as soon as her eyes fall on my arm, hanging lopsided and bruised and swollen like eggplant. The pain is now unbearable and I'm holding my bad arm with the other.

I tell her everything, skipping the part about the pedophile. She quickly turns to her husband: "He needs to go to hospital right away! Hurry up. Get dressed."

Baba leans deeper into the cushion behind his back: "I just ate and feel too bloated to move. We'll talk about it after my nap."

"Shame on you! My son is dying on my hands and you want to take a nap?"

"Don't make a big deal out of it. It's nothing, just a sprained muscle that needs time to heal on its own."

"What're you talking about? I see bone shards sticking out! He may need an operation."

"Here you go exaggerating again," he says and hauls himself up to get ready, cursing and groaning.

His frustration is now turned on me: "Are you living in a fog or something, running headlong into a crate? You have this bad habit of walking with your eyes up to the sky. It is all her fault for pampering you two all the time."

"Why do you blame the poor boy?" Mama jumps to defend me. "You have no tolerance for stress. If they get hurt you want to punish them rather than try to help."

"He does deserve punishment! This is just what I needed, spending a fortune on medical bills when I'm so broke . . .

230

"And you—" he goes on, still addressing his wife, "you want to see a doctor for every little thing, as if we owe those greedy bastards. You think money grows on its own like weeds."

"Mom, he's right—maybe I don't need a doctor." I rush to avert a fight. "It doesn't really hurt that much."

"You stay out of it! When I say you need a doctor, you need a doctor."

I shut my mouth, worried how Baba is going to pay for the bills. Then it suddenly occurs to me that I have medical insurance, provided by the principal to promote his school as a modern institution.

"Baba, Baba, don't worry about money! I have insurance. It'll cover everything."

"What insurance!" he says, cautiously interested.

"It is a complementary gift from the principal . . . came automatically with the enrollment package."

"It's probably crap." He ties his belt.

"No, it is real. It pays up to eighty percent of the costs."

"Like hell it does. Does it cover your damn tuition too?"

"There are several bone fractures," the doctor say, looking at X-rays. "He needs an operation under general anesthesia."

"What does that mean?" Baba asks.

"We have to put him to sleep. The surgery will take the whole day."

My father is suddenly concerned, as if my tragedy registered late. He keeps smoking and pacing the waiting room, and his eyes fill up with tears, although he tries hard to hide them. Every time the surgeon comes into the room, he bothers him with a question.

"Is he going to live?"

"We'll see."

When I wake up, Baba is standing by my bed with red eyes. He has called in several of his friends to give him heart, including the Colonel and the butcher. The Colonel tussles my hair and mouths some of that "prince" crap, and the butcher opens a bottle of cola with his teeth to raise my spirits. Baba's mood has picked up; he keeps joking and laughing.

"Oh you're back, my son," he plants a juicy kiss on my cheek. "Let's get out of this depressing dump before you fall back into sleep."

The doctor wants to keep me there a little longer, but Baba is in a rush to beat it. At the cashier, he waves the insurance card, but they don't honor it.

"You must pay in cash now."

"I don't have any money."

"Then we can't release him."

"So what's this insurance good for? Why did I pay for this crap?"

"We'll give you a receipt to make a claim for it."

"But I only have a few coins in my pocket."

"Ask a friend," the cashier says with a cold look.

My father turns to look at the Colonel. The officer gropes his own body earnestly, as if frisking himself. But there are no pockets on his uniform to carry money. Baba's eyes then turn to the butcher, who hesitates at first, but eventually fishes out a fat roll of cash. He slips off a few bills from the wad and hands them to the cashier, and we are free to leave.

For the first few weeks life is ideal and I'm in no hurry to get well. The cast is a little cumbersome, but it keeps me out of school and so it's worth bearing. All day I laze around the house reading melodramas, and Mama and I gossip like two old ladies. Sometimes well-wishers come with a present, and I enjoy their pity as much as their sweets and flowers. The highlight of the period is Houri's surprise visit, her first to our new house.

I'm excited and run to get her present, a pink pair of fishnet stockings that started out as a Mother's Day gift to Mom. But I decide to give it to the nymph because they'll look nicer on her. Mama may have sensed something though, as she never leaves the room so I can slip the present to Houri.

The day after my release from hospital, Baba runs to collect the insurance money, supposedly to pay off his debt to the butcher. But we all know he wants to keep it for himself. The insurance agent says that I have to get well before he can release the money.

"What? He's well as he can be, or he'd still be in hospital!"

"He must make a full recovery. We need a clean bill of health from his doctor."

"Listen, cut the nonsense and let me have the money. I badly need it."

"Sorry, but we have to go by the rules."

My father though doesn't leave the agent alone.

"I got there before the janitors," Baba tells us the day after. "I wanted to catch the agent before anyone else. But the bastard won't come down. Next time I'll take the Colonel with me to scare them into paying."

That doesn't work, either. The agency has dealt with bigger shots and holds its own. So Baba leaves them and tries his luck with the hospital about a week after the surgery, talking me along to improve his argument in case they need to see me.

"I need a certificate," he tells the nurse.

"Where's the patient?"

"Right here. Look—he's healthy as a bull!"

The nurse gives the cast a few tap-taps with her knuckles and then shakes her head.

"No. It's not dry yet. Give it a few weeks."

"What do you mean it's not dry? It's dry as an oven. Here, feel it," Baba says, trying his own knuckles on the plaster.

"What's the big hurry?" the nurse comes back, annoyed that her professional opinion is challenged. "Leave the poor kid alone."

"Hey, don't tell me how to treat my own son. I know what's best for him."

"Okay, go ahead and kill him, if that's what you want to hear from me," the nurse says and walks off.

Baba stands there stymied for a few seconds and then pushes me toward the waiting room.

"I should have come alone," he growls, then traps the unsuspecting surgeon when he shows up at the front desk.

"Doctor! Doctor!"

"I'm busy right now . . . in the middle of an operation."

"No problem, I'll wait until you finish," Baba says and follows him to the operating room.

"Wait a minute!" the doctor pauses. "You can't come here . . . all right, what do you want?"

"Just write a line saying my son is healthy as a bull."

"Where is he now? I need to see him."

"He's in the damn gym lifting weights! Just write a few lines saying he's recovered and I'll bring him later to prove it."

233

"I can't. I must examine him first."

"Okay, so write what you can," Baba says holding a pen and a hospital pad.

He keeps hassling the doctor until he scribbles a note, something vague that wouldn't bind him to anything. The next day my father takes it to the insurance company but they've now stiffened their requirements, demanding for the cast to be removed before they pay.

Baba is utterly hopeless, looking to clutch at any straw. He tries the usual channels for cash, but they all turn out to be dry. Even the butcher, the ever-willing creditor, is hanging back. He's now so desperate that I almost do something stupid: tap into my cache and offer him a loan myself.

A week passes, and one day my father comes home asking about my health.

"How're you doing with that carcass hanging from your arm?" he points at the cast. "It must be a drag to carry it around . . . bet you can't wait to get rid of it."

"No, it's actually fine, as long as it keeps me out of school."

"Don't be silly! You need your hand to do your homework."

Mama comes into the room and catches the gist of the conversation.

"What! The cast is so fresh on his arm. You want to make my child disabled for life?"

"No knife ever cuts its own handle." It's a Persian proverb to underscore the protective bond he feels with his son. The arm will heal better exposed to air and sun."

Baba is now moving heaven and earth to find a doctor to remove the plaster, but no one is willing to take the risk. When he gets a bug in his pants, nothing can stop him until he sees it through.

"Shahed! Get ready to go to the clinic down the street. See if we can get it removed."

"But they only give injections," I say.

"A little bribe will make anyone an expert."

We go there but again no luck! Turned away by the world, he decides to rely on his own resources, put his magic touch on the stubborn cast.

No one will scratch my rear but the nail of my own finger is another Persian proverb he keeps repeating.

Early one morning, I wake up to a whisper: "Get up! Get up! Follow me to the yard—and quiet!"

"Ha? What?"

"Don't make any noise. I don't want your mother to wake up and stick in her snout."

I lumber out of bed and stagger out after him. In the yard, he runs to grab a hammer and a screwdriver from his uncle's shed and comes back to settle down to work. He's still examining my cast when the door opens and Mama emerges with a horrified look.

"What in the world are doing?"

"Mind your own business!" he says, knocking his knuckles on the plaster. He pushes me down, then kneels, and positions my arm on the ground

"Are you out of your mind?"

"Go back to bed. I won't let you play hell with my plans again."

"I had a hunch you were up to something rash and foolish."

"I know what I'm doing!" he growls, still not lifting his head to look at her.

She falls silent and he takes a few gentle taps with the screwdriver.

"Hang tight, son!" he consoles. "It may sting a little at first . . . just a pinprick . . . but you'll be okay."

"This isn't a vaccine shot!" Mama comes closer, but cautiously. "You're going at him with a sledge hammer."

Baba ignores the sarcasm and goes on with words of comfort: "Like I said, you'll soon be able to do your homework, which you must have missed a lot." He adds a chuckle to distract me, and then the blows rain down.

Baba who can't even hammer a nail straight is pounding like a slave in a labor camp. I feel a dull pain in the very marrow of the bone inside the cast, but the vibrating ring of the blows is even scarier. He carves a few dents, but the plaster is solidly packed. He holds my fingers sticking out of the cast, and pounds harder. He's made a small hole by now.

"Seems like your mother is right . . . maybe . . . is a bit too early to remove . . . not quite ripened."

"So what are you going to do now?" Mama asks, biting the tips of her fingers.

"It's too late to back out. I'll go get the saw."

He comes back with a saw and runs it back and forth over the cast. The grating sound gives me shivers, but I feel no pain. It takes about fifteen minutes to cut through and finally take it off, and I'm horrified to see the thin bruised stick, all that is left of my arm.

The night after the brief romantic spell with Tracy, I had a dream about Mary, or rather this strange creature with Mary's head and the body of a dog. It was an unsightly monster, but loving and obedient. She didn't speak a word, but her big exaggerated eyes begged for caresses. I held back, as usual, and felt the scalding guilt for not responding. She appeared hurt, shedding tears the size of a balloon. The balloons kept rolling down her cheeks, forming a pool and eventually a river. The river swelled and flooded over, washing me away and everything else in its path. I desperately looked for a rock or a log to cling onto, but there was nothing except for colorless balloons filled with water. They were everywhere: big squishy blobs spreading for miles around, falling from the sky, filling the air. Then I woke up in terror, drenched in sweat and overcome with guilt. I wanted to call Mary, beg her forgiveness, and plead for another chance . . . .

Summer is approaching and the heat is already unbearable. There hasn't been a drop of rain, and a thick pall of smog and dust has hung over Pleasure Land for weeks. The vivid images of the belly dancers have blistered and peeled off, hanging from the boards in shreds.

One place that hasn't seen much change is the compound of brothels. Herds of steaming stallions flock down the narrow path, jostling into each other. In the brutal heat and absence of glitter, their lust feels even more ferocious and intimidating.

A few dull weeks pass after my surgery and Mama and I are both getting restless. We get fewer visitors in this house. Grandma and her sister Khaleh are too religious to come see us. They think their mandatory daily prayers wouldn't be accepted by God in the neighborhood of sins. So we are lonely and miss our old house, even its rats and cockroaches. But there's no hope of our moving back there soon, with Baba and his father still at loggerheads.

Around this time the butcher offers to put us up in his basement garage converted into a flat, and since he's not asking for advance rent, my father jumps at the offer. Mama is at first a little reluctant to move into the same house with the butcher, but she eventually relents.

"After all, it is better to live around a well-to-do thug than a bunch of pimps and drug addicts," she reasons.

The butcher's house is in the same neighborhood where my aunt, Houri, and the coalman live. It is a relatively clean area with lots of old plane trees, and my mother has always dreamed of living in one of those big brick houses.

We stuff the trunk of the Bride with our belongings and tie the bulky pieces up on the roof rack, including the mattresses and quilts. I'm nervous all along the way, worried that my precious money-holder will be blown away. But the Bride safely carries us out of the red light district and finally Baba parks outside the butcher's grand house. We go upstairs to meet him and his wife. His two teenaged sons are away in college in another city.

It is a big house with a spacious living room, stacked with silk carpets of different colors, and hung with a chandelier big enough to light a stadium. Walls and curtains are in a gaudy peach color and the furniture has red velvet upholstery, with gilded arms and legs.

The butcher's wife is a friendly woman, encrusted with layers of jewelry, with two columns of gold bracelets hanging from her thick wrists. Mama is quite intimidated by the loud display of wealth and sits stiffly on the edge of a fancy chair. But Baba acts like he was born to it, and is busy entertaining the landlady, while the butcher and I run to move our stuff into our flat. The butcher looks happy to have his favorite friend close to him and tries to act humble.

He's a strong man and carries the whole bundle of bedding inside, and I walk behind him hauling the moth-eaten rugs. In a few minutes Mama joins us too, and then the butcher's wife. Baba shows up at the very end, faking a backache.

Mama gets embarrassed every time the butcher's wife comes down to visit and has to sit on the frayed rugs. But the landlady doesn't seem to care and the two women become friends soon. The men, too, are chummy as ever, so close in fact that my father has forgotten he has to pay rent, which is due every two weeks. We've been here for a couple months and the butcher has yet to see a single *rial* from us. At first, he acts cool about it, leaving it to my father's sense of fairness.

I've seen Mama worried about Baba's running up debts before, but now she's really mortified about the late rent, especially since the landlords are so nice to us. The butcher brings good treats from his shop and doesn't charge a single *rial*. Meat is no longer a novelty in our house and our stomachs are fuller than they've ever been.

This is too good to last long. When the butcher sees my father shows no intention to pay, or any shame, he becomes alarmed. He throws out subtle hints like: "This month is coming to an end" or: "Time really flies, doesn't it? It's already two weeks." But Baba doesn't hear or feigns ignorance.

Around mid-July, over two months since we moved in, things begin to change. The solid bonding between Baba and his friend becomes unraveled like a ball of yarn. The butcher seems to suddenly realize his pal owes him some money in back-rent and a fortune in overdue debts. First he holds back all privileges: no more evening treats, no more cash handouts and no more faithful laughs at Baba's jokes. He's waiting on an opportunity to recover his money, but the problem is that he can't find my father. Baba either doesn't come home or slips in and out when the landlord is not around.

After a week of evasions, Baba and I accidentally bump into the butcher in the hallway. The big man is full of hurt.

"Is this the way you treat a friend? Is this how you return my favors . . . stabbing your bosom pal in the back?" The landlord eyes well with tears of self-pity.

"I'm so ashamed. I can't even lift my head to look at your eyes," my father says and reaches to kiss him. "Give me until tomorrow and your money is ready."

"Is that a manly promise?"

"It's a supermanly promise."

"Tomorrow" becomes a week, but my father still has his disappearing act. Feeling betrayed, the butcher comes down to the garage with an eviction notice, which we obviously have to ignore. So he comes back two days later to throw our stuff out in the street. Filling the doorway like a monster, he's drunk and his tongue rolls in his mouth like a worm. His cheeks and eyes are flushed red, matching the color of his notorious shirt.

The minute he lays eyes on my mother, with my brother and me hiding behind her, his heart goes soft.

"I could finish off your husband with a deft stab of the knife . . . could slice him to pieces and run it all through the meat grinder," he threatens with a thick tongue, massive arms stabbing and slicing. "I could open up his gut and make a feast for the alley dogs . . . .

"But how can I bring myself to make a widow of a nice lady, and orphans of these lovely children?—children more neglected than any orphan I know. How can I throw your stuff out in the street when there's nothing to throw out?"

"Please, sir. Have patience. He'll eventually show up."

"All right, you can stay. But I'll have to teach that ingrate a lesson. It's not the money, mind you, but the breach of trust, our loyalty pact. He's cheated me and no one does that! He'll pay the ultimate price for it."

The butcher waits a few more days and then makes good on his threats. One day he and his gang trap my father in our quiet alley. I see them just as I come home from school: they're setting on him like a pack of wolves. Baba lies there half-dead on the sidewalk, where the butcher has straddled him, slapping in rapid-fire, with his friends cheering on. I stand back and watch with a bleeding heart, but too scared to act.

I must have looked too miserable because in a minute the thug lets go and swaggers off, with his sidekicks in tow. I take a couple of steps and timidly survey my father in his pathetic state: his shirt ripped, his face smeared in blood and his foot dangling in the gutter. He's teetering on the brink—now lucid, now delirious. My heart aches but I'm afraid to touch him or look closely. I pause for a long moment and then take a good look, as if to make sure it is my father lying motionless, so crushed and humiliated.

His eyes, already purple and swelling, open a crack, a stupefied stare that doesn't recognize me at first. Then, with great effort, he struggles to his feet and staggers toward the door—his shoulders slumped, his legs refusing to work right. It is such a sorry way to see my father, so unlike him and contrary to the invincible picture in my mind. He stumbles a few times and I rush to hold his hand, which he refuses to give at first. Then come more wobbly steps and he keeps

239

bouncing from wall to wall in the hallway, before crumpling to the ground, like an old man losing the grip of his crutch.

I slip my hand under his arm and try to brace him up. As I struggle with his bulk, our eyes meet; and I see the shame, the fear, the need. He looks helpless, blameless, so boyishly innocent, and that fills me with rage, an intense desire for revenge.

I take him inside, spread a futon on the floor and help him lie down, and pull a quilt over him. Mama is not at home, so I get a bowl of warm water and softly wash blood off his face and mud off his arms. He stares at me steadily. There's love in his eyes, gratitude, remorse—feelings normally lost under his big ego. It is as though the beating has shaken loose latent emotions and brought them to the surface. It is as if the cowardly attack has given birth to a new intimacy between us, a new tie sprouting from the rubble of his crushed bones and ego.

ROMANCE

After this incident, Baba swallows his pride and agrees to move back to Grandpa's house. But he still puts on a brave face, promising to eventually get even with his old man. He soon forgets his beating, however—long before his cuts and bruises heal. Once again he is his mischievous self, tearing around the city chasing *houri*s.

So I settle into the old schedule: washing the Bride, giving Baba a bath, and shuttling between the cleaners and the shoeshine stand. Life keeps its usual routine: there is the idiot with his wretched donkey, the barber with his wretched perversion and the rats with their wretched fate in the claws of the cat.

Going back to the old house revives my memories of Houri. I haven't seen her since she came to comfort me with my broken arm—it's been many weeks—I have no idea where she is. She's now constantly on my mind and I miss her terribly. My adventure in Pleasure Land and the disappointing encounter with its tattered whores makes her even more precious to me.

Then, one sultry summer evening, she appears out of nowhere, laughing and flirting as always. She's in skintight pants and a cotton shirt, open to show a skimpy tropical halter.

"Where have you been?" Mama asks.

"Been busy. But my husband is away on assignment now and you'll see more of me."

She peels off her shirt and sits exposing herself unguardedly. Luckily Baba is not around to horn in on my date again and I can have her all to myself. I go to the closet and dig out the package of fishnet stockings, now crumpled and dusty, and wait for the right opportunity.

After dinner, Houri asks my mother if I can walk her home and then sleep over at her house. She doesn't want to be alone with all the freaks on the loose. Many people in our neighborhood bed down on the roof on hot summer nights, and that leaves sleeping beauties like Houri exposed to predators.

Mama has no objection, to my great relief, and we set off together, holding hands and laughing like drunken lovers. Finally! This is the moment I've been counting days for, spending a romantic night with her under the stars.

The air is cooler outside, saturated with moonlight and her sweet perfume. Walking close to her side, I'm a few inches shorter, but I stand on my toes every now and then to appear taller. Like a clingy child, I hang from her bare arm, trying to slow down our progress and make the journey last longer. I take a chance and slide my hand under her shirt and work it up her back and bare shoulders, and then move it down over the curve of her lower waist.

"Young man, what are you doing?" she yells, shaking off my hand.

"Houri?"

"Yes?"

"Do you want to run away together?"

"Run away? Where to?" she giggles. She's taken my hand again and pulls us along with her swaying walk. This late there are only a few men on the street, but Houri makes every one of them turn their heads. Again I try to look as tall as I can—her protector at the very least.

"I don't know. Anywhere: Paris, London, Hollywood—somewhere no one can find us."

"I don't think your mom would like that—or my husband."

"You don't take orders from your husband. You don't love him."

"Who told you that?"

"Everyone knows this."

She stops, alarmed, and turns to face me. "Tell me, what did you hear?"

"That . . . that you married him for money." Suddenly I'm not sure if I ever did hear that.

"Did your mom say something?" Her face tightens and I realize my mistake.

"Oh no—no one said this . . . but it's true, isn't it?"

"That's my business."

"Okay, I promise I won't talk about it . . . but let's go somewhere. I have money."

"Oh? And just how much do you have, Shahed?" She's swinging along again, looking over her shoulder at me. The amusement is back in her voice.

"About ten thousand."

"What?" She shakes her head, "Where would you get money like that?"

"I can't tell you yet. I'll tell you once we're safely away."

We reach her house and she goes to change into a nightgown, and I take the present out of my pocket waiting for her to come back.

"This is for you." I say, holding out the package.

"What's that?"

"Open it!"

"Well, thank you, but what is it for?"

"Because you're so special."

"I am! All right, I'll open it tomorrow. Let's go to bed now. It's getting late."

We climb up on to the roof where rugs and mattresses have been set out under a huge mosquito net draped like a tent. We climb under and she gestures to the bed, looking so soft and luxurious with a brocade cover.

"Time for you to go to sleep, Shahed. I'll be back up in a while." Embarrassed, I don't know if I should take my clothes off in the filtered moonlight, it seems she is smiling at me. Then she's gone. I decide to leave my clothes on, in case I have to protect her. It takes a while before I fall asleep. It's probably past midnight when I wake and hear her gentle breathing. I have an urge to hug her. Slowly, I turn on my side and lean on an elbow, staring at her in the faint light. The small lines around her eyes and mouth have loosened and blended into her smooth skin, and her full lips are more inviting than ever. Cautiously, I put my hand on her leg and let it wander carefully over the silk gown, while remaining alert to her every stir. My heart beats fast and I feel a prickling sensation all over my body, not to mention my *dool* which is frightfully stiff. I have this strange fear that it may blast off like a rocket and blow up in the moonlit sky.

I am totally lost in the act when I notice a huge shadow moving back and forth outside the tent. I jerk my hand back and roll away, my heart beating even faster. Is it a beast coming to violate the sleeping beauty? How am I going to protect her? I freeze for a moment and then crawl over to the tent's flap to take a peek. It is the cuckold, to my dismay, stripping down to his long shorts. I can see a dark mat of hair covering his chest and shoulders. He is walking around the

243

roof, checking out the surroundings. Then he turns and lumbers to the mosquito net like a grizzly bear, his hulk blocking the moonlight and casting a heavy shadow over my sweet dreams. I quickly drop the flap, crawl out to a corner and hide under a thin blanket, waiting for my destiny. In a second, I hear the stomp of his elephant feet and just pray to God they won't land on my back.

I can't see anything and just hear a massive body plop down.

"Houri . . . Houri," he calls a few times, but she just moans, asking to be left alone. It doesn't take long before his snores fill the air, and then I crawl out from my hole and into the night. There's really nowhere to go. I'm too afraid of walking back home alone or staying in that house. I look at the neighbor's roof which is a one-yard drop from ours. No one is sleeping there, so I jump off and move on my hands and knees to a corner by the smoke stack, and there I plunk down for the night.

I wake up just as the sun is coming out. The air is chilly and I'm crumpled into a ball, already sniffling from a cold. The events of the night before come back to me like a bizarre dream hard to shake off. I struggle to my feet and climb the wall onto Houri's roof and sneak past the see-through tent. They're still in bed and the bear still rumbling. I hurry down the staircase into the yard and out the door. Streets are still empty and shops are closed, except for an eatery serving boiled lamb head. It's too early to go back home and I'm not so eager to see the sour look on my mother's face while she waits for her husband to show up. I shake my pockets and there are a few coins. I slip into the eatery and order a lamb tongue and a pair of hoofs. The waiter brings them in a bowl of soup and I settle to eating, trying to make sense of just what happened the previous night.

Saturday
12:00 midnight,

Shahed,

I'm taking the time to write you so as not to be misunderstood later and/or have my words fall on deaf ears. In my emotional state I might spell something wrong, not write in proper English form, or even make sense. I couldn't care less. Find fault somewhere else. I'm very disappointed. Oh, no not in you but in me for being such a fool to put up with your bullshitting for this long. Now that my rose-colored glasses have finally fallen off, I see clearer. I see a child living in a world that demands him to become a man. A boy not willing or able to grow up because he doesn't know the difference between growing up and growing old.

Shahed, you are a frightened killjoy who's not at all interesting any longer. My time is too valuable, too precious to waste babysitting your ever-changing adolescent moods. A while ago you said you didn't want pressures, a serious relationship, or to get married in the next few years. Our relationship has become mundane you said. You said you wanted to be left to yourself. It was your choice and I said o.k. You didn't think I could handle it. But to your dismay I did. But the freedom you so hungered for must have not been all it was cracked up to be. You called me in the middle of the night and cried for me to come back. You said "I made a mistake," you loved me, you didn't really want to go out with anyone else.

Now that you find out I can live my life without you, you are scared. You know I found the right man and we have a bright future ahead of us. We communicate on such a level that we both admit we love each other, how much we need each other. This guy really makes love to me. He's not like you. You don't make love. You masturbate with a generic woman's body. So get this into your head—I'm not home for your 'beckon calls' anymore.

Again, you set my emotions on a roller coaster confusing me and negatively setting off my life. I can't afford to let you do this. I'm not old enough to qualify as your mother or have the patience for you to mature. I know exactly what I want, what I'm looking for with no apologies to anyone. Don't bother dishing out any more of your complements, like "you're so strong, so solid, so full of life." Don't get me wrong, Shahed. They are all appreciated. They helped me grow a lot. But now I've grown so much that I've become unaffordable to you. What I need and obviously what you need are not the same. So go and search for your distant dreams. God be with you.

Mary

WEDDING

About a week after my disappointing night on the roof, we attend a wedding that turns out to be a memorable night for me, if not for the bride. The bride is the coalman's daughter and she's marrying a cousin, someone close enough for the zealot to entrust with his daughter and money. Houri, a friend of the coalman's second wife, is invited to the event and she takes the liberty of inviting Baba, Mama and me. I'm eager to see her. Maybe her husband will really go on an assignment; I plan to offer my protection again.

I love weddings, and even more, the exciting buildup to them. I love the flutter, the mood of expectancy, and the endless gossip: who's the winner in this union, the bride or the groom? Who has the social edge, the better looks, more education, and so on.

Houri comes to see Mama every day with the latest news on the negotiations between the two families: what has already been agreed upon and what needs to be worked out; at what rate the bride price is set and how much gold is going to change hands. I listen to and absorb every crumb of gossip, especially those related to sex, like the bride's fear of losing her virginity. If there's something I don't understand, I run to the barber for explanation.

The excitement reaches its climax on the wedding day, as women rush to get ready on time. At our house, too, there's a whirlwind of activities: first an appetizing session waxing Houri's legs and then visits to the beautician and the dressmaker.

At the beauty salon, I wait a long time for Mama and Houri, but I don't even feel time pass in the bright atmosphere fragrant with perfumes. On a table before me is a stack of fashion magazines, and I go through them all, appreciating the glamorous models. Some of them, the brunette ones, look like Houri and I think she, too, deserves to be there, even on the cover. Every few minutes, I go to check up on her, see how she's coming with her makeover. I stand by her chair, fiddling with the accessories on the counter and giving instructions to the beautician. For an hour Houri has curlers on, sitting under a black hood. I don't like her in that look, but soon she comes out of it prettier than before.

At the dressmaker's, I try to squeeze my way into the fitting room, where Houri is trying on her gown. Mama already has her outfit: a big black maternity dress. She's sitting down fanning herself by the shop window, unaware of my intrusion.

"No!! Don't come in! I'm naked!" Houri shrieks, rushing to shut the door.

For a boy so hungry for love, there's nothing more inviting than hearing this from a woman: *Don't come in, I am naked!* It's like someone closing the gate of heaven in your face. You think—what is she trying to hide from me: what precious secrets of life, what forbidden fruits, what dazzling spectacles?

I pay no attention and push my way in like a maniac. She's in her lingerie, folding her arms, but covering little. I throw my arms around her bare waist and press my face into her chest. She gives a gasp but doesn't seem angry, just lets off muted screams and soft giggles. Like a cat, I brush myself against her, savoring her scent. With no small effort, she finally pries me loose, but doesn't shoo me out.

"You can stay if you promise to be a good boy."

"I promise. Please. Please."

She wriggles into a skin-tight dress of maroon velvet with a slit down one side, and I help to close the back. Then she puts on her high heels and looks in the full-length mirror. There, she stands for a long time striking fashion poses: resting her hands on her hips, keeping her arms akimbo, with a knee forward, or doing pirouettes— as Mama and I stand back flattering her silly.

The wedding party is held that evening in the coalman's spacious garden, surrounded by high walls. A sheet of canvas hangs in the middle, dividing the venue in two parts: one for men and the other for women. Boys under twelve or thirteen can swing both ways, and I'm right on the borderline. Strings of electric lights in white, pink and blue festoon the walls and hang from the trees, brightly illuminating the garden.

Most of the guests have already arrived, sitting around rows of long tables covered with white tablecloths. They're laden with bouquets of flower and trays of pastry and fruits, with precious bananas sitting on top. The bananas are there mainly for decoration, to give distinction to the coalman's party, and people hardly touch them, trying to be discreet. An all-male band plays subdued music in the men's section, but it is loud enough for the women to hear, too.

The coalman himself stands by the door greeting guests as they arrive. He's in his ceremonial best—a funeral dark suit and a white shirt open at the neck, with no tie to be religiously correct. He has washed the soot off his face for the first time since the New Year celebrations, exposing the white stubbles that accentuate his red eyes. He doesn't look so healthy and keeps coughing, deep retching coughs that might be a sign of tuberculosis. Every time a bare-headed woman walks in, he jerks like a dog on a leash and lets loose with a flurry of coughs—but he has enough sense to control his zeal for just one night.

Soon the place is packed with guests, and many more. Those not lucky to be invited are perched atop ledges and surrounding balconies, enviously watching the action below. I keep on the move, eager to take in all the action, mainly in the female section. Women are more fun, singing and dancing to whatever tune that comes from the other side. The male half is cheerless as a funeral. All they do is eat, yawn and talk about business, and I only go there to steal a banana.

A little after ten Houri finally arrives with a regal air, looking magnificent in her shimmering velvet gown and brocaded silk shawl. Her husband, her butler rather, is in tow, walking a few steps behind. The couple has never looked so mismatched, and this seems to be the ultimate puzzle on everyone's mind.

He helps her off with the wrap and stands back dumbly holding it, like a walking coat rack. Freed of the shawl and her escort, Houri roams freely through the garden like a *Nymph of Paradise*, talking to women and flirting with men. She knows no boundaries, respects no taboos, behaving as her whims dictate. In defiance of the coalman's code, she shakes hands with men, even pecking a few on the cheek. I can see the host and his fellow fanatics giving her disapproving eyes—but their outrage pales in the face of the overwhelming admiration for her. As she sashays about, men turn to stare and women point her out to each other. She's the most glamorous of the guests and everyone wants to record a proud moment with her. People line up for a quick snapshot with her, and Houri doesn't let anyone down.

Like a queen of hearts, she shows no haughtiness, allowing herself to be loved and admired.

Before long, her subversive influence catches on and other young ladies follow her lead. Women walk into the male territory and men make an incursion in the other direction. Soon it becomes a mixed party and the divisive curtain falls from so much tugging. The moralists, the bores, the tight-asses get up and leave one by one, in useless protest—and then the real fun begins. The men's band haul their instruments to the dance floor in the women's section, and soul comes back to the party and to the revelers.

Houri is too busy to spend time or even notice me. But I follow her everywhere: to the dance floor, to meet the other guests, and even to the bathroom where she refreshes her make-up. Every time she poses for a picture, I jump right in and spoil it. She's in the limelight and I want part of the glow. But I may be overdoing it at times, because I notice people pointing at me and whispering to each other. Mama keeps telling me to stop being such a pest, but I pay no heed. I'm crazy tonight, drunk with love and happiness.

A car pulls up outside the garden honking steadily, and everyone knows it is my father announcing his arrival. Some children run outside to have a look, and I follow. The Bride is decked out with even more finery and smothered in flowers, ready to parade the "just-married" through the streets after the party.

Baba parks his car right by the entrance, in the glare of light from two tall kerosene lamps, and tips some of the boys to stand watch. He walks in and gets a cold reception from the coalman, who still stands by the door.

"What's the matter, Hajji? You look like you're at a funeral," he says. "This is your daughter's wedding, not a wake. You should have left the soot on and dressed in red, so you could dance like a *Hajji Firouz*."

The coalman gives him a hateful look, followed by a spell of coughs. My father ignores him and his eyes begin searching for Houri, who's sitting a few seats away from my mother, talking to a handsome young man. I realize Mama and her friends have been quiet the whole night. I saw my cousin, Reza, whispering to her earlier, and that makes me a little worried. For a second I wonder if something is wrong . . . but I'm not going to let it ruin my night and run to sit in the empty seat next to Houri before my father takes it. Baba and I may be in for a big fight tonight over our common love.

And here he is, towering over me like a bulldog contending for a juicy bone.

"Move over! Make some room!" he says. He hasn't even greeted my mother before homing in on Houri.

I sit still.

"I said move over!"

I wiggle my butt a little without really moving. He reaches to move the chair and I press my ass down hard to bolt it in place. Then he turns around and drops his butt in the empty space between Houri and me and wiggles to edge me out. Houri's still talking to the young man and misses the struggle she's provoked.

Baba finally makes himself comfortable and skillfully steals her attention from the young man. The guy isn't much of a fighter; he gives up the prize and walks away. Next, my father wants to get rid of me.

"Why are you here, Shahed?" His smile is big but his hand on my shoulder is heavy. "Go play with the kids!"

"I like it here."

"No, this place is for adults."

"I'm not going anywhere. You can't force me."

"Don't talk to your father that way! You should be hanging out with kids your age."

"I don't know any kids here."

We spar for a few minutes and neither side is willing to back down. It is as if we have the nymph between us and are tugging her in opposite directions. I pull and he pulls, he pulls and I pull, until I finally score a point. When the band plays a love song, I grab Houri's hand and drag her onto the dance floor. As we rock slowly, I press my body against hers and enjoy the warm sensation of the touch. It is a long, slow song and I keep tightening my squeeze, as if to reach something deep in her. But she is hardly moving.

"You are kind of rigid tonight, Houri."

"Am I? I don't know," she says with a tired smile.

"I wonder if Baba has told you something."

"Like what?"

"I don't know—some lies to turn you against me."

"What're you talking about?" She moves back and holds my arms away from her. "Are you really twelve?"

"Almost thirteen."

Baba stares with a sly look on his face, flashing a conspiratorial wink every time our eyes meet. That makes me nervous because I know a teasing remark is zooming toward me like a torpedo.

"Nice going, boy," it finally comes when the music ends, loud and clear for everyone to hear. "I didn't know you could dance so well."

"But hey!" he goes on, now louder. "Don't drag it on too long. Let me have a turn, too."

Houri gives a ringing laugh and I turn my back to Baba to hide my embarrassment.

"Why are you blushing?" Houri asks, still laughing.

"I'm not blushing," I say, burying my hot face in her breasts.

"Is that because of what he said?"

"Everyone knows he's jealous," I mumble, "but he could be more delicate about it."

"That's his style." She lightly pushes me away from her and I turn to look at my mother. She is staring hard at us.

"He should be spending more time with Mama . . . look at her, she's sitting there sad and lonely."

"She looks pathetic in that maternity dress."

"I think Baba doesn't deserve a good wife like my mother," I said. "She'd be happier with another husband. I could work on her to get a divorce. But you know what? I'd be afraid of Baba marrying you."

"Where do you get these ideas?" she laughs.

I cooked up another excuse to call Mary: I'd wish her a happy wedding, which was coming up soon. We actually talked awhile, and Mary confessed to feeling confused. Somehow I ended up inviting her to meet in a motel—just casually to talk out misunderstandings and try to stay friends. At first, she didn't want to come, but I talked her into it with a persuasiveness I didn't think I had. Either she fell for my trick or it was something she wanted herself. Perhaps Mary still harbored the futile hope that things could be worked out between us.

Once in the room, I talked about my dreams.

"You should have called me. We're still friends."

"Only friends?" I said, sitting tentatively on the edge of the bed. She sat across from me in a chair, keeping a tense distance.

"What . . . more do you expect to hear?" she said with a deadpan look.

"I don't know . . . when is your wedding?"

"Next week."

"Are you sure you want to go ahead with it?"

She rolled her eyes and her face twisted uncertainly. "Of course. Why?"

"Just curious."

"Look, I already met Joe's father and stepmother. They're such a nice people."

"What about Joe himself?" I stiffened, as if to brace myself for the answer.

"He's nice, too. Why do you ask these questions?"

"Just curious."

"No, tell me. What's in your mind? I want to know. Why did you call me?"

"To wish you a happy future life."

"You're lying." She narrowed her eyes, as if I'd insulted her. There was that anger mixed with doubt I had seen so much from her.

"Okay . . . I also wanted to make sure you're not angry with me."

"What difference does it make now?"

"It does to me. I can't stand to be resented by someone I care so much about."

"You only care for yourself. You called me because you want me to beg you to come back," she went on, "so you can have a chance to reject me again. You know what? You're sick."

"I may be, but I still miss you. I need you, Mary." I stood and reached out to hold her. She held herself stiffly, but didn't resist. I took her hand and eased her over onto the bed, and there I sat with my arms wrapped around her. She felt so soft and fresh, as if I was hugging a long-desired stranger. I was looking to revive those divine moments in the fitting room with Houri, the intense adolescent lust heightened by grand dreams. But a stinging urge for release seized me, something I knew I would later regret. I threw myself on her, kissing her wildly and in a few moments, I burst into a forceful orgasm—a release induced by smell alone, a vague and distant scent.

Panic hit hard and I was unable to breathe freely. I stood up trembling, like a naked child out in the cold. Doubt and fear came back into my heart, followed by the bitter taste of remorse. I felt terrible for reopening the wound of separation, rekindling her doubts, confusing her plans. We were back to where we'd started, and this time the burden of her dependency was even more unbearable. I wanted to drop on my knees and beg her forgiveness, ask her to forget that foolish lapse of judgment, that rude distraction from her straight path to happiness. What I did was plant a hurried kiss on her forehead and rush out the door.

WOOING HOURI

My mother and Houri have been cold to each other since the night of the wedding, for reasons I don't understand. Mama now paints a totally different picture of her former dear friend:

"She's very shallow. All she cares about are looks and style. I'm not sure if she's even read one book in her life, or anything more serious than a fashion magazine.

"Well, of course it's all because of her poor childhood. She desperately wants to get things she was deprived of as a child . . . that's why she submitted to a loveless marriage . . . ."

This is just what Mama says, and I don't give it the slightest credit. She's a woman and any woman tends to be jealous of a nymph. But it doesn't matter. Nothing matters. I have no way to see Houri now and my days are as empty as before, especially since there's no school in summer. It is not that I miss school; I just don't have an excuse to go out and spend all the money. The heat, too, has reached the summer climax and life is unbearable in this cramped house.

One day my father comes home ordering us to pack our bags and get ready to go on vacation, to a mountain resort.

"You're telling me now?" Mama starts immediately with her familiar complaints. "I hate traveling on short notice . . . need more time to get ready."

"You don't have to go if you don't like. I'll go by myself." He says this so quickly she looks at him with a sudden knowing.

"You were looking for an excuse to take off alone, weren't you? That's your new tactic."

"Are you going to sit here and analyze me or go pack?"

She spreads a sheet on the ground to bundle a few mats and blankets, and I stand there to make sure the magic mattress is not included. I don't want to carry all my secret fortune with us to an exposed summer resort. Done with the pathetic bedding, we go down to the basement to pack kitchenware and other necessary stuff. Through it all, Baba just stands there rushing us along, not raising a finger to help, until we're in the car.

"By the way," he says, when the weighted down Bride is primed to hit the road. "I've invited Houri and her husband to join us."

"Why—why did you do that?" Mama turns to him, horrified.

"So we'll have the pleasure of their company. We're meeting them at the resort."

Mama reaches for the door handle. "Then I'm not coming!"

"What's the matter with you?"

"I can't stand that—phony brainless—doll."

"Ah, don't be childish. I thought she was as your best friend."

"Who's my best friend? Houri?—the seductress trying to snatch my husband right under my nose?"

He laughs it off. "Your husband is not one to fall easily for her snare."

"I know you've been sharpening your teeth for her."

"I wouldn't worry about it. Her husband will be there. He's going to watch her like a hawk."

"That's right—like a blind and castrated hawk."

There is one more surprise that Baba doesn't let out until we're well on the road and it's too late to turn around.

"Oh, by the way—I forgot to tell you. Taj is also coming along."

Mama almost hits the roof of the Bride. "What! That ranting lunatic!"

"Yes, he can keep us entertained with his antics and also run errands for you."

"I don't need any help. Please cancel this one. Where is he now?"

"He's at the village looking for a babysitter for his donkey. We'll pick him up on the way."

"Stop right here! I'm hitchhiking back home."

"Come off it. He's not so bad."

"He's dirty . . . stinks like sewer."

"Don't worry. I had him take a bath and put on clean clothes."

"But what about his rotten brain, mister? What can you do about that? What if he has a fit of insanity and attacks vacationers with his donkey prod?"

"I've thought of that one, too . . . brought horse tranquilizers to calm him."

Taj is coming along because Baba needs someone to play his tricks on and make others laugh, and the idiot is a perfect prop with his demented looks and bulging testicles. Taj is also a safe target for pranks. My father makes a punching bag of him and he never gets the urge to hit back as Uncle E does, for example. This way, Baba can steal the show and impress women more.

As the idiot enters the car, Mama gives a shudder of revulsion and closes her eyes, but there's nothing she can do, but suffer in silence. Even with a bath and fresh clothes, the idiot smells worse than a gutter. His beard is as unkempt as a bird nest and his pants are full of holes, with a rip running along the crotch from too much scratching.

Taj climbs into the back with the children and my father empties a bottle of cologne on him to make the smell bearable. Mama speaks not a word throughout the ride, but the idiot keeps my brother and me amused with his bizarre tales about himself and his donkey.

The retreat is a narrow stretch of woods tucked deep into the mountains, running along a roaring river. It's a rare patch of green in a craggy and dry landscape; all through summer, the place is packed with holidaymakers. The garden we check into has a row of furnished cabins on the edge of the river and a cluster of thatched huts out in the back. Houri and her husband rent one of the cabins and of course we go for a low-rent shack: a three-walled log structure finished out with leaves and twigs.

Our hut is a bit far from the river and closer to the road, but still well-shaded and secluded, except for the fact that it doesn't have a door and we're all exposed. Once again I'm glad I didn't bring my mattress along and I compliment myself for being so smart.

Everyone is exhilarated by the change of climate and Mama and I run to unpack the bundles and furnish our shack with the few rugs and blankets we've brought along. We stack up the pillows against the walls for cushions and spread the mats on the floor; once we're done unpacking, I go to scope out the terrain. There's a small playground with a rusty swing and seesaw, and also a recreation hall with soccer and billiard tables—but the latter is more for rich kids. Farther up the road, there's another club offering dance and music classes and courses in horseback riding—that too is for those who can afford it. For the poor folks, there are old muleteers renting out their skinny beasts for rides, and shooting practices at a firecracker-studded board with old air rifles.

At first, I'm a bit self-conscious about our doorless tumbledown shack, where other vacationers can peer in. Every time rich teenagers pass by the hut, I run to hide, ashamed of being associated with our shabby furniture. But soon I get too busy to care any more, with my days full of fun activities.

Every morning, Baba wakes me up early and we go shopping for breakfast at a nearby village. Small shops stand in a row, selling bread fresh out of the clay oven; homemade dairy products crudely packaged but looking healthy and appetizing; and vegetables and fruits piled in bright mounds, filling the air with their scents. By the time we get back, Mama has laid out a *sofreh* on the riverbank, waiting for us to come back with food. We all sit around the spread and enjoy the meal in the cool breeze to the roar of the river and chirping birds. After breakfast, I hang out a little in the playground and then go for a swim, until it is time for lunch. In the afternoon, there's some more splashing, followed by a pleasure stroll with Baba and Houri; in the evening, a riot of fun, games and dance parties around a campfire. By the time we hit the bed, it is way past midnight and we're dead tired. We huddle together in the pleasant chill of the night, sleeping in excited anticipation of more play and fun on the following day.

The outdoor dance parties are the high point of the vacation, with trendy teenagers rocking and twisting to whatever is the rage in Europe and America. These are mostly affluent kids and rather snobbish, but once my father has worked his special charms on them, they accept me as an insider.

Although much older, Baba becomes a fixture, the main center of attraction. He has no problem relating to boys and girls less than half his age. In fact, he prefers their company to those of their fathers, who fritter time away fishing or playing backgammon. He also has his sidekicks: Houri and the idiot.

With the nymph to cheer him on and the idiot to beat over the head, Baba is hilarious as a court jester, entertaining the kids every evening with rough and raucous humor. Taj and his testicles are of course the biggest joke, and my father never leaves them alone.

"His balls have ballooned so large that they put those of his jackass to shame," he says, pointing at the "balloons" with a stick, as in a university lecture. "Watch out for them. They're a sign of his animal sex drive."

257

The kids laugh themselves to tears and before long, they're all addicted to my father's company, chasing him everywhere like a pack of autograph hunters. Baba, too, is never short of ideas for adventure. At times, he takes it a little too far and parents become alarmed. One day he takes his fans on a wild cruise up the mountain road, him leading the way in the Bride, which in spite of the dust is one of the most magnificent things ever seen at the resort. The kids follow on motorcycles, all hooting and shouting like a gang of soccer hooligans. On the way back down, they almost run a car off the road; unfortunately, it's the camp director and the kids get grounded for a day.

I can't always keep up with Baba's energy, but feel proud of him, a man so popular with these arrogant kids. Of course, I would have liked to be popular in my own right, but it still feels good to be the son of an idol.

Even Taj is having a great time. Like a guest of honor, Baba takes him everywhere, and the idiot is more than glad to participate—be it dance parties or bikini picnics on the riverbank. He's temporarily forgotten some Islamic codes, not making too much fuss when women show their hair or take off their clothes.

"This is because of the change of climate," Baba opines. "If he stays here long enough he may even regain his full sanity."

Weeks pass in a flash and we're still having a jolly time. While busy entertaining, Baba is also in amorous pursuit of Houri. He trails her everywhere she goes, on foot or with his eyes, looking for an opportunity to be of some service to her: polishing her nails or rubbing suntan lotion on her back. When she goes out for a solitary stroll, he shadows her like a lovesick Romeo in an Indian movie, hiding behind rocks or tree trunks, nervously shifting routes to fake an accidental encounter. I am shadowing their every step. Baba chases Houri with lust and I chase him jealously. Luckily, she is elusive as ever, constantly ebbing and flowing, blowing hot and cold. She laughs at his jokes and gives meaningful stares and that's about as far as it goes.

Once I hear him whispering to her, during a walk on the river bank. They slip onto a patch of grass and I stand a few yards away behind a tree, pricking up my ears.

"I wish I knew where I stand with you," Baba says. "You're so annoyingly difficult to figure out."

"We're only friends. You know that," she answers while playing with pebbles, in a meditative mood.

He picks up his own pebbles to fiddle with, a little show of sensitivity to impress her: "You're an enigma, Houri. You don't reveal yourself."

"What do you expect me to reveal?"

"It would be nice if you let slip your intentions."

"Intention? There's no particular intention. I'm just trying to be free and have fun."

"I want to discover everything about you . . . the truth, the lies, the mystery."

"You're in a poetic mood again," she giggled, juggling with the pebbles.

"I only bare my poetic side to you."

"Ah, you're such a charmer. What do you want from me?"

"To pin you down, body and soul."

"No one can pin me down."

One early evening, off to buy groceries for Mama to make dinner, Baba and I see Houri wandering bored along the river path. Baba pulls the Bride to a smooth stop so he can give her his best smile.

She leans down and says wistfully, "Where are you off to?" .

"Shopping," my father says. "You want to come along?"

"Of course. There's nothing to do here."

My father turns to me with a look which I understand too well.

"No, I'm coming," I insist, if only to spoil his fun.

"Pooh! You're so clingy!"

Baba opens the door to the Buick, pulls me out, then waves Houri in with a flourish. I look back through the trees at our shack and see Mama staring out at us. I wave and get in the back quickly.

We start along the road and I hope it will take a long time to get to the store. In the back seat, I touch the fall of Houri's hair and sniff for a breath of her perfume. Then, just before we hit the village, Baba swings the Bride into a side road and climbs the hills. We drive up a winding scenic route and in a while come to a grade, where the entire landscape opens out before our eyes. Baba parks and invites Houri out for a stroll.

"You can stay in the car if you don't feel like walking," he says, leaning against the door so I can't open it.

259

"No, I'm coming." I scramble to the other side and jump out.

The lovers walk ahead and I follow like an unwelcome chaperone. Houri looks gorgeous in her blue top and white pants. Her silky hair is gathered behind her neck and held together with a clip, exposing the sexy sunburn on her slim shoulders. My eyes are fixed on her hips swaying gracefully and my father's hand hesitantly straying above.

They move on silently and his hand grows more restless, until it finally settles on hers, clasping it tight. Houri pulls away and turns to look at me with a blush. Baba changes tactics; he runs to a bush and plucks a rose, coming back to slip it into her hair, while licking his pricked thumb.

Houri turns redder and lets a sigh of exasperation. Baba turns to me with an accusing look and signals to me to get lost. I ignore him. He is about to thrash me when he sees a man pulling a mule with a rope along the path. "Hey Shahed, here is a horse for hire. You want to go for a joy ride?" he says, pointing at the mule with hollow rib-cages and sad eyes.

"No, that animal looks too miserable to take it for a ride."

"Don't be a bore. What's wrong? Are you afraid?" he says to provoke me.

"I'm not afraid of anything," I answer, looking down in disgust.

"Don't worry, it won't kick. Come here, I'll help you mount."

Before I can object, he puts me up on the beast and it ambles off into the thick forest.

It turns out to be a lousy ride. The mule is too lazy and stubborn and pauses at every step to sniff at grass. The earth under his hoofs is moving faster than us. The sun is sinking behind the mountain and the sky is turning darker. I'm scared and a little angry, too, for being tricked into going on this ride. I want to head back, but the mule doesn't take any orders, refusing to move in any direction. I give it a few slaps across the neck and some pokes in the ass with a stick, but it is all in vain. Frustrated, I slide off the beast and set off on foot, leaving the animal there to do as it damn pleases.

It's getting dark fast, with the sky blotted out by thick forest leaves. I pick my way through thorny bushes, stooping under low branches, zigzagging sharply to sidestep lizards and tiny snakes, or whatever it is that skitters away from my feet. But the trail seems to lead nowhere and panic sets in. I scream out for my father a few times, but there's no response. The only sound to be heard is birds chirping and distant howls of dogs or jackals.

Maybe an hour later I come to a clearing, and there I find them lounging on a hollow log, lost in what looks like an amorous act. Baba is pawing her like a cat, and she makes only a half-hearted effort of defending herself. It must have been an intense struggle, as his shirt has come loose and her hair undone; the rose has lost all its petals. Her face is tense and forbidding and she is twiddling nervously with her ring. Then her gaze falls on me. She shoots up to her feet and shakes her clothes. My father, too, turns to look at me. "Where have you been, Shahed?" he snaps. "We've been looking for you all over."

I just stand in silence.

"Why do you look at me like that? I said where the hell have you been?"

"Come here!" For an instant, Baba looks astonished. "I—I want to talk to you," I say, surprised myself at the role reversal.

He ambles over coolly, and once we're out of Houri's hearing, I let loose with a hoarse cry of pain.

"What do you think you're doing carrying on with a married woman? She's taken—didn't you know that? And your wife is waiting for the groceries to cook dinner."

He pops his eyes wide, feigning shock.

"Excuse me?"

"This is immoral . . . unfair . . . You must stop it now!"

He bursts into a guffaw. "Ha-ha . . . ha-ha . . . what's the matter, little fellow? Are you jealous?"

"Hell no . . . I'm angry."

"Ha-ha . . . ha-ha . . . ," the laughter echoes through the valley. "Don't you think she's a little too old for you, a tough chew for your baby teeth?"

"Why did you have to choose her? There are lots of whores you could have taken up with. Why can't you leave her alone?"

A sob rips out of me—I have to turn away from him. That triggers another burst of guffaws, followed by the bitter truth I'd hoped not to hear.

"I 'm afraid . . . ha-ha . . . my little fellow . . . ha-ha . . . you had your chance and you blew it. Now, if you don't mind, I'll have a crack at her . . . ha-ha . . ."

He spins on his heel and swaggers off in her direction.

After months in the grim world of fundamentalist rule, I had found there were few left who could remember the turbulent history of one small family. I still clung to the notion that I should find out who had betrayed the young Shahed, but who was there to help me understand the loss that scarred my heart? My mother enshrined my father's memory with blind loyalty, my brother's selective amnesia was all too understandable . . . Hajji and Grandma, nosy Khaleh, the butcher, the barber, and even the relentless dwarf Khan were dead.

My increasingly listless searches took me through streets I had walked with Houri. I realized that unconsciously I had been hoping to find her, wanting to feel again the heated excitement of touching her silky skin, hear her bold laugh, watch her electrify a room of staid couples. I longed for a breath of her musky perfume in the sere air of Tehran.

I began to look for her everywhere, curious to know how her beauty had stood up to the test of age and the mullah's purges. But she was either not around or unrecognizable in the mandatory veil. There were rumors: she'd been hanged . . . she'd fled the country . . . she was hospitalized with severe depression . . .

I asked my aunt about it when I visited her.

"She and her husband escaped to Switzerland just in the nick of time, before the borders were closed . . . her husband had salted away a lot of embezzled money in Swiss banks . . . their house was confiscated and is now occupied by war-displaced refugees."

How smart of the cucumber, I thought. At least he had the sense to stash his ill-gotten hoard in a safe bank, not in a mattress!

"I heard your other neighbor, the coalman, is dead?"

"Yes, he died a long time ago. His sons are now living here with their wives and children. The mansion was torn down and converted into apartment flats. One of his sons fell martyr though, and another lost his leg . . ."

My aunt's once elegant garden was also broken down into two separate quarters with cheap marble façades, one of which was occupied by her stepson Reza, and his wife and children. Reza had grown out of his wildness and become wrapped up in domestic cares and the

262

hustle for money. He'd inherited his father's carpet business but was blowing it because he also inherited his opium addiction.

Aunt Fatima was in black, still mourning her brother and also her father, who'd died more recently. She looked shorter and a lot wider, the thick hair on her head turned silver. But the warmth and generosity had endured and she never stopped weeping for joy while I was there.

Uncle E was stuck in a bedroom, confined with severe Alzheimer's, losing all contact with earthly or extraterrestrial beings. I visited him briefly in his dim room and he just stared at me vacantly. His white mane of hair had thinned to threads. His rosy cheeks had dried. Death was certainly around the corner.

I looked around the house. There was no sign of the romantic ambiance: the sun-raked parlor, the soothing voice of Nat King Cole, and the aroma of opium and charcoal. The persimmon and pomegranate trees had been uprooted and the cold little room where I hid to spy on feasting women had been razed from the corner of the yard.

"Auntie, there's one more thing." I said while we stood by the patient's bed.

"What, my love?"

Suddenly I found it hard to breathe. "My father . . . your late brother . . ." To my chagrin, I was losing control. My voice choked, tears burned my eyes.

"God bless him." She pulled me into her arms and kissed me, a noisy kiss coming from the depth of her heart. "I know . . . we all miss him . . . What a man!"

I wiped my face with my coat sleeve. "How close were you really to him, Aunty?"

"As close as he let me be. You know he was too self-centered . . . responded only to his impulses. Of course I tried to talk to him many times, but he never took my advice seriously."

I glanced at Uncle E, my one-time prey. He lay there flat, eyes tilted upward, chest flat—no wad of cash stuck up his shirt pocket.

"Did . . . Baba ever talk to you about Grandpa's stolen money?"

"Oh, son, don't mention it. You were just a little kid. The devil crept under your skin and you were too defenseless."

"That's not what I mean, Aunty. Did he ever talk about it—tell you anything else?"

"Yes, I cornered him when I saw you with those terrible bruises. He said he was very embarrassed. He wanted to make sure you wouldn't do it again. But the punishment he gave you was too severe. It still makes my heart bleed to think about it."

"But—did he tell you he stole the stolen money from his own son? I wonder how he justified it."

"No, Shahed, but . . . to be honest, I suspected the same thing." She took my hand and looked up. Her old face was filled with compassion for me, her own eyes had tears. "But what's the use of lingering on it? Wash resentment out of your heart. Try to forgive, my love. Forgiveness is the answer."

By the time we get back it is late, and my mother's worried sick. The teens have camped outside our shack waiting for my father. He ignores them and thumps right into bed. Houri, too, disappears quickly to avoid Mom, joining the cuckold who's snoring away in their cabin. As soon as her husband falls asleep, Mama calls me out for interrogation, but I evade all the questions, refusing to give her a shoulder to cry on again.

Early the next day, Houri leaves the resort with her husband, before she can face Mama and answer for her whorish behavior. My father, too, says he has to go back to the city to "tidy up" his business, promising to come back in a few days. Before Mama can object, he's out the door with his stooge in tow.

With Baba gone, the wheels grind to a halt at the resort and it gets too quiet. His young pals go on their own way and I never get invited to their parties. All day there's nothing to do but sit on the riverbank and juggle pebbles, or watch old men fish for trout. A few times, my brother and I try to amuse ourselves with card games, but it is no fun with just the two of us and we end up bored and fighting each other. All day we go around nagging to Mom, and there's nothing the poor woman can do to cheer us up.

I rather miss Houri, though not as much as my father and his wild games. After the incident at the forest she kind of fell from my eyes, but her thoughts haven't totally dropped out of my mind. I think she should be given another chance. I didn't even see her kissing my father. Two dull weeks pass and still no news of my father. We're running out of money to pay for food and rent and Mom's worried to death. The fall season, too, is approaching and our neighbors pack and leave one by one to get ready for their children's school. Soon the resort becomes deserted and takes on a gloomy look.

Around mid-September, a chill wind blows from the north, bringing thick clouds and scattered rain. Our thatched hut is no shelter from rain and cold, and with leaves turning yellow and falling, we're more exposed to the elements of nature. Every other night we wake up to the thud of raindrops on the roof and rush in panic for cover, only to remember it doesn't exist. We've come on this trip ill-prepared, with just a few blankets to keep us warm. At night, we feel the chill to our bones and there's only our warm breath under a thin quilt. There's also no telephone to announce our distress. We're hopelessly stranded in the middle of nowhere.

Feeling sorry for us, the director of the camp and his wife offer to shelter us in their house until my father comes back. But Mama is too proud to accept, already too embarrassed over the late rent. So the couple stops insisting and just gives us extra blankets to hold off the night cold.

Two more weeks drag by and there's still no sign of my father. Mama has absolutely freaked out and never stops cursing her husband.

"Even a wolf wouldn't do this to its cubs, leaving them alone in the middle of nowhere to fend for themselves," she sighs, pacing the hut and wringing her hands.

Then she turns to me: "I'm mostly worried about your school. A long absence could kill what little desire you've got for studying."

Another thing she's obviously worried about, but doesn't speak of, is her delivery, which is approaching fast. With no doctor or midwife around to help, I may have to perform my first medical procedure.

Mama now sees things in a bad light and cries for no reason. Like a cat, she jumps at every sound. Whenever the rare car comes up the road, she runs out to see if it's the Bride pulling up.

One day she sends the landlord to the city for some news of her husband. Two days later the old man returns empty-handed. Mama is then utterly desperate:

"I know why he doesn't show his hide. He doesn't have money to pay for rent. In other word, he's hocked us. I guess I'm going to give birth in a pit, like a stray dog."

One day a severe storm lashes through the valley and rain comes in torrents, filling the river and flooding its banks. We're having a cold skimpy dinner in our hut when there's a crash, followed by jagged streaks of lightning. Then all the heavens crack wide open and water pours down in buckets through the threadbare roof, soaking everything inside. We quickly roll up our possessions into a couple of sheets and wait for the rain to slacken, then hoist the bundles onto our shoulders and squelch through mud and dead leaves toward the landlord's house.

Mama waddles ahead like a duck, holding the bundle in an awkward clutch. At one point she slips and sinks up to her ankles in the mud, and I fear that is the end of the baby. Then I see the landlord and his son looming through the downpour—a pair of angels. They pull Mama free and carry our mud-covered loads to their house. The landlady is filled with pity to see us in this miserable state and puts her foot down for us to move in. Mama is not so stupid as to refuse this time.

A couple days later my father finally shows up, when the weather is fair, as usual. His smile beams widely, as if nothing has happened. He just doesn't see his wife's furious glances. His back is turned on her and he's talking passionately to the landlord and his son about his adventures in the city.

"Lots of things are happening. New fancy buildings are going up every day. You people are wasting your time here, missing out on all the fun and action."

"Really! Tell us more," the son says, wide-eyed.

"I will later. Now we have to run."

Baba takes a thin fold of banknotes out of his pocket and hands it to the landlord.

"This is for you. I really appreciate all you've done for my family, taking them under your wings while I was away."

"No problem. It was my duty," the old man says shyly and starts counting. In a moment his face sets into a surprised grimace.

266

"Is . . . this all?" he beeps out hesitantly, as he counts once again. "This is short."

"I know—ha!—I know—it's not all of it," Baba responds with dismissive laughter. "Keep this for now and I'll soon come back with the rest."

"We don't really deal on credit here." The landlord frowns but I can tell he's no match for Baba.

"I know, Hajji, and that's why we're not taking everything with us. We'll leave some stuff as collateral."

"What can you leave as deposit? I'm sure it won't be gold?"

Baba pats the landlord's back and laughs: "You don't have much choice, Hajji. You either accept that or get to keep my family here longer . . . ha-ha-ha."

FUNERAL

We return to the city and the autumn air is as hot and polluted as a summer day. Our house, already under-furnished, is bone bare, as if gnawed by hyenas. After hitting bottom, Baba has sold everything around the house he could turn into cash, including the worm-eaten rugs my mother had tenaciously guarded. With no rugs, and no blankets, which we have left in hock at the resort, there's nothing to sit on but newspapers and mattresses, one of which I'm using as a safe. Mama wants to prepare something to eat, but there's not even a pan to fry an egg in.

We have a light meal of bread, watermelon and Bulgarian cheese and then everyone retires for a nap under the ceiling fan whirring away. With all the windows curtained off to give Baba a peaceful rest, the house has become dark and quiet. I putter about the room looking for something to do, but there's nothing and I grow more restless. After a long vacation, even one that has gone awry, our matchbox of a house feels more cramped and depressing. I think of going for a walk, but it's too hot outside and streets are empty on Friday afternoon, the holiest time of the week. The only thing left is go to the basement and check up on the cat.

I skip downstairs and before reaching the basement, a foul smell, the awful stench of death and rot hits my senses. I descend deeper and turn the switch on and there, in the dim yellow light, I find the decaying corpse of the cat, circled by grisly remains of several rats. While away, we'd left the feline to survive on a diet of rats alone, but that must have been too poisonous even for her.

I stand back staring at the nauseating scene, until the smell becomes unbearable. I'm sweating like a horse, unable to breathe. Suddenly, hit by a panic attack, I turn and shoot up the stairs, heading out the door and onto the street.

Our neighborhood is a ghost town on a Friday afternoon—deserted, forlorn, and depressing. Not a single soul is seen around and the hum of flies is the only sound to be heard. Shops have pulled down their gray shutters, adding to the desolation. I walk up the dusty pavement under the blazing sun, past the coal warehouse, the bath-house and the mosque—which has also given in to languor, silencing its *azan*.

Further up, Taj is slumped against a wall, resting. By his side, the donkey cart is laden with rotten cantaloupes and watermelons, drawing swarms of flies but no customers. The idiot keeps slicing the melons and eating them himself, drooling on his shirt and spitting the seeds out in long arcs. A short distance away, two mangy dogs are passionately entangled, with all the lust they can muster in the furnace heat. Taj has spotted them. He shoots to his feet, grabs his spur and sallies forth. As he approaches, the dogs let out frightened howls and try to pull apart so they can make a run for it. But the idiot is upon them, and brings down the prod in repeated thrusts.

"No sins allowed here, shameless beasts. No sins!" he screams.

I keep walking and find myself drawn to my aunt's decent neigh-borhood, longing for her lush garden and her loving hospitality to give me a break from the gloom. Closer to her house, there's a commotion. Men in black are carrying a coffin on their shoulders, chanting "There's no God but Allah." Death notices are all over the walls, with a black-and-white picture of the coalman peeking out from a corner.

The pallbearers parade the coffin, a trunk of rough plywood fit for packing coconuts, and then take it to the coalman's mansion, finally setting it down in the garden in holy display. Mourners pay their respects and take sweets passed out by the family. The gate is wide open and I take a look inside. The garden is rich with romantic asso-ciations for me, recalling my drunken tango with Houri on the night of wedding. The zealot lies peacefully in the box, wrapped in a spot-less white shroud, not a speck of soot on his face; he looks healthier than he did when he was alive.

Some of the mourners get carried away with grief, most of all the deceased's second wife, the queen of his harem. She loses herself so completely that her veil slides off her head, exposing a mat of hen-naed hair. I half expect the coalman to spring up and drag her down under with him, meting out one last holy punishment before bidding farewell.

I get home just in time to wash the Bride. While sweeping the inside of the car, I come upon a ring: a loose diamond ring that Houri had fumbled with out in the forest. I quickly pick it up and shove it in my pocket before Mama can see and throw a tantrum. I think about giving it back, but decide it's mine for keeps.

Baba takes off for the evening and doesn't come home three nights in a row. He must think that Mama has been hardened by those lonely weeks out in the resort and won't mind his short absences. Surely, he's acting strange nowadays and Mama is convinced there's a "new whore" in his life, and that it is certainly Houri.

So she's been seeing a lot of her clairvoyant advisor. So far her medicines aren't having any effect. This new whore is even tougher to dislodge. Nevertheless Mama still has hope and we're going there again today, to give it double push. It is not just Houri's tentacles we need to unclasp. The butcher, too, has popped back into our lives, the mentor for decadence. Baba is definitely out carousing with his nasty friends and mistresses.

Off to see the mystic, we pass by the pawnshop down the street, where Baba auctions off our belongings. Mama is tired already and stops to lean against the window. Her swollen belly pushes out the chador she's taken to wearing because nothing else is big enough. She realizes she's staring at her shabby rug, and pain crosses her face. She shakes her head and sighs nostalgically, as if mourning a dead son. I take her hand and pull her away.

The mystic lives deep in the slums in a filthy alley, bisected by a shallow gutter. We give the knocker a tap-tap and a sour-faced old woman comes to the door. She's just a sack of bones wrapped in a creased skin, with shags of hennaed hair sticking out of her headscarf. We follow her down into a dingy basement, where she sees her clients. Weird concoctions sit around in sooty tin bowls, like love potions to feed to unruly husbands like my father. We sit cross-legged on the cement floor and Mama pours out her sad story. The witch hears it all coldly and then hobbles off to a side room, where bins of herbs are stored. From one of the bins, she scoops herbs into a cone of newspaper and walks back to hand it to my mother.

"Feed him this and *Inshallah* you will have your husband back," she says and then pulls an amulet out of a tin box beside her. "Take this, too. Hide it under his pillow every night."

"From your mouth to God's ears," Mama says. "How long will it take before I see results?"

"It depends. Change will come gradually. First he will start coming home early and then he'll lose all interest in women."

"All women? You mean even his wife?"

"Don't be a fool, woman. Why do you even want to sleep with a man like him? You've got more important things to worry about, like raising your children."

"You're right," Mama seems ashamed. "May you see rewards for your good deeds."

While waiting for her husband to be lured back to the straight path, Mama is banging on every door to sign me up at school. But the principal won't accept me on credit again and wants the whole tuition in advance. That's unthinkable because Baba can't come up with that kind of money, at least not for his son's education. So Mama has no choice but to settle for an inferior public school. We go to the one nearest to our house, but it is so dirty that she doesn't want to set foot there at first.

In any case, they refuse to take me in so late in the school year, no matter how much my mother begs. We try another one, and they too give us the same answer. So there's nothing to do but wait for a miracle. Once again I'm tempted to tap into my bank and finance the tuition, but think better of it. I may be thirteen, but I'm not stupid.

I knew Uncle E didn't have much more time to live when I visited Aunt Fatima and saw how wasted he was, bedridden with Alzheimer's. Three days ago he finally gave in to the inevitable and bid farewell. But at least he outlived my father, his bitterest rival. What the old fox didn't get though was the splendid last rites extended to my father. From what I heard from Aunt Fatima, far more people had shown up for Baba's funeral, and the event eventually turned into a political rally against the Shah—a common occurrence in those days.

As his coffin was being paraded through the street, Taj, his loyal stooge, ran ahead shouting slogans, blaming the embattled monarch for his master's death. He acted as if my father was a hero, an icon, a martyr. But if he was a hero, it was to his fair-weather friends and grasping mistresses.

271

The idiot himself died a few months after, either out of grief for his idol or disillusionment with the revolution. The revolution and its rotten fruit must have proved too far removed from his vision of utopia. It was either too potent or too diluted for his demented taste.

Uncle E's memorial service was held at the mosque in my old neighborhood. The building was even more decrepit than I'd last seen it, eroding faster than the faith of its worshippers. But it's crooked dome still rose stubbornly, refusing total ruin or renewal—just like our repressive traditions.

I stood by the door with my cousin Reza, who welcomed male mourners and accepted their condolences. They were mostly older men, their faces deliberately set in sorrow, all fingering prayer beads and mouthing prayers. By the entrance was a makeshift shrine erected to the deceased, hung with religious trinkets and ablaze with colored light bulbs: a glittery image of the nirvana Uncle E's soul had taken off to. Inside the mosque, men went around offering dates and sweet pies, as if to make the taste of grief more palatable.

"It's good to see you, Shahed, after so many years," Reza said once all the guests were inside and Qu'ran verses began to ring out.

"My condolences to you. Your father never thought he'd die one day."

"Yes, he was full of air. You are the one who deserves condolence. It was your father who left a vacuum with his departure."

"Reza, do you remember those feasts, when we sneaked in to see the women?"

For a moment his face softened, his lips parted as if to speak. Then he smiled cynically, baring his rotten teeth. "No, cousin, I don't . . . Life's hardship has wiped all sweet memories from my mind."

"But—do you remember when you took aim at the donkey's penis?"

"Which one? I took out many donkey pricks, as many as sparrows."

"Have you heard from Houri recently? Do you know what happened to her?"

"Who . . . that whore? Not after your father knocked her down. What a man! Really!"

272

HOLY VIRGIN

The miracle finally happens one day, and my father stumbles upon an unexpected fortune, coming from an unlikely source: his father. Grandpa has stepped into a big mess and is desperate for help.

The whole thing started when his darling son came back from Europe on summer vacation. Turned into a Don Juan with long hair and film star sunglasses, he's been tearing around the city seducing gullible young women, and using our house as a love nest while we were gone on holiday. He knocks scores of girls out of their virginity, drops them, and gets away with it, but then he runs into this "bitch" who isn't so disposable.

My uncle actually met the leech through my father. She's the younger sister of the butcher's mistress. If you ask me, Baba set them up intentionally to get his brother in trouble and then shake down his old man. You know, I wouldn't put anything past my father. At first Baba wanted to show off his cosmopolitan brother, but he ended up framing both him and his father.

Anyway, they go out one night on a triple date: the butcher and his mistress, Baba and his new concubine, and my uncle with his new date. I heard all this from cousin Reza, who is shadowing his uncle as before.

The bitch never lets go of my uncle's arm, and they go over to our empty house and make out, perhaps even on my treasured mattress. This is repeated over several nights and then the leech comes up with her ultimatum:

"You have ruined forever my chances of finding a good husband. Come on, marry me right away or I'll sue." This is what she said according to Reza.

Whether it's true or not, she also claims to be pregnant by my uncle, refusing to settle for anything less than a solid marriage, backed up by a bride price equal to her weight in gold.

So Grandpa is absolutely desperate, willing to kiss the hand of anyone who can pull him out of the mess—even his "good for nothing" son's.

A couple of weeks after we return from vacation, Hajji comes to our house, despondent and weary as a defeated soldier. He has none of the aggressive look he had the day he came looking for the thief. His head is hanging and his face has aged even more. The wad of handkerchief is in his hand, and he keeps wiping sweat and tears. I can't help thinking: What goes around comes around.

"What scares me the most," he whimpers in a cracking voice. "is the court junction stopping my son from leaving the country. This has dashed my hopes of having a doctor-son."

"So, what do you expect me to do?" Baba asks. They are sitting on our last two cushions around a meager tea laid out by my mother. The feudal lord has been wise enough to avoid any mention of stolen money, and Baba's playing the role of devoted son.

"You speak the language of whores. You know what the bitches want." Grandpa shows his usual level of tact. "I know nothing about the evil ways of the city and the sophisticated tricks of street sluts."

"You've cursed me all my life for chasing my dick, and now it's suddenly an asset?"

"Sinners may come in handy one day, too," Grandpa says, looking down at the floor, covered with a blanket in the absence of rugs.

Baba doesn't argue and instead recognizes the air is thick with opportunities. He voices solidarity with his old man, but does anything he can to scare the hell out of him.

"This is a holy big shit laid at your door, Hajji. You ought to prepare yourself for the worst."

"What do you mean the worst?" The old farmer is getting alarmed. "Be clear."

"I know this bitch and I know her mother," Baba says, putting a steadying hand on his father's shoulder. "This woman can make your life miserable. She'll stop at nothing to get what she wants."

"Like what?" Hajji asks, horrified.

"I know the mother is already feeding her daughter like a pig to fatten her and get more gold out of you."

"Oh Lord! What am I supposed to do?"

"To be honest, I don't know. This is no slap on the wrist. The 'light of your eyes' has committed a horrible crime: deflowering a virgin and knocking her up. I'm not really sure I want to get involved." Baba gets up slowly, and goes to stare out the window, like he's trying to decide if he should take on a national crisis.

274

"Please. You're my only hope. I have no one else to turn to."

"I know, I know. And I do want to help . . . but . . . okay, I'm going to have to think about this," Baba says with a sigh. Then he goes to get dressed to prepare for his evening out.

"Please don't leave me alone in this!" Grandpa calls out. "My whole reputation is at stake."

"Your reputation!" Baba yells back. "Wait until all the shit comes out. You haven't even seen a fraction of it."

"Oh, God! I can never live down this shame." Grandpa says, on the verge of tears. "What did I do to deserve this? Accursed be those who brought this wretched fate upon me."

Baba waits a few days to let his father sink deeper into despair and then he and I go to see him at the farm with some bad news, and the glimmer of hope only he can provide. The old man has come down with the flu, looking even weaker than last time, and has wrapped himself in a thick quilt, constantly drinking tea.

"I don't want to scare you, Hajji," my father says as soon as he steps in the door, trying to look pessimistic, "but things are more complicated than I thought."

"What is it? Tell me!" Hajji sniffles.

"It turns out that the girl is married—separated from her husband but still not officially divorced. Do you know what this means? Adultery! And you know damn well what they do to you for adultery in a Muslim country."

"Oh Lord! What a disgrace! Rue the day I planted his seed. He's no longer my son. I'll disown him, cut him out of my will," Grandpa says, punching the air with a thick finger for emphasis.

"Good. I'm glad you finally see who's been a true son to you."

Hajji tries to grasp this idea. "You're right. He's worse than you. So, what should I do now?"

"Nothing. You need an out-of-court settlement. But let me try and get a feel for what they want . . . how much they hope to reap off this scandal."

"All right, you have my full trust. I'll leave it all to you."

"No problem." Baba's got the old man right where he wants him. "I'm going to need some money to launch the case," he says smoothly.

"What do you need money for?"

"To pay my way around—you know nothing works in this country without bribes."

"Who do you have to pay?"

"People at the court, the guys pulling strings—I need to persuade them to bend the rules a little in our favor."

"How much do they want?" Grandpa is swaying weakly from side to side.

"I have no idea yet. Leave a couple thousand with me, just in case."

"Two thousand!" he throws off the blanket. "I—I don't have that kind of money!"

"How much do you have, Hajji?"

"Right now? Not—even a thousand."

"That won't cut it. Make it fifteen hundred at least."

"A thousand is all I've got, counting every *rial*," Hajji says, pulling his pockets inside out to prove it.

My father pockets the money and we drive off, promising to return soon with happier news. He immediately drops me off at home and disappears. Days later he shows up with a tan. He has obviously been out vacationing at a seaside retreat instead of working on the case. The minute Baba arrives, his wife corners him to ask for money for herself, as if for a ransom to keep her mouth shut in front of Hajji.

"Don't worry," Baba says. "A big fat load of money is coming our way soon. Just be patient."

He doesn't go to see his father, though; then Grandpa shows up, demanding news on the case. He still looks weak, and climbs the stairs with slow steps instead of thundering up as before.

Baba studies the old man and takes a long drag of his cigarette. "Sorry it took so long, Hajji, but you know it's hell cutting through the red tape in this country. I've been running out in the sun like a dog, trying to push this damn case for you. The good news is that I finally made a dent."

"How far did you get? Tell me quickly!"

"The women seem to be ready to settle."

"Good! How much do they want?"

"Not all that much—about five thousand."

"Five thousand! You think I'm sitting on a treasure trove? No, I'm not paying that kind of money. I don't even have it."

"Don't be a tight-ass, Hajji; you want to be out of this jumble you must cough up."

"No, I won't pay! Let them fight it."

"Suit yourself, but there will be hell to pay. You know I'm no amateur at this business. I've knocked around quite a lot. And I'm warning you, these women are pure venom, lethal as they come."

Grandpa mops sweat off his brow. "Okay, let me think about it."

"Hajji, there's not much time for thinking. The enemy is ready to pounce and I can't hold them off forever."

The old man shakes his head in disbelief, then takes his wad out and unfolds it with trembling hands.

"Hajji, your hands shake like you're opening a human heart."

"This is no time for jokes. Here, take this, but I'll be damned if I'll pay a *rial* more."

Baba must not have taken the vow seriously because he's back to see his father the next day asking for more. By now Grandpa is getting suspicious.

"You take me for a fool, don't you?"

"Hajji! Why do you say that?"

"You know damn well why. This is starting to look like another of your swindles."

"Let me set you straight on something, Hajji. I'm not making a single *rial* in this. I'm just doing it to help my kid brother."

"Like hell you are."

"Hey, wasn't it you who came crying for help? Alright if you don't need me, then goodbye."

"This is no help. You don't know the meaning of the word. You're milking me dry."

"You want your problems fixed—you have to loosen the strings. I know this little romp your sweetheart had is costing you a lot."

"I won't pay. That's final!"

"Then you're on your own. I'm not begging you to let me help you," Baba says and makes for the door.

"Wait! Don't turn your back on me, please. All I'm saying is . . . why do we have to pay again?"

"This one is for an abortion."

"What!" Grandpa snaps out. "You want me to pay to end a human life? Never!"

"Hajji, don't try to look like a virgin to me. I know where you come from," Baba responds, arching his eyebrow. "Your darling son knocks up a girl and you expect others to pay to get rid of his bastard?"

"There's no way I'll stoop to such a sin."

"You talk like you have any choice. Do you know what it means to have a bastard in the family?" Baba says, pausing for it to register. "Try to be reasonable, Hajji. Paying a few thousand won't kill you, but imagine the bitch making a claim on your whole estate, using the child as a lever. You'll be finished. You'll be camping out in the streets."

A look of terror comes to Grandpa's face and he breaks into a stutter.

"I . . . I don't know what to do . . . don't know what the hell to do." Silence, then, "Okay, how much?"

"Speaking off the cuff, three thousand."

"That's a lot.

"Pooh. Hajji, you really don't get it, do you? Abortion won't really be the end of it. We'll have to pay the bitch up to sew herself up too."

"Sew what?"

"Her cunt, so her mother can pass her off as a virgin. You know no man wants a used wife. They all want zero mileage."

This last is utterly beyond Grandpa. He shakes his head and lets a puff of air.

"Okay, here's five hundred. Take it and don't come back again."

"You must be joking, old man. You can't even get a baby circumcised with five hundred."

"That's all I have."

"Raise it to two thousand and I think we have something to make a deal with."

Baba is quite happy with his profit. The money he squeezes out of his father keeps him afloat for a while and even pays my tuition. The principal is more than happy to take me back, even so late in the year.

At school, there's a lot to catch up on—studies as well as treats at the cafeteria. It takes a few weeks before I get back in the groove, but then I go at it ferociously. The school environment revives my appetite for good food and I go on a frantic bout of shopping, until I run out of the small notes. I tap into the cache for a few big orange notes, but they are not so easy to pass off for a boy of my age. So I decide to lay low for a while until the opportune time.

The news came as a shock, although I thought I was accustomed to tragedies, always waiting for one to happen. Mary died in a car crash while driving her orange VW—her first car, one of her big dreams that had come true. The impact was brutal and her car was crumpled into a ball of scrap, like all her ambitions. The van that hit her was driven by a diabetic patient prematurely released from hospital. Once again, she was in the wrong place at the wrong time, just like the day she met me.

Grief and guilt flooded my heart. I crawled around the room, biting into anything—shoes, carpet, books—trying to ease the pain and hold onto my sanity. When I calmed down a little, I sat amidst the rubble and called Mary's aunt to offer my condolences, but more to hear that I wasn't to blame. Laura hung up the phone in anger, and when I called again, it was Bill who answered. He threatened to kill me if I called again or dared to turn up at the funeral. "You're the one who killed her," he yelled, and I couldn't agree more.

Mary would have been alive had I gone along with her wishes and married her, if I had a trace of that self-negation my mother knew so well. So I was guilty, guilty of denying happiness to a woman who so deserved it. I was guilty of hanging onto a life I don't know how to live. It was me who should have been in that car. She was full of life, full of hope, and I was just a waste of life, a tombstone disguised as a man.

In front of Mr. Johnson's fading mirror, I stood, studying myself from different angles—front, back, in profile. I saw no James Bond, only a coward trying to survive at any price. I've shamed myself deeply, I thought, past all forgiveness and beyond redemption.

Mary and I had both had difficult childhoods, each a victim of a broken household of different kinds—hers, openly in ruins but devoid of lies, mine glued together with my mother's spit to keep up a false appearance of familial bonding. Mary at least had the will to turn hers around into something positive, brief though it was. What had I done, except to cling to dusty memories and nurse deep grudges?

FUTILE HUNT

The baby is late, and Mama is howling her head off day and night. Grandma has come to help, but she's helpless as a lamb. Her nosy sister, Khaleh, is also here, taking the opportunity to crash again. But she, too, is useless, spending more time snooping around than comforting Mom.

With the baby's arrival on hold, Baba decides to take a little break and go hunting with his friends.

"It's such a beautiful autumn day. It would be a shame to miss it, especially since I can't be of any help around here," he says.

Mama is too weak to challenge his arrogance, but somehow steals a breath to throw in an obstacle.

In a hoarse voice she says, "Take Shahed with you. He'll get depressed sitting here listening to my screams all day."

She actually wants me to be there to spy on her husband, see if all the potions she's been secretly feeding him are working.

"You must be joking. He'll be even more bored with us old guys," he says, while rummaging in the closet for his hunting gear. "He'd better stay home. You'll need a man around."

This time, he can't get away with it and I'm finally on board.

In the car, he launches into a long sermon, trying to coax me into a promise that I would keep my mouth shut.

"Listen, my son, you're a big boy already—almost a man. But if you want to be a man, be accepted as one, there are certain rules."

"Like what?"

"You have to show you can keep a secret, if you want to be let in on the action. This trip will be a good test to see how much you can be trusted."

I don't quite understand what he's getting at but tell him okay. We drive for half an hour and then stop outside a modern villa, where the butcher is waiting with his mistress and another woman—who turns out to be Houri. I'm very surprised to see her, but not unhappy. Since the incident at the national park I've lost respect for her, but all my resentments ebb once I set eyes on her.

The men go out to pack hunting gear into the Bride and I find myself alone with Houri in the butcher's gaudy living room. There's an uneasy silence between us, each waiting for the other to say something.

"How is your mom?" she finally asks in a mournful tone.

"She's—all right," I say, hanging my head.

"Is the baby here yet?"

"No."

"Are you angry with me, Shahed?"

"Why should I be? Actually . . . yes."

"Why?"

I'm grateful I don't have to answer because the butcher hurries back in just then and calls for his mistress.

The bathroom door opens and out walks a fattish lady in a red outfit of scaly texture, tightly hugging her plump figure. With her bleached blond hair and heavy makeup, she looks like a painted egg. But the butcher seems very proud of his baby and never takes his hand off her big butt.

The men are finally done loading and we pile into the car. I get in the front seat between Baba and Houri, and the butcher and his concubine slide in the back, cuddling and moaning away throughout the ride. The nymph, too, is holding my hand and running her fingers through my hair; I'm lulled into a fairytale serenity, basking in the pleasure of our romantic revival. Once again, I start fantasizing about our long-overdue dream trip and am already planning which routes to take to America.

Why go on holding a grudge against her, I think to myself. Everyone has his or her foolish moments at times. She definitely deserves another chance.

On the way, we make a couple of brief stops to buy groceries and pick up a used rifle for me so I can join the hunters. The gun is a piece of junk with a scuffed butt and a cracked barrel bandaged with tape, but I'm still happy to have it.

After a long drive we turn onto a gravel side road, bumping through a flat stretch of barren land peppered with trees and brown patches of grass. We stop the car at the greenest spot and pile out. The women run straight to set up a picnic and the butcher retires under the shade of a tree, relaxing by a stream of clear water. Baba hauls the guns out from the trunk, props them against the trunk of a tree and then goes to join his friend, who has peeled down to his undergarments and is drinking from a bottle of vodka. He looks so disgusting in those long shorts that I have an urge to grab my gun and shoot him. Unfortunately, my rifle leaks and the bullets probably won't reach that far.

Baba chats with the butcher a little and then goes to check up on the women, who are busy making sandwiches at a folding table. I stand by the thug, hearing the vodka gurgling down his throat, but my eyes are fixed on my father. He sidles up behind Houri and wraps his arms around her, resting his chin on her shoulder. Then his right hand veers toward her buttocks, an inspiration from the butcher. But Houri slaps it off and turns to me with a shy face. Baba also turns to look at me, but doesn't seem to mind my presence this time—he must have already accepted me an insider in his male club. He grabs my broken gun and walks toward me. "So big boy, are you ready for the hunt. Millions of hares are out there waiting to be taken out. So run before it gets dark!"

I don't see any damned hares, don't even know if there's one, let alone millions.

"You're sending me on a fool's errand!"

He ignores my objection. "Listen: try to go easy on them. It's a damn powerful gun and we don't want to kill off their race," Baba says with a booming laugh.

I strike out into the open field, a parched, dusty plain dotted with scruffy bushes, stretching on for as far as the eye could see. I run for a few minutes and pause to get the lay of the terrain, spot the hares my father imagines will be there. There are no clouds in the sky and no hint of a breeze. The earth shimmers under the blazing midday sun. The caws of crows and the crackling of brush under my feet are the only sounds in the deep silence.

I push farther and the clumps of thistle grow larger and scarier, like porcupines braced to fire their quills. There's the rustle of some creatures darting through the scrub. Thinking they're rabbits, I cock my rifle and aim. But the creatures, whatever they are, move too fast and I'm only chasing shadows. I keep jerking the gun and pull the trigger a few times, but there's no pressure and no pellets fly—like my syphilitic great uncle, I'm shooting blanks. Frustrated, I give up and plod over the rough terrain, blinded by burning sweat and the intense glare of light. I keep tripping over dry bushes and my face and limbs are all covered with scratches and dust. Every few minutes, I pause to try my luck again, circling around myself like a fool, desperately looking for something to take back so I can show off maybe one dead rabbit. But it is a futile hunt and I tramp back empty-handed.

The couples might not have expected me back so soon, as they're heatedly at it in their separate corners. The butcher and his baby are rolling around in the shade of a tree, rumbling with their drunken laughter. Several yards away, Baba and Houri lie on a patch of green next to the stream. Their heads are joined, their shoes kicked off, their feet dancing in the air; they peck and coo like a pair of doves. The nymph has puckered her lips, frowning sexily and inviting more kisses. My father isn't letting her down.

Houri's short skirt has hiked up to her black panties, exposing her full coppery legs. With sudden pain, I remember how they felt when I helped her shave them. But it is Baba's hand now skating excitedly over the smooth skin.

I pull behind a tree and watch them carry on, hurting inside, screaming silently. It's a sickening sight: Houri squirming against my father, his big hands roving over her silken skin . . . moving further and further up . . . over her buttocks, in her crotch and under her panties—unknown territory I could not have reached even in my wildest imagination. I laugh at myself for having thought the same thing about my father, when I naively believed I was the one who had her, not him.

I observe for God knows how long, through a blur of tears, until Houri looks over and sees me. She jumps up as if a wasp has stung her. She pulls her skirt down. We stare at each other for some painful moments and then a screaming sob tears out of me. With nowhere to go, I turn around and hit the field again, this time running madly and tirelessly. "I hate you! . . . I hate you! . . ." I keep yelling.

Fifteen years later, as remembrance of that phony hunting trip, comes to me unbidden, I can still feel the heat of that intense hatred for Houri. Somehow it's grown into self-loathing, for the memory always reminds me of that final intercourse with Mary. As memories of all my failures with women collect into a cement block at my feet, it's that picture of exposed flesh and groping hands under the hot sun that plunges me into the river.

It was a moment that savagely ended my childhood and launched me into a vacuum that became my future. That mad dash into the open dusty field, those wild screams could not silence my pain. I could never shake off her spell, the curse of that ill-fated affair. My whole life became a frustrated obsessive labor to loosen that leech that just wouldn't budge.

It's such a drag to have lots of money but not be able to spend it. I'm stuck with those big orange notes in my mattress safe, too afraid to try and break them. Once again, I'm back to my impoverished days, deprived of all the fine food dished out at the cafeteria. Now that I've had a taste of those hamburgers and cakes, the lash of hunger is even more painful.

One day I can take it no more, and tear into the futon to dig out one of the bills from deep in the wadded cotton. I've brought needle and thread to sew it back up. After my long apprenticeship at Grandma's school, no one could tell the mattress was opened. While hard at work, I sense a shadow passing by. But when I turn to look, there's no one there. I figure it's Khaleh on a spying mission and don't give it much thought, just hoping that she hasn't seen much.

I duck out the house and take the one thousand-*rial* orange note to a bank to break. The clerk looks at me as if I'm trying to palm off a counterfeit bill. Before he can call his boss, I grab the note and fly out. I try breaking it at several other places, but they all turn me away. Even the unscrupulous banana man shies away this time, although I offer to buy a whole box of bananas. This is a real cause for worry since Seyed doesn't usually decline any money, whether it is clean or dirty.

Desperate, I almost do something stupid: try and spend the bill at the school cafeteria. But I control the urge at the last minute. It would have been a deadly mistake. Not even rich kids dare to flash that kind of money. If they're caught, they'll have to answer directly to the principal.

All those tiring trips to the military conscription center with my mother were in vain and we could not make a dent in the cold frowning bureaucracy. I had all but given up, already planning an illegal exit. I had talked to a human trafficker and he wanted three thousand dollars to get me out of the country, a perilous camel ride through rugged terrain and across the border into Pakistan.

I decided to give it one last try at the passport office, pull a string with my boyhood tormentor, Edison, who had a position there. The Colonel came to my mind, the tightwad my father hung around with, in case his clout came handy. I wondered what the Colonel was up to in a time when his crisp uniform no longer cut any crap, the royal insignia and glittering medals now worthless as trash.

I got to the passport office early, but it was noon before I finally made it to the line outside Edison's office. I waited until my turn came and then stepped forward and slapped my useless passport on his desk, still labeled as "Brother Husseini."

"Brother Husseini or Brother Edison, whoever you are, will you help an old pal?"

He became stiff and alert, but didn't look up, slowly flipping through my passport until he got to the picture.

"Sha—Shahed?" he finally looked up and stared at me, squinting to recall.

"Shahed. Shahed. Where do I know you from? . . . Are you . . ."

"Yes, the Mushroom-head . . . Elephant ears"

His eyes shone and filled up with tears. He jumped from his chair, circled the desk and pounced on me.

"Oh my God! Oh my God!" he kept saying as he kissed my cheeks, my forehead, my elephant ears.

"What are you doing here, man?" he gasped.

"What are you doing here?"

His face tightened as he tried to control himself and he took out a handkerchief to wipe his eyes.

"Life . . . fate . . . you know?"

He looked around and his office mates were watching in surprise and too much interest.

"Let's get out of here," he hissed to me. "These are nice guys, but walls have ears."

He grabbed my hand and pulled me out of the office and down the steps into the courtyard. We sat on the ledge of a flowerbed with no flowers.

He was silent for a while, then patted my shoulder. "You're staying for lunch. They're serving *Ghormeh Sabzi* today." A popular Persian dish. We looked at each other for a moment and then I spoke.

"Edison—how can you stand this job, the place, your new identity?"

"I have no choice. Even this I may not have for too long."

"What do you mean?"

He took out his prayer beads and started to thumb them, then stopped and lit a cigarette. His teeth were hopelessly stained and decayed. His Elvis cowlick had thinned to a gray mat pasted on his skull. His bright green eyes were dull now and full of sorrow.

"My father was executed last year. He was a colonel working for SAVAK—you know—the Shah's secret service."

"I'm sorry to hear that."

"Now they're purging the so-called anti-revolutionaries from government offices and universities. I know I'm on the hit list."

"What about your new name and identity, can't they help you?"

"I don't think so. My past is far too exposed to cover up."

"You can always find something else."

He looked at the ground, taking a deep drag. "It's not that easy. I have no money, no proper training. They confiscated our house and everything else my father owned."

"So how did you end up with this job?"

"It used to be an okay job—secure. My father got it for me, pulling strings, like six years ago. You know I was never a good student. I thought I was set for life, until this damn revolution came . . ."

Edison put his hand on my knee and sighed deeply: "So, what about you? What have you been doing?"

"I haven't fared much better. I went to America after high school . . . didn't do a damn thing there. I made a mistake and came back . . . now I'm trying to escape."

"What do you need, an exit permit?"

I nodded. "Right. And I need your help, Edison."

"But what can I do?"

"Stamp that goddamn thing on my passport."

He stared at me helplessly for a long moment and then opened his mouth to say something.

"I know . . . but find a way to do it. I can't stand it here anymore."

"Let's—go upstairs," he answered uncertainly.

I followed him to the second floor and a rather big office at the end of the corridor. "Deputy Director, Colonel Hejazi" was embossed on a plaque on the door. He went inside and reappeared fifteen minutes later.

"Colonel Hejazi is an old friend of my father, but no one knows about it here," he said softly. Then even quieter: "He's a closet anti-revolutionary, like all of us. Okay, let's go in."

The colonel was standing at prayer in a corner of the room. His shirtsleeves were rolled up to his elbow and his feet were bare. We sat down waiting for him to go through the mummery of devotion. It didn't take long, far briefer than Grandpa's prayers. He greeted us warmly, put on his socks and jacket, and went to sit behind his plain desk, under a large portrait of Ayatollah Khomeini.

"Edison said you came from America," he said while lighting a cigarette. He was in his midforties but already had white stubble in his beard. His navy blue uniform draped his slumped shoulders like a rag. His teeth were unsightly from smoke and neglect. I felt pity for the man, a once honorable officer reduced to a hireling of the mullahs, having to feign piety to keep his lousy job.

"Yes. Now I'm hoping to go back."

"I understand. May I see your passport?"

I handed him my passport.

He thumbed through it and then set it down on his desk and stamped a page.

"Here you go. My best wishes to you."

I wanted to say something, but Edison quickly grabbed my arm and rushed me out of the office. He started to walk briskly down the corridor, suddenly busy with more folder-clutching lackeys.

I followed on his heels, trying to convey my gratitude to my former classmate, but he turned to me abruptly, the warmth gone from his face. He was obviously scared. "You know what? You won't be able to take lunch here. Your appointment is finished." Then he moved his mouth close to my ear: "Let's make it another day, my friend . . . maybe in America."

My mother has been hollering all night and there's no sign of the baby. The little rascal must have caught a sense of what is waiting outside and is holding fast—and poor Mama has to pay for it as always. She's melting like candle wax, and we just watch in helpless pity. Aunt Fatima has now joined forces to try and break the deadlock, but the job is even beyond the iron lady. It's a tough labor, by all accounts, and she needs professional help. So we're nervously waiting for my father to show up and take her to the hospital.

There's finally the sound of the key turning in the lock and my aunt runs to hold my father by the door. I hear them arguing it out.

"I don't see why everyone is rushing it!" he says. "Give the baby time. It can't stay there forever."

287

"Shame on you!" his sister shouts in a trembling voice. "How can you be so cruel? One wouldn't even do it to his enemy."

"Oh you're with them, too, blaming me for everything? I'm losing my last ally in the world."

"I can't watch her suffer like this. Go wait in the car and I'll bring her."

"Forget the hospital. I haven't had a good experience with them."

"At least run to get the midwife."

"All right."

"Wait!" my aunt shouts after him. "Take Shahed with you. I don't want you to get distracted and pick up the wrong woman."

So I get to miss school once again, but this time it is worth it. We're talking about saving a human life. What's the point of my becoming a doctor if Mama won't be around to feel proud?

There's lashing rain and terrible rush hour traffic. A chain of smoking cars, trucks and buses are locked in bumper to bumper and we can hardly move. It takes an hour to finally pull free and hit the main highway, driving fast to the city outskirts where the midwife lives. A Jeep pulls up on our left and keeps honking. We turn to look, but our windows are too steamed up to see.

My father at first ignores the honking. Then he curses and steps on the gas pedal. But the Jeep keeps apace, still hooting. Baba rolls down the window for another look and then freezes. It is Khan, the persistent creditor, sitting in the back, with two other men in front. The guy on the passenger side has a face rutted with scars and red from some skin disease, or maybe anger. His mean eyes are fixed on my father, as if to hypnotize him into surrendering; his mouth works angrily with curses.

My father tears his eyes away and guns the big engine, but the Jeep won't let up. The thug has now leaned out of the window, ordering us to pull over with loud screams and frantic gestures of his hands. Baba is obviously scared and keeps looking at the speedometer; his knees, too, are jerking and beads of sweat run down his sideburns.

The Buick is more powerful and at first we take a good jump ahead of them, but we can't shake off the tail for too long. When some farm trucks slow us down, the jeep catches up and draws level. We race side by side for a few minutes and then the jeep bangs into our car, trying to edge us off the road. Baba tries to hold his own, but the attacks won't stop. One is so heavy that it sends me flying into the dashboard with a noisy thud. I'm too scared to feel the pain and just wonder what they're going to do to us.

The jeep keeps sideswiping us until the Bride skids and fishtails to a halt. The jeep screeches up next to us. Baba jumps out to see the damage and finds his side of the Bride bashed in, the wheels tilted inward, and the door hanging from one hinge. He bangs his fist on the hood, cursing aloud, but still not ready for a fight. After making a lot of noise, he jumps back in behind the wheel, waiting for the enemy to make the next move. The enemy also remains in their car, just gesturing to my father to join them for a talk.

"I'm not going anywhere," Baba shouts at them. "If you want to talk to me, come here."

The macho test of will lasts for a good minute, until the men give in and make to step out of the jeep. But before their feet touch the ground, my father hits the gas pedal and the Buick goes flying, with the broken door swinging in the air. We drive on for a while and then the Buick careens off the highway and roars through a shantytown at breakneck speed.

The jeep is in full chase. Baba zooms past crumbling mud houses, bumping over potholes and turning sharp corners, until we come up to a mud wall and a brick kiln blocking a narrow street. The jeep pulls up right behind and boxes us in, and the men charge out. My father also leaves the car, but I slip down onto the floor and cower under the dash. I hear them screaming at each other and tremble like a shivering chick, until I hear Khan's voice trying to call a truce.

"My good men, we live in a civilized world. Let's settle this amicably."

I creep up and look through the windshield and see the midget standing between the warring parties, with his arms outstretched to keep them separated.

Eventually my father joins them in the jeep for a "civilized" talk, I suspect he makes some "manly" promises, because in an hour he climbs out and the jeep roars off.

Baba stands there stricken, looking at the battered Bride. He's so upset he forgets about the midwife and the baby, and heads back home.

Mama is lying on the mattress, soaked in sweat and looking pale. Next to her is my aunt, kneeling on the floor, blowing air into the mouth of a bruised lifeless baby. Her hands are smeared in blood and her eyes puffy from crying.

289

DOOMSDAY

One day, I finally risk it all, in a rash moment, as if flinging myself into a terminal shopping spree. I take the one-thousand-*rial* note to the cafeteria to spend, placing a big order to make it plausible. The sales clerk takes the note and gives it a close examination, and then disappears into the backroom, obviously suspicious. My heart goes into a free fall and I damn my thoughtless act.

A minute later, the clerk returns with her supervisor, an older woman with a sulky expression. She has the orange note in her hand.

"Where did you get the money?" the manager demands.

My mind won't work. Why didn't I think up some good excuse? I give the lame explanation I gave the banana man: "It's my monthly allowance."

"Nonsense! Even I don't make that much in a month." She tells me to wait, then leaves, taking the note with her. I'm so frozen with guilt I don't even think to tell her she should give it back to me.

I feel sick, delirious, going through unimaginable horror. The thought of escape comes to my mind. But where to, being hemmed in by high walls?

Minutes tick past and there's still no sign of the clerk or her supervisor. A long line has formed outside the snack shop and boys give me dirty looks for holding them up. Finally Bam the disciplinarian looms across the yard. He's marching in long, determined strides, as if off to capture a fortress. He draws close and walks past, heading straight to the snack shop to talk to the women. A while later he comes out to hassle me with a cross-examination, waving the bill in his hand as hard evidence.

"Where did you get this?"

"It's—it's mine." He's furious. He grabs me by the scruff of the neck and shoves me ahead toward the office. There's a double line of students standing in watch. They all whistle and heckle us as we pass.

The general sits sprawled behind his desk, talking to the teachers—the same cast of shoe polishing cowards. Bam plants me

290

in front of his boss and pins the orange note to my chest, like a jail number. He keeps fiddling with my appearance, as if to measure me for a new suit. Once I'm groomed to stand trial, the principal leaves his chair and lumbers in my direction.

"Where did this come from?" he says, clamping a pudgy hand on my shoulder.

"It's—it's m-my money." I can barely stutter it out.

"Look me in the eyes and say the honest truth," he says.

"I'm t-telling the truth."

"Cut the crap! Wheeeere did you get the money? Come on, tell me!" he says and grabs my ear with his other hand, giving it a sharp twist.

"Ouch! . . . it's mine . . . I swear."

"The TRUTH . . . I want the TRUTH . . . YOU HEAR?"

It comes in a deafening boom, followed by slaps and backslaps, finally knocking me to the floor.

"It is the likes of you who bring shame to my school and to this great land," he leans over with a face twisted in disgust, his voice quivering with hurt pride. "You have fouled up the image of my school and will pay for it. Now, say who you stole the money from!"

There's no point to keep on lying and I'm about to burst into tears and make a full confession:

Yes, I did it, but I'm innocent. It wasn't my choice to be a thief. The habit crept up on me, seized and consumed me like a snake eating a rabbit. It was born of desperation, of hunger—for food and attention. Give me one last chance and I promise to behave. I'll bear the pang of hunger, the stab of desire and won't complain so much as a peep. I'll resist the temptation of your hamburgers, the lure of your toys, and other fancy stuff you showcase in your cafeteria. Never again will I dare to crave things I don't deserve to have, things not meant for my sort. I will not try to rise above my means and seek out a taste of the good life you exposed me to. I'll stay happy with what I have and what I don't have, and I'll be grateful for it all, too. I'll be content with the shabby coat on my back and my busted shoes, and the rag I carry around for a school bag, bulging with junk and a tacky sandwich. I will live life happily ever after amongst the rats, the cockroaches, the losers, the perverts, the morons, the sadists—and even the cast of lepers, cripples, and epileptics in the public bathhouse. I'll spend my holidays relaxing by the open sewer running outside my house, under the protective shade of diseased trees landscaping my street . . . .

Here the general gives my shoulder a jerk and shakes me out of my horrified trance.

"I'll count to ten and you come out with it." He's spitting with rage now. "One . . . two . . . three . . ."

Suddenly the door flies opens and my mother bursts in with fear on her face.

She's pale, gaunt, with two black circles under her eyes. Her dress is sloppy, her hair messed up—signs she left the house in panic. The principal must have sent someone to our house to inform my parents. The moment her eyes fall on Grandpa's note draping my chest, she lets out a shriek and faints. One of the teachers runs to get her sweetened tea and another, a woman, rubs her shoulders. In a few minutes she's back to life—and joining the interrogators.

"Are you the thief, Shahed? Please tell the truth," she begs in a slow mournful voice. "Are you the one who robbed Grandpa?"

I keep my head down, but know the moment has arrived to come clean. So I give a hesitant nod, affirming the bitter truth she'd hoped against hope not to hear. It must have been devastating, judging from her agonized cry. I reach for her hand, hoping to ease the blow, and look into her eyes pleadingly. There's a wounded expression there, changing to flares of terror as I tighten my hold on her hand. She jerks her hand away and turns her back to me, out of anger or helplessness. It is all too late anyway. A woman who's always stood in the way of harm coming to her children, there's nothing she can do to help her son.

Mama pours out more apologies and drags me out of the office, heading toward home. My father is certainly waiting for me, ready to really dish it out with rage and vengefulness. I've already seen the previews of what's coming: his furious retaliations against the banker, Uncle E, and his own father. On the way to catch a bus, I try to get a conversation going, get her to say anything to ease my anxiety.

"Where are we going, Mom? Where are you taking me?"

She's sunk in her own thoughts and deaf to my pleas.

"Hah, Mom? . . . please tell me . . . Mom, can you say something? Is Baba home waiting for me? Is he going to punish me?"

"Of course!" She's gasping, out of breath. "You—you just wait! He'll fix you!"

She hastens her steps, her cold hand gripping mine and pulling me along, as if to bring me faster to my doom. I don't have the courage to face Baba and drag my feet, trying to delay the inevitable, the final moment of reckoning. But every time I pause, she gives my hand a jerk and I lurch ahead like a mule under blows.

My mind goes back to the thief in Pleasure Land, the young man pummeled by the gang of vigilantes. Now I feel for the thief, more for him and less for the rough justice he faced.

Buses are full and we take a shared taxi, which drops us off a few blocks from home, and we slog the rest on foot. We advance down the lousy street, past grimy shops and ruined landmarks. The banana man is standing outside, sprinkling his fragrant fruits with murky water from a bucket. He flashes a malicious grin as I walk past, as if he knows where I'm headed and is happy to see dark fate finally asserting itself. Closer to home, Usta is perched atop his stool, his head flicking like a horny rooster's. He too must have smelled blood, as the mean leer is back on his face. We're no sooner inside than the trapdoor flings open and he sticks his head in.

Mama leads me down the balcony to the last room, the scene of the crime and where Baba is going to greet me. The guestroom is chosen because it's the farthest from the street, and less likely for strangers to hear my cries of pain. She opens the door, throws me in like a carcass to feed a caged lion and slams the door closed.

He's lounging on an elbow paging through a magazine. Behind him on the wall is the coat rack from which Grandpa's trousers hung on that fateful day. He raises his head just enough to pin me. His expression hardens and a ferocious glow comes to his eyes. He sits up and leans back, lacing his hands together behind his head and looking straight at me, as if to mark his prey before pouncing.

I press back against the door, looking back in terror—my knees trembling, my heart racing and my head pounding. I can feel the heat, the intensity of his anger, the painful stab of his gaze. He makes no move, however; just sits staring, as if to melt me into shame. I feel compulsion to do something to please him. But I'm motionless, speechless, breathless.

He goes on staring for a while, his jaw set hard, his eyes getting red; I stare back—not out of defiance, but to be prepared for the attack. Then he bounds to his feet and starts toward me—full on, in heavy steps, arms spread like an eagle. With every stomp, the floor shakes, the ceiling rocks and my head whirls; and the moment his hand lifts, I feel the trickle of warm urine down my leg, the chill down my spine. His hand freezes up in the air, for an infinite time, and then it swings hard, coming down like the furious lash of an elephant trunk.

One slap is all it takes to knock the breath out of me, but not enough to quench his thirst for revenge. The blows keep coming, one after another, from different angles, each heavier then the one before—until I lose all control and my bladder bursts. With what energy I have left, I creep out of the pool of my own piss and crawl into a corner—where I coil up like a worm, using my puny arms to shield against what may come next.

Mama must have finally been satisfied with the punishment because in a minute she steps in to stop the fight and collect my whimpering remains. Now that I've received proper justice, she's her nurturing self again, ready to cradle and nurse me.

I come out of this horror black and blue, crushed in body and spirit. I can't raise my arm, and my eye is swollen shut, so I think that's why Mama keeps me home from school. Or maybe I can't go to school any more—not that I want to now. But there's one thing I still hold on to: recovering the hoard of cash I've stashed away. Now that I've paid dearly for my crime, I can go on and enjoy the fruit of my pain, relax by a pool with a beautiful date and drink soda from a tall glass. No one can prove I still have the money, and if anyone asks, I have a good answer: I spent it all. After all, you can't be punished twice for the same crime.

I wait a few days for the dust to settle, for the house to be empty—and then go to get the money. I open the stitches on the mattress, the one I've marked, and dig through lumpy masses of cotton. But the notes aren't there! I fall into a panic and go to open another, thinking I may have mixed them up. This one, too, I give a thorough search, but still nothing! I rip up the rest, one after another, clawing my way through the puffy innards like a madman, tossing the stuffing into the air. The room fills with cotton, showering over my head like snow, giving me the demented look of the damn fool I am. I stay in the room for hours, picking frantically and swimming amid white fluff—like an earthquake survivor sifting through rubble, searching for loved ones. I search and search until all energy drains out of me and I sink into black despair.

I never found out who stole the bills from me. I was too scared to ask all those years. I can only guess: Someone who could betray a son and walk away with a clean conscience. Someone who embellished his car with more finery. Someone who bought all new sets of jazzy clothes to wear to nightclubs. Someone who . . . .

A few days before I bid farewell to this land for good, my stamped passport secure in my pocket, I made one last trip to my old street. A last ditch hope to find the answer. I had an itch to go straight to the house, give it one last search, every notch and crack, in case that spellbinding bankroll had been accidentally swept there. But then I realized my folly. I wouldn't be welcome, whoever lived there. The barbershop next door was as close as I could get to the scene of my lost dreams.

Lewd Usta was no longer there, replaced by a dapper young man with an absurd, old-fashioned Elvis Presley hairdo. The trapdoor was gone, patched over and blended into the wall. The walls had been repainted and peppered with posters of American idols and European landscapes. Standing in the doorway, I stared at a luscious scene in Switzerland inviting me to Travel on Swiss Air. My spirits lifted suddenly; I thought: I've seen that kind of idyllic landscape, and it's even within my grasp. In a few days I'd be returning to a colorful land. And I would find my way back to the Butterfly Town.

The handsome barber shook out a fresh white towel and invited me to sit in the old chair.

"How would you like your hair cut?"

"Painlessly." I smiled. He looked puzzled.

"You have nice pictures all over the walls. But aren't you kind of worried?"

He knew what I meant. "They don't bother us here much. They harass people in chic areas. Besides, my brother is a martyr."

He gently pinned another warm towel around my neck. "What did you mean by painless haircut?"

"Usta's haircuts were a torture."

"Did you know Usta?" He combed my hair softly, as if it were a baby's.

"Too well. Do you know where he is?"

"He's dead . . . suffered a painful death in a madhouse." He began to snip with quiet sureness.

"He had a paranoid streak about him."

"How did you know him?"

"I lived next door."

He lifted the scissors from my hair and stared at me in the mirror. "Oh, you're the son of . . . ."

"Yes."

"Everyone talks about him."

"Who is living in this house now?"

"An old lonely widow. She has a sad story . . . snitched on her rebellious son to the mullahs . . . it led to his death . . . now she refuses to come out of the house."

Elvis went on to tell the story of the old widow.

This old mother was a devout soul who fell too hard for the revolution and its lies. To help further its cause, she snitched on her carefree, unruly son. The son was too deeply into "decadent" pleasure, partying and boozing regularly. He loved American culture and tried to copy its popular icons. He could sing and dance like Michael Jackson, and dressed and swaggered like James Dean, sporting frayed jeans and riding big bikes.

As much as he worshiped the sparkling American images, he hated his own culture of grief, the restrictions imposed in the name of faith. So sick he was with all the anguish around him that he joined a rebel movement, fighting the system blindly out of desperation.

Every day, with nothing better to do, he zipped through the streets on his motorcycle, throwing petrol bombs at religious sites and government offices. He was an elusive saboteur, too, able to get away with it all for quite a while—until his mother found out and reported him. Now remember, she meant her son no harm—just wanted his behavior corrected. She was given this promise before being tricked into cooperating.

It took only one week for the rowdy young man to be reformed and handed back to his mother, but it was only his lifeless body.

Come, mother, take delivery of your son.

But this is his corpse!!

That's right, mother. Children are a gift from God. The Lord takes them away as easily as He gives them.

But, Hajji, you promised!

Don't question the wisdom of divine order!

But I meant well. I had his best interests at heart.

So did we, mother. But don't you worry. His soul may still have a chance to be saved.

This matter-of-fact account of a horror story struck me like a fuzzy nightmare. It was bizarre and yet familiar. I saw my own mother in the old zealot. Like Mama, she fed her son to the wolves with the best of intentions: to instill honesty and virtue in him. I felt I knew the old zealot intimately. Her tale evoked sympathy as much as disdain. But I didn't feel disdain for my mother at that moment. I missed her. I cherished her youthful zeal in guarding a family beset by problems, rats, cockroaches . . . all alone. She gave it all and held no grudges, not even against a husband who denied her existence.

I left the barbershop in a daze and looked at my old house again, my heart aching for the old widow cloistered inside. Her sad tale had awakened dead feelings toward my mother in my heart. It was ironic that my hazy mission to recover the long-lost treasure, the secret key to happiness, should result in a renewed bonding between me and my mother.

I crossed the street and sat on a stoop outside the coal ware-house, my eyes resting on the decaying door of my old house, shut firmly to protect the privacy of the grieving mother. My mind resumed the futile search for the elusive orange notes, the elusive thief, and the elusive love. It all came to look so petty and ridiculous. Suddenly something hit me with the glow of insight: there is no way I can ever be sure who stole my money—but if it was my unscrupulous late father—Congratulations, Baba! I salute you! You deserved it more than anyone I knew. You had a birthright to it, more to that than all the land you inherited and laid waste to. I hope you enjoyed my money as you did with all the other "little loans" you hustled out of all and sundry. *Nooshejan!* Food to your soul! I wish from the bottom of my heart that the loot I paid for so dearly became flesh around your muscles and juice under your skin—juice and flesh that Mama could never pump into my body despite all her sacrifices.

You know what, Baba? I don't resent you any more, because now I realize there was a purpose to your mad pursuit of fun. Hell, there was even a prophetic vision in your mania to grab life with both hands while you could still live it. My broken bones, my trodden spirit, were just a token contribution from a son-follower to advance your cause and make sure your mission succeeded. I was only a foot-soldier destined to fall so that you could pursue joy full throttle, celebrate life and pleasure and negate death and grief.

So no more tears, my faithless father! Let's clean house and move on! Still, there is something I'm dying to know: why did you feel you deserved the money more than I did? What went through your mind the moment you took the notes from my safe? Did you think stolen money re-stolen would make it any cleaner, or did you just want the money out of your son's hand to make sure he wouldn't go astray . . . regardless of its final destination.

But . . . let's forget it. All I need to say is that now—I miss you. Miss you even in my nightmare memories of you. You made me laugh as you caused me pain, kept me amused even while you were skillfully stabbing me in the back. Some people seek security and comfort in money, religion or patriotism. For you, humor was the end. You chose to laugh in the face of hardships, thus making life's heartless moments bearable.

One more thing, Baba: I want you to rest content wherever it is that your soul has landed. If there's any truth to the delicious promise of paradise, you found it here on earth, and there's no need for you to search for it in heaven or hell: the *hours*, the fragrant fruits, the flesh of all fowls, the . . . your son, on the other hand, still walks in fog, with his eyes fixed to the sky, groping for that obscure object of desire.

"Verily, the Hour is coming . . . and I'm almost hiding it from myself . . . that every person may be rewarded for that which he strives." (Surat Ta-ha, 20-15)

Before flying back to America, I made my way back to *Behesht-e-Zahra,* this time alone, to praise my father at his grave. The cemetery was crowded as always, with no end to the grief of this wailing nation.

Dozens of trailers were parked along the road, stacked with layers of coffins. They were draped with Iranian flags and bore unidentifiable remains, often as little as a few charred bones and the brass key to heaven. Mourners clung to the trucks, shouting slogans and punching the air with their fists, some risking a stampede to touch the holy caskets. A jeep full of laborers arrived to unload and haul the boxes to a bottomless market with its insatiable appetite for death.

I squeezed through the crowd, holding high a bouquet of flowers, my first touch of sentiment since that gift to Houri fifteen years earlier. I walked past the holy fountain, gushing red water, a dowdy symbol of the massive blood spilled for the country and Islam, and headed straight toward *Lanatabad*, the unholy ground holding my father. Some stooped old women in black were moving in the same direction, in anonymous silence. All they wanted was a quiet moment with their inglorious dead.

With no clear marking, it was hard to find my father's grave and I had to remember the formula to locate it: down to the lone dead tree, then four steps to the right and five steps to the left, as Mama had instructed. I finally came to a mound of dirt, one looking fuller than the rest, and I made a wild guess it was Baba's. I knelt there, still holding the bouquet, trying to think of how to mourn. At the next grave, a woman kept her weeping vigil, holding a blood-stained rag to her face. I put the flowers down and started plucking weeds from around the grave, as I tried to conjure up a few lines of prayer to intone. No memory came, so I made up my own elegy, Baba's favorite song that he used to play over and over. In that state of mind, the sappy lyric had a haunting edge.

My heart has gone mad again with love . . . it is lost in a lonely alley . . . knocking desperately on every door . . .

I was lost in the song and must have been too loud, as I felt a hand tapping my shoulder.

"What are you doing? This is no place to sing such a song." It was the woman grieving at the next grave. She was in a black robe and hood, a substitute for the chador that nonreligious women wore.

"I'm singing praises to my father. It's his favorite song."

"Is this his grave?" she asked, still holding the bloody shirt.

"I'm . . . not sure. I think so."

299

"I'm here for my son Farrokh. He was a communist, a true angel with a heart of gold . . . he lived to help others . . . and eventually paid for it with his blood . . . met the fate of all anti-revolutionaries."

"Of course."

"Farrokh disappeared for six months. Then one day they called to say his corpse was ready to be taken away. They even charged for the bullets they pumped into his body. This is his shirt."

She burst into tears, put her head down and pressed the stained shirt to her eyes.

"I'm truly sad to hear it." I wanted to hold and comfort her, but didn't dare.

"I wish them eternal suffering . . . all the torments of hell," she went on falteringly. "I only live for the day to see them suffer."

The vague hope steadied her a little and she looked up at to me.

"Was he an anti-revolutionary, too?"

I heard distant shouts, and turned to see a gang of zealots in rags, taking pebbles from their pockets to throw at shameful mourners in *Lanatabad*. "Death to God-denying communists! . . . Damn you and your dead infidels!" I didn't feel threatened.

"Who?"

"Your father."

"Yes. Yes, in a way."

"Which group did he belong to?"

"Group?"

"Which side did he fight on?"

"On the side of life."

NEW DAWN

On the bus from the Los Angeles airport, I noticed as if for the first time that the streets looked clean, orderly, with plenty of green on parkways and lawns. Cars were quiet and shone with newness, the brilliance of wealth and prosperity. The smells were right for this land: the fresh ocean air was fragrant with ever-present colorful flowers; even lavatories were hung with artificial deodorants. Expressions of personal freedom—fluorescent shorts on tubby women and youth with bleached hair sticking straight up—were just that, not bland and silly indulgences of the spoiled Americans.

The orderliness was soothing to me, not stifling as before. What a systematic mind behind this tidiness, I thought. What a developed sense of civic life! The memory of the hostages, too, was fading and I was greeted with more smiles than apprehensive curiosity. Glances didn't linger and I felt more secure. Everyone appeared engaged in his or her own world in a land tolerant enough to embrace diverse opinions and cultures.

I took a shuttle bus to Monrovia. A "For Sale" sign was posted in front of Mr. Johnson's house, right by the front porch, where he used to wait and fish for companionship. I knocked on the door a few times, but there was no answer. The windows, too, were curtained and I couldn't see the inside. I went to my shack in the back; a padlock was on the door and the small window was boarded up.

I came back to the sidewalk and looked for a familiar face, someone who could give me news of the landlord. Bill's pickup truck was parked on the street, with the image of the blond licking at the banana still pasted on the windshield. I moved well away and stood waiting. Not a soul was around. It was not a street that fostered neighborliness. There were no corner stores, no neighborhood boy who would take even a cursory interest in the fate of an old man a few doors down.

I thought about ringing a bell, but was too shy. I didn't think I had a good reason to drag an elderly person to the door. So I took my pen out and scribbled a note for my landlord, informing him that I was moving out and had his money ready. Just as I was slipping the note under his door, an old lady emerged from the house opposite with a little mutt in tow.

"Who're you looking for?"

"Mr. Johnson."

"Oh, son, Frank is dead. He passed away a few months ago and his sister put the house for sale. Can I ask you who you are?"

"I'm his tenant. I mean . . . I've been away."

"I see. You're the nice guy living out in the back. Frank told me about you. When did you come back?"

"Just last night."

"Oh, I'm glad you made it back safely. Now, do you need to get into your place? I believe it's locked and I don't know what they did to your stuff."

"That's okay. There wasn't much there."

"I wish I could help. Do you need a place to stay now?"

"No, I'm looking for a bigger place to live with my mother. Anyway, it won't be in this town."

"Does your mother live here?"

"She will come soon, once I settle down."

Before taking the bus to Monterey, I decided to go and see George at the gas station. I didn't want to have come all the way to Monrovia without doing anything.

When I got there, he was predictably arguing with a Latino man over the restroom.

"For customers only!"

"I buy gas here all the time," said the Latino.

"I don't remember you. Get out now!"

"Let him use the bathroom," I called with a smile.

"Shahed! You're alive!" He hurried round the counter and reached out to hug and kiss me.

It was good to have someone welcome me, even George, who peered into my face with a huge grin. I saw the Latino man furtively take the key to the restroom and slip out.

"As alive as I can be."

"They didn't take you to the front?"

"They didn't need me. They had enough."

"So, you want a job again?" he said, draping his arm over my shoulder.

"Yes, but not here."

"Then where?"

"Up north somewhere . . . around Pacific Grove, maybe."

"Where the hell is that? What're you going to do there? You have no experience."

"I learned a few things while I was away."

"All right, *habibi* . . . I wish you good luck."

What drew me to the Butterfly Town was its postcard image, a bright toytown nestled amid a lush forest, overlooking a quiet ocean. I was attracted by the memory of that parade I had attended with Mary. I wanted to see more of those carnivals and appreciate them from my new standpoint, and if possible, try and blend into the picture. I hoped to take active part in those parades, wear a bunny costume of pink or orange or the red outfit of *Hajji Firooz.* I wanted to saunter through the thick woods, watch deer roam free and butterflies lay eggs.

As I stepped off the bus, I looked around. No such spectacles were in sight, but the bright colors were still there. So were the smiles and the serenity. I was in deep contemplation.

"You're a lucky man! Let me read your palm," someone spoke in a foreign voice. I looked up and saw a swarthy man pointing a forefinger at me. He looked South Asian, wearing a red outfit and a green turban, an orange dot painted between his eyebrows. A silver ring pierced one of his nostrils and a parrot was perched on his right shoulder. His whole stylized appearance and mannerism said con man. Yet he also reminded me of *Hajji Firooz,* the harbinger of a new dawn in my homeland. The only difference was that his dark skin was real and his bright outfit didn't look fake against the sunny landscape.

"No, thanks," I replied.

"You're a fortunate man. I can see it on your forehead," he said as he kept closing in. "Let me tell you all about the bright future ahead of you."

"That's okay, I know where I'm going," I said and quickly turned away.

* * *

We seek other conditions because we know not how to enjoy our own; and we go outside of ourselves for want of knowing what it is like inside of us.

So it is no use raising ourselves on stilts. We have to walk on our own legs. And sitting on the loftiest throne in the world we are still sitting on our behind.

—MONTAIGNE